I0657767

COLLECT THE PIECES

Lost Kings MC #25

AUTUMN JONES LAKE

COPYRIGHT

Collect the Pieces (Lost Kings MC #25)

Cover Models: Masson & Evanya
Photographer: Wander Aguiar Photography
Cover Design: Shanoff Designs
Proofreading: Julie Barney
Digital ISBN #978-1-961848-14-6
Paperback ISBN: #978-1-961848-17-7
Alternate Paperback ISBN: #978-1-961848-18-4

ABOUT COLLECT THE PIECES

Everything I thought I knew about my woman has been shattered. Now, it's up to me to collect the pieces and decide if Margot and I are a match made in heaven—or destined for hell.

This the second book in Jigsaw and Margot's story. Twist the Knife should be read first.

GLOSSARY OF CHARACTERS AND TERMINOLOGY

The Lost Kings MC™ World © Autumn Jones Lake

THE FOLLOWING MAY CONTAIN SPOILERS IF YOU ARE NOT CAUGHT UP ON the series or have skipped books.

Please note, this glossary only pertains to my romantic fictionalized motorcycle club world. It should not be construed as applicable to any other fictional clubs or a real-life motorcycle club.

THE LOST KINGS MC: UPSTATE, NY ("EMPIRE," NY)

President: Rochlan "Rock" North. Leader of the Upstate NY charter of the Lost Kings MC.

Sergeant-at-Arms: Wyatt "Wrath" Ramsey. Protector or enforcer for the club.

Vice President: Blake "Murphy" O'Callaghan. Murphy was the road captain up until *White Lies (Lost Kings MC #15)*

Treasurer: Marcel "Teller" Whelan. Handles the money and investments for the club. In After Glow (Lost Kings MC #11) Rock and Teller discovered they were father and son. In *Reckless Truths (Lost Kings MC #21)* they let the whole club in on their secret.

Road Captain: Dixon "Dex" Watts (newly appointed to the position in White Lies) His books are: *Rust or Ride (Lost Kings MC #22)* and *Agony to Ashes (Lost Kings MC #23)*

THE LOST KINGS MC: DOWNSTATE, NY ("UNION" NY)

President: Angus "Zero" or "Z" Frazier. As of *Zero Apologies (Lost Kings MC #14)*, Z is the president of the Downstate, NY charter of the Lost Kings MC.

Vice President: Logan "Rooster" Randall: Rooster's story is told in *Swagger Sass (Lost Kings MC #14.5), Rhythm of the Road (Lost Kings MC #16), Lyrics on the Wind (Lost Kings MC #17),* and *Diamond in the Dust (Lost Kings MC #18)*

Sergeant-at-Arms: Grayson "Grinder" Lock as of *Throne of Scars (Lost Kings MC #20) His books are Crown of Ghosts (Lost Kings MC #19) and Throne of Scars.*

Treasurer: Hustler (he hasn't gotten a legal name yet!)

Road Captain: Jensen "Jigsaw" Kilgore; Jigsaw, Rooster's best friend from childhood. His books are: *Twist the Knife (Lost Kings MC #24), Collect the Pieces (Lost Kings MC #25)* and *Scatter the Bones (Lost Kings MC #26)*

THE LOST KINGS MC: PORT EVERHART, VA

President: Cypress "Ice" Caldwell

Vice President: Farmer

Sergeant-at-Arms: Pants

Treasurer: T-Bone

Road Captain: Boots

THE LOST KINGS MC: DEADBRANCH, TN

President: Squiggy

SAA: Steer from the Downstate NY charter moved to TN in *Throne of Scars.*

Retired President: Digger, we first met him in *Lyrics on the Wind.*

He passed away and the Lost Kings attended his funeral in *Agony to Ashes*

OTHER LOST KINGS MC MEMBERS

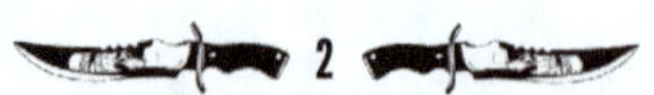

Thomas "Ravage" Kane: We've gotten to know Rav and his snarky humor a little bit better in each book. Ravage is a general member who helps out wherever he is needed.

Cronin "Sparky" Petek: Sparky is the mad genius/hippie stoner behind the Lost Kings MC's pot-growing business. He is rarely seen outside of the basement, as he prefers the company of his plants.

Elias "Bricks" Serrano: We have seen Bricks and his girlfriend Winter throughout the series. He's one of the few members who does not live at the clubhouse.

Sam "Stash" Black: Lives in the basement with Sparky and helps with the plants.

Hoot: We've seen glimpses of him since Slow Burn when he was a lowly prospect. He finally got his full patch, but still gets a lot of the grunt work.

Birch: We also met him as a prospect. He's been voted as a full-patch member but shares in a lot of the grunt work with Hoot.

Priest: The Lost Kings MC's national president. We first met him and his wife, Valentina, in After Burn.

Malik: Prospect for the Lost Kings MC. Helps out at Crystal Ball. Owns the Lucky Duck pawnshop in Ironworks.

Sway: Former president of the downstate charter of the Lost Kings MC. We've seen Sway and his wife Tawny off and on in the series since *Strength From Loyalty,* usually annoying Rock in some fashion. After some legal troubles in *Throne of Scars,* Sway disappeared to Florida and has not been seen since.

THE LADIES OF THE LOST KINGS MC

Hope Kendall North, Esq.: Nicknamed First Lady by Murphy in *Corrupting Cinderella (Lost Kings MC #2),* Hope is the object of Rock's love and obsession. Their daughter is named Grace after Rock's mother.

Trinity Hurst Ramsey: Wrath's angel. Former caretaker of the club. She now has her own photography and graphic design business.

She is married to Wrath, fiercely loyal to the club, and best friends with Hope. Although she loves her niblets, **Trinity and Wrath are happily childfree by choice and intend to *stay* that way**.

Heidi "Little Hammer" O'Callaghan: Murphy's wife and Teller's little sister. Heidi just graduated from college and works at Empire Med. Murphy officially adopted her daughter, Alexa Jade. In *Reckless Truths,* Heidi and Murphy had another daughter, Brittany, affectionately nicknamed "Bit-Bit" by her big sister.

Charlotte Clark, Esq: Teller's sunshine. Often credited with taming the brooding treasurer of the Lost Kings, Teller. As of *Fighting the Forbidden,* she gave birth to twins. In *Collect the Pieces,* we meet Ivy and Ivan.

Lilly Frazier: Z's brave and devoted siren. The new queen of the Lost Kings MC's downstate charter. One of Hope's best friends. Z and Lilly's son is named Chance.

Shelby Morgan: Rooster's sassy little chickadee. Country music singer from Texas. We first met Shelby in *Swagger and Sass.*

Serena Cargill: Former downstate club girl. Abused by Shadow, the former VP of the downstate charter. Found love with her Grinder, her "murder daddy" in *Crown of Ghosts.* She gave birth to their son Lincoln in *Agony to Ashes.*

Emily C. Walker: Engaged to Dex. Serena's best friend. Introduced in *Throne of Scars.* She is the guardian of her teenage sister Libby.

Margot Cedarwood: Daughter of the owner of the Cedarwood Family Funeral Home, a business the Lost Kings MC invested in as of *Reckless Truths.* Jigsaw has had his eye the pretty blonde mortician her since the day they met. She's shy, sweet, and has a dark side.

Liberty Isabel Walker: Libby is Emily's teenage sister. The Walker sisters have no other family. Grinder is protective of them.

Willow: Bartender at Crystal Ball, but once or twice we've caught her sneaking in or out of the basement with Sparky.

Swan: Lost Kings MC club girl and dancer at Crystal Ball. Swan has found a new calling as the yoga teacher for the old ladies of the

Lost Kings MC and is slowly moving away from dancing at Crystal Ball.

OTHER RECURRING CHARACTERS IN THE LOST KINGS MC WORLD

Griffin "Stonewall" Royal: Remy's best friend and business partner. We first meet him in *Renegade Path*. He has been in and out of the series since *Beyond Reason*. He helped Grinder out in *Crown of Ghosts*. In a relationship with Remy's little sister Molly. Their books are *Fighting the Forbidden (Ruthless & Royal #1)* and *Repairing the Wreckage (Ruthless & Royal #2)*.

Roman "Vapor" Hawkins: *Renegade Path* is his story. He is married to Dex's "niece" Juliet. We first see in in *After Burn*.

Remington "Ruthless" Holt: Owns "The Castle" with his best friend, Griff. An underground fighting ring Murphy used to participate in. We've seen him most recently helping out the club in *White Lies, Crown of Ghosts, Agony to Ashes, and Twist the Knife.* Guardian of his younger sister, Molly. Considering forming a support club for the Lost Kings MC with Griff, Eraser, and Vapor.

Easton "Eraser" : Owns Zips, a racetrack near the Lost Kings MC territory. Married to Ella. We first met him in *Renegade Path,* and again in *White Lies*.

Dawson Roads: Famous (fictional) country music singer in the Lost Kings MC world. He's been mentioned here and there since *One Empire Night,* but we didn't officially "meet" him until *Rhythm of the Road* when Shelby was on tour with him. We see him again in *Repairing the Wreckage*.

Carter "Scribbles" Clark: Charlotte's goofy, often inappropriate, younger brother. Most recently rescued by the club in *Reckless Truths.* Given the road name *Scribbles* by Wrath.

Loco: Business associate of the Lost Kings MC. He covers the Ironworks area of the Lost Kings MC's territory. He has appeared throughout the series and become a strong LOKI ally.

Lynn Morgan: Shelby's mother. May or may not have hooked up with Jigsaw or Steer at some point.

Russell "Chaser" Adams: President of the Devil Demons MC in Western NY. (The Hollywood Demons series contains his story.)

Mallory "Little Dove" DeLova-Adams: Chaser's wife. Daughter of mafia boss Anatoly DeLova.

Angelina Adams: Mallory and Chaser's daughter

Linden "Stump" Adams: Chaser's father. Former president of the Devil Demons MC.

Sullivan Wallace: Jake's brother, and the owner of Strike Back Fitness. He's a significant character in *Bullets and Bonfires* and has his own book, *Warnings and Wildfires.*

Jake Wallace: One of Wrath's business partners in Furious Fitness. Jake has appeared off and on throughout the series since Tattered on my Sleeve. He sometimes holds self-defense classes for the ladies.

The mysterious "Quill" who we met in *Diamond in the Dust* and again in *Crown of Ghosts.*

Anatoly DeLova: Mallory's father. Leader of the Russian mafia. Sometime business associate of the Lost Kings MC.

Stella: Pornographic film actress. The downstate charter is the sole investor in her production company. Ex-girlfriend of Z. Current… something of Sway. Her *Sex in Every City* series sometimes requires members of LOKI to work as bouncers on her film sets.

Inga March: Porn star, and former dancer at Crystal Ball. Sued the whole club for paternity of her son in After Burn (Lost Kings MC #10) We last saw her in *Rust or Ride.*

Tawny: Sway's ol' lady. The former "Queen B" of the downstate charter of the Lost Kings MC.

Anya Regal: Porn princess of the Lost Kings MC, Virginia charter.

Shonda: Club girl from the Lost Kings, MC Virginia charter.

Lala: Club girl from Downstate NY.

Bonnie: Club girl from the Downstate club.

OTHER MCS: FRIENDLY CLUBS:

Devil Demons MC: Based in Western NY. Long-time friend of the

Lost Kings MC. Their clubs are intertwined and share a lot of history. More of this is explored in the *Hollywood Demons* series.

Wolf Knights MC: Mostly an ally of the Lost Kings. They used to run Slater County but said they were dissolving their charter in White Lies and turning it over to the Lost Kings. As of *Reckless Truths,* Slater County is officially Lost Kings MC territory.

Iron Bulls MC: (From the Iron Bulls MC series by Phoenyx Slaughter): Southwestern outlaw club. Meets up and does business with LOKI once in a while.

Savage Dragons MC: (From the Iron Bulls MC series by Phoenyx Slaughter): Texas outlaw club.

ENEMY CLUBS:

Vipers MC: Used to run Ironworks until the Lost Kings took over that territory. Still active in other parts of the country.

South of Satan MC: Vermont MC who has stirred up trouble for LOKI in the past. Last disposed of in *Reckless Truths*.

LOST KINGS MC TERMINOLOGY

LOKI: Short for LOst KIngs. Only to be used by members of the Lost Kings MC.

War room: Where the Lost Kings hold "church."

Property patch: When a member takes a woman as his old lady (wife status), he gives her a vest with a property patch. In my series, the vest has a "Property of Lost Kings MC" patch and the member's road name on the back. The officers also place their patches on the ol' lady's vest as a sign that they always have her back. Her man's patch or club symbol is placed over the heart. Rock's patch is a crown. Wrath's is a star. Murphy's is a four-leaf clover. Teller's is a dollar sign. Z's is the letter Z. Rooster's patch is a rooster wearing a crown. As a joke, Wrath gave Rock and Hope a "product of" patch for baby Grace.

PLACES IN THE LOST KINGS MC WORLD

I use a mix of real and imaginary names to describe the places in my series. Again, I bend and shape geography to my needs as this is a fictional world that I have created.

Empire, NY: The territory run by the Lost Kings MC upstate charter. This is a fictional version of Albany, NY, the capital of New York State. Many of the Lost Kings MC's businesses are located in and around Empire.

Slater, NY: Loosely based on Schenectady County. Until recently it was the Wolf Knights MC's territory.

Ironworks, NY: Loosely based on Rensselaer County (Troy, NY). At the beginning of the series, it was run by the Vipers MC. It is now considered territory of the Lost Kings MC.

Union, NY: A fictional area two hours south of Empire, NY, where the "downstate" charter is located.

Pine Hollow, NY: Where the Cedarwood Family Funeral Home is located. About an hour west of Empire, NY.

Crystal Ball: The strip club owned by the Lost Kings MC and one of their legitimate businesses. They often refer to it simply as "CB." Located in Empire County.

Furious Fitness: The gym Wrath owns with Murphy and Jake. Often just referred to as "Furious." Located not far from Crystal Ball.

Strike Back: Owned by Sullivan Wallace but members of the Lost Kings MC and Ruthless & Royal have worked and worked out there in the past.

Johnson County/Johnsonville: Fictional area where Heidi grew up. About an hour west of "Empire." Where Strike Back Gym, The Castle, and Zips are located.

Zips: Racetrack owned by Eraser where all the illegal gambling/racing in the area happens.

The Castle: Formerly a juvenile detention center. The building is now used to house the underground fighting ring run by Remy and Griff. Murphy used to fight here. Other LOKI members also blow off steam in the cage here from time to time. Located in the middle of nowhere, NY, it once-upon-a-time housed Griff, Vapor, Eraser, Sully, and possibly Teller during their "troubled youth" days.

Kodack, NY: Another fictional NY area located in Western New York. Somewhere near Buffalo, perhaps. This territory is run by the Devil Demons MC.

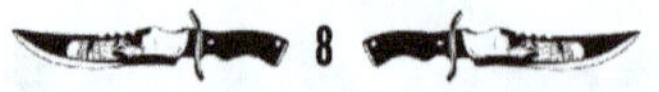

Empire Medical Center: Local hospital where all the Kings receive medical treatment. Heidi also works there now.

OTHER MC TERMINOLOGY

Most terminology was obtained through research. However, I have also used some artistic license in applying these terms to my romanticized, fictional version of an outlaw motorcycle club. This is not an exhaustive list.

Cage: A car, truck, van—basically anything other than a motorcycle.

Church: Club meetings all full-patch members must attend. Led by the president of the club, but officers will update the members on the areas they oversee. (Some clubs refer to the meeting room where they hold church as the "chapel." My club refers to it as their "war room."

Citizen/civilian: Anyone not a hardcore biker or belonging to an outlaw club. "Citizen wife" would refer to a spouse kept entirely separate from the club.

Cut: Leather vest worn by outlaw bikers and adorned with patches and artwork displaying the club's unique colors. The Lost Kings' colors are blue and gray. Their logo is a skull with a crown. The Respect Few, Fear None patch is earned by doing time for the club without snitching. Brother's Keeper patches are earned by killing for the club. Loyal Brother is for a brother who's spent more than five years with the club.

Colors: The "uniform" of an outlaw motorcycle gang. A leather vest, with the three-piece club patch on the back, and various other patches relating to their role in the club.

Fly colors: To ride on a motorcycle wearing colors.

Muffler bunny or "bunnies": A girl who hangs around to provide sexual favors to members. Old ladies in my series will sometimes refer to them as "friends of the club," depending on the girl in question. Some clubs refer to them as club whores, patch whores, or cut sluts. These terms are not regularly used in my series. Sometimes simply referred to as a "club girl."

Nomad: A club member who does not belong to any specific charter, yet has privileges in all charters.

Old lady/ol' lady: Wife or steady girlfriend of a club member.

Patched in: When a new member is approved for full membership.

Patch holder: A member who has been vetted through performing duties for the club as a prospect or probate and has earned his three-piece patch.

Road name: Nickname. Usually given by the other members.

Run: A club-sanctioned outing, sometimes with other chapters and/or clubs. Can also refer to a club business run.

I'm sure I'm forgetting something! But this should be enough to get you started!

CHAPTER ONE

Margot

My emotions have never followed a straight path. They twist, turn, coil, and knot into pieces I can't always identify—some smooth, some jagged. Sometimes they devour me. Other times they disappear.

So many experiences have carved into me, reshaping me into something sharper, softer, or in between. Growing up in my family's funeral home taught me lessons in silence and death. Whispers behind closed doors and endless tears.

But the cruelest lesson came too early. Touched too close. The world showed me the rot that can live inside people who look friendly on the outside. Long before I was old enough to understand what true suffering looked like, I stumbled upon it and accidentally saw the kind of cruelty some people are capable of inflicting on those weaker and more trusting than them.

No one warns you about the aftermath of that discovery—the lingering sense of hopelessness that will drive you crazy when you realize no amount of justice will ever be enough. Nothing will ever replace a life that's been stolen or trust that's been broken.

And now, with Jigsaw standing here, his broad, naked frame crowding the back of my closet where I keep my special *trinkets*, horror carved into his face as he stares at me like he just discovered he's been sleeping with a monster, that same familiar sense of hopelessness slams into me. Like an old unwelcome ghost, it spooks every bit of confidence I've gained over the last few months.

Now he's seen every piece of me. The woman he taught how to enjoy kissing also has a dark side.

He hasn't said a word, but the silence feels like shattered glass at our feet, the pieces too scattered to ever put back together. I should say something, right? Explain myself. Or maybe lie to him.

But resentment, or maybe stubbornness, keeps my mouth shut.

I wasn't ready to share this part of myself with him yet.

He knows my secret; well, not *all* of it. Not the *how* or the *why*. Or even the *who* or the *when.*

If he learns those details, he'd have the power to rip my life apart.

But I don't think he'd betray me. One thing I've learned is that his loyalty runs deep.

Losing him, though? That would devastate me more than any prison cell ever could.

After years of self-doubt, I thought I'd found the person who saw me—all of me. And didn't flinch.

Until now.

CHAPTER TWO

Margot

Margot, 8 years old...

Ominous white moonlight glows around the edges of my curtains. A faint thud from downstairs. Why's fear crackling through my chest?

Momma's sharp, quick whisper. Daddy's heavy footsteps. I toss back my purple quilt and sit on the edge of the bed, listening to the sounds below.

Another voice drifts up. I don't recognize it. It's muffled.

Chills run over my toes as I tiptoe over the hardwood floors, careful to avoid the creaky spots. I quietly twist the cool metal knob until the lock clicks open. My stomach tightens. I shouldn't sneak out of my room. Momma's told me many times not to wander through the house at night. And *especially* not to go downstairs.

I'm not allowed to visit the dead.

I peer into the hallway, heart jumping with fear and curiosity. Shadows snake along the walls. My feet sink into the carpet as I tiptoe to the wide staircase and peer over the banister. No one's below. Voices drift up to me—Momma, Daddy, and another man. Familiar but not clear.

Slowly, I creep down each step, careful to press my body close to the wall where the steps won't make a sound. I'm used to being quiet upstairs. During a service, Momma says I can't make a sound that might disturb the families below.

A door slams. Metal clangs. Outside an engine hums to life.

Momma's voice pulls tighter like a balloon about to pop, broken by a soft sob. Daddy's calm voice soothes. Then silence. I reach the last step and peek around the corner. The hallway leading to the cold room is empty. Light spills over the carpet from an open door.

Burning with curiosity, I hurry toward the open door. Just a quick peek. I can be fast. Momma and Daddy will never catch me.

"How do we keep Margot safe when monsters like him are running around loose?" Momma says.

Fear chills me to a stop. Monsters? Real monsters? Where?

The shadows suddenly seem bigger. Scarier. Can the monsters get into the house?

"Such a nice boy. That poor family," Daddy says. "Good God, he's Margot's age."

Quiet falls over me. Who? What happened?

Momma's harsh sobs cut through the stillness. "What are we going to tell her?"

"Margot understands death better than most children," Daddy says.

Death. It happens to everybody eventually. Nothing to be scared of. Granny tells me that all the time. It still makes me sad every time I think of not seeing her one day.

My family helps other families say goodbye to their loved ones by making them look nice and celebrating their life, Momma explained to me.

I felt good about that until I realized kids don't like to play at my house. Or play with *me*. They make fun of me for living with ghosts and zombies. They whisper that my house is haunted. No matter how many times I try to explain that's not true, they still say it.

Curiosity pulls me closer to the open door. The prep room. I'm not supposed to go in there.

Just a peek. Then I'll sneak right back upstairs. No one will ever know.

My eyes go to the tall, shiny silver table first. A small body, mostly covered with a white sheet. On the counter next to the door rests a blue duffel bag stuffed so full the zipper won't close all the way. Small, shiny black shoes sit on top of the bag. The kind of shoes my older brother James would call "dressy" shoes and only wear to church.

"We'll need to start with a base layer to neutralize the bruising," my mother says. "He's so young." She lets out a harsh sob. "I'll go soft with the foundation. Those purple tones will be stubborn on his delicate skin," she finishes on a whisper.

Daddy rounds the table and gently touches Momma's elbow. "Darling, let's take a break."

She's shaking her head before he finishes speaking. "No. He must have been so afraid. In pain. Terrified. Alone with that monster. I want to stay with him until..."

I slide my gaze back to the table. To the sheet tucked under a pale chin. Freckled cheeks. A wild mop of messy brown hair.

Recognition flips my tummy upside down. I gasp loud enough to draw my mother's attention.

"Margot!" Her eyes widen and she hurries toward me, blocking my view.

"Is that...is that...Hoyt Harris?" The boy who lives down the street. We play together in his backyard and walk to the bus stop together. His mom is nice and makes us oatmeal cookies with chocolate chips instead of nasty raisins. Hoyt never makes fun of me and isn't scared of my house. He even lets me play with his Hot Wheels and doesn't think it's weird that a girl likes cars.

"What are you doing down here?" my father asks, his voice low and calm.

"I heard noises." I tilt to the side, trying to peer around my mother, but she rests her hands on my shoulders, stopping me. "Who is that, Momma? What happened?"

"You should go back to bed, Margot."

Curiosity, too painful to ignore, pushes me out of my mother's grasp and I hurry toward the table.

Hoyt. But he doesn't look like the same boy I play hide and seek

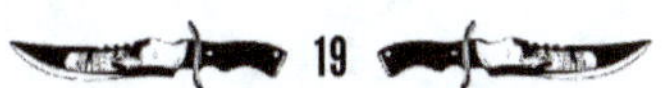

with. The boy who can never contain his laughter while he's supposed to be hiding.

But he's not laughing now.

Or even breathing.

He's *still.* So still he looks like a life-sized doll.

My nose tickles and my eyes burn. "Why? What happened?"

"You know how we always tell you not to go anywhere with strangers?" Daddy says.

"James!" Momma scolds. "Not now."

"No, she needs to know this." Daddy squats in front of me so we're eye-level and grasps the tops of my arms. "It's not just strangers. Even people you think are friendly can be dangerous. Never, ever go into anyone's house without letting one of us know. Not for a minute. Understand?"

Numbly, I nod, but inside I'm a tangle of confusion and fear.

"Never get into anyone's car, either," he adds. "For any reason."

I glance up at my mother. "I know. You told me."

She clasps her hands together and stares at me. "We just love you and want you to be safe."

I peer around Daddy to stare up at the table. "Is that what happened to him?" My small voice shakes. "He went into someone's house without tellin' his momma?"

Daddy clears his throat and pulls me away from the table, closer to Momma. "Something like that."

"But why?" I choke on a sob.

Momma rests her hand on the top of my head, brushing my hair off of my forehead. "Sometimes bad things happen to good people, and it's hard to understand. Hoyt was hurt by someone, and now he's no longer with us. We'll take special care of him."

"Who hurt him?" My voice comes out small and squeaky. "Why? He was so nice."

Momma and Daddy share a look.

"You know Mr. Gade?" Momma says.

My eyebrows pinch together. Mr. Gade lives a bunch of houses down the road. He's weird but always hands us candy when we go by his yard.

"Don't," Daddy says, touching Momma's arm. To me, he says, "The police have him. He won't hurt anyone else."

Tears burn my eyes. "What about Hoyt's momma and daddy?"

Another sob escapes Momma. She closes her eyes briefly.

"We'll do everything we can for them," Daddy says.

"Can I say goodbye to Hoyt?" I stare up at the table.

"Yes. At the service," Momma promises. "Now, come on. Back to bed."

She settles one hand between my shoulders and presses, turning me toward the door. My throat tightens and my stomach churns. My heart pounds so loud it drowns out the sounds of my feet shuffling against the cold tile.

Momma doesn't take her hand off me, guiding my steps as if she's afraid I'll return to Hoyt's side. But the heavy feeling in my chest won't allow me to move anywhere but forward.

Upstairs, Momma tucks me under my purple quilt with the rainbows and unicorns, tucking it under my chin and smoothing it out around me. The unicorns are such a bright white, I can practically see them glowing in the semi-darkness. She leans over and kisses my forehead. "Go back to sleep," she murmurs. "I love you more than anything."

"Love you too, Momma." I curl my fingers in my quilt and pull it higher, then turn on my side.

My door quietly clicks closed behind her. Hoyt's pale face and still form won't leave my mind. My eyes pop open but staring into the darkness is even worse.

CHAPTER THREE

Jigsaw

PANTS.

I need to put on my pants.

My brain might be slow to clunk its way into action, and it's definitely having trouble instructing my body to move, but one thought keeps hammering against my skull—I can't have this conversation with Margot while my dick's swinging in the breeze.

"Can we…" I wave my arm toward the bedroom, but it doesn't do anything to stop the prickling sensation creeping over my skin. "Talk about this in there? I'm not a big fan of enclosed spaces." I don't even give a fuck about admitting that to her. I just need to get out of *this closet*.

Margot blinks and steps back. Her lips purse, and a flicker of sadness or disappointment ripples over her face. That's the last thing I want. I hurry past her and down the long corridor, leading into her bedroom. Once I'm free of the closet, I inhale a long, sweet breath.

What the fuck?

Pants? Where did I leave my pants?

There. Draped over the bottom of the bed.

That's not where I left them. Did Margot put them there?

Who cares?

Images of Margot's souvenirs dangle in my mind. Twisted trophies turned into ornaments.

Pants first.

My Margot. Soft and sweet. But also dark and deadly. How could I not suspect…anything?

Maybe I did, and that's why I started calling her *little lady death.* Is that why I've been drawn to her since the first time we met? Have I always been drawn to the darkness in her even if I didn't recognize it right away?

Nope. I'm not that deep.

I yank my jeans on, buttoning them and fumbling with my belt like I've forgotten how my own hands work. Why am I so rattled? I've killed more than my share of people. Watched my brothers kill. Helped my brothers clean up *after* they killed. I keep my own box of murder souvenirs. Who am I to judge anyone?

This is different.

Why? I don't know.

I've only known one side of Margot—the sweet, shy, kind woman who captured my interest the first time I saw her. It's not her kill trophies that have my heart tied into a knot. It's the religious bullshit she started spouting that unnerved me. *That's* where it all went wrong.

I slip my shirt on and scrub my hands over my face, still trying to make sense of it all.

"Are you leaving?" she asks in a low, uncertain voice.

I turn and find her with her back to the now-closed closet door—the door to so many mysteries I don't want to solve.

But I kinda do.

Call me Detective Murder, but I *want* to know every last detail.

"No. I'm not leaving." I might be freaked the fuck out, but I'm not a damn coward.

She blows out a relieved breath and closes her eyes.

"Meeoww."

Gretel slides her sleek body through the open bedroom door and hurries toward Margot. She weaves herself around Margot's ankles, then gracefully sits, wrapping her tail neatly around her legs. She tilts her head up and stares at me as if she demands I hear Margot out. *"Meeorrww."*

Freaky-ass cat.

"You…" My voice comes out rougher than I intended. "How long have you been… doing *that*?" I vaguely gesture toward her closet of horrors.

"A few years," she admits, her gaze steady now but still guarded. "Only in…extreme cases."

A few *years*. I stare at her hands, clasped in front of her. The same hands I've seen tenderly care for the dead…have also caused death.

"When you say 'extreme cases'…"

Her chin tilts up, her eyes brimming with a mix of defiance and vulnerability. It's possible I'm the only person she's ever told about her murderous hobby.

"I mean exactly *that*." She crosses her arms over her chest.

I force a smirk onto my face that probably looks deranged as fuck. "I'm still gonna need more details, sweetheart."

She shoots me a glare that could freeze blood.

Fucking hell, she's hot.

Have I found my Harley Quinn?

"Are you sure you want those details, Jensen?" The grave way she uses my given name snaps me back to our discussion.

"Every fucking word."

She nods once and pulls her robe tighter around her body. "Let's go out there." She tilts her head toward the living room.

Yeah, this isn't a bedroom conversation. I nod and hold the door open for her.

Gretel scurries out ahead of us, leading the way.

When Margot and I are seated at the counter, she swivels her stool to face me. Gretel bats her little paws at Margot's legs until Margot leans over and settles the cat in her lap.

"What?" I reach over and rub behind Gretel's ears. "My lap's no good anymore?"

She purrs and rubs her cheek against my fingers but stays right where she is.

Margot absently strokes her hand over the cat's shiny black fur. "When I was about eight years old, a friend from the neighborhood—a boy my age—was…" She swallows hard as if it's too painful to share. "Murdered."

The word lands between us like a cement block. Whatever explanation I expected, it didn't start with the death of a kid.

"He was m…murdered by a…a…a predator in the neighborhood." She stutters through the words, then takes a deep breath.

"Jesus. I'm sorry. That must've been awful for you."

Margot nods, her face pale, fingers still stroking Gretel's fur even as her gaze turns distant. "I…I saw him. His body." She tilts her head slightly toward the front door of her apartment. "Downstairs. I…used to sneak around the house at night when I was little." She lets out a soft laugh. "Aaron, one of my brothers, thought it was funny to teach me all the ways to avoid getting caught. That night started out no different than many others. I heard a noise downstairs and trotted off to investigate."

Dread curls in my stomach. This story isn't going anywhere wholesome.

I lean forward, resting my elbows on my thighs and slide my fingers around one of her hands. "Take your time."

She squeezes my hand briefly. "I wasn't supposed to go in there. I knew what we did—the family business. But Mom always told me we helped families give their loved ones a proper goodbye. I didn't really understand what that meant. Like, the behind-the-scenes stuff."

"Yeah, eight seems young to explain the nitty gritty of funeral prep." That sounds stupid to say to someone who grew up in a funeral home. When death is literally her family's business. What do I know about what's appropriate or not?

"So, I peeked. And I saw him on the table. Heard my mother talking about what they needed to do…" She swallows hard. "To cover all his bruises." She chokes on a sob and shakes her head.

I wait while she gathers her composure. "My mother sent me back to bed. We had the funeral here. It was…surreal. All of my classmates were here. Some didn't understand and made horrible jokes…"

"Kids can be fucking awful."

She nods once. "After that, my parents were different. They'd always given me these really intense stranger danger speeches. But now they kept reminding me that sometimes the people you know—neighbors, teachers, friends of the family—weren't safe either."

Smart move. I remain silent so she doesn't stop talking.

"At the time, I didn't understand what had happened. But later, when I learned the truth..." She clears her throat before continuing. "It wasn't until I was in high school that I looked up all the information I could find about what happened to Hoyt. That's when I finally realized how bad it had been," she finishes on a whisper. "How much he suffered."

My stomach tightens. I don't think *I* want the details, and I didn't even know the kid. I can't imagine Margot as a teenager piecing it all together.

"Hoyt and I used to walk to the bus stop together," she says softly. "He was one of the only kids who didn't make fun of me for living in a funeral home." The corners of her mouth tilt into a sad smile. "He'd try to defend me when kids bullied me, but he wasn't much bigger than I was."

"Sounds like a good kid."

"He really was." Her eyes shine and she drops her head, hugging Gretel closer. "He loved to be outside doing stuff. I was allowed to walk down the street to play in his backyard. His mom was really nice. She used to make us these magic cookie bars on the weekends. Sometimes he'd come over here to play. Nothing scared him."

By eight I'd already had a brutal education in how evil people could be. I almost envy the childhood Margot's talking about, except I know the dark turn that's coming.

"One day Hoyt didn't show up for school. When I came home the police were here. They questioned me about the last time I saw Hoyt. I'd said goodbye to him on the sidewalk in front of his house the day before. That was all I could tell them."

The guilt in her voice tears me up. I reach over and rest my hand on her knee, offering my silent support.

"There was a man in the neighborhood, Mr. Gade. He seemed harmless—always tending his garden and giving out candy. Someone must've told the police they saw Hoyt near Mr. Gade's house." Her hand strokes over the cat's fur faster. "He was a man who lived down the street. Hoyt and I always ran into him. He was friendly enough but kind of…strange. He'd stop us to ask questions about school. I used to be jealous because he'd give Hoyt candy, and little toys. Hoyt loved Hot Wheels. I did too but Mr. Gade never had any for me. As a kid I was jealous. Later on…"

"You were just a kid," I remind her gently. What kid wouldn't be jealous?

"When I was eight, I didn't understand all of it. All I knew was that Hoyt was gone. But later, I learned the truth about Mr. Gade…" She shakes her head quickly, as if she's eager to purge the rest of these memories. "They found Hoyt in Mr. Gade's house a few days later. Stuffed into some cubby in the walls like insulation." Her voice cracks. "The things that man did to him…" She takes several deep gulps of air. "I briefly saw his body…but I didn't comprehend…"

"Margot." I slide off my stool and wrap my arms around her. "It had to be traumatic to see your friend like that." What the fuck were her parents thinking? Why didn't they take better precautions to protect Margot? Something so deliberate and cruel happening to a friend at that age had to be devastating for her.

"It was. The neighborhood was so different after that. Even though they arrested him rather quickly for Hoyt's death, there were stories that he'd abused a lot of other kids over the years. Kids stopped going outside to play. My mom or dad always drove me to school after that. But the worst thing was that he was only sentenced to fifteen years in prison."

Fifteen years. Grinder, the SAA of my charter, served that much time for a crime he didn't even commit. Some fucking child-murdering sicko did the same amount of time? "Jesus Christ."

"I remember how angry my parents were. They called representatives and judges. My father worked on the campaign for the man who ran against the DA in the next election. It was a pretty big deal out here."

"I can understand why."

Her lips tighten into a flat, angry line. "He didn't even serve the full sentence. I had just graduated from college when there was an uproar about him possibly returning to the neighborhood."

"Really?"

Margot nods. "His mother had passed away and left the house to him."

"Are you fucking kidding me?"

"I wish I was." Her hands clench into fists in her lap. "I was so… furious. That wasn't *justice*. All I could think about were Hoyt's parents. They never recovered from losing their son. They moved away. But that disgusting creature was out and about, free to live his life."

The answer to my question is dangling in Margot's closet but I ask anyway. "What did you do?"

She lifts her head. Slowly, a wicked gleam replaces the sorrow in her eyes.

"I started planning."

CHAPTER FOUR

Margot

Margot, 22 years old.

No trespassing. *We don't call 911.* A drawing of a handgun sits in between the two warning sentences.

Since Mr. Gade is a felon, I highly doubt he has a gun in the house. The sign is meant to scare all the people who protested when he moved into the neighborhood after being released from prison. That must make for a fun visit when his parole officer stops by. Or maybe his parole officer hasn't had time to visit yet. Who knows, maybe he thinks the sign is funny.

A gun wouldn't save him tonight anyway.

Considering I saw Mr. Gade strolling near the elementary school Monday afternoon and caught him talking to a kid yesterday, it seems the parole board was misguided in allowing this murdering freak his freedom so early.

Another example of the many ways the justice system fails children.

Ignoring the sign, I circle to the back of the house. Layers of darkness remain around the white rustic Victorian home. For a man who'd had dozens of death threats when he moved in, you'd think he would've installed some motion detector lights.

A window on the rickety back utility porch is partially open. I could probably crawl through it but I'd rather not risk getting my clothing caught on a stray nail. My blonde hair's slicked into a neat bun, tucked up under my tight, black knit cap. The slick black jacket I'm wearing is brand-new and zipped to my chin. My tight black pants are also brand-new. I wanted to avoid leaving any evidence after tonight's visit. Nothing from my home to be accidentally left behind and tied to me. The small black backpack slung tight to my shoulders and stuffed with supplies has never even been inside my home.

Still, I'll probably make a mistake. But it's a risk I've accepted.

For Hoyt. Little Hoyt who never got to grow up, to finish school, decide if he wanted to leave town or stay. A child who didn't receive justice. Not as far as I'm concerned.

Stop. Don't think about him now.

Let's get this done.

Slowly, I curl my fingers around the small metal handle on the screen door. A low screech echoes as I turn, turn, turn the ancient knob.

I stop. Wait. Cock my head and listen.

The sound probably didn't carry as far as I think it did. I tug and the door lurches open with a weary, metallic groan.

Another pause and listen.

I open the door just wide enough to slip through and onto the enclosed porch. It's so dark, I can barely see in front of my nose as I step onto the bouncy wooden floor. I don't dare take out my mini flashlight, though. Not yet.

A faint shine ahead of me must be the glass window on the door leading into the house. Beyond that a faint, blueish flicker.

Fear crackles through my stomach.

Mr. Gade must be awake.

There's still time to leave. Go home. Forget this madness.

I curl my fingers around the brass knob and twist.

It doesn't move.

I crouch down to inspect the knob. It's a simple, single keyed lock. Same as you can buy at any hardware store. I pull out the master key I'd bought for this occasion. It's supposed to work on a variety of simple household door locks.

Metal on metal grinds and clicks as I ease the key into the hole and meet resistance.

I swear under my breath and pocket the key. Although I have a small hammer in my little bag of tools, breaking the glass is a last resort. Instead, I finesse a small, thin, flexible piece of metal about the shape of a credit card out of my jacket pocket. Gripping it tight between my thumb and index finger, I wiggle it into the gap between the door and the doorframe, then slide it as close as I can to the doorknob. I'd practiced this at home on every door in the house. Once I get the feel for the mechanism, I tilt the metal toward the doorknob and quickly pop it back the opposite way. The latch springs free with a sharp click.

I push the door open a few inches and wait.

A hot wave of onions, garlic, and something more putrid rolls through the gap. I turn my head and gag. In all of my planning, I never considered how bad the house might smell.

There's a slight whine as I push the door a few more inches.

Based on the photos I'd studied from the listing when the house had been for sale, I'm entering the kitchen. My eyes slowly adjust to the gloom, and I can make out old, white appliances—refrigerator, a crusty looking stove, and a battered microwave. It's almost Christmas, but a filthy pair of Fourth-of-July-themed dishtowels dangle from the oven handle.

I close the door with the softest *snick* of metal on metal. Inside, the smell's even worse. Like the man scrubs every surface and appliance with garlic cloves and onion peels instead of Formula 409 and a sponge.

The flickering from the TV in the front room catches my

attention. I can't see what's playing on the screen but the sounds… they're not innocent. My skin crawls and my heart lurches as if it's trying to leave my body and run into the night.

No. I won't give into my fear. This gets done tonight. Tomorrow, the world will be safer. One less fiend preying on children.

Or you'll be the one who's dead.

Or in jail.

Doesn't matter. It'll be worth it if I spare another kid Hoyt's fate.

I'm not delusional. I don't think I'm a savior or better than anyone else. I just don't want to see another kid brutalized and murdered.

With my breath trapped in my lungs, I tiptoe across the tile floor. Even with my shoes on, it feels gritty or dirty under my feet.

Bam! My hip slams into something solid. A scrape of furniture against floor rips through the air.

My body freezes. I squeeze my eyes shut and wait. Blood pounds through my ears.

The awful moans and whines from the television continue.

In small increments I ease my body away from the kitchen chair I'd bumped into and edge forward. Silently, I slide the backpack off my shoulders and rest it on the chair I'd knocked away from the table. Feeling my way with gingerly outstretched hands and soft sweeps of one foot in front of the other, I continue toward the flickering blue light.

The living room is straight ahead. Long dark curtains cover the windows facing the street.

There he is. Dimly lit by the glow of the television. Unruly tufts of hair sticking out all over his head. No awareness that I'm creeping up behind him. Guilt and unease about invading someone's private space prickle around the edges of my conscience.

No. He doesn't deserve peace or privacy. The state of New York might think he's "paid for his crime" but I strongly disagree. I'd bet my life Hoyt's parents would agree with me.

I pull a syringe out of my pocket and uncap it. Two more full syringes are rolling around in my pocket—just in case. Full to the brim with a popular tranquilizer I'd helped myself to at the lovely veterinarian's office when we did a pickup there last month. The poor man had a heart attack while tending to the animals overnight. One of the dogs who'd been boarded at the vet's office stood guard over the old man's body all night long. The vet techs had to gently coax the pup away so we could tend to the body. I suffered a twinge of guilt at the theft, but I didn't have an easier way to get my hands on what I needed, and I knew this man had to be dealt with soon.

A sharp bleat of pain from the television's speakers almost jolts my soul from my body. In the chair, Mr. Gade moans.

With great reluctance I turn toward the screen. Maybe my subconscious already knows what's playing and my brain refuses to accept it. It takes great effort to force my gaze toward the sound of the awful noise. Finally, I take in the images. My stomach plunges.

I slam my eyes shut and bite back a whimper.

Children. That's where the horrible sounds have been coming from. From children. Young ones. So small. Grainy images on the television. Being forced to do things no child should ever witness or be part of.

My fear and determination slip away, replaced with a sorrow that fills my heart, yet also leaves me frozen and empty.

Then my gaze drops to Mr. Gade. His hand shoved down the front of his sweatpants. His slack jaw and glazed eyes focused on the screen of horrors in front of him.

Enjoying himself.

Anger blazes my fear and sorrow into ashes, leaving nothing but the bone-deep need to end this sick creature's life.

He's so engrossed in his disturbing home movie, he hasn't even noticed me.

The high back of his chair partially blocks my aim. I have to sneak in close—too close for my comfort—yet somehow he doesn't see me in his peripheral vision. A dark, angry shadow about to plunge a needle into the side of his neck.

Now! I pierce his skin and jam the plunger down.

Stunned, he turns and jerks to the side, staring up at me with wide, confused eyes. His shoulder twitches up as if he wants to bat the needle away but his wrist is still trapped in the waistband of his pants.

His body jolts, the tendons in his neck standing out. Completely rigid, he slumps to the side of the chair, eyes wide and staring at me.

I'd been worried a dose meant for dogs might not be enough for a human, but it seems to have stunned him for now.

His lips move like a fish gulping air, but no words come out.

"Who am I?" I taunt. "Is that what you want to know?"

More fish-gulping.

"A friend of Hoyt's," I answer. "I've waited a long time for this night." I tilt my head toward the screen without looking at it again. "I see you haven't changed at all. The world's going to be a whole lot safer with one less pervert in it."

His limbs jerk as if he's willing his body to move or run away. Still worried I might have the wrong dosage and he could escape, I pull out another syringe. Usually I'm sucking fluid *out* of bodies, but I still know exactly where to poke—right into his fat, juicy jugular vein.

He chokes and gurgles, his body curling in on itself like a dried leaf. *Whoopsie*. Maybe *that* was too much.

"I'd like to leave as little evidence behind as possible," I warn, moving in front of him while turning my back to the television screen. "I wanted to stuff you into the wall. The way you did to Hoyt. But I feel like that's going to take a lot of time and effort on my part." I tap my chin as if I'm pretending to review all my options. "I don't relish the idea of making your death look like a suicide, though. Because clearly you have no remorse for your actions."

More choking sounds.

I pull a knife out of my pocket. "I really do want to take a souvenir, though, so I guess that will make it obvious it's *not* a suicide."

Now I'm just babbling. I wish I'd come up with a more solid plan before tonight. Stun and paralyze him with an injection so I can take my time killing him was as far as I'd gotten.

"Maybe a closet will work? It'll take a while for anyone to find you. Give any evidence some time to deteriorate."

I pull a thick black zip tie from the cargo pocket of my pants.

Grabbing the sleeve of his grimy sweatshirt, I tug and pull until his hand pops out of the waistband of his pants. I grip his other wrist and bind them together, cinching the zip tie tight. Just in case the drugs wear off before I finish my search of the house. Keeping an eye on him, I squat in front of the chair and bind his ankles together.

"Guh-guh-guh," he sputters.

"Gun? You have a gun you want me to shoot you with?"

He squeezes his eyes shut.

I'm not sure how to interpret that, nor do I care. Instead, I return to the kitchen, where I grab one of the gross little Fourth-of-July towels. I return to the living room and force it in his mouth, tying it tightly behind his head. "Just in case those two doses wear off. I didn't precisely measure them." A wild laugh escapes from my lips. His eyes bug impossibly wider as if a little unhinged laughter is more terrifying than anything else that's happened to him tonight.

"People think guys like you get 'prison justice' when they're inside, but that's not always true, is it?" I tsk. "You had a nice, cushy, segregated area of the prison where you had the luxury of associating with more sickos just like you, right?"

He grunts unintelligible sounds through the dishtowel.

I sit back and squint at him. "Are you working your way through the alphabet or something? I can't make out what you're trying to say." I flick the dishtowel out of his mouth.

"Puh, puh, puh-lease."

"Please?" I ask in a high, mocking tone.

He blinks his eyes.

"Please. Huh. That's interesting." I swallow hard. "Did Hoyt say please? Did he beg you not to hurt him? Did all those other kids before Hoyt say please too?"

He stares at me.

I stand and grab the remote off the side table, then punch the *mute* button. Silence, except for Gade's gasping breaths and my pounding heart, descends over the house.

"You stay put." I laugh and shake my head. "Who am I kidding. You're not going anywhere."

With the final notes of uneasy laughter dying in my throat, I move out of the living room and into the long hallway stretching to the back of the house. On the left, a nightlight throws off enough dim light to make out a shadowy bathroom. Across from the bathroom, I push open a light door with enough force that the knob bangs into the wall with a harsh clang. I wince at the sound and throw my arm out to stop the door's violent swing. I don't want to turn on a light but then I notice the heavy curtains over the sole window. I thumb the switch on the wall and squint at the harsh, yellow glare from a single bulb overhead.

Piles and piles of clothing are scattered over every surface. Some of it in baskets. Some just heaped on the floor. The scent of detergent mixed with foul funk triggers my gag reflex. Someone must not like doing his own laundry.

A colorful stack of boxes in the far corner snags my attention and I hurry closer. Disbelief and dread battle inside me. Candy. Not even good candy. The generic, colorful, sugary candy that looks pretty but tastes like fruity chalk. The kind that appeals to young kids who haven't yet discovered that better candy exists.

What's Gade doing with such a large stash of treats? Nostalgic for his own youth? Or am I looking at the bait he'll use to attract new victims? He used to give Hoyt and me candy all the time when we were kids. He even gave Hoyt little toys sometimes. I search the colorful boxes. Just candy.

Has Gade already harmed another kid? I've kept tabs on him, but I can't devote every second to the man without raising suspicions.

Whatever the reason, the candy stash seems like another sign that I'm doing the right thing. As I stand, the curtains catch my eye. They're thick and heavy but that's not the only reason it's so dark in here. A sheet of plywood has been bolted to the wall, completely covering the window.

Gade *really* wants to make sure no one can peek inside.

Still pondering the window situation, I wander into the next bedroom. It's dark. Absolutely black inside. Probably more plywood covering the windows. I search the wall for a switch, flip it, and a small lamp in the corner blinks on, casting a soft pinkish glow around the room.

A child's room.

Disgust and fear churns in my stomach. Who the hell would allow him to have a kid visit? Or is he setting up a trap for his next victim? The walls are painted a soft blue. A blue bookshelf holds rows of children's books. The blue metal-framed bed is neatly made up with a bright red-and-blue race car comforter. Even the little lamp, now that I can see it better, is in the shape of a red race car.

Is this Gade's room? From what I remember of him from when I was a kid, and in the interviews I've studied more recently, he acts childlike. It almost makes him seem non-threatening. When in reality, he's a monster.

Does he sleep in this childish room to feel closer to his victims?

No, never mind. I can't…I can't dwell on the implications of this room. That's not why I'm here. He's a bad guy. He killed my friend. That's all I need to know. Let the police do their jobs and discover the rest when they find his body.

I flick the light off and move to the last bedroom across the hall. The overhead light flickers to life, revealing old, heavy wood furniture with ornate carvings. The elevated four-poster bed is almost too big for the bedroom, taking up most of the floor space. A small step stool sits near the side of the bed. The covers are rumpled and tossed to the side. *This* is his room. An adult's room, which makes the children's setup across the hall even more concerning.

Sweat and something muskier seems to hang in the heavy air. I wrinkle my nose and slide one of the dresser drawers open. Empty.

The small closet holds a few jackets on hangers but not much else.

As I'm about to close the closet door, a small cut in the wall behind the jackets catches my attention. I search for a light inside the closet and find one of those small, round tap lights. I push the *on* button, praying the batteries are fresh.

The harsh white glare helps illuminate the back wall of the closet. The cuts in the wall are roughly the shape of a small door. My own house has plenty of little oddities, strange doors, and closets. But those have been there for decades. The house was designed with them.

This looks recent and sloppily done. Like Gade was in desperate need of a hiding place and took a utility knife to the drywall.

Dread fills my body.

What's behind that makeshift door?

I tease my fingernails into the seam and pry the rectangle of drywall loose. It swings toward me like a broken piece of cardboard. Cool, musty air drifts over my exposed wrists. No scent of decay, thank God.

Edging closer, I thrust the light forward and peer inside. VHS tapes. Stacks of them against the walls. Shoeboxes also stacked in neat rows. I don't have to be a criminologist to know what's on the videotapes. Probably more of what was playing out in his living room.

I duck inside and pick up a large, yellow padded envelope sitting on top of the stack of tapes. It's addressed to Gade at this address from a PO Box in Kentucky. Inside, it feels like another VHS tape.

Sure, knowing his parole officer would be monitoring his computer usage, Gade had to go old school—all the way back to videotapes. Amazing that he's only been out of prison for a few months and already managed to track down this appallingly large collection of depravity.

Curious about the shoeboxes, I flip the lid off of one of them.

No, no, no.

A photo of a child in pajamas with terror written all over his face rests on top.

I slam my eyes shut. *I can't.*

The box is full of photographs that I assume only get progressively worse.

I rest the lid on the box without closing it fully, afraid the malignancy of what's inside will somehow wear off on me if I touch it too much.

Slowly, I back away from the tapes and boxes. A whispered *zing* of metal against the nylon of my jacket stops me. I turn my head to the side and stare. A large silver nail that has to be at least five or six inches long juts out of one of the wall studs at a sharp angle. That could've hurt if I'd backed into it. More large nails stick out from different spots. I can't tell if Gade is planning to hang items or the contractor who built the house went wild on his nails budget, but it does give me an idea…

Otherwise, I've seen enough.

It's time to finish what I came to do and then get out of here. The longer I stay, the greater my risk.

Gade's eyes are glued to the screen when I return to the living room. They have a distant, far-off dreamy quality that crawls over my skin. He grunts and twitches as I stand in front of him, blocking his view.

"You've been worse than I expected." I stare down at him, already weary of this disgusting man.

His throat works hard to release whimpers and muffled pleas of innocence. His fear and desperation only disgust me. I take no pleasure in torturing him and I certainly don't want to drag this out.

My mind spirals with the dark possibilities. In a perfect world, no one person should act as judge, jury, and executioner. But the price of following the "law" in this case is an innocent child's life being forever altered.

The videos.

The photos.

In my limited observation of Gade, I've already caught him wandering too close to the local elementary school. It's all proof that it's only a matter of time before he harms another child. He can't help himself.

Should I try calling his parole officer first? What will they do—send him back to prison? Then I'll be doing this in two to four years when they release him again.

No one else is going to put this man down. It *has* to be me. Besides, I'm already here and he's already drugged.

We're halfway there.

I've fantasized about this for fourteen long years. I can't turn back now.

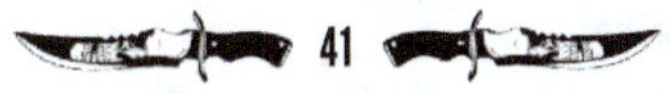

"I'd like to do this as quickly and cleanly as possible." I pace in front of him, weighing my options. "I have my scalpel." I pat my pocket. "I bought a new one, just for you." I toss him an evil smile. "But that might get messy." I look down at my black jacket and pants. I'm planning to burn them after tonight anyway, but I don't want to encounter anyone between here and home with blood on my clothes. "That giant four-poster bed gave me some ideas though. I don't need to get you high off the ground to—oh." My nose wrinkles. "I found your disgusting stash. Your hidden room."

His eyes widen and more gurgling noises work out of his throat.

"Yes, I think we'll do it in your special little hidden room."

The pieces of my macabre puzzle fall into place as I turn back to the kitchen and grab my small backpack of goodies. I take out the rope, hitch the backpack over my shoulder, and return to the living room.

"I was worried the drugs might not knock you out so I—"

Gade's belly-crawling and wriggling across the floor like a snake slithering for freedom.

"Oh no you don't." I knew I'd gotten too cocky. Hurrying to close the distance between us, I land on his back with one knee. "Where do you think you're going?" I brace my other foot against the floor and loop the rope around his neck, yanking hard.

His forward motion stops but he thrashes underneath me. I yank the rope tighter and tighter, thankful for the gloves protecting my palms. Finally, he stops moving.

"You better not be dead yet." Wary it might be a trick, I slowly ease myself off of him, still holding tight to the rope and breathing hard.

Now what?

Thankfully, he's not a big man. I thread the rope through the zip ties around his wrists and use it to drag him to his bedroom. His body rustles and scrapes over the floor. Damn, the police will probably notice the drag marks through all the dustiness and grime of the house.

Then again, they're going to find him stuffed in the wall and missing at least one body part, so that'll kind of make it obvious it wasn't suicide.

Dragging him down the hallway isn't hard. Making the turn into the bedroom is a little more difficult. Pulling him into the closet and then through the space in the wall—is like pushing dough through a keyhole.

His wrists are raw and bleeding. Definitely no hiding that. Even if he's here for a while, decomposing before he's found, evidence that he was bound will still be there.

It's awkward in the tight space. I end up crouching over him to tie the rope around his neck in a noose knot. Underneath me he wakes with a shuddering gasp. His body flips, his shoulder banging into my thigh and knocking me off balance.

"Shit!" I land painfully on my knees.

Still bound by the zip ties, he awkwardly flops and rolls to his hands and knees, then pitches forward, hitting the floor with his shoulder.

"Enough of this," I growl, yanking the rope hard. The knot slides down, tightening around his neck.

He chokes and curls his thumbs under the rope, trying to tug it free but it's sturdy rope and I practiced this particular knot over and over before tonight.

Groaning in pain, I stand and limp toward the wall. Dragging the rope with him flailing at the end with all my might, I lasso my end around the nail I almost impaled myself on earlier and tug straight down.

Gade gets to his knees and tries to crawl toward the door.

The knot around his neck tightens. He pitches forward but the rope keeps him from hitting the floor. I hurry to tie the loose end into another knot, tightening it, effectively hanging him in mid-air. I've assisted with a few bodies of people who accidentally strangled themselves during solo-sex sessions. I always thought it would be a fitting way for Gade to die. If I hadn't found the nail, I probably would've used those tall bedposts that almost reach the ceiling. But this is better.

I pull on the rope again, wanting to choke every wisp of life from this evil man.

His body twitches and struggles as I step in front of him. The nail in the wall should hold. Even if it doesn't, Gade's too close to death to do much about it. I set my backpack on the floor and pull out the small glass lab jar, unscrewing the cap and setting it on the floor. I shake out a large plastic bag with a zippered seal at the top and set it next to the jar.

Gade's eyes dart wildly while he chokes and drools, his skin turning an ugly shade of red.

"Hopefully for you, that anesthetic hasn't worn all the way off." I pull out my scalpel, gripping it tightly. I can't feel the coolness of the metal through my gloves, but I don't need to.

Gade's tongue pokes between his lips. Red dots speckle the whites of his eyes as his body swings wildly to the side, desperate for oxygen.

"I have to listen to a lot of sermons in my line of work. Even took some theology classes in college." My tone remains conversational and steady, even though inside I'm shaking. "And you know which quote always resonated with me the most?"

Gade's eyes widen and he shakes his head.

"Don't worry, I'm not a religious nut." A wicked smile stretches across my face. "My job's turned me into an atheist, if anything. No, actually—" I pause, allowing childhood memories to sharpen in my mind. "*You* did that. Taking my friend. In such a brutal way. At the funeral, I asked my mother how God could allow something so awful to happen to Hoyt. Spoiler alert—her answer didn't satisfy me."

His throat works as if he's trying to gasp for air or speak, but only scratchy, pathetic sounds escape.

"If your right eye causes you to stumble, gouge it out and throw it away." I lean in close, my tone soft and almost reverent. "*That's* the quote. People don't talk about it enough."

Gage's eyes bug out. Poor guy. He must sense where I'm going with this.

"Everyone says Jesus was being hyperbolic, but he said it *twice*. I think he meant it—avoid sin at all costs. *All costs.* Not commit your sins, pretend to ask for forgiveness, then do it all over again."

His face really is turning purple now. Not much longer.

"You know, it reminds me of men who blame women for 'dressing provocatively' when they rape them. Like, what kind of bullshit is that? What's the excuse when it's a child, huh?" I slap his cheek. "I'm actually asking here. What was Hoyt wearing that got you so worked up, you sick fucker? His Optimus Prime T-shirt? Or maybe it was his kind smile. The way he'd wave hello to you in the morning when we passed your house?" My voice cracks but I continue, "We all would've been better off if you'd plucked out your own damn eyes. Better to enter heaven with no eyes than to sin."

He thrashes, arms clawing at the rope.

I snort with laughter. "It's not my place to judge, but I'm pretty sure if there's a hell, that's where you're headed."

Grabbing his head with one hand and holding him steady, I slowly sink my thumb into his eye socket. The soft, squishy tissue gives way easier than you'd expect. "It's fitting that you were watching that homemade filth when I got here—I'm going to leave the television on, so the cops get a good look at what you were up to." I probe and wiggle until there's a wet, sickening pop and the eyeball comes free, still connected by nerves and tissue.

Thin, reedy, airless screams tear from Gade's throat and his body sways from side to side, still tethered by the rope.

I flick my gaze to where the rope's tied to the nail. The knot slides against the long, shiny metal but seems to be holding. All good.

Before I lose my nerve, I slice the blade of the scalpel through the connective tissue all around the eyeball. Gade's head jerks once, then slumps forward, the rope still holding his dead weight.

I pop the eyeball in my little jar, secure the lid, and carefully wipe the blood on my scalpel off on a clean corner of Gade's shirt.

My gloves are messy, and I carefully roll them off, turning them inside out as I do. I drop them in my open backpack and pull a new pair from a separate front pocket.

Exhausted but numb, I stand and stagger toward the boxes of

photographs. Grabbing the one with the loose top, I dump the photos around Mr. Gade's lifeless body, still suspended by the rope. Thankfully, many of the photos land face-down. But far too many assault my eyes.

Tears burn my lids, blurring the horrors in front of me. So many different children. Too many. Some have adults in the photos, too. I doubt these are all Gade's victims. Probably photos he traded for or bought from other creeps. I can't look at them too closely or I'll break down.

I still have so much to do.

I squeeze my eyes shut, but the images are forever seared into my brain.

I should've taken both of his eyes.

Will the cops ever be able to piece together who these children are and where the photos came from?

Slower now, I grab a pair of snips from my backpack and cut the zip ties from Gade's wrists and ankles, then stuff them in my pocket.

Blood from his eye socket drips and hits the wood floor with a soft *splat, splat, splat.*

Bile sizzles through my stomach but I can't afford to get sick here.

Vigilante justice might sound romantic, but the reality is bloody disgusting. The stench in the tiny hidden room revolting.

I grew up in a funeral home. I've seen more dead bodies than I can count, made it through mortuary school, and dealt with every kind of death imaginable. There aren't many smells I can't handle. But prepping a body is sterile and detached. Compassionate even.

What happened here is visceral. Messy.

I step out of the small door, leaving it open. The musky bedroom air is a welcome relief. Should I close the door? The longer the body decomposes, the better for me. But the sooner the police find those videos and photos, the sooner they can try to find those children.

I leave the hidden door as it is. And I leave the closet door wide open.

Part of me is shocked and sickened by what I've done. The other part hoists my backpack over my shoulders and carefully retraces my steps, checking the house for anything I might have left behind. Hopefully, I've left no trace. But I've always known this was a gamble. All it takes is one footprint or hair I missed, and everything could unravel.

I'm okay with that.

Justice for Hoyt. That's all I wanted.

And now I have it.

I'll never murder again. One and done.

If only I'd known it was just the beginning.

CHAPTER FIVE

Jigsaw

Good versus Evil.

Some people think it's easy to see the difference. Society might think I'm evil for killing my father—never mind all the evil things he did to me when I was a kid, what he did to my sister, or all the ways he destroyed so many other lives.

Margot wants justice for innocent people—not herself. She's not motivated by selfish reasons.

She's an angel of goodness.

Someone who needs to be protected at all costs as far as I'm concerned.

I don't care if she's killed a few predators. She's right. The world's safer without them.

As she finishes her story, I release the air trapped in my lungs.

"You could've gotten hurt." She'd been so reckless with her own safety that first time. "Shit, Margot. Zip ties? You didn't bring a bigger weapon than some rope and a scalpel?"

Why am I questioning her when she obviously did just fine? Am I really mansplaining murder to her?

She doesn't seem bothered by my questions, though. "He was a wuss. The second guy—he was much more dangerous. *That* one was close."

Anxiety I didn't even know I was capable of leaps into my throat.

She stands and walks to the refrigerator, taking out a can of seltzer and cracking it open. She takes several long sips, then sets the can on the counter. "Can I tell you about that one another time? I really don't like dwelling on those memories for too long."

I slide off the stool and hurry to her side, pulling her into my arms. The remorse she carries still weighs her down, even though they deserved everything she did, I'm sure of it. Me? I never think about a man I've killed again. Unless it's with relief that they're no longer a problem. I certainly don't have any guilt about it.

"You can tell me anything you want any time you want," I assure her, holding her tight.

"Thank you." She returns the embrace, burrowing her face against my chest. "Thank you for not hating me."

"I could never hate you."

Margot's pure goodness. Nothing she just told me changes my mind.

Destroy the world or save it? Good versus evil is more complex than that. I'd rather burn down the world to protect the people I consider family.

And I'd absolutely slaughter anyone who tried to hurt Margot.

Margot

I never expected to be having this conversation with Jigsaw so soon. After he told me what he did to his father, I knew I'd be able to trust him with my own secrets one day—just not today.

Yet, here we are.

The weight of fear I'd been carrying slowly evaporates, replaced by calm settling over me. I squeeze him tighter, rubbing my face against his shirt.

"You don't have to give me details about the others," he says, his words rumbling beneath my cheek. "But were they pedophiles too? How'd you…"

I sigh and pull away, meeting his gaze. He seems more relaxed now, curious even. Not the man who almost bolted from my closet earlier. But what if his calm curiosity morphs into judgment? Will he rescind his acceptance if I say no? Some men don't think rape is a big deal—certainly not execution-worthy. Although, if he is that kind of man, it's better I find that out now, isn't it?

It doesn't matter. I'm in too deep. I promised to answer his questions, and I will.

"No. One was a professor who raped one of his students." Pain blunts my tone as memories of other students I spoke to at the funeral return. "We handled her funeral. I prepped her body."

He drags his hands through his hair and staggers backward, bumping into the counter. "Have they *all* been connected to you in some way?"

"I didn't know her before she passed," I explain.

"That's not what I mean." He throws one arm wide, gesturing toward my front door. "They've all been connected to the funeral home in some way? That's risky as hell, Margot. Someone could easily piece that together."

"Why should they?" I shrug, although I've worried about that myself. Many, many times. "We handle most of the funerals in the area. Of course I would've come into contact with them."

"Margot." He lets out a pained huff of air and takes my hands.

"It's only four people." I scoff. "Four vile criminals that the justice system didn't punish sufficiently, if at all. No one's going to dig too deeply into their deaths, because secretly everyone's relieved they're gone." I slap my hands together like I'm dusting off remnants of ashes.

"My opinion of law enforcement couldn't be lower," he continues in that maddeningly patient tone that suggests he's about to disagree with me. "But some zealous detective might start sniffing around one day. And a prosecutor eager to make a name for themselves might think putting the 'cute blonde mortician who secretly murders bad guys' on trial would make a hell of a story."

"Wouldn't it, though?" I widen my eyes, allowing a hint of crazy to slip out. "Can you imagine lil' ol' me on the stand, testifying about all the horrible things I've witnessed and how it drove me insane?" I twirl a finger around my ear in a chaotic loop. "And my lawyer could argue that I've inhaled so many embalming fumes, they must've impaired my judgment?"

He stares at me. Shocked I've given it so much thought? Rethinking our relationship? Thinking we're soul mates? I can't tell.

"When the jury learns about the horrible things those men did to innocent women and children, do you really think they'll convict me?" I ask, my tone sharpening to force a response from him.

"The system is broken, yeah. It *could* go that way." His serious expression remains. "But a soulless prosecutor could also argue you're a privileged woman who decided to seek vigilante justice against men who'd already done their time."

"My version's better," I counter.

His lips quirk with frustration. "It is." His expression hardens to stone. "But please join me here in the real world for a minute. Realistically, they'd probably go at you with everything they can. To make an example of you. To stop any other would-be vigilantes from following your path."

"Jury nullification exists, you know," I argue, crossing my arms over my chest. "All I'd need is a few mothers on that jury to hear what that monster did to Hoyt, and I think they'd set me free."

He exhales another long, slow breath. "Or maybe they'd feel self-righteous and want to punish you because you had the strength to do what they couldn't."

That's too scary to dwell on. "They found a mountain of evidence at Gade's house. *That* was all over the news. They didn't talk about his missing eye. Just all the child abuse media that was found and the investigation into where it came from. The assumption was that one of the other victims' fathers killed him."

I'd been a little insulted, actually, that they assumed a man killed Gade.

He nods faintly yet his skepticism seems to linger. "Makes sense, but still…"

I need him to understand that these weren't rash, emotional decisions I made in some hormonal fog. Every choice was well-thought-out and rational.

"Every time, I ask myself, *is this one worth me potentially ending up in prison for the rest of my life?* So far, the answer has been yes." I stand taller, my voice growing steadier. "A woman who killed pedophiles, rapists, wife beaters, and baby killers would probably be treated okay in prison."

He stares at me for the longest time and as the silence stretches, I brace myself for the worst.

Finally, he exhales a long, slow breath. "You might be right about that last part. But I don't like the risks you've taken. Forget going to prison. What if you get hurt while you're *hunting*?"

"You're not bothered by the morality of me committing murder?"

"What?" He snorts. "Fuck no. Not the pieces of filth you're talking about. *Your* safety concerns me, though."

"I'm very careful." I glance down at my hands. "As much as I'd love to chop them into pieces, I'm cognizant of the fact that I don't have the physical strength or size to overpower them." I flick my wicked gaze at him again. "I have to be more thoughtful. Deliberate. Plan ahead. Use the element of surprise."

Jigsaw

"You work so many hours. How do you have time for all this planning?" I ask, trying to get a better handle on Margot's safety precautions.

"It's not like I have a long list. There've only been four targets." Margot rolls her shoulders, like a bird ruffling her feathers. "I'm not a psycho."

I cock my head and pinch my thumb and index finger a millimeter apart. "You're a *little* psycho."

Her mouth turns down. Are her feelings hurt? She admitted to murder. Multiple murders. She's smart enough to know that's not exactly normal behavior. "You're *my* little psycho," I add. "Tell me more. Are they always connected to people who've come through the funeral home?"

"Do you know how many dead bodies I've seen?"

That's not an answer to my question. "You grew up here. I'm guessing a lot."

"Accidents, natural causes, weird stuff, and lots of normal, mundane deaths." She pauses, swallowing hard and looking away. "The worst, though? The cruelty people inflict on others. On the most vulnerable. Children. Babies. Pregnant women. Those bother me the most."

Her voice wobbles as she tips her chin up, and the sadness in her eyes punches me right in the chest. "Do you know murder is the leading cause of death for pregnant women and new mothers?"

My stomach clenches. "No."

"It is."

"I believe you."

"Do you know how many children are molested—usually by someone they know—and never get justice?"

Unfortunately, I've known more people who survived horrible shit at the hands of someone who was supposed to protect them than I care to think about. "Too many."

"So you're not unaware."

"Margot, I didn't kill my own father just because he beat me when I was a kid." No, if I wanted a pound of flesh, I would've whipped him raw and left him bleeding the way he did to me so many times. I hesitate, the words crawling up my throat like splinters. "It was the things he did to Jezzie, and the other children on the farm after I left, that made me slit his throat."

My entire body feels like it's balanced on the tip of a knife as I wait for her to deflect the conversation away from her and ask me for more details.

She studies my face but doesn't say a word.

I blow out a relieved breath.

"It's not just *what* he did to Hoyt," she continues, breaking the silence. "If I thought he'd been rehabilitated when he was released, I *might* have left him alone. Maybe."

I don't think even she believes that.

"But once I saw him casually strolling by the elementary school, checking out the kids..." Her voice shakes with disgust. "I knew he hadn't changed one bit."

I let out a disgusted snort. "Pedophiles rarely do."

"I couldn't stand it if another kid had their life forever altered because of him. Ruining a child's life and future is unforgivable. I don't care what the Bible or anyone else says. There's no justification for it. Ever."

"Agree." I run my hand over my chest, considering how to phrase my next question. "You don't have to tell me everything. But who did you *take care of* while I was away?"

How long had she been planning that one? The whole time we were having our "lessons," she was plotting to kill a man? Shouldn't my dark, barren soul have sensed her murderous intentions?

Her eyes gloss over with tears, and she ducks her head. "I told you babies are the hardest. Sometimes, it's natural causes and there's nothing anyone can do about that. Or accidents—they're sad, but normal. Other times..." She swallows hard and takes a deep breath. "Do you remember the night you came over and I was too upset for 'lessons,' so you took me out to dinner instead?"

"Yeah." Upset isn't how I'd describe her. Despondent and lifeless would be more accurate.

She explains the vicious beating that ended her client's pregnancy only a few weeks before the baby was due.

Acid rolls through my stomach. An ex-brother did something similar to Serena—a club girl at the time. Only none of us knew the full extent of what that piece of shit put her through until well after we'd buried him for other offenses against the club. Before we put him down, I learned about the horrible shit he'd done to his wife, and *that* had been heavy on my mind when we took the vote to strip his patch and put him in the ground. It still *haunts* me that we shared a patch with Shadow and none of us knew what a monster he really was.

"When I found out this was the *second* time she'd lost a baby because of him…" Margot shrugs. "That's when I knew he had to go."

"Jesus Christ," I mutter, my voice full of raw frustration. "I wish you'd told me. I would've helped you…or something."

"It was a delicate situation." She runs her gaze over me, her lips tugging into a half smile. "You don't blend in well. You're very…recognizable."

"What are you talking about?" I run my hands over my hair, probably forcing it to stick up in every direction. "I'm a tall, blond-ish white dude. There're hundreds of guys walking around that look like me."

"No." She reaches up, curling her fingers around my wrist and tugging my hand away from my hair. "You're quite striking and memorable."

That warm, shivery sensation I only get when Margot's hands are on me tingles along my spine. "You're only saying that 'cause you kinda like me," I tease.

"I more than like you." She peers up at me with shiny eyes. "I don't want…I don't want to lose you," she finishes in a whisper.

The vulnerability in her voice and expression cracks me wide open. "I'm not going anywhere."

How could I ever leave her now? Margot's already my dream woman. That she dabbles in a little murder now and then? Just icing on the Margot cake.

CHAPTER SIX

Jigsaw

The stillness wakes me the next morning. I'm not used to waking up in a place this quiet. No rumble of bikes. No background noise of brothers shouting or girls moaning. No strumming of Shelby's guitar somewhere in the background.

Just silence, broken by the occasional creak of the old house, the soft hum of the refrigerator, or birds chirping outside the window.

It's...peaceful.

How can I feel peace after everything she confessed last night?

Margot sleeps curled up on her side, her face turned toward me, her breathing soft and even. She looks so small, so damn fragile, it's hard to reconcile this woman with the one who calmly admitted to planning and executing four murders.

Not that I have room to judge.

If anything, I'm impressed.

I've seen darkness before. Hell, I've lived it. But Margot's is different. Her darkness isn't a choice. It's a calling. A fight against the horrors in her small corner of the world.

I watch her for a long moment, trying to untangle what I'm feeling. Protective, sure. Drawn to her more than ever, yup. But there's something else. Something I can't quite name.

Awe. Knocked-on-my-ass kind of awe.

My brothers have sent plenty of fuckers to the demon's dinner table. Hell, we eliminated half of the South of Satan MC a few months ago. Before that, we offed a few of their associates and a college kid who went after Murphy's ol' lady. With the help of our Virginia brothers, Rooster and I rescued Shelby when she'd been kidnapped by one of her crazy stalkers. Rooster let me go at the guy's fingers with the garden shears, but we had to turn him over to the cops, so I couldn't kill him like I wanted. None of that violence was done on a whim. We were reacting to the situations we found ourselves in.

Margot, though. She *chooses* her "projects" carefully. Her targets don't even know they're on her radar. They never see it coming. My own tiny, curvy blonde angel of vengeance.

She stirs, her fingers curling into the pillowcase.

I should stop staring at her like a goofy fanboy and let her rest.

The door creaks and cool air drifts over my shoulder. I turn my head toward the widening bedroom door. Gretel pokes her nose inside, then pushes it open wider and stalks across the room. Ah, here comes the black, fuzzy alarm clock.

This morning, she's quiet, though. No warble to announce her arrival. She gracefully leaps onto the bed, landing light as a feather.

"Oh, so you *can* jump lightly," I whisper, extending my arm and rubbing my fingers together to entice her closer.

She purrs and bops her forehead against me, her silky fur sliding over my skin. Then, like the disrespectful little beast she is, Gretel climbs onto my hip and walks her pokey paws over my ribs. I scoop her up before her sharp claws have a chance to pierce my bare skin not covered by the blanket and settle her on the bed in the space between Margot and me. She flops on her side, facing me and purrs louder, kneading her paws against my chest.

Margot's nose twitches. She reaches for Gretel without opening her eyes. "Furball," she murmurs, rubbing behind Gretel's ears. The cat's purring revs up another few decibels.

"You're still here." Margot brushes her knuckles against my chest, then opens her eyes.

"Told you I wasn't going anywhere." I wrap my fingers around her wrist, tugging her closer. "You sleep okay?"

"I really did. I had the softest, fuzziest, most pleasant dreams."

Maybe unburdening herself was a good thing. "You've really never told anyone…what you told me last night? Your dad doesn't know?"

She closes her eyes as if she hadn't planned on waking up to this conversation. "God, no. I don't ever want him to know that about me. I think it would break him. He's very 'normal moral.'"

"Normal moral? What's that mean?"

"I mean, I don't consider what *I've* done immoral."

"Agree. But my morality lives in the gray area anyway."

She chuckles lightly. "They were a clear and imminent threat to innocent lives." The smile slips off her face. "I have access to so many creepy, sad, and uncomfortable secrets no one thinks about. And when we take someone into our care who's been violated or abused…I don't know. I can't help myself. I want to know everything and then that knowledge makes me feel like I have a duty to protect others." She winces and shifts her gaze to the cat. "Wow, that sounds like I have some crazy God complex, doesn't it?"

"No," I whisper, completely caught up in every word.

"I don't *like* killing people," she continues in a harsher tone. "It's not a crazy itch I need to scratch. My targets come to me. In a manner of speaking."

"I understand what you're saying." If anything, I want to be the Joker to her Harley—without the crazy, just the devotion.

Her phone buzzes.

"Ugh." She rolls over and grabs her phone, swiping her thumb over the screen and quickly scanning the text. "Yes, Dad, I know," she mutters, quickly typing out a reply. "Rose-colored light bulbs. I know. He acts like I didn't spend a semester studying color theory and stage lighting or something." She sighs and returns the phone to the nightstand.

"What?" I ask, curious. "Color theory?"

Pink spreads over her cheeks. "Well, yeah. Sometimes, it's grisly business creating that peaceful facial expression families see at the end." She bites her lip as if she's afraid to gross me out with her mortician secrets. "But in some circumstances, even after embalming, the skin remains a bit grayish. So, we'll set them under rose-colored light bulbs during the visitation. He's just reminding me to add them to an order I need to place today."

Now I can't stop thinking about gray skin and pink light bulbs. I don't want to hurt Margot's feelings, so I force a tight smile. "Learn something new every day."

She winces. "You kinda wish you didn't know that now, don't you?"

She reads me too easily. "It's my fault for asking."

Gretel's clearly had enough of our lazy morning conversation. She flips and twists her body until she's on her feet, then uses my legs as a launching pad.

"So violent," I laugh, turning to watch her streak through the open door.

"Sorry," Margot says.

"It's fine. She jumped onto the bed so daintily earlier, I got worried." Uncomfortable sensations prickle against my neck. I hate letting Margot think I don't want to learn about her job. "Hey, I like all your little mortuary secrets. I think it's...nice that you do so much to make sure the last moments people get with their loved ones are as pleasant as they can be."

Relief or gratitude spreads over her expression. "Thanks."

"What does today's schedule look like?"

"A service for a nice man from the neighborhood. His kids have been sweet. They're just...heartbroken."

"No one fighting over his stuff yet?"

"No, thankfully. He was a friend of my dad's, sort of—like grab morning coffee at Stewart's and have a chat kind of friends..."

Somehow, I don't picture Mr. Cedarwood running down to Stewart's in his suit and tie to have coffee with the locals, but maybe I've been judging him too harshly.

"...So, he did the restorative work."

"Wait, what? You...he...you work on people you know?"

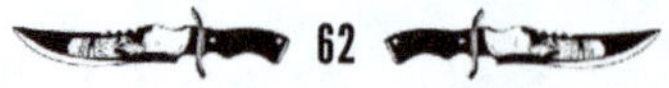

"Well, *yeah*," she says with a large dose of *duh* in her voice. "I don't think Mr. Lewis would've been comfortable having a woman he's known since she was a toddler working on him."

"Huh." I frown, giving it some thought. "It's nice someone still cares about what they think after they're…gone."

"It's important."

"Still thinking I really want to be tossed in a bonfire, though." I grin at her, but she doesn't laugh.

Her face scrunches as if she's in pain. "Don't joke about that. The world would be so much…duller without you in it."

"Trust me. I'm not going anywhere."

I lean in and kiss her cheek. She's got a long day ahead, and so do I if I plan on sticking close. But my gut's telling me to stick around.

To keep her safe.

From the world. And from herself.

Maybe it's paranoia. Or maybe it's knowing how the world works. Maybe I've seen people I care about get burned by their pasts too many times. Secrets have a way of crawling into the light. But if someone starts sniffing around Margot's?

They'll have to get through me first.

CHAPTER SEVEN

Margot

Jigsaw's acceptance came easier than I anticipated. He's still here. I half expected to wake up in an empty bed and get a "this call cannot go through…" message when I dialed his number.

And even though it clearly makes him uncomfortable, he lets me tell him a little about my job. Why does it feel so nice to talk about it with someone who isn't a mortician and still have them understand?

My phone buzzes and I grab it off the counter. I release a sigh as I read the text.

"Your dad again?" Jigsaw asks.

"No." I type out a quick reply, then open my notes app and the details of the text. "A client who wanted a slight change to her grandmother's obituary. I need to make sure I do that before it gets sent to the paper. Her grandmother raised her and she's having a really hard time."

Jigsaw moves closer and eases his arms around me. "You can only take on so much grief. I know you're good at your job, but the emotional side will suck you under if you let it."

As much as I want to deny it and tell him to mind his own business, I know he's right.

My phone buzzes again. "The accessibility and personal

connection is why we've been in business for three generations." I reach for my phone and read the text. "But it's exhausting sometimes, too," I admit.

Jigsaw stares at me for so long, fear swirls in my stomach. What's going through his mind?

"Is this what you've always wanted to do?" he asks.

I open my mouth to say yes, of course. But the truth stops me. I'd wanted to be a cosmetologist—for the living. "Well, I wanted to do makeup—just not for the dead." I shrug, suddenly uncomfortable talking about this. "But I feel like I get to help people more this way."

"I know you do." He curls his hands around mine. "Your clients are lucky to have someone as compassionate and kind as you are to help them through difficult times." He hesitates and looks away for a second. "But what about the toll it takes on you?"

Suddenly, it feels like we're talking about something else. "Do you mean I wouldn't murder people if I chose a different career path?"

"No. That's not what I meant." He squeezes my hands. "You see a lot of bad things that vigilante justice can't resolve." He shakes his head. "Jesus Christ, you told me you have an entire month dedicated to funerals for teenagers because they're all driving drunk after proms and graduations, for fuck's sake."

"Sometimes the one who caused the accident survives...but they don't really fit my criteria."

He blinks and stares at me.

"Although," I continue, turning the idea over in my head. "A repeat offender...that might be a different story."

"All right. Easy," he growls. "I wasn't trying to give you any ideas. I don't want you risking your freedom more than necessary."

Now that I've had the thought though, I can't resist it.

No.

I always told myself I'd stick to one thing. Jigsaw's right. I'm not a comic book anti-hero. I can't punish everyone. *Stay in my lane.* Stick to my criteria, it hasn't led me astray yet.

After breakfast, I have to run downstairs to set up the viewing room. Unease rolls through me as I step into my closet to get dressed.

Jigsaw hovers outside the door, his keen gaze focused on me as I choose a somber black skirt, thin, dark red sweater, and black blazer.

"Guess you're never setting foot in here again?" I ask.

A sharp scowl darkens his expression.

Great, now he thinks I'm insulting him. "I meant because of my *ornaments,* not that you don't like enclosed spaces…" Damn, what's wrong with me.

"No. You'll have to give me a tour one day." He wiggles his fingers toward the closet door. "Show me what's in the weird, hidden little door space back there."

Shocked, I let out a snort of disbelief. "You sure got a lot of snooping done in a short amount of time."

"I wasn't *snoooooping.*" He draws out the word as if he's offended. "I was curious. There's a difference." He zigzags his finger through the air. "The house design is wild."

"Oh. That's true. It's nothing. Just like a little mini closet where I keep some…supplies and a few other…oddities." *And a collection of newspaper articles about all of my victims.*

He nods slowly. "It wasn't just the confined space. It was—"

"Finding out your girlfriend's a serial killer?"

"You're not a serial killer," he says in a much more patient tone than I think he's feeling based on his lingering scowl. "You're motivated by justice, not personal gratification."

"That's true. So what were you going to say?"

"The Bible quotes." He shivers with disgust. "When I was little, after a beating, my father would read lengthy passages from the Bible to us. When I was older and he graduated to whippings, he nixed the biblical story time, so a bit of an improvement," he finishes with a strained laugh.

The clothes in my hands flutter to the floor and I hurry to throw my arms around his middle. "I'm so sorry. I was just…you kind of surprised me. I didn't expect…I mean, I wanted to tell you but—"

He wraps his arms around me tight, cutting off my bumbling explanation/apology. "It's okay. You didn't know." He pulls away, still keeping his hands on my shoulders. "You wanted to tell me what?"

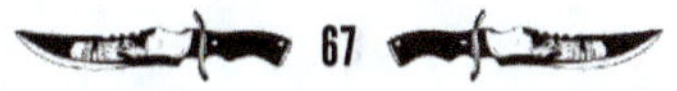

I tilt my head toward the closet. "That. Not yesterday or today but, you know, eventually."

"You trust me that much?"

He hasn't given me a reason not to, yet. "Yes."

His lips part as if he has something to say, but then he shakes his head and hugs me again.

Gretel bursts into the room, loudly announcing her arrival.

Laughing, I back away from our embrace. "I think she's playing alarm clock for me. I need to get dressed."

"Do you need help this morning?" he asks.

"No, you can hang out here." I drop onto the bed and roll my stocking up my leg. Maybe he wants this chance to escape after everything he learned about me yesterday. "If you want to."

Keeping his gaze focused on my hands as I work the thin black material over my knee, he leans over and scratches behind Gretel's ears. "I don't mind hanging out with G-kitty for a bit. But it sounds like you have a busy day." He stands and flexes his biceps. "Let me get the grunt work done for you. Put these to use." He pats his upper arm.

Laughing, I stand and shimmy into my skirt, tugging at the zipper in the back. Having him watch me get dressed is messing with my motor coordination. "I'd be silly to turn down that offer, wouldn't I?" It *would* be a big help. My father and Paul are busy until later this morning.

He spins one finger in the air, urging me to turn around. I grab my sweater while he tugs at the skirt and slowly zips it into place.

"There." He pats my behind. "I hope you understand how painful it is to watch you put clothes *on,* let alone help."

"Well, I appreciate the assist. Having you watch me get dressed has made me forget how to use my hands." I wiggle my fingers in front of his face, and he laughs.

Gretel scurries out of the bedroom as Jigsaw and I head toward the living room. I stop and slip into my sensible, black heels while Jigsaw laces up his boots.

I close the door behind us, double-checking that it's locked.

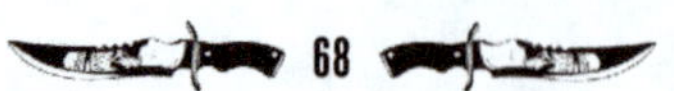

“Can’t be too careful on days where we’ll have a lot of people wandering around,” I explain.

Jigsaw’s face pinches into a frown but he nods.

It’s dark and quiet downstairs. I flip on the hall lights, then wind my way into the parlor to turn on the lamps. I lead Jigsaw into the viewing room and show him the closet where we keep the wooden folding chairs stacked.

“I got this,” he says. “Go ahead and make your phone calls or whatever you need to do.”

“A few deliveries might come to the back door, but I’ll hear the bell.”

“I can get those too.” He sweeps one hand in front of him. “Everything’s going in here, right?”

I quickly flip through my mental list of items. “Um, except the food. That’ll go in the kitchen.”

“Got it.” He leans down and kisses my cheek.

We part ways at the door of my father’s office. I’m used to doing the morning prep work alone, with Paul, or one of the part-time attendants. For these smaller services, my dad only comes in to do a last-minute check these days. At least he trusts me with this much. I’m not sure what he’ll think about Jigsaw helping me.

I’m almost through with my list when the front doorbell chimes, cutting through the muffled silence and occasional thump of chairs being moved around.

I flick my gaze to the small black-and-white video monitor that shows the front porch. Two men in suits are waiting by the front door. Family members arriving early to check on things? That’s always possible.

I hurry down the long corridor, my heels thudding over the hardwood.

“Want me to get it?” Jigsaw asks.

I smooth my hands over my skirt. “No, I’ve got it.”

He retreats into the viewing room to where he can still watch the front door.

My own personal bodyguard.

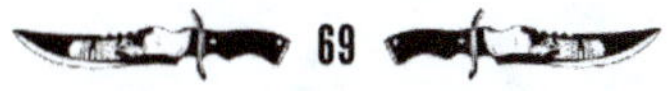

Laughing to myself, I twist the knob and pull the heavy door open.

"Good morning." The young, slender man runs his gaze over me. Not in a leering manner, more like he finds me lacking in some way. "Margot Cedarwood?" His deep voice sends an ominous shiver through me for a reason I can't name.

"Yes. Are you here for the Lewis celebration?"

"No." He pulls a black leather wallet out of his breast pocket, flips it open and holds it out to me to inspect the badge inside. "Dan Wood with the Slater County Sheriff's Department. We'd like to ask you a few questions, Ms. Cedarwood."

CHAPTER EIGHT

Margot

Cold fear streaks down my spine.

My heart thumps wildly.

Detectives have stopped by before. Wanting to observe a service or ask questions about a family member. We've certainly organized funerals for several members of law enforcement over the years.

This visit could be totally normal.

Or the end of my freedom.

An ominous cloud hovers over me. Like somehow my conversation with Jigsaw last night was overheard by the universe and it ratted me out to the sheriff.

Grabbing my professional composure by the throat, I force my lips into a gracious and welcoming smile. "How can I help you?"

"May we come in?" the short, older, pot-bellied man asks.

"Of course." My voice settles into the soft, dulcet tone I use with clients, concealing the chaos gathering inside me.

I step back to allow them inside.

Detective Wood crosses the threshold first.

The older detective stops and hands me a business card embossed with the shiny red sheriff's insignia and the man's name across the top. *Walt Wearmouth.* Strange name.

Walt hesitates as he steps into the foyer. Maybe he's arrived at an age where he fears the reaper.

To further unsettle him, I lead both detectives into the viewing room, instead of the cozier parlor across the hallway.

The younger detective tucks his hands in his pockets. "Do you know a Patrick Larsen?"

Holy shit.

"I know *of* him." I clasp my hands in front of me and tilt my head, like I'm a good little citizen eager to help.

"He was found dead a few weeks ago."

"Oh." I refuse to say "that's too bad," or express any sort of sympathy for that monster. But I'll happily play dumb. "Well, my father usually handles the logistics…I can call him—"

"No, no. That's not why we're here." The young cop gives the old one a sideways glance. "Do you know Laurel Larsen too?"

"Yes. Is she okay?"

"*How* do you know her?" Detective Wearmouth asks.

They should have this information somewhere, shouldn't they? "We took care of her daughter's cremation after Mr. Larsen beat her so badly their baby was stillborn." I enunciate each word clearly, hoping they understand just how little of a fuck I give about Patrick Larsen's death.

"Have you spoken to her since then?" Detective Wood asks.

"Not since the service." I turn and peer into the hallway. *Where'd Jigsaw go?* "She sent me a thank-you card but I haven't spoken to her."

"Can we see the card?"

"Uh, yeah." Where'd I put it? Dad's office probably. I wouldn't have taken it upstairs. I incline my head, indicating they can follow me.

No sign of Jigsaw in the hallway. I try to casually glance into the parlor but unless I stop and crane my neck around the corner, I can't see much.

Inside my father's office, I round the desk and walk straight to the wall where he often tacks up personal notes from family members. Laurel's card is tucked into the corner with the envelope behind it.

It's nothing fancy. A small, simple white card with a white rose on the front.

I quickly flip it open even though I already know what it says.

Dear Mr. Cedarwood and Margot,

I don't have the words to fully express the depth of my gratitude for your kindness and generosity during one of the most painful times in my life. The care and compassion you showed in arranging and caring for baby Ashley is a comfort to my heart in a way I didn't think was possible.

Forever grateful,

Laurel

Tears sting my eyes. *Not the time to get emotional.* I close the card and hand it to Detective Wood. He flips it open and slowly scans the note, then passes it to his partner.

Without looking at the card, Detective Wearmouth asks, "Did you have any personal interaction with Mrs. Larsen?"

"Of course I did," I answer in a tone meant to convey what a dumb question that is. "The normal interaction I'd have with any family. She also stopped by before the service to give me a baby blanket that she knitted." I have to stop to take a breath. "She asked to have her daughter wrapped in it."

This man must be made of stone, his expression doesn't shift at all. "Is that normal?"

"Nothing about the situation was *normal*. But yes, parents especially, will give us items to put in with their children."

Detective Wood groans.

Oh, sorry. Did that make you uncomfortable?

Detective Wearmouth flips the envelope over and studies the blank side. "No return address," he mutters.

"She said she was going to stay with her mom or her sister," I offer. "But I didn't ask for the address."

"Why not?"

I only stalk bad guys. "We didn't need it."

"No final bills or anything?" he persists.

I drop my gaze to the floor. "There were no bills. My father didn't charge her for the service. For any of it."

"What about the remains?" Detective Wood asks.

"They were ready for her at the service."

"Is that normal?" Detective Wearmouth asks. "Not to charge for a funeral?"

"As I said, nothing about the situation was normal." After a breath, I add, "Thankfully."

"Did your father know Mrs. Larsen before she came to you for the funeral?"

My eyes widen in surprise. Why would they think that? "No. As far as I know, she was referred to us by the hospital."

"Then why the free funeral?"

Why are they so stuck on this point?

How do I explain human decency to two people who probably don't see a lot of it?

"It was an awful…tragic situation. We often waive costs for stillborn babies or infants." I swallow hard, fighting for composure. "The cost and work for us is much less in those cases. It just seems like the right thing to do." I straighten my spine, lift my chin, and stare Detective Wearmouth down. "Three generations of Cedarwoods have operated this way. We're not unique. Other funeral homes have similar policies."

April says even her soulless, corporate funeral home waives the cost for a simple infant burial.

"I see." Detective Wearmouth grunts and hands the card back to me.

They still seem suspicious. They're detectives who deal with death on a regular basis. But they're on the ugliest end of it. Their job isn't to care for the dead and bring families peace. It's to bring bad men to justice.

If they didn't fail at their jobs so often, I wouldn't have to be standing here as nervous as a mortician awaiting her own autopsy.

CHAPTER NINE

Jigsaw

As soon as I realized two of Slater County's finest were at the front door, I slid out of the viewing room, into the hallway, and slipped up the first few stairs. Unless the cops want a tour of the entire house, I'll be out of their sight but still able to hear the highlights of the conversation.

The less law enforcement knows about Margot's involvement with my MC, the better.

Once Margot moved the detectives to her father's office, I tiptoed into the parlor, staying out of sight but within listening range.

Didn't I just warn her about this exact situation?

If I were superstitious, I'd think I jinxed her.

I lean against the wall, cocking my head to follow the conversation. They stick to asking about Laurel. Sounds like they think she offed her husband. Why the fuck are they even wasting the energy on such a piece of shit?

Margot's calm and controlled voice drifts through the house. As the probing questions continue, I relax. If anything, they seem more interested in Margot's father, not Margot. Maybe they think the old man was involved with her and killed her husband for revenge?

Still, my guard stays up. Protecting Margot's my first priority, but I don't want her father implicated in a murder either.

"Three generations of Cedarwoods have operated this way," Margot says, her voice strong and clear, tinged with disdain for the stupid questions. "Other funeral homes have similar policies."

That's my girl.

"I see," grumpy cop huffs like a walrus lifting himself out of the water.

Margot answers more inane questions, her tone shifting to polite but firm, just distant enough to give nothing away. Every answer sounds reasonable, logical, leaving no room for suspicion.

"Just out of curiosity," the other cop says, "do you know where you were the night of…" he hesitates, then rattles off a date that falls right in the middle of my trip to Deadbranch. *Fuck.* At least if I'd been in the state, I could've been her alibi. But law enforcement from New York to Tennessee knows all the Lost Kings MC charters were in Deadbranch for Digger's final farewell.

"Here, probably," Margot answers smoothly. "I'd have to check my schedule to be sure."

"Pretty woman like you wasn't out on a date?" one of them asks.

My hands curl into fists.

Margot lets out a nervous laugh. "Unlikely. I work a lot." After a few seconds she says, "I would've been prepping for the Walsh funeral."

They don't ask if anyone can confirm her whereabouts.

Relieved, I blow out a slow, silent breath. If they seriously suspected Margot of being involved with that guy's death, they would've asked for someone to confirm where she was. They're only here to check items off of their list.

Still, do I need to bring this to the club? Or at the very least inform Teller? Cops sniffing around a business we have a stake in could be an issue. I *can* present it as they had a question about one of Margot's clients, can't I?

Except that I *know* Margot is involved. It borders on lying to my club. Not that I think anyone will have an issue with what she did—*if* it was a one-off. Hell, they probably wouldn't care, even applaud her. But once I mention her kill list has a few more entries, *that* might be a red flag for my brothers. If she's ever caught, it could bring unwanted attention to my entire club.

Fuck me.

My gut's screaming to *protect Margot at all costs*. From everyone. Even my club.

"Did you ever interact with Mr. Larsen?" walrus cop asks.

"Absolutely not," Margot snaps. "As far as I know there is a restraining order in place. We would have called the sheriff's department if he showed up here."

"Man can't say goodbye to his daughter?" the older cop presses.

Fuck that dude. And fuck you too.

"The *man* was directly responsible for his daughter's death." Margot's sharp tone pierces the otherwise somber atmosphere. "In a brutal, deliberate act. So no, we would not have opened our doors to him."

"Of course," the younger cop says, trying to sound reasonable.

"It was a small service. Very short. Only Laurel, her mother, and her sister attended," Margot adds in a calmer tone. She's playing this perfectly. No nervous giggle or guilty stammering. Just straightforward answers as if she has nothing to hide.

"You haven't heard from Laurel since then?" the younger cop asks.

"No. But I wasn't expecting to, either." Margot pauses. As if it's an afterthought, she asks, "Wait, *how* did he die? You don't seriously think Laurel had anything to do with it, do you?"

Good girl. They'll think it's odd if you don't ask how he died.

"Unlikely," the younger cop says. "Guy overdosed in a motel room."

"Oh," Margot says, in a voice devoid of emotion or further interest.

"You don't seem surprised," the older cop prompts.

"Laurel mentioned that he had a substance abuse problem," Margot explains. "I'm a little ashamed to say this, but at the time, I thought she was just making an excuse for…what happened…for what he did to her." She strikes just the right note between contrite and judgmental.

Damn, Margot's a good liar. Scary good.

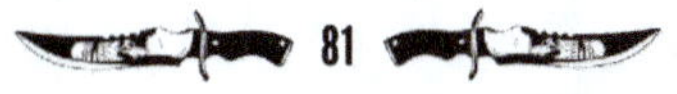

"No, it looks like she was telling you the truth about that," younger cop agrees. "Well, if you hear from Laurel, please let us know. You have my card."

"Will do," Margot promises. "I'll let my father know as well."

"When will he be back?" the older man asks.

"In a few hours, but we'll be busy with the service. I can have him call you tomorrow if you want?"

"Sure," he answers, as if he doesn't care one way or another.

They're silent for a moment, then low murmurs and thuds over the carpeted hallway alert me that they're on the move. I quietly track their movements, following the length of the parlor room as they head toward the front door. I stop before the parlor room's open archway to stay out of their sight.

The front door releases a long, low squeak as it opens. Margot must be making it clear she'd like them to leave now.

"Thank you for your time, Ms. Cedarwood," the younger cop says, his voice coming from farther away now.

"Of course."

I risk peering around the corner. The detectives are on the porch, angled toward the street. I catch a glimpse of Margot's profile. Her arms crossed over her chest.

"That motorcycle out there belong to you?" one of them asks.

Well, fuck. Guess they took time looking around the house before they knocked on the door. I parked my bike in the same place I always do, tucked into a nook where it's not quite visible from the street or back porch.

Damn, it's killing me that I can't see more of Margot's face. I creep closer to the front door.

"Gosh no," she says in a wide-eyed, scandalized tone. "I've never been on one."

I've known this since the beginning, but a pang of regret still hits me.

"Nice woman like you shouldn't be gettin' mixed up with bikers," walrus cop says in his gravelly huff.

Weird that's their first assumption.

Without skipping a beat, Margot says, "We serve all of our clients equally."

"I'm sure you do," the older detective says. "What I'm trying to say is Slater County's home to the Wolf Knights Motorcycle Club," he says in the slow, patient tone you'd use to educate a toddler on the finer points of finger painting. "Looks like a skull and crown on that bike. Doing business with a rival club could be dangerous to you personally."

For fuck's sake. As if we'd ever start some petty turf war over the location of a funeral or involve civilians. Lying assholes.

A smirk spreads across my face, cutting through my annoyance at their lies. These dumbasses don't even realize the Wolf Knights aren't running shit in New York these days. Slater County belongs to the Lost Kings now. Cops need to update their *NY Outlaw Biker Clubs for Dummies* handbook.

"I appreciate the concern," Margot says in a tone that doesn't sound appreciative at all. *Could she be more perfect?* "But we serve a wide variety of clientele and haven't had an issue yet."

From my limited view, Margot's posture remains strong and steady. She doesn't giggle and gush about how her boyfriend's a member of the Lost Kings MC. She doesn't try to convince the cops that we're really a bunch of nice guys. Nope. Her manner stays distant and indifferent, giving them *nothing* at all.

Just like a perfect ol' lady should behave when talking to the cops.

CHAPTER TEN

Margot

Thoroughly rattled by the two detectives, I watch their unmarked black sedan drive away before going inside.

"You think they'd have better things to do," I grumble as I close the door behind me.

Two big hands clamp down over my hips, spin me around and yank me backward.

Jigsaw swallows my startled yelp with a kiss.

"What are you doing?" I ask between greedy slides of our lips.

He stares down at me with reverence in his eyes. "You handled that like a queen."

Embarrassment heats my skin. I press my hands against his chest, pushing myself back. "You heard everything?"

I hated pretending I didn't know whose motorcycle they were talking about. I hate that he heard me claim I don't know anything about his club.

Worse, I'm embarrassed that I bragged about how careful and clever I am with my kills. Having two detectives drop by to ask me questions today feels like a Karmic nudge not to get too cocky.

But Jigsaw doesn't say "I told you so" or lecture me about the risks I've taken.

No, he's staring down at me with nothing but affection and admiration in his expression.

His hands, still firm on my hips, give me a gentle squeeze. "I caught the highlights of the conversation. You were perfect."

"Perfect? I thought I was going to puke." I lower my voice to a whisper. "Do you think they suspect me? Why did they have so many questions?" I cast a glance around the house, still worried they're somehow listening nearby or bugged the place.

"Not saying that I'm an expert." A hint of a smirk twists his lips. "But if anything, I think they're suspicious of your client."

He thought so too? "I'd confess and go to prison before I'd let her get in trouble," I warn him, in case he thinks I'm the kind of person who would let an innocent person pay for my crimes.

His expression doesn't change. "It sounds like they wanted to confirm he had a drug problem and when they couldn't find her right away, they needed to talk to some people so they could check it off their list." He throws a quick glance toward the front door. "Sounds like you could've been one of the last few people in the area to see her."

"Oh, I guess that makes sense." I blow out a relieved breath. My heart slows and the panic wrapped around my lungs slowly unravels. "How can you be so level-headed and calm?"

He raises his eyebrows. "You sounded calm. Kept things polite and professional. The right amount of interested and mildly annoyed."

"Great, so I guess I've nailed the recipe for talking to the cops."

"Yup." He grins at me.

"Why are you so…strangely happy about that?"

"It's a useful skill to have." He glances down at me and his smile fades. "Real talk? Ol' ladies get hassled by the cops from time to time just for being involved with a member of an MC."

How unfair. "Yes, I got that from their 'warning' to me outside. Why, though?"

He tilts his head and gives me a *let's be serious* stare. "To get dirt on the club. Doesn't really happen around here. We try to maintain a good relationship with law enforcement in our territory. But they've approached some of our ol' ladies when we've been on the road and stuff." He shrugs as if it's a minor inconvenience. "You handled yourself well, that's all."

I poke his chest. "I told you I'm good at keeping secrets. My dad was always friendly with the old Wolf Knights' president, so I didn't care for them talking about them that way, either."

He lifts his chin and slowly nods as if he's had some great revelation.

"What?" I ask.

"Nothing. I wondered how Teller and your dad crossed paths."

I blink, not understanding the connection.

"Upstate's had an alliance with the Wolf Knights for years. They came to Teller when they decided to leave Slater County."

"Oh." The bell at the back door rings, halting our conversation. "It's probably the flower delivery." I pat his chest. "I have to get that."

"Okay." He sweeps his arm in front of him, as if asking me to lead the way.

"I deal with them all the time," I say over my shoulder. "You don't have to follow me."

"I don't like that you're here all by yourself."

"I'm usually not," I grumble, reaching for the door and twisting the knob as the bell rings again.

The man on the other side has a large wreath of white roses in one hand and the easel display stand in the other. "Morning, Margot." He flashes a quick, friendly smile, then his gaze shifts over my shoulder and his lips flatten. "Uh, the Lewis arrangement." He nods to the wreath.

I can only imagine Jigsaw standing behind me scowling at Carl.

"Hi, Carl. Come on in." I open the screen door for him, and he turns sideways to enter.

"Morning," he says to Jigsaw.

Jigsaw dips his chin but doesn't respond.

I shoot him a glare, then follow Carl to the parlor. He sets the arrangement near the podium. I'll probably have to move it later but for now, it works. "Thank you."

"Not a problem." He slaps his hands together, dusting off his palms. "The daughter called and made several changes. I hope we got it right."

I sigh. She should've called *me* and I would've handled it. "It's lovely. I'm sure she'll be pleased."

He flicks his gaze to Jigsaw again, hovering behind me like my personal bouncer.

"I've got one more," Carl says. "I'll be right back."

I wait until Carl's footsteps pound over the back porch, then turn to Jigsaw. "Must you hover behind me glaring at everyone?"

"You didn't introduce me."

"I wasn't sure if you wanted me to."

His expression remains steady and possessive. "I want you to."

My heart jumps. "You do?"

"Fuck yeah I do." His voice is low but firm.

Warmth fills my chest. "You want me to introduce you as my boyfriend?"

"Yes."

"Jigsaw or Jensen?"

His lips quirk. "I'm not crazy about people outside the MC world calling me by my road name." He brushes his fingers against my shoulder. "Except you."

Carl's footsteps clatter over the back porch again. I straighten as he reappears with the second arrangement, carefully maneuvering through the door. "Same place?" he asks.

"Yes, please." Still giddy over Jigsaw's request but needing to do my job, I follow Carl, directing him where to place the arrangement.

When he's finished, he dusts off his hands and hands me a small electronic signature pad to confirm I received the arrangements. While I'm scrawling my name across the screen, Carl's body shifts.

"Are you new to Cedarwood?" he asks Jigsaw.

"No." I hand the stylus and pad back to Carl. "Forgive my rudeness, Carl, this is my boyfriend, Jensen."

Carl's jaw drops but he recovers quickly, sticking his hand out. "Nice to, uh, meet you."

"Likewise."

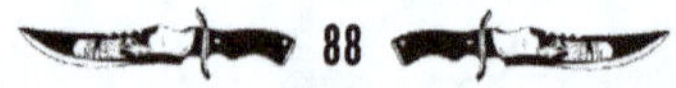

They shake hands, Carl staring at Jigsaw and nodding. Should I be insulted? Does he think I'm that undateable or something?

"Well, that should be everything. If you have any issues, just call." Carl hesitates for a beat then mutters a quick goodbye.

"Bro didn't hide his disappointment well," Jigsaw says, watching him go.

"What? Be serious." My gaze skips from the door to Jigsaw's face. "Are you happy now?"

"Yes." He shifts the full weight of his attention to me, stepping closer, crowding against the wall. Not touching, yet. But close enough to notice how much space he takes up and how protected I feel in his orbit.

At the back door, several other voices converge. Whatever's happening between us has to wait. I press my hands against Jigsaw's chest. "I...I have to get back to work."

He shifts his body to the side, allowing just enough space to slip through.

My dad's voice rises above the others, knocking all the fuzzy feelings right out of me. My nervous gaze darts around the room. Chairs—almost done. Flowers—still need to be moved. Supplies—still need to be brought up from the basement. I haven't accomplished much this morning. "Damn. Dad's back already," I mutter.

"I'll finish lining up those chairs." Jigsaw clasps his hand over my shoulder. The heat and possessiveness in his eyes have been dialed back to a slow simmer. "What else can I help you do to get ready? Between those cops wasting your time and me not being able to keep my hands off you, you're running behind."

I slide my hand down his chest. "I'll never complain about having your hands on me."

"Good." He lifts his chin. "Tell me. What else?"

"Ah, the chairs. One more row, there." I drag my finger through the air, indicating a space near the podium. "And then I have to run downstairs for some bulbs. I need to change out the ones over there."

He nods once. "I saw a ladder in the closet back there. Okay to use that one?"

"Yup."

"Got it."

I hurry into the hallway and meet my father at the back door. "Flowers are here." *Duh, he just ran into Carl.* Why am I so flustered, acting like a teenager who got caught making out in the driveway after curfew?

"Good." He lifts his gaze, staring down the long hallway.

"I'm still working through my list," I say before he starts firing off questions. "Two detectives stopped by earlier. Talking to them set me back a little."

"Detectives, why?"

I shrug. "I guess Laurel Larsen's husband died? They wanted to know if we'd spoken to her recently. I have their cards."

His forehead wrinkles. "It'll have to be later. Sorry you had to deal with that."

"It's fine." I drop my gaze and pluck at an invisible piece of lint on my blazer. "Jigsaw's helping me prepare the viewing room."

"That's…" He pauses for so long, I drag my gaze up to his face. "Very nice of him," he finishes.

"Coming through," Paul shouts.

My father and I side-step away from the door. Paul bustles in, balancing platters of snacks in his arms and heads straight for the kitchen.

Footsteps thud along the floor behind me. It can only be Jigsaw and my heart flutters in anticipation.

A smile lifts my father's face. "Morning. Margot says you've been helping out. Thank you."

"Not a problem." Jigsaw stops behind me, so close his warmth spreads over my back. "I didn't want to leave Margot alone when there were so many people coming in and out."

His tone carries an edge of judgment. And here I'd been worried he was going to mention he spent the night—not that Dad couldn't figure that out on his own. Instead, he's implying, what? I need a babysitter to do my own job?

Anger heats my blood. I grit my teeth and force a smile.

"Yes," my father says smoothly. "We're a bit short-handed this morning."

"I need to run downstairs," I say.

Dad nods once. "Meet me in the office when you're done."

I take a right, heading down the hallway. It's not until I pause at the basement door that I realize Jigsaw's right behind me.

"Are you my shadow now?" I ask, pushing the door open and hurrying down the stairs.

"What?" He pounds down the stairs behind me.

I stop at the bottom and glance up. He left the door open.

Shaking my head, I turn the corner. "You realize I've done this job for a while, right? I don't need you telling my dad you stuck around to babysit me."

He scowls. "What are you talking about?"

"You didn't want to *leave me alone,*" I mimic in a deep voice that sounds nothing like Jigsaw's.

"Because you said you'd have vendors coming in and out." His voice rises with frustration. "I wasn't implying you're not capable." He clenches his jaw. "I don't trust people. *You,* of all people, should understand *why.*"

I *have* been alone with more than one vendor who made me uncomfortable, but I'd rather bite off my tongue than admit it right now.

"You know I'm right," he insists.

I glare at him, my stubbornness digging in. "I know no such thing."

He jerks his chin. "Come on, get your bulbs."

I let out a huff of annoyance and spin around, heading for a large metal supply cabinet.

Jigsaw doesn't move or say a word.

I grab a small stepladder and drag it closer to the shelves.

"*Demons give me strength,*" he mutters behind me. "Why are you being so difficult?" He grabs the stepladder, pushing it aside. "Put that away. I'm standing right here." He runs his gaze over the shelves. "Which ones?"

I point to the second highest shelf. "The first two white boxes."

He stretches, his shirt lifting slightly, and easily reaches what I need. "You weren't reaching this with that itty bitty stepladder."

A scream of frustration bubbles in my throat—because again, he's right, I'd still have to be on my tiptoes. "Don't be smug, Stretch."

He chuckles, tucks the bulbs against his side, and heads for the stairs.

I slam the cabinet doors shut and hurry to catch him. "I can carry my own bulbs."

"Too late."

A growl of frustration bursts out of me.

Jigsaw stops at the bottom of the steps and turns to face me. "You need to get it through your head, if we're together, I protect you. If you can't deal with that, tell me now."

Pain constricts around my throat. "That sounds like an ultimatum."

"An *ultimatum*?" He draws out the word as if tasting its absurdity from every angle possible.

CHAPTER ELEVEN

Jigsaw

The fear rippling over Margot's face tamps down my annoyance.

She's afraid I'd leave her?

I don't think I've ever had someone in my life who wanted to keep me this much. It's unfamiliar but comforting.

And fuck knows she's out of her mind if she thinks I'd let her go now.

Margot's stubborn. So am I. This is still so fucking new to me.

"I didn't mean to make it sound like an ultimatum." I dial down my dickishness. "I don't know how to explain it better. If I don't feel right about a situation, I can't *not* protect you. It's just not who I am."

"You said you've never been in a relationship before."

Not sure what that has to do with anything. "If I can easily do something for you, why would I stand there and watch you struggle to do it? I'm not an asshole." I throw my hand out, gesturing to the cabinet.

"I do it all the time," she argues.

"Cool. When I'm not here, go nuts."

The corners of her mouth curl up. She's trying hard not to laugh.

"Glad that's settled." Shaking my head, I wave my arm toward the stairs. "Now go up first, so I can stare at your cute ass."

She lets out an outraged squeal, followed by laughter. "What?"

"You heard me."

She hurries up the stairs, her heels *click-thudding* all the way.

The overly floral scent of the funeral home hits me when we reach the main floor. Is the smell always that strong, or do they start pumping in air freshener before a service?

More people are milling around the house now. Margot's expression switches to smooth and professional in an instant.

I glance down at my outfit—jeans, boots, and T-shirt. I don't exactly fit in with all the dark suits. "Let me get those light bulbs switched out for you, then I'm going to take off."

"Thank you."

I'd also rather not be here when they move the body into the viewing room but that seems disrespectful, so I keep it to myself.

When I'm finished with the bulbs, I store the ladder away and find Margot in the hallway setting out a guest book, prayer cards, and mints on a small table.

"Hey." I stop next to her. "I'm going to head out. But call me later, when you're done."

"This will be long and then we have back-to-back consultations." She bites her lip. "And I'll be working all day tomorrow too it looks like."

Disappointment hits me hard.

Why am I getting so clingy?

The way I just want to be near this woman all the time can't be normal. "All right," I answer evenly. "You think you'll be able to take off next weekend?"

"For the bonfire at the clubhouse? The whole weekend?"

"Yeah." I shrug. "We can stay over. It'll probably be busy there all weekend. Or we can take a ride, and I'll show you Downstate's clubhouse or my place?"

Her eyes light up and a softer smile curves her lips. "I'd really like that."

"Good." I have to at least pretend I don't want to kidnap her indefinitely. "If you can't get off the whole weekend—at least Friday night?" Christ, I sound like I'm begging now.

"Okay." Her whole face scrunches into a frown. "Unless there's like a mass-casualty pileup on the Thruway or something, Friday won't be a problem."

I huff a laugh—then stop. She's not kidding. "Yeah, of course."

She casts a quick glance around, then leans up on tiptoes, hooks her arm around my neck and drags me closer. "Thank you." She brushes a quick kiss against my cheek.

I turn, catching her lips for a longer kiss, then drop my forehead to hers. "For what?"

"Everything." She lifts her gaze to the ceiling. "For hearing me out. For all your help this morning."

"You don't have to thank me." *I think I love you and I'd do anything for you.*

"Well, I do."

Letting her go feels like breaking my arms out of concrete.

"Be careful," she warns.

"Always," I answer automatically, but her words linger as I move through the house. A sobering reminder of everyday danger.

Outside, the back parking lot has more cars than usual. I stop at my bike and send Teller a quick text.

> Me: You available to meet at the clubhouse for a few minutes?

I stare at my phone, waiting for a response.

Nothing.

The man's busy changing diapers and whatever the fuck else you do with babies but come on now.

"Jensen?" a rough voice hesitantly calls out.

I stuff my phone in my pocket, glance up, and find Margot's dad coming down the porch steps.

"Everything okay?" I ask.

"Yes, yes." He stops in front of me and slides his gaze over my bike.

The corners of his mouth twitch. Is that a *smirk* on Cedarwood's face? "Thank you for helping Margot this morning."

"Of course. Not a problem."

He interlaces his hands in front of him. "And you were here when the police stopped by as well, right?"

Oh fuck. Is he really going to grill me about spending the night with his twenty-eight-year-old daughter?

When I don't answer fast enough, he scoffs. "Do you think I haven't noticed your bike parked outside all this time? You do a good job tucking it close to the house, but it's not invisible." He cocks his head, leveling me with another give-me-a-break stare. "And it's certainly not quiet."

Heat creeps up my neck. Am I *blushing* over my girlfriend's dad busting me for sleeping over?

"Are you good to my daughter?" he asks, not waiting for me to deny the obvious.

Except for ticking her off with my overbearing ways. "I try to be, sir." *She's stubborn, though.*

He studies me for a long, uncomfortable moment. "You seem to respect what she does." He gestures toward the house. "What *we* do here."

"Yes, I do."

"It doesn't *scare* you?" he asks.

I glance at the funeral home looming over us. "Uh, not really."

He lowers his voice to a low, spooky tone. "You're not worried the house is *haunted*?"

I lift my eyebrows. "No. Should I be?"

His jaw tightens. "You're not weirdly *fascinated*?"

A shudder works over me when I realize what he's *really* asking—do I get my rocks off playing with dead bodies? "Definitely not."

He chuckles. "I didn't think so."

I hope he's not waiting for me to ask permission to date his daughter.

"The cops who were here earlier, did you speak with them as well?"

I'm already shaking my head by the time he finishes the question. "No. I stayed out of sight. But I tried to overhear as much as I could."

A knowing smile turns his mouth up, as if he enjoys the thought of me sneaking around and pressing my ear against the door. "And?"

I swallow hard. Is Margot sure her dad doesn't know she killed that guy? "Uh, they seemed interested in locating one of your clients. Her husband died and I guess they can't find her. They just asked how well Margot knew her, stuff like that. She handled herself well."

"Good." He flicks his gaze toward my bike again, and I can't shake the feeling he has something heavier on his mind. "If there's ever anything you, or your club, have questions about, you can just ask me. You know that, right?"

I frown as I puzzle that one out. Is he implying… "Mr. Cedarwood, I'm not with your daughter because my club asked me to spy on her." *Actually, my president specifically asked me* not *to get involved with her.*

He lifts his eyebrows.

I hold his stare, waiting to see if he has more questions.

I'm sure as fuck not telling him I'm in love with his daughter before I say it to her. I'm not even sure my mouth knows how to form the words to express *how* I feel.

After a long beat, he nods. "I'm glad to hear that."

My jaw twitches. "Are you?"

"I want her to be happy." He tilts his head and runs his gaze over me. "But you also seem like someone who can keep her…safe."

From what?

It doesn't matter. He's right, I'll protect her from anything. "Absolutely."

"Good." With that, he turns and heads inside. "I'm sure I'll see you soon," he calls over his shoulder.

I need to write this down in my *never expected to fucking happen* journal.

My phone buzzes and I pull it out.

Teller: When?

Me: About an hour.

Teller: I'll be there.

I grab my helmet off the handlebars and snap the chin strap into place.

Swinging my leg over the bike, I settle into the seat and fire up the engine.

I'm not sure what Cedarwood's agenda was with that conversation. But the cops came sniffing around Margot, and that's something my club needs to know.

Now.

CHAPTER TWELVE

Jigsaw

The bizarre conversation with Margot's dad sticks with me all the way to the clubhouse. He's really not bothered about a biker dating his daughter? Thought for sure he'd want her to marry another mortician or something.

Whoa. Why's my brain going to marriage? That's been on my *never, ever happening* list for years.

When I finally reach the clubhouse, at least ten different bikes are parked out front, including Rooster's and Z's. Rock's SUV is in the garage and his bike is parked along the fence—so he's here too. I should've known if I was meeting with Teller, he'd have Rock join us.

As I get off my bike, a weird sensation hits me. Last time I was here, I didn't know Margot was a murderer. *No—angel of justice.* She was just my shy, sweet girlfriend that I told my club I've been seeing. Oh, and I threatened to stab anyone who made her uncomfortable.

It doesn't matter. Her confession didn't change how I feel, did it?

Nope.

If anything, I'm more in...whatever I am with her, than before that knowledge bomb landed on my head.

"You finally get here?" Rooster calls out from the front steps. He jogs down and crosses the parking lot.

"I asked to meet with Teller." I brace myself for the bruising hug Rooster inflicts on me. The fucker always squeezes like he's testing how sturdy my ribs are. "What're you doing here?"

"I was helping Z with his back deck." Rooster points toward the trees in the direction of the cabin Z built up here for his family.

I squint at him. "Since when are you a carpenter?"

"He just needed an extra set of hands." He glances at my bike. A slow grin spreads across his face. "Did you come from your sweet, sunshiny girlfriend's love palace?"

I blink. "What kind of weird-ass shit just came out of your mouth?"

"Why so grouchy?" Rooster holds up one hand. "Never mind. I don't want to know, do I?"

I blow out a harsh breath. "She's not *that* sunshiny." I can't share Margot's secrets with him. Not yet. "She's got a bit of a dark side too."

"Good." He lets out a deep, satisfied chuckle like I just confirmed a bet he had with himself. "Sounds like the perfect woman for you, then."

Great, he probably thinks I'm talking about bedroom kinks, not murderous tendencies.

But he's not wrong. She *is* the perfect woman for me. In so many ways.

That's why I need to do what I can to keep the cops away from her without ratting her out to my club.

The screen door opens, and Teller sticks his head out. His gaze flicks to Rooster, then me. "You coming inside or not?"

"Yeah." I slap Rooster's chest as I step past him. "Thanks for holding me up, motherclucker."

He elbows me and falls in step next to me. I bound up the short steps and yank the door out of Teller's hand. "Right here, boss."

Seeing him up close, I take in his droopy eyes, messy hair, and generally grim expression. Brother looks like the sleep deprivation truck ran him over. "You look like shit."

"Thanks, asshole. I haven't slept in weeks." He yawns loudly and obnoxiously in my face. "Not even sure what day it is."

Well, now I feel even worse for asking to meet with him. "How's Charlotte doing?"

He scrubs his hand over his face. "Same. Tired." His voice softens just a fraction. "But she's the one with at least one baby attached to her at all times. Heidi's at the house with her now, helping out until I get back."

Sounds like a nightmare to me.

My aversion must show on my face. Teller jerks his head toward the war room, his scowl deepening. "Come on, you didn't want to meet up today to hear my babies' first weeks home journal entry."

I chuckle and move into the clubhouse's entryway. "Nah, it's a great reminder to stop and buy condoms on my way home."

Rooster smacks the back of my head.

Teller snorts with laughter. "For you—yeah, definitely. We were actively trying for this—we just didn't expect two at once."

In the war room, Rock, Z, Murphy, and Wrath—*for fuck's sake, Wrath too?*—are already seated at one end of the long table. I stop short and frown. "Uh, I'm not sure what Bishop Babymaker here," I point to Teller, "told everyone, but this isn't that big of a deal."

Wrath squeezes his eyes shut and shakes with laughter.

Murphy kicks out the chair across from him. His grin is pure mischief. "Sit your ass down, commander chucklefuck. We were here anyway."

Commander chucklefuck. I'll have to remember that one.

Grinning, I take the chair and drop into it. Rooster sits next to me.

I nod to Z. "How's everything at the house, Prez?"

"Coming along nicely."

I tap my fingers against the table. "Rooster said you need an extra set of hands." I hold my hands up in the air and wave them around like a magician. "You know I'm more talented than he is."

Z chuckles. "Knock yourself out when we're done here."

I turn my attention to Rock. "Prez." I nod in greeting.

"What's on your mind today, Jigsaw?" he asks, his patience clearly on its last thread.

I sit back, resting my elbows on the arm of the chair and clasp my hands over my stomach. "Well, like I said, it's not that big of a deal. But Margot had two Slater County detectives stop by today—"

"Fucking hell? You don't think that's a big deal?" Teller snaps.

"Relax." I hold my hands out in a calming gesture. "Has nothing to do with us." *It's her kill they were worried about, not ours! Never saw that coming, did you?*

Murphy mutters under his breath. "Jesus, this oughta be good."

"The husband of one of her clients died," I explain. "They can't find the woman, so they were just asking Margot questions."

"Did the woman kill him?" Teller asks.

"No. Cops said he died of an overdose." *Neither of those things are technically lies.*

Teller stares at me, unimpressed. "Okay?" His exasperated tone jabs at my annoyance button. "That's it?"

"Yeah." I answer in a tone that sounds more like *yeah, dumbass*. "But it's a *club business*." I draw out the words, since Teller obviously needs the reminder. "So I wanted to keep *the club* informed."

"No, you're right, Jigsaw," Rock says.

I throw a smug look Teller's way, and he rolls his eyes.

"What's the woman's name?" Z asks me.

Shit. Laura? Lauren? Think, motherfucker. "Laurel Larsen, I think. Husband's name was Patrick? I didn't exactly pop out and introduce myself to the cops. And I didn't want to explain to Margot that I was planning to sprint here and share with the club."

"Good call. No reason to worry her." Wrath arches an eyebrow. "Sounds like it's nothing." He glances over at Z. "Who do we know in Slater?"

"No one," Teller says. "Whisper didn't have a lot of pull with the local law."

Murphy exhales sharply, his usual humor gone, and raises his hand to halt the conversation. "Wait a second. Margot's clients are dead people. Were the cops looking for a dead person?"

"No." I let out a long sigh and flash an apologetic look at Teller. Christ, his wife just had two babies, I don't want to put this story in his head. "Uh, she had a miscarriage. The husband beat her up pretty bad, I guess—"

Teller flinches like I punched him in the stomach. "Jesus Christ. Who fucking cares if he overdosed?"

"Good riddance," Rock adds.

"Yeah," I answer slowly, weighed down by the burden of knowing the whole truth. "My thoughts too." *And my girlfriend's!*

The room quiets as everyone lets the information sink in.

"I think they were going through the motions," I add. "Margot's probably one of the last people who talked to Laurel at the service. They kinda pressed her on why her dad didn't charge the woman for—"

"Wait, Cedarwood didn't charge her?" Teller asks.

"No, I guess he doesn't charge for infant cremations or whatever."

Teller nods approvingly.

"Cops were kind of dickish about it," I add. "But Margot set 'em straight."

"Sounds like you overheard a lot." Wrath jerks his chin at me. "How'd she handle talking to cops?"

I grin like a proud outlaw boyfriend. "Smooth as butter." Then I realize, she'd have no reason to be lying to the cops and I dial it back. "She was polite but didn't take any shit from them. Oh! The best part—" I look Wrath straight in the eye. "You'll appreciate this. I guess they noticed my bike parked in back. They warned her how Wolf Knights run Slater County so she shouldn't be mixing with anyone from another club."

"Heh." Murphy lets out a dry laugh.

Wrath shakes his head. "Dumb motherfuckers don't even know what's going on in their own backyard."

"What'd the guy overdose on?" Rock asks.

My stomach clenches. I thought we'd moved past the details of Patrick Larsen's death. "Uh, cops didn't say. Just that he overdosed."

Rock glances at Z and Wrath. "I'm hearing more and more about certain substances moving into the area. Stuff we used to make sure stayed *out* of Empire. It starts landing in Slater it's only a matter of time before it ends up *here*."

Z holds up his hands. "The fucking government can't get a handle on some of this shit. We may have expanded our territory, but we haven't expanded our numbers enough to be running around playing outlaw DEA agents."

"Fucking doctors and pharmaceutical companies are responsible for a lot of what's going on now," Murphy adds. "Ain't no one holding them accountable."

Z points a finger gun toward the window. "*Someone* should."

"Look who's up on current events." Wrath slaps Murphy's back like he's a good little student.

"What?" Murphy scowls. "I watch documentaries and stuff."

"Since when?" Teller laughs.

"Since Heidi makes him," Z says.

"We can debate the politics of it another day," Rock says. "I'm more worried about our business interests out that way. I don't want to see Remy's bar getting held up at gunpoint because some tweaker needs cash. Or Sully's gym." Rock sends Wrath a pointed look.

Teller snorts. "It'll only benefit Cedarwood's if bodies are dropping from overdoses."

Rock's mouth twitches with irritation but he nods. "True. I still don't want to start seeing a problem. Once it gets out of control, it's hard to contain."

Murphy's jaw tightens and he shifts his gaze to the empty end of the table.

"I'm out that way a lot now," I say. "I can stop into Remy's place more often." I tap my cut. "Make our presence known. And I've gone over to Sully's a few mornings to work out. Things seem dull as ever in that part of town. But I'll check in there more."

Rock stares at me for a few beats then nods. "That's good, Jiggy. Thank you."

"Dex is pretty much living at Emily's place now," Z says. "Take him with you on some of these visits."

I hadn't realized Dex was there that often. "Yeah, I'll do that."

"Aw, the four of you can double-date," Murphy jokes. He smirks at Rooster. "Unless you're going to be jealous."

Rooster reaches over and rests his heavy palm on the top of my head. "He's allowed to have other friends."

"Fuck off." I laugh and slap his hand away.

"All right." Rock slaps his hand against the table, then focuses on me. "Will Margot tell you if the cops come back?"

"Yeah, definitely."

"Whoa, whoa." Wrath holds up his hands, calling a time-out. "Go back. You said the cops saw your bike and told her not to associate with other clubs. What'd *she* say?"

A wide grin spreads across my face. "Not a damn thing."

"She didn't say it was her boyfriend's bike?" Murphy asks.

"Nope. She said the funeral home has a varied clientele, they don't discriminate, and it's never been an issue, in her most polite *fuck off* voice. She was great. Pretended she had no idea what they were talking about."

Wrath nods with approval. "Good girl."

"Yup." I knew he'd appreciate Margot's discretion.

"Orrr," Rooster drawls. "She's embarrassed to admit she's taken a walk on the wild side with a biker."

Slowly I turn my head his way and give him the wounded puppy eyes. "Really? I'd expect that from Z or Murphy but not you."

Murphy cracks up. "Even I wouldn't say that."

Rooster just stares at me with that maddeningly steady expression, like he's trying to stare inside my skull and implant some words of wisdom. "Let's not forget, she's your first real girlfriend."

And my last. "What's your point?"

"Yeah, what *is* your point?" Z asks. "Half of us at this table married their 'first real girlfriend.'" Z adds air quotes and a *you're-a-moron* tone to punctuate his thoughts.

Rock laughs. "*I* have an ex-wife."

"Marrying evil incarnate isn't anything to be proud of, Rock," Wrath reminds him.

I continue glaring at Rooster. "Your 'dating' history could've been an entire season of *American Horror Story*. So how about you shut the fuck up about mine." Considering his first girlfriend did everything she could to ruin his life, and his second girlfriend's father tried to shoot him, that was low of me.

He started it.

Rooster strokes his hand over his beard a few times. Either I hurt his feelings or he's thinking up more obnoxious comments. "No lies detected."

"Not to pry, but I'm still curious *how* the fuck you two hooked up." Murphy holds up his hands as if he means no harm. "Respectfully, she doesn't seem like *your* type, Jigsaw."

Wouldn't my brothers *love* to hear that Margot asked me to be her sex coach. The endless jokes would never stop raining down on me and they'd eventually spill onto Margot whenever she's around the club. She'd be hurt and mortified to find out everyone knows that's how we started.

"I always kind of pictured her dating a banker or something," Teller adds.

I shoot a glare at Murphy, then Teller. "Well, I've been pondering how two intelligent women could possibly settle for your two dumb asses for years, but here we all are."

Murphy snorts with laughter but I continue glaring at him.

What am I so pissed about? That their comments have a ring of truth to them? Whoever Margot's dickhead ex is, he made her feel so bad about herself, she asked *me* for sex lessons. That's the only reason we ended up together.

Fuck, I still wish I knew what he said to her. And who he is so I can track him down and maim him.

Will she ever trust me enough to tell me something *that* personal?

"All right." Wrath's authoritative growl cuts off any additional chatter. "Sounds like Margot knows how to deal with the cops. Z's going to find out what he can about the Larsens. Teller's going to go home, get some sleep, and take a shower because he smells like baby shit."

Laughter erupts around the table. Even from me.

"What?" Teller pulls his T-shirt away from his chest and sniffs. "No, I don't."

Murphy tilts his head like he hates to be the bearer of bad news. "Don't take this the wrong way. But…"

I press my fist to my lips to keep from losing it.

"Shut up." Teller stands and stares at Rock like he's a kid about to shit his pants, waiting for the teacher to give him a bathroom pass.

Rock waves a dismissive hand toward the door. "Go. I'll check in on you later."

Teller leaves, slamming the door behind him.

Shaking his head, Rock turns toward Rooster and me. "You two can go too."

"Trin's in the kitchen making pancakes for lunch if you're sticking around," Wrath offers.

I fake a horrified expression. "I thought you didn't eat pancakes." I clutch my chest and roll my eyes skyward. "Think of all the sugar."

Wrath's lip curls. "I didn't say *I* was eating them. She's making *me* steak and eggs."

"Isn't it kind of embarrassing a man your size can't make his own food?" Murphy snort-laughs.

"I *can*." Wrath's head tilts, slow and deliberately, like he's weighing the pros and cons of kicking Murphy's ass. "But I'm here, listening to your disrespectful mouth."

I push my chair back and stand. "As much fun as this has been, I'm going to go get my pancakes on."

I nod at Rock, then Z. "Thank you."

Rock inclines his head. "Thanks for keeping us up to date."

"No problem." I punch Rooster's shoulder on my way out, relishing his exaggerated grunt of protest.

Happy to be free and not asked to stick around, I make a beeline for freedom. Rock, Z, Wrath, and Murphy seem to have things to discuss. Since I prefer to mind my own business, I head out of the war room, intent on putting some distance between myself and both presidents.

"Look at you leaving the table like a big boy today," Rooster jokes, coming up on my left.

"One time, motherclucker. One time." I roll my eyes. "You act like I'm always staying for detention or something," I growl at him, still annoyed that he questioned how Margot feels about me in front of everyone and pointed out she's my first girlfriend. As if I'm too dumb to figure out how relationships work.

Anger rising as I keep thinking about it, I stop and slap my palm against Rooster's chest, halting him in his tracks. He glances down at my hand and back to my face.

"What the fuck's your problem?" I growl, low enough that we won't be overheard. "Why'd you question Margot's motives like that in front of everyone?"

A deep frown creases his forehead. After a second, he brushes my hand away. "Has she told *anyone* in her life that she's seeing you?"

"Huh? Who, the corpses?"

"No, her friends, her dad? She must have other people in her life." He closes his eyes and shudders. "Besides corpses."

"I'm pretty sure her dad already knows—he talked to me this morning before I left."

His eyes widen. "Yeah, and how'd that conversation go?"

"Fine." I shrug. "Basically, he wanted to let me know that I'm not as slick as I think I am, parking my bike alongside the house where I thought he wouldn't see it."

Rooster snorts and ducks his head. "Smooth."

"Other than that, he wanted to make sure I'm not weirded out by what they do there."

"Are you?"

"Not really. I don't exactly go wandering around the house, though." I blow out a breath. "I guess he was concerned I might only be seeing her because the club asked me to spy on her."

He scoffs. "If only he knew Z told you not to."

"Right."

"I'm sorry," he says.

Holy shit, is an asteroid about to hit the planet? "Did you just apologize?"

He lets out a heavy sigh, as if he already regrets it. "Something about pretending not to know you rubbed me wrong…" He shrugs. "I don't want you involved with someone who doesn't even want to acknowledge you're together."

"I can't decide if I'm deeply touched." I press my hand against my chest. "Or deeply offended."

"Fucking hell. I should've kept my mouth shut."

"Well, yeah." I nod and punch his shoulder. "If it makes you feel better, *Dad*," I sneer, "I think she told her cousin about us. Same thing —he's seen and heard my bike there a lot."

"Okay. Good."

"You realize the whole point is *not* to tell the cops anything personal about ourselves, right?" I ask since he seems to have forgotten Outlaw 101. "I was fuckin' proud of her for not saying anything. Wrath agreed."

"You're right. Jesus Christ, I already apologized. You need me to beg too?"

"Gee, could ya?" I wave my hand at the floor. "Maybe puff out your chest, strut around, flap your arms at your side and yell cock-a-doodle-do a few times? Then I'll know you're truly sorry."

"You're insufferable."

"It's part of my charm."

Out of the corner of my eye, a flash of green catches my attention.

"Jiggy?" Hope lightly touches my arm, stopping me from hurling more insults at Rooster.

Even though I'm rethinking staying for breakfast—I'll always make time for Rock's wife.

"Greetings, upstate First Lady." With an exaggerated flourish, I press my hand over my stomach and dip my head in an overly dramatic bow. "How may I help you?"

"Christ," Rooster mutters.

"Don't be jealous." I elbow him in the ribs. "No one's interested in your big, bearded face."

Hope mashes her lips together, but a snort of laughter slips out.

"I'll see you in the dining room." Rooster slaps my shoulder.

Hope says goodbye without taking her eyes off me.

"I'm not used to having the full force of your attention focused on me, First Lady," I say once Rooster's vacated the area. "What's on your mind?"

Her pink lips tilt with amusement. "Are you still bringing Margot to the bonfire this weekend?"

I should've known mama bear would be excited that another one of her cubs has found a mate.

"That's the plan," I confirm. "She's trying to find someone to cover the whole weekend. But if nothing else, definitely Friday night."

Hope's forehead creases. "It must be hard for her to take time off."

"It is. She's looking forward to this."

"Since the party's here, it should be..." She waves her hand in the air like she's searching for the right word.

"Free of muffler bunnies?" I add helpfully.

She rolls her eyes and blows out an annoyed huff. "For the most part, yes."

I jam my hands in my pockets and check out the toes of my scuffed boots. "I already warned her."

"Well..." Her voice wavers for so long, I lift my gaze. Her lips are curved into an amused smile but her gaze shifts to something or someone behind me. "That's more than I had before *my* first clubhouse party, so that's very kind of you."

"What's that, baby doll?" Rock steps up behind Hope and slides his arms around her waist, hugging her close.

No need to stake your claim in front of me, Prez.

He whispers something against her ear that sounds awful close to, "Do you need me to take you upstairs?"

Pink spreads over Hope's cheeks but she leans into him, murmuring, "Maybe."

For fuck's sake. Don't married couples usually fuck all their horniness out of themselves by now?

I clear my throat—loudly. "Ah, Hope was giving me some info about the bonfire."

"Yes." She pats Rock's arm that's still firmly curled around her waist. "I was trying to reassure him that there won't be a pack of muffler bunnies roaming around the clubhouse to ambush Margot her first time visiting us here."

Rock groans and briefly closes his eyes. "Were you now?"

She nods quickly.

Rock's so overprotective of Hope, I can't picture him throwing her to some of the she-wolves who used to hang around the MC without any warning. Then again, ol' lady of the president has a lot more responsibility than most ol' ladies. Old-school brothers like Rock and Wrath could've decided to test Hope to see how she'd handle herself. On second thought, *Wrath* would come up with some twisted test, for sure. Big fucker has a sadistic streak wider than the Grand Canyon.

Margot…she's stronger than she looks. Brave as hell underneath her sweet exterior. Still, the thought of anyone fucking with her for shits and giggles turns my thoughts down a rage-fueled path.

"I know you're not sure about the whole weekend," Hope says. "But are you at least staying Friday night?"

"I'd like to." As long as Margot's comfortable and having a good time.

"I'll make sure there's a room available for you two." Hope lifts her chin toward the staircase. "Or, if she's not comfortable here, our guest room is open."

Rock side-eyes her but doesn't say anything.

I'd rather sleep outside and take my chances with the bears roaming through the woods, than sleep under Rock's roof. It's well-known that our upstate president values his privacy, and I have no intention of being the asshole invading it.

"I won't keep you." Hope squeezes my arm. "Go get breakfast. Or razz Rooster. Whatever you usually do for fun."

"I think I'll mix it up and razz Rooster *while* eating breakfast today." I grin at her.

She returns the smile. "Good plan."

"Thanks for keeping your knife in its sheath." Rock pierces me with a stern stare. Not a trace of amusement to be found on his granite-cold face.

Fuck me, he's never gonna let that one go, is he?

Instead of reminding him I came here today like a good little soldier to keep the club informed, I vacate the area.

I head down the long, empty hall to the dining room. The hum of lively—and vulgar—conversation drifts toward me before I even reach the swinging doors.

But my appetite's already fading.

I'll have Margot with me here this weekend.

The last time she was around the whole club was Teller's wedding and she spent most of the night baked out of her mind on Sparky's brownies.

She'll be stone-cold sober this time. Instead of the peacefulness she's used to, it'll be loud and rowdy.

It'll be fine. Right?

Except...what if it's not?

What if one of my brothers makes her uncomfortable? What if the old ladies—hell, what if Hope, the closest thing to a mom the club has—senses the darkness in Margot and starts asking the wrong questions?

I roll my shoulders back and crack my neck, pushing the thoughts down. Not going to happen. Margot's used to dealing with all sorts of people.

This is different.

Whether they admit it or not, the brothers will want to test Margot. And MC parties are rarely completely bunny-free. One or two will find their way up here.

Doesn't matter. I'll protect her. From the outside world. From the club. From anyone who looks at her wrong.

Still, the thought lingers as I shove through the doors.

What if bringing her here is a mistake that ruins everything?

CHAPTER THIRTEEN

Margot

WHAT DOES A WOMAN WEAR TO A PARTY AT HER BOYFRIEND'S motorcycle club? I had joked with Jigsaw about wearing something that would allow us to be frisky in the woods, but it's supposed to be chilly tonight. It's a bonfire in the woods—doesn't seem like a dressy affair. I stroll through my closet, running one hand along the long row of clothes to my right. I want to look nice. What if I run into one of those muffler bunnies Jigsaw warned me about? I need to look like I belong with a man like him when I'm on his turf.

Although having him chase me through the woods and pin me to a tree while he lifts my dress has been a fantasy playing on a loop in my head all day, I'd rather be comfortable and not risk flashing my underwear to the whole party if we end up sitting on a blanket near the bonfire.

My phone chirps and I hurry into the bedroom to grab it off my dresser.

Shelby.

We'd traded numbers but I didn't really expect her to call me.

I click accept and answer with a tentative, "Hi."

"Hey, Margot!" Shelby drawls, her rich, warm twang drawing out my name to *Mahhr-guh.* "Jiggy's on his way but he's gonna be a while. I thought I'd check up on ya in case ya got any questions? I know it's your first clubhouse party."

"Well, uh." This is embarrassing. Am I really asking her for wardrobe advice like a teenager? "Jigsaw said it's a bonfire in the woods, so my instincts say a dress isn't the way to go?"

She laughs softly. "I mean, if you want to, go for it. I'm a Texas girl. When it gets below sixty, I'm wearing long johns under my jeans and a winter coat, ya know?"

"You've got a point. I don't like to be cold, either. Jeans and a flannel sound better than a dress, then."

"Yup. Anyway, I feel duty-bound to warn ya. Since I'm not sure Jigsaw will think of it," she says.

"Warn me?"

"Since it's your first clubhouse party, some of the guys will want to razz ya a lil' bit. Test your mettle, ya know?"

"The guys? Jigsaw warned me some of the…uh…muffler bunnies might…" But I have to worry about his brothers picking on me too?

She lets out a disgusted sound somewhere between a snort and a whistle. "Yeah, that shouldn't be a problem upstate. Most of the girls are nice but a few are snotty lil' hags. But I got your back, don't worry 'bout them."

Tears prick my eyelids. Shelby sounds protective of me already even though we barely know each other. And, she's younger than me. "Thanks. I don't want to do anything to…you know, embarrass him." My cheeks flame hot. I can't believe I just admitted that.

"Please. Jiggy's so dang smitten with you. If one of them bunnies looks at you funny, he'll probably send them cryin' to their momma."

He's smitten with me?

Obviously, I know we're…something. And I'm important to him or he wouldn't be bringing me to this party. But to hear his best friend's fiancée so casually say it sends a shiver of pleasure through me. Like it's just a known, common fact. *Jiggy's smitten with Margot.* I bite my lip to stop myself from squeeing into the phone like a teenager.

"Well, the feeling's mutual," I assure her. "So, if any of those girls get too close to him, I might push them off a ledge."

"Ooowee!" she shrieks into the phone. "That's the energy you need. I knew we were going to get along, Margot. I just knew it." When she stops laughing, she says, "Anyway. Rav's a lil' rascal. He loves tryin' to embarrass any newcomers. He's just playin' though. But don't be surprised if he tries to get you to admit how or where you lost your virginity."

I burst into laughter. "Wow. Okay. Am I allowed to make up something?"

"Huh. Dang it. Why didn't I think of that?"

"He got you, huh?"

"Sure did. But Charlotte put an end to that game, I doubt he'll try it again." She pauses and I hold my breath, waiting for whatever advice she has next. "Lord knows what he'll come up with instead."

An idea so brilliant pops into my head, I blurt it into the phone without thinking. "I thought people tell scary campfire stories when they're in the woods around a *campfire*."

"Like, *Legend of Bloody Mary* urban legend type stories?" she asks carefully.

Not exactly. "Sure."

She lets out an almost nervous-sounding laugh. "That might be more fun. Anyway, the guys like to joke around and bust on each other. It's not personal. And like I said, Jigsaw won't let anyone get carried away."

I interact with different personalities every day. I've got this. It's still nice to have a heads-up, though. "Thanks, Shelby."

"You got it. I'll see ya a lil' later."

We say goodbye and I set my phone down. I wander into my closet and find a bag big enough to hold a weekend's worth of clothing. I have a hard time narrowing it down, but I end up with a few outfits that should work—including one dress. Just in case.

I can't stop thinking about what Shelby said. The guys might want to test me tonight—have me share an embarrassing story or detail about myself in front of everyone.

Not happening.

After dropping the clothes off on my bed, I return to my closet.

This time, I go all the way into the back, past all my work clothes, shoe collection, jewelry, and special "ornaments," to the small hidden door in the corner.

The latch sticks for a second before popping open. Inside, newspaper clippings and other…oddities I've collected over the years wait in the dark. I reach for one particular item and carefully wrap it inside a velvet sack.

I don't know if I'll have the guts to actually use it.

But if I do…

It'll be the last time anyone tries to embarrass me at a party.

CHAPTER FOURTEEN

Jigsaw

The ride to Margot's place is a hell of a lot different in my cage. The old 4Runner handles like a tank, stiff and bouncy over every crack in the road. Feels like I'm steering a cinder block on wheels. It's survived years of New York winters, potholes the size of craters, and my general lack of giving a shit, so I should be thankful it's running at all.

I made one of the prospects give it a thorough detailing, so it's clean for my girl and she won't be brushing road salt off of her jeans when she climbs in. It's not classy enough for my pretty little lady death. But it wasn't built for class—it was built for survival. Just like me.

Wind whistles through the driver's side window, a reminder that the seal is barely hanging on. I should've fucking fixed that.

I tighten my grip on the wheel. Driving always makes me feel like a raccoon trapped in a giant dumpster. I'm more than ready to be out of this steel cage. Unfortunately, I've got at least another hour to go to get to Margot's and then an hour back to the clubhouse. I might be out of my skull by the time we get there.

Nah, I'm taking my frustration out on my trusty old cage for no reason. Am I worried about officially introducing Margot to the club as my girlfriend? Is that what's giving me the itch to claw my way through the windshield? I've never had an ol' lady. Never specifically brought a woman to the clubhouse to introduce her as *mine*.

In fact, I've talked a lot of shit about never wanting an ol' lady and how I relish variety in my bedmates. I'm more than willing to eat my words if my brothers want to razz my ass—I deserve it. But I'd rather not have them say that shit in front of Margot. It's one thing for *me* to tell her I never did relationships before her. It's totally different to have it confirmed in grotesque detail over and over by every member of my club…and probably a few bunnies too.

Fuck.

Hope said the party should be bunny-free. *Please let her be the one who had final say over the guest list.*

I glance over at the passenger seat. A small brown gift bag with a red and black plaid ribbon tied around the twine handles waits for Margot. I've never gotten a girl a gift before. Usually, my presence is enough of a gift. But I saw it and immediately thought of Margot.

Will she think it's weird or too much?

Too soon?

No. It's practical. Useful. She'll like it.

Finally, her house comes into view. I tap the brakes, grimacing as the 4Runner dips forward too hard. Forgot how stiff the front suspension is. Instead of detailing it, I should've replaced the shocks.

The parking lot's empty, so I stop right by the porch stairs. Before I even take the key out, Margot's trotting down the steps with a hot-pink backpack that's almost as big as her slung over her shoulder and a long, wide Tupperware container tucked under her arm.

I jump out of the truck and meet her at the bottom of the steps. "I'm more than happy to come to the door, you know." I slide my fingers under the strap and pull her bag off her shoulder.

"Yes, but I'm eager to see you." She hooks her arms around my neck and lifts on her tiptoes to press a warm kiss to my lips.

"I approve." I curl my free arm around her waist, pulling her closer. "Do I really have you for the whole weekend?"

"Sure do. Paul promised not to let my dad call me for any reason." The first hint of nervousness ripples over her face. She stands back and sweeps her hand over her outfit—sleek, dark jeans, dark green lace-up boots, and a green and blue flannel shirt—utterly fucking adorable. "I hope this is okay. I know I promised to wear something with easier access if you wanted to chase me through the woods." The corners of her mouth curl into a hesitant smile. "But it's supposed to be chilly."

"Trust me, if I want to get those pants off, they're gone." I pinch the soft flannel material of her sleeve and rub it between my fingers. "You look perfect."

"I talked to Shelby." She ducks her head, almost shyly. "She said she was wearing jeans and a hoodie, so I thought this would be okay."

Thank you, Shelby. I hadn't even asked her to call Margot. "I've got a sweatshirt or two in the truck if you get cold."

"Or *you* can keep me warm."

Chuckling, I turn her toward the truck, open the back door, and toss her bag inside, then walk her to the passenger side. "I plan to. Don't worry."

I swing her door open and wince as the hinges squeak. "Ahh, it's not really…" *worthy of you.* "In the best shape. It runs great, we won't get stranded or anything," I hurry to add. "But I usually only drive it in the winter, to get groceries, or big stuff."

Why am I acting as nervous as a high school sophomore going on my first date?

"It's got four wheels and a roof, I'm happy." She grips the side handle and lifts herself up into the seat but pauses midway.

"Oh! Yeah. This is for you." I pluck the bag off the seat and hand it to her once she's settled inside. I slam the door and hurry to my side.

She's still staring at the bag once I get behind the wheel.

"What is it?" she asks.

"Open it."

"I didn't get you anything," she murmurs, as she gently tugs the plaid ribbon free.

"You don't have to give me anything." I reach over and rest my hand on her leg. "You coming up there with me tonight is already a gift."

The sweetest smile lights up her whole face as she pulls out the long, flat box.

Please don't think it's weird.

I don't want that smile to leave her face.

She pries the lid off.

A tiny wrinkle forms between her eyebrows as she takes in the hand-stitched leather case. Her fingers skim over the smooth surface before she unsnaps the button at the top and carefully tips it sideways.

Her eyes widen, and her lips part as the knife slides into her open palm.

"Oh, wow!" she gasps, tracing her finger along the handle.

I knew she'd like it.

The abalone shell gleams in the afternoon light, the swirling blues and greens shifting like moonlight over the ocean. It's elegant but tough, just like her.

She rests the box and case in her lap and carefully flicks the blade open. "It opens so smoothly. I hate when I break a nail trying to work the blade free."

"Yeah, it was designed to be easy for daintier hands to use." I trace my finger over her knuckles, wanting her to understand that wasn't meant as a criticism.

She turns the knife slightly, watching how the light catches the blade's dark rippling pattern. "That's from the layering, right? That's what gives it the design—kind of like a fingerprint."

I exhale a slow breath. She knows just by looking at it. Could she be more perfect for me?

"Yeah. It's handmade Damascus steel, layered, welded, then hammered." I tap the side of the blade. "It holds its edge. Stronger than it looks."

Her lips curve into a small smile at that last part.

"It's beautiful." She picks it up, balancing it carefully in her palm.

Then her gaze flicks up to mine, sharp and assessing. "Jigsaw," she says, almost like a gentle scolding. "This must've been expensive."

I shrug. "I thought it suited you."

She raises an eyebrow. "How so?"

"It's small but elegant. Beautiful. And—most important—*deadly*."

She laughs softly. "I really love it."

I exhale a sigh of relief. "Good."

"Will you be upset if I stick it in my pocket right now?" she asks. "Instead of putting it back in the box?"

"No, why would that upset me? I want you to use it."

She shifts to the side slightly and wiggles her hand into her front jeans pocket. "Well, I don't want to lose it."

I should've gotten it engraved. Something sappy like "J loves M?" *No, I haven't actually said that to her yet.* How weird would it be to give it to her on a knife? Maybe something funnier she'd appreciate, like *slay all day*?

"I can take it and get your initials engraved on it if you'd like?"

"That might be nice."

I twist the key in the ignition to get us moving. "We don't want to be late for dinner or everyone will mercilessly rag on us."

She turns and sets the bag on the back seat. "We wouldn't want that." I wait while she clicks her seat belt into place. "I thought it was just a bonfire? Like hotdogs and s'mores."

"It started out that way but then Murphy said he was going to make chili since it's chilly out." I roll my eyes. "His dad jokes are reaching a new level of annoying lately."

Margot titters with laughter.

"Heidi wanted to make cornbread to go with the chili—oh, and the chili meat is probably venison because a bunch of the guys hunt up at the property."

"I like venison," she says.

Thank God. I'd been bracing myself for a lecture about how mean hunting is. But I should've known Margot's more practical than that.

"Shelby's allergic to tomatoes," I continue, listing off the bits of the menu I remembered, "so Trinity said she'd make mac and cheese."

"Ooo." Margot lets out a delighted moan. "I love homemade mac and cheese."

"I'm sure there will be other stuff—I should've mentioned earlier that the menu expanded. You didn't eat dinner, yet?"

"Nope. I was planning to stuff myself with s'mores." She turns slightly, gesturing toward the back seat. "I didn't want to come empty-handed, so I made a batch of inside-out chocolate chip cookies."

Cookies? I'd been too nervous about giving her the knife, I didn't think to ask what was in the box. "Inside-out cookies?"

"They're fudgy chocolate cookies with white chocolate chips. Sometimes I put pecans in them too, but I wasn't sure if anyone was allergic to nuts."

"Those sound awesome. Give me one now."

"What! No. They're for the party."

I turn toward her and smoosh my face into pleading puppy mode. "Come on, *please*? You know how much I love cookies."

Laughing, she turns and stretches, reaching for the container. After some muttering and cursing, she settles back into her seat and hands over a dark brown cookie speckled with white chips. The sweet, chocolaty aroma hits my nose and my stomach grumbles. "They look tasty. Smell good too."

"I'm happy with how they turned out."

I bite it almost in half and groan with happiness. They're chewy at the edges and softer in the middle. Too good to share. "You leave these right where they are tonight. They're all mine."

"No!" she laughs and slaps my thigh. "They're for the party. I'll make you your own batch next time I bake. Promise."

I'm too busy munching on the other half to complain. "Mrfkay," I mumble around the cookie.

Margot uncaps the bottle of Coke in my cupholder and hands it to me. I take a long swig and hand it back to her. "Thanks."

I hit a jagged piece of road and from the corner of my eye, catch Margot bracing herself against the door.

Shit.

My sour mood about the truck roars back to life. *For fuck's sake,* she's going to think the only kinds of vehicles I like are death traps. "Sorry." I tighten my grip on the wheel. "The suspension is kinda stiff. Gonna be even bumpier when we reach the clubhouse."

"I'm fine." She bounces once in the seat, testing it like it's an office chair she plans to bring home. "Don't forget, I'm used to my tiny classic car. It'll rattle your teeth on rough roads sometimes." She leans forward, staring straight ahead. "Besides, I really like how high up this sits. I don't feel like a bug some monster truck could drive right over."

She's just being nice, but her words take the edge off of my frustration.

After that our conversation dwindles down to not much. It's not the usual comfortable silence we're able to share. It leaves me tense and itchy. I glance over at Margot a few times. Her hands are clenched tight in her lap and she's staring out the window with a grim expression.

"You all right?" I ask, reaching over and resting my hand over hers.

She slowly unclenches her fists.

"Margot, what's wrong?" I try again.

"Are you sure you want to take me to your club?"

Why is she asking me that now?

"Uh, yeah." I wave one hand toward the windshield. "We're literally halfway there. Why would you even ask? I thought you were excited?"

"I mean, now that you know what I am…about my *side hobby.*" She draws out the words for emphasis, as if I can't figure out her meaning.

If only she could understand how well she'll fit in. "What you are is a deeply compassionate person with a strong stomach and even stronger sense of justice. You'll be right at home."

"Can I ask you something?"

Anyone else posing that question would clang my danger alarm. Not Margot. "Anything."

She hesitates for a few beats as if she's rethinking her question. "The night your club came to—*borrow the facilities*—who went into the retort? Were they random club enemies or was it more…personal?"

We're already in *that* crime together, so I don't hesitate. "Both. But what sealed their fate that night was that they kidnapped Charlotte's brother and chopped off his toe."

"Holy hell. Really?"

"Yup. Sent it to Charlotte in a fucking box."

"Is he okay?"

"Yeah, he's a tough little dude. But I've overheard Charlotte say it was bothering him for a while, he just didn't want anyone to know."

"That's awful." She's silent again. Probably debating if the loss of a pinky toe was worth killing over.

"They were also holding a girl, June, hostage and did some pretty heinous stuff to her." I glance down and frown, brushing my hand over my side. "They stabbed Rooster…"

"Wow." She blows out a breath. "I read about motorcycle clubs and how a lot of disputes stem from petty beefs over territory or perceived insults. But that's a lot more than riding through town wearing your colors and not calling ahead."

Pleased she remembered that bit of protocol, I nod. "That's an interesting way to put it. You're right. Some clubs aren't very level-headed and beef over dumb shit." I consider my words more carefully. I want Margot to feel comfortable in my world, not live in fear that we try to murder each other. But I also want to be honest with her. "My first charter could be that way sometimes. It's gotten them into trouble more than once over the years."

"Is that the reason you and Rooster left?" she asks. "Bad decision making?"

I nod once, then let out a dark laugh. "That, and the old president wanted to pump him full of lead for dating his daughter."

"You're kidding."

"Rooster's big, white ass wishes I was joking."

"I'll never tell anyone you shared that with me," she says in a solemn tone, understanding my club might not approve.

Even so, I need her to understand the stakes. "We try not to drag the women into club specifics." *Sometimes that's easier said than done.*

"Kinda hard to do that when someone sends your wife her brother's *toe*," she points out.

"Uh, yeah," I agree. "Each brother decides for himself how much he shares with his ol' lady." I swallow hard, wary of even the potential sting of betrayal. "If she ever betrays the MC, *he's* the one who suffers the punishment from the club."

"What form of punishment?"

"Depends on the depth of the betrayal." Am I really sharing this much detail with her already? Worse, am I doing it right before I take her to hang out with the club for her first visit as my girlfriend? Truth is, if an ol' lady snitches to the cops, they'd probably *both* end up six feet under. "Most punishments come in the form of cash or blood."

"So, a fine or a beating?" Her voice is full of curiosity, like she's trying to swallow our brand of family justice. "No permanent disfigurement?"

Good God, her mind is fascinating and sharp as a blade. I want to crawl inside her brain and *live* there. "Like cutting off a finger or something? No. If we strip someone's patch, and they don't end up in the ground, they have to get rid of any and all Lost Kings MC ink. Method is up to them." I gesture to my arms and shoulders. "But you've seen how covered a lot of us are."

"Covering all that ink could be disfiguring in its own way."

"Right, and if they don't do it in a specific time frame..." I let the idea hang for a few beats. "Then we do it for them—"

"And not in a neat, artistic fashion, I assume," she says with a healthy dose of sarcasm.

I tilt my head to the side in answer.

When she doesn't say anything, I glance over.

She lifts her eyebrows, silently demanding more detail.

"I've only seen that happen once," I say. "When I was a prospect in Washington."

"Let me guess, the president wanted you and Rooster to watch, so you'd fully grasp the price of betrayal?"

My brothers have no idea how much Margot's going to deserve that property patch I'm giving her one day. "I'm sure that had a lot to do with it. It doesn't happen often, though," I hurry to add. "Club here spends a lot of time vetting brothers before we vote them in, and they get their full patch. Especially now."

"Now?"

I sigh and shift my gaze to the approaching highway sign. Our exit's coming up. Can I finish this before we get to the clubhouse? This story might be giving Margot too much history.

Fuck it.

"Our old president was a little too busy enjoying the benefits of his position instead of actually running the club. Some bad apples slipped into Downstate's barrel. Or they turned rotten over time. He paid a price for his laziness." Sway got a fucking bullet to his head and somehow survived. But it opened his eyes to what a piece of shit his VP Shadow had been. "He's retired now."

"Did he have to cover his ink?"

"No. He didn't betray the club and get kicked out…it's complicated and not really important. Our national prez strongly encouraged the retirement and appointed Z to take over."

She nods slowly. "How political."

I tighten my grip on the steering wheel. "Yeah, we're a regular outlaw democracy."

"You'd die for your brothers?" she asks.

"Yes." I flip my blinker on and slide into the exit lane.

"Would they die for you?"

"Yes," I answer without hesitation. "They'd die for you too, Margot. Because you're mine."

Her laughter's lighter than before. Teasing. "Not because I have the keys to the oven?"

"That doesn't hurt," I answer honestly. "But it's not important enough to take a bullet."

Margot

Betrayal. Punishments. Cash. Blood.

The words repeat over and over in my mind. A grim reminder of the world I'm about to visit. I wish I hadn't asked Jigsaw so many questions about the club. Now I'm even more nervous that I won't fit in.

As he steers the truck through back roads of Empire County I never knew existed, a dark weight of disappointment or regret hovers over me. Except for college, I haven't ventured far from Pine Hollow in my life. Jigsaw has lived in different states and traveled all over the country, seeing places I've only read about or visited through YouTube videos.

So much of my life has been consumed by death instead of actually living.

"How many states have you visited?" I ask.

He's quiet for a few seconds. "Probably all of them? Except Alaska and Hawaii. And the ones in the middle." He swerves one hand between us like an airplane. "Nebraska, Kansas, Oklahoma. No desire to see them. But I only traveled through a lot of those places to get to the next stop. Like when I've been on one of Shelby's tours. Didn't always have a chance to *see* a lot of stuff."

"Still, that sounds like fun."

"It's a blast. When I'm traveling with the club, we usually rough it. Sleep in tents and stuff." He laughs. "The older brothers started putting a stop to that. Wrath says he's too big to be sleeping on the ground."

"Yeah, that doesn't sound appealing."

"You have somewhere you want to go?" he asks.

"Everywhere." I glance out the window again. "Somewhere."

He clears his throat. "We can do that. Not roughing it on the bike," he hurries to add. "Fly somewhere, I mean."

Why does that simple promise cut through my doubts so easily? "I'd like that."

The roads look more familiar now. Jigsaw must've gone some back way I've never used. After a few more miles, I recognize the big rooster mailbox at the end of Teller's driveway.

"That's Teller's house, right?" I ask.

"Yup. In case you couldn't tell, Rooster got him the mailbox."

That must've been a moment. "It's cute."

Not too much farther down the road, Jigsaw flips his turn signal on. The anxiety growing in my stomach expands like a balloon. He turns onto a road that stretches into the trees, but then he makes another sharp left and approaches an open gate. The truck bounces slightly as it moves from the dirt to the paved driveway.

Straight ahead, a golden Buddha statue seems to greet us with a serene expression that seems odd for a motorcycle club whose emblem is a grinning skull wearing a crown.

"Oh my gosh, that's huge!" I laugh as we pass it, the vehicle following the driveway's gentle curve to the right. The truck lurches as it climbs the steep hill. A huge building that almost looks like a log cabin but is the size of a boutique hotel comes into view.

"My goodness," I breathe out. "*That's* your motorcycle club's clubhouse?"

"Were you picturing a shack in the woods?"

"No, but I wasn't expecting *this* either."

"Legend has it that it used to be a spiritual retreat center or something before Upstate bought it."

"I believe it."

"Don't, um, get too excited. Downstate's clubhouse isn't this nice."

I open my mouth to ask why, what's the difference, but he already mentioned their last president wasn't as dedicated.

"Under our old president, Upstate and Downstate didn't mix that much. I hardly ever came up here, but since Z took over as president, the two clubs mingle a lot more." He lets out a short laugh. "I think we've finally moved past that awkward blended family stage."

"Why not just merge them into one club, then?" Unless two iron-willed MC presidents don't want to consolidate leadership. I better not say that out loud.

"Honestly—I think we're moving in that direction. Especially since Upstate built a new clubhouse down in Empire. Some of the guys have houses and stuff down near Union, though. And we have a few businesses down there too, but yeah, I think eventually, that'll happen."

"The club doesn't tell you where you have to live, though, right?"

"No. As long as we get to church on time and we're available when needed, we can do whatever."

It still sounds restrictive. But I guess it's not my business. Besides, who am I to judge when I'm basically on call twenty-four hours a day, seven days a week?

Motorcycles are lined up tight against a tall, wooden fence—its rough planks shadowed by towering pine trees. The fence itself cuts a clear boundary between the clubhouse parking lot and the looming forest, with wide dirt paths branching off at each end, disappearing into the woods. Across the asphalt, two sprawling garages sit in a loose L-shape. One has its massive bay doors thrown open, bright lights flooding the interior where folding tables have been set up. Tucked around the far side of that garage, a narrow trail sneaks into the thick evergreens. Beyond the brush, the silhouette of a small house or cabin peeks through the foliage.

Jigsaw glances over, then follows my line of sight. "They built Sparky a small cabin over there for him to do his 'special baking' without it stinking up the whole clubhouse."

It takes a second for that to sink in. "Oh! Where he makes the pot brownies. Got it."

"Yeah." He scratches his jaw, gaze lingering on the cabin. "Murphy wasn't too thrilled about the idea of Sparky leaving 'treats' lying around where the kids might find them."

I wince. "Yikes, that would be bad."

"That never happened," Jigsaw says quickly, as if he's worried I'll assume the worst about his brothers. "But—"

"They wanted to be safe. I get it." I nod, still staring in the direction of the cabin. "That was smart."

Just how much money does the club have that they can afford to build an entire house for one member to bake pot brownies?

That seems way too intrusive to ask, but I can't stop thinking about it.

Jigsaw ends up backing the truck into a grassy spot along the driveway.

Anxiety over meeting everyone rushes in and pushes out my curiosity about the clubhouse. I drag my sweaty palms over my jeans, then flip the visor down and check my hair in the mirror. My lipstick's faded and I pull my purse into my lap, searching for my lip gloss.

The passenger door swings open, letting in a rush of cool air. "What's wrong?" Jigsaw asks.

"Nothing." Nervous with him watching, I quickly swipe the mauve-pink gloss over my lips, screw the cap on, and toss it back in my purse. "Sorry."

"Don't be." His gaze drops to my lips. "That color's pretty on you."

I've only ever had women compliment my makeup. Boyfriends I've had either didn't notice or complained. "Thanks."

He takes my hand and helps me down from the truck.

"There ya guys are!" Shelby jogs over the parking lot, her cowgirl boots hitting the pavement with hard *thwack, thwack, thwacks.* Rooster's following behind her at a slower pace.

Jigsaw laughs. "Where'd you even come from, songbird?"

"Sparky's cabin." She stops in front of us and whips her head around, her blonde curls fanning around her. The light scent of sandalwood and blue tansy fills my nose for a second. How about that? I use the same shampoo. Maybe we're meant to be friends.

"I assume he's doing a lot of baking for tonight?" Jigsaw asks.

"Ohhh, yeah." Shelby nods slowly. "Be careful. He's got brownies and these big sugar cookies with green M&Ms in 'em. You see them, steer clear unless you wanna be floatin' in the clouds all night."

My cheeks warm. Did Jigsaw tell her I accidentally got high off brownies at Teller's wedding? Or is she just delivering a general warning?

"Hey, Margot." Shelby leans in and gives me a quick hug. "Good to see ya again." She tilts her head down. "You look great. Told ya." She tugs at the hem of her oversized sweatshirt. A crabby looking pink flamingo takes up a good portion of the front. *Flock around and find out* is written in a spiky, rough-textured font underneath. "Casual on bonfire night."

"That's my kind of flamingo." I nod to the sweatshirt.

A slow grin spreads over her face. "Ain't she cute? Trinity helped me design it. I'll have to get one for you."

"Thanks."

"Hey, Margot. Welcome," Rooster says, moving in behind Shelby and resting his hand at her waist. His gaze shifts to Jigsaw. "Not quite a full house yet. But everyone's inside."

Jigsaw tilts his head toward me. "I'll grab our stuff once I know where we're staying. That okay?"

"Sure."

"I think Trinity was puttin' y'all in the room next to ours," Shelby says.

"Great," Jigsaw groans.

"Hush it!" Shelby blushes and laughs.

Rooster just rolls his eyes.

The four of us cross the parking lot. Shelby keeps up a steady stream of chatter, but my anxiety about stepping inside seems to drown out everything else. I smile and nod, but I'm not quite sure anything she's saying penetrates my fog.

Inside is even more overwhelming. We step into one large, high-ceilinged great room. Close to the door, there's a wide coat closet, its door left open to reveal a cavernous space full of jackets, footwear, and farther back what looks like a gun safe the size of a small vehicle.

My questioning gaze lands on Jigsaw's face, but he doesn't seem to notice my surprise.

"Trinity's got all the room stuff sorted out here," Shelby says, pointing to what looks like it's usually a bar, but tonight is being used like a hotel reservation desk.

Jigsaw looms behind me like my lethal protector as he nudges us closer to the bar. His hand rests at my waist, keeping me close to his body. Is he worried I'm not safe in his club's house? Or does he realize how nervous I am?

The blonde behind the bar lifts her head and flashes a welcoming smile. "Hey, Jiggy!" Her pretty, light-brown eyes slide to me. "Welcome, Margot."

"Are we checking in now?" Jigsaw asks.

She lifts one shoulder. "Since a lot of people were coming up, Wrath and I thought it would be easier to keep track of where everyone's staying and hand out rooms early instead of waiting until the last minute." Her lips quirk with amusement. "When everyone's high and horny."

That's quite a mental image Trinity just painted. And now it's seared into my brain—the whole place teeming with bikers drunk, high, and desperate to get their hands on someone.

"If I'd known that, we would've come up sooner, "Jigsaw says, casting a stink-eye at Rooster.

Trinity laughs and shakes her head. "Come on now. I got you." She picks up a tablet and taps her fingers over the screen. "I put you in the room next to Rooster." She points her finger toward the ceiling at an awkward angle. "Two doors down from the end on the left."

"Thanks," Jigsaw says.

"Oh! And we installed new locks on all the doors." She grabs a green sticky pad, glances at the tablet screen, then jots down a four-digit number. "That's your code for the weekend. If you have any issues, just let me know."

Jigsaw glances at the number, then hands the piece of green paper to me.

1051

Easy enough, but I'm still so nervous I'm not sure it'll stick. I shove the paper in my back pocket.

While we're still crowded around the counter, a woman in a green sweater and dark jeans walks toward us. "Hi!" She throws her hand up in a quick wave.

Trinity glances up and grins. "Hey, mama bear. Where'd you come from?"

"That's Hope," Jigsaw whispers in my ear.

I nod quickly, remembering her from the wedding. Did I say anything embarrassing to her that night?

Hope stops in front of Shelby. "You made it!" she gushes. "I'm so happy to see you."

"I missed ya!" Shelby throws herself at the woman and they embrace like long-lost twins who'd been separated at birth. I'm so focused on them, it takes a second to notice the man close behind Hope. *Rock.* The president. The man, according to Jigsaw, who probably decides how the brothers get punished for their bad behavior.

"Relax," Jigsaw whispers in my ear. He reaches down and pries my hand off the hem of my shirt and curls his fingers around mine.

How does he know?

Hope turns toward us and flashes a smile so warm and welcoming, I'm finally able to take a breath.

Stay present. Don't retreat into yourself. I organize entire funerals. Why is this stressing me out so much?

"Hi, Margot. I'm so happy you could join us." Her arms hang awkwardly at her sides as if she wants to embrace me the way she did Shelby, but hasn't decided if I'm a hugger, yet.

"Yes, thank you. I've been looking forward to it all week." I work my mouth into a smile and pray it doesn't look as uncomfortable as it feels.

Forget my palms. With all this attention focused on me, I think my butt is sweating now.

Jigsaw

Margot presses tight to my hip, like she's trying to crawl inside me and hide. She deals with people all the time—counsels families, talks to vendors on the phone, consults with religious leaders and who knows what else. At the car show, she talked to lots of people. *Why so shy here?*

"What's wrong?" I whisper in her ear once Hope has moved on to talking to Trinity.

Her lips tremble into a smile. "I want your friends to like me and not think I'm weird."

The way she automatically turns to me for safety satisfies some caveman need I didn't even know I had. Who am I kidding? The urge to protect her showed up the day we met and never left. I fight off the urge to kiss her.

Tonight isn't a business transaction or a passing hobby. Meeting my family is important to her. Making a good impression matters. *That's* the difference.

I wrap both arms around her, turning her to face me, and pull her close. "If you're weird," I say in a low tone, "it's the good kind and everyone accepts that here."

She lets out a nervous laugh.

"Margot." I dip lower, pressing my forehead against hers. "My brothers and I all ride two-wheeled death machines and wear matching outfits. That's a little weird, right?"

She giggles harder. "I guess."

Much better.

"Are you planning to swallow her whole?" Rooster slaps my arm. "Let the woman breathe."

I shoot a glare at him, and he backs off. His gaze darts between Margot and me, his brow furrowing slightly. The big dope must figure out that Margot's nervous. "I hope you're prepared for Murphy's chili. My eyes were actually watering when we went in the kitchen."

"I like spicy food," Margot says.

"You're in luck, then." Shelby crosses her arms in front of her like a shield. "I gotta stay far, far away from it."

"Jigsaw said you're allergic to tomatoes." Margot's tone is so solemn, I'm worried she's having a flashback to a client who died of a tomato allergy or something.

Shelby must be having a similar thought. She tilts her head and squeezes Margot's shoulder. "Sure am. Best thing about not being dead broke now is carrying a couple epi-pens with me wherever I go."

Margot sighs. "That's good."

"I was gonna tell Murphy that real, traditional chili doesn't even have tomatoes in it—it's called chili for a reason—but I didn't wanna be *that* person." Shelby titters with laughter. "And I don't even like it that way. Unless it's over a Frito pie, it's basically a big ol' bowl of braised meat on its own."

"I thought the big disagreement was whether beans belong in chili or not?" Jigsaw says.

"True, in Texas it doesn't have beans," Shelby explains. "But not everyone has the luxury of being able to hunt or *afford* all that meat, especially if you got a big family to feed. Beans stretch it out, ya know?" She waves her hand in the air dismissively. "I never liked the beans or not argument. Seems classist to me."

"I never knew you had all these opinions on meat and beans," I tease.

Shelby clutches her stomach. "I know, right? I think I'm hungry."

"Hey." I nudge Margot. "I'm going to grab our stuff so we can put it upstairs, okay?"

"I'll go with you," she says, pivoting toward the door.

And here I thought she'd been easing into things.

"We'll be right back," I say to Rooster.

Outside, I curl my hand around Margot's and lead her to the truck. The driver's side is facing the woods, giving us a little privacy.

"You all right?"

She leans back against the side panel. "Yeah, just overwhelmed. I like everyone," she hurries to add.

It'll be a lot more overwhelming once the whole club and all their guests arrive. "Everyone already likes you, Margot." I brush her hair out of her eyes. "When I told the club about us, they were more concerned about *me* corrupting *you* than anything else."

That seems to help. A soft smile curves her lips. "Did you tell them that you have thoroughly and irrevocably corrupted me?" She pushes away from the truck and loops her arms around my neck. "Did you tell your brothers what an excellent *teacher* you are?"

"No." I dip down and catch her lips in a quick kiss. "Do you want me to?"

"No! I was kidding." She stares up at me with wide eyes. "You really didn't...you know, share locker room talk?"

"We don't have a locker room." I glance toward the clubhouse. "Okay, yeah, technically there is a locker room. But no. I told you before, none of the wifed-up brothers share stories about their ol' ladies. It just doesn't happen. Lost Kings guard that information with their lives." I squint toward the forest. "Honestly, the only time we get a hint of that is when Heidi brings her sex toy catalog in, and everyone wants to place an order."

Margot releases me and takes a step back, like I've completely scandalized her. "You're kidding?"

"Nope. Right at the breakfast table." I slap my hands together. "She'll smack that catalog down and take orders." I squeeze my eyes shut and laugh. "She didn't think it through though, because when Charlotte orders—"

"Oh, ew. Yeah, I'd die if my brother's wife ordered sex toys in front of me."

"Exactly. Out of all of us, Sparky's the only altruistic one. He likes to order these little vibrating cock rings for the whole house."

"Little, huh?" She lets out a small, nervous burst of laughter. "Well, those won't do *you* any good."

"I've never tried one on but thanks for the compliment." I reach for the door. "I promise everything will be fine."

She lifts her chin and nods quickly. "I trust you."

That means more than anything to me.

Margot

Back inside the clubhouse, Shelby's waiting for us. "Everyone went down to the dining room for dinner."

Jigsaw glances at me. "I'm going to run this stuff upstairs." He lifts his chin.

"Come on." Shelby grabs my arm, leading me toward the long wide hallway that seems to end in a set of swinging double doors. "We'll stop in the ladies', give Jiggy a chance to catch up with us."

"I'll be right back." He pops a kiss on my cheek and hurries toward the stairs.

Shelby watches him for a second, then squeals. "What'd I say? Smitten."

The same warmth I'd felt when she said that over the phone returns, spreading across my cheeks.

"Come on, I'll give you the tour as we go." She slaps her hand against a door as we pass it. "Men's room—avoid at all costs."

"Noted." I laugh.

At the next door, she pushes it open to reveal a large, multi-stall restroom. Small, square and a few taller, rectangular lockers line the wall to our left. They're big enough to store a purse, coat or other small personal items. Some are secured with a padlock; others are open or open with items inside.

"You can store your purse in one of these." Shelby points to the lockers. "You just gotta carry the key around all night." She tugs one key out of the lock of an empty locker and dangles it by the stretchy band it's attached to.

"I just leave mine up in our room." She pats the front pocket of her hoodie. "Keep the important stuff in here."

I clutch the narrow strap of my small black purse. "I'll keep it with me for now."

We each do our thing and meet at the sinks. I blink at my reflection—paler than usual, eyes a little too wide, hair flat. I smooth my hands over my cheeks, as if I can swipe some color onto my skin. It doesn't help. I still don't like what I see. I pull my gloss out and lean closer to the mirror to dab it on.

I screw the gloss shut and drop it into my purse.

Shelby meets my gaze in the mirror and gives me a reassuring smile. "Come on, we wanna get there before the guys eat all the food on us."

I nod, but my feet feel heavier as I turn toward the door.

As we step into the hallway, the sound of low voices and laughter, punctuated by shrill screams from babies or arguing children, fills the hallway in waves. A chorus of familiarity from people who consider themselves family.

"That's the yoga room." Shelby points to a closed door as we pass it. "We'll probably have class tomorrow morning while the guys are in church. You should join us."

"Oh. I'd like that. I don't think I brought anything to wear for yoga, though."

She shrugs. "Someone's always got extra clothes around here. We'll find you something if you want."

Another hallway stretches to our right. Shelby points. "Gym, laundry room, and I'm not sure what else is down there."

She pushes the double doors open, and I'm immediately overwhelmed with the size of the dining room. It's more suited to a college dining hall than a retreat. One very long table—or more likely several tables arranged together—splits the space in half. A shorter round table set up near one end has tiny, colorful chairs around it and toys scattered over the top.

A long buffet has been set up against the wall, underneath large windows where weak late afternoon light beams. Against the back wall, an actual bar is set up with more bottles than most actual bars probably carry. In front of it, there's a table set up with coffee and tea.

Shelby nudges me. "I need to check on something in the kitchen real quick—we usually sit on this end. Jiggy should be down here soon."

"Oh, sure. Go ahead, I'm fine," I say, still staring at the scene in front of me.

Brothers in black leather vests just like Jigsaw's prowl around the table, some greeting each other with laughter and complicated handshakes or back slaps. Other brothers pull out chairs for their wives or girlfriends—some doing it one-handed because they're carrying a kid in the other arm.

It's an unexpectedly domestic scene.

And I stand right inside the doorway with my back to the wall, hands clasped in front of me. The same stance I usually take when I'm working at a service. Still as a statue. Observing everything.

"What're you doing?" Jigsaw's warm voice pulls me out of observation mode.

"I…" How can I explain that I'm more comfortable lurking outside of events than being a seated guest at the table? The night he took me to the racetrack was different. Outdoors and less formal.

"Come on." He slides his arm over my shoulders and steers me toward the table.

Shelby's returning from the kitchen, and she lifts her arm high, throwing a big wave. "Jiggy there you are!" She hurries over, her cowgirl boots thudding against the terrazzo floor. "Come on."

I'm introduced to several people along the way. It's almost a relief to sit in my chair and fade into the background.

One of the biggest men I've ever seen cups his hand over his mouth and shouts, "Form an orderly line. Serve yourselves!"

"Wrath's gotta direct traffic now?" Jigsaw says to Rooster.

Rooster's lips tilt with amusement.

A burly man with a tidy beard and red hair leans forward. "He just loves bossing people around, everywhere."

"Margot," Jigsaw says. "You remember Murphy? He's our VP upstate and he made the chili tonight."

"Hi, Murphy."

A tall woman with long, dark brown hair, carrying a wiggling baby, sits next to Murphy. "She's feeling sassy tonight," she says, kissing the top of her daughter's head.

Murphy holds out his arms, taking his daughter and tilts his head toward the woman. "Margot, this is my wife, Heidi." He settles the baby in his lap. "And this is Brittany."

"Oh! I remember Brittany from the wedding. My goodness, she's gotten so big."

"Tell me about it," Heidi laughs. "Hi, Margot. It's so great you were able to come up tonight." She waves her hand around the table. "Sorry things are a little more chaotic than usual."

Murphy squints at her. "Are they though? Seems about normal to me."

Dinner is a long, leisurely, but lively affair. The chili leaves a pleasant zip on my tongue, smoky and rich, with just the right amount of heat. Thick, creamy mac and cheese balances it out, each bite decadent and buttery. Golden cornbread crumbles easily between my fingers, slightly sweet, the perfect companion to soak up the spice.

The room hums with energy, conversations overlapping, laughter spilling freely. A few of the guys tease Murphy about using too many chilis.

I shake my head vigorously. "This is excellent, Murphy." I dab a napkin over my lips. "The heat sneaks up on you but in a good way."

"Thank you." He nods.

"Stash is just mad because he thinks a sprinkle of black pepper is too spicy," Dex says loud enough to be heard all the way down the table.

Laughter drowns out Stash's response. Dex's girlfriend pokes his side and smiles at him.

Jigsaw warned me the guys love to pick on each other, and he wasn't wrong. Their banter is relentless, the insults sharp—but underneath it all, there's an unmistakable bond. Even their rudest jokes land with the warmth of familiarity, not cruelty.

A shiver of envy works over me. I lost my mother young. Never had playful siblings who knew me well enough to develop cute inside jokes. But these bikers—the same men who delivered several bodies to my crematorium under the cover of night—laugh easily, share stories freely, and pull their wives and girlfriends into the fold like they belong. The affection they all have for one another is palpable.

Under the table, Jigsaw slides his hand over my leg, gently squeezing my thigh. "You all right?"

"I am, yes." I clutch my stomach. "I'm trying not to stuff myself so I can save room for s'mores and cookies later."

After finishing his dinner, one of Jigsaw's brothers grabs a cup of coffee and returns to the table. Instead of sitting, he stands behind his chair and surveys the room.

Shelby elbows my side and discreetly points her finger. "That's Ravage. Ten dollars says he's conjuring up something obnoxious in that head of his." She says it with more affection than annoyance, as if it's regularly scheduled programming.

"So. Now that we're all seated around the table." Ravage claps his hands, drawing everyone's attention to him. "And filled our bellies—thanks to the hard work of Trinity, Heidi, Murphy, and Shelby."

Trinity lifts her head. "And Swan, Stitch, and Layla for helping us out in the kitchen."

Murphy lifts his hand. "And Teller for donating the deer meat."

"Yeah, yeah." Rav rolls his eyes. "Everyone's awesome. Blah, blah, blah."

"Aw, he tried to be polite," Shelby laughs. "Lasted about fifteen seconds. Good for Rav."

Rooster chuckles and wraps an arm around her shoulders.

"Now, for the most important question on everyone's mind." Rav rubs his hands together, a playfully devilish gleam lighting up his eyes.

"Here it comes," Jigsaw mutters.

"Tell us about our brother, Margot," Rav says. "Is Jigsaw treating you right or do we need to kick his ass?"

I cough and choke, my mouth full of chili, and quickly reach for my glass of lemonade.

At the head of the table, Rock and his wife are busy helping their daughter, but Rock stops and frowns in Ravage's direction.

"Can we eat in peace, instead of doing…whatever you're doing?" Teller scolds.

Ravage flicks his hand in the air like he's batting away the suggestion of inappropriateness. "I'm not talking about in the bedroom, we'll get to that later." He steeples his hands under his chin like he's having difficulty maintaining his composure. "Is Jigsaw a good boyfriend? Does he know how to open doors? Bring you flowers? That's all we want to know."

A few of the guys snicker or cough.

"Who is this *we* you're referring to?" Teller asks.

"No way Jiggy's doing any of that," someone mutters.

Charlotte leans forward and turns toward me. "*This* is Ravage being respectful," she whispers, loud enough for everyone to hear. "In case you're curious."

Still feeling like a bug under a microscope—even though half of the people at the table are paying more attention to their dinner than me—I smile to acknowledge Charlotte.

"It's probably the most respectful he's ever been." Wrath crosses his arms over his chest and squints at Ravage. "You all right, bro?"

"I'm excellent." Rav's gaze remains trained on me. "Margot, please enlighten us?"

"Knock it off," Jigsaw growls.

Rooster makes a squeezed and twisted fist gesture that seems mildly threatening, then points at Rav.

"No, it's okay. I don't mind answering this one." I sit up straighter and rest my hands in my lap. Jigsaw said sticking up for myself would work best here. I just hope I don't accidentally insult anyone in the process. "To answer your first question, I don't like flowers, so that wouldn't be an item on my 'good boyfriend traits' list. As to your second question, I learned how to open doors when I was four or five. I can show you how if you need help."

The brothers howl with laughter, some even slapping their hands against the table.

Jigsaw grins and kisses my cheek.

Rav nods as if he's pleased.

Another brother, Stash, I think, leans forward, resting his elbows on the table. "I thought all chicks like flowers?"

"Well, I can't speak for all *chicks*." I roll my eyes again. This time, the women at the table laugh. "But I have to order a lot of flowers at work. Then I have to deal with moving them and transporting them to another location." A sneeze tickles the back of my nose just thinking about it. "They're delicate and expensive, so I always have to be careful with them. They're also messy and leave residue everywhere." I sigh. "Although, I've become an expert at removing pollen stains."

My gaze skitters over the beautiful, full-color sleeve of roses Z's wife has covering one arm. "I prefer paintings or pictures of flowers. Bonus—they last longer too."

"She's right," Heidi says. "They die so fast. It feels like a waste of money."

I blow out a breath, relieved no one seems insulted by anything I said.

"Hush, little hammer," Ravage says to Heidi. "We all know Murphy isn't romantic enough to buy you flowers."

"No, he buys me cars and jewelry," Heidi says, leaning in to pop a kiss on her husband's cheek. "And deadly weapons."

"We can all agree that's *much* more romantic." Lilly raises her water glass.

"Damn," one of the guys says. "If I ever bring another ol' lady around, you keep all that to yourselves. I don't need you to set high expectations for my future woman."

"I don't think that's going to be an issue for you, Butcher," Z says. "Moving on."

More laughter rolls around the table.

The conversation shifts to other topics. Jigsaw leans closer to me. "See, you're doing fine. And now I know you don't like flowers."

I pat the knife in my pocket. "I think you already suspected since you picked out a perfect gift for me."

Jigsaw was right. Ravage's teasing had been aimed at him more than me. But as I reach for another piece of cornbread from Shelby, I catch Ravage watching us, mischief still glinting in his eyes.

He's not done with me yet.

CHAPTER FIFTEEN

Margot

After dinner, a group of guys head out into the woods to start the bonfire. Others stick around to help clean up the dining room. Trinity and a few other women pack up food and drinks to go. Parents gather up their kids and all the supplies that go with them.

I curl my hand around Jigsaw's arm. "Do you mind if we run upstairs for a minute? I want to drop off my purse and maybe grab a sweatshirt."

"Yeah. Let's go." He stops to say a few words to Rooster and then we leave the dining room.

"Shelby gave me a short tour." I draw a line with my hand. "Well, of this hallway."

"You all right?" he asks. "Dinner was okay?"

"It was *so* good." I rub my stomach.

"No, I mean everything else."

"Oh, yeah." I lower my voice as we climb the stairs. "I just didn't want to…you know, insult anyone accidentally."

"Rav had it coming." He turns right at the top of the stairs with the familiarity of someone who's spent a lot of time here.

"Do you stay here a lot?" I ask.

He stops in front of one of the doors. "Not a *lot*. More often, lately.

I don't always get a room near the presidential suite, though." He tilts his head toward the door at the end of the hall and winks at me.

"Is that my doing?" That seems to be what he's implying.

"Maybe. The rooms at this end always belonged to officers or were saved for important out-of-town guests. The ones at the other end share a communal bathroom."

"Ohhh."

"But now that most of the officers have their own houses on the property, they usually assign these to downstate officers or couples."

"That's sweet." On second thought, though, "A lot of organizing and planning has to go into assigning all those rooms every time there's a party up here."

"Trinity and Hope take care of most of it, I think." He shrugs as if he's never given it much thought. "At our place, Lilly oversees room assignments now."

"Do all of the wives have a role in the club that sort of matches their husband's?"

He frowns and tilts his head. Oh, boy. If being with the road captain means I'm supposed to handle anything trip-related, the club's in for a rude awakening. I've always taken my car to a mechanic. I don't ride and I'm scared to even *sit* on a motorcycle. Considering he's the one who maintains the vehicles, plans, and leads the club's trips, I'd be absolutely useless.

"Interesting question," Jigsaw finally answers. "From what I understand, Trinity already ran the house before she and Wrath got married. But with him being the enforcer, it makes sense she does that stuff. And I think she just really likes planning and organizing things."

"That's what I'm good at."

He gives me a soft smile. "I'm happy you're thinking about stuff like that but tonight is just about you having fun and getting to know everyone."

Why do I always have to overthink things?

He punches the code Trinity gave him earlier into the silver keypad. A green light flashes. Jigsaw turns the knob and opens the door.

"Wow, I've seen hotels that aren't as nice as this." A large king-sized bed takes up one whole corner of the room. Our bags are on a chair in another corner. But it's a silver basket on the nightstand next to the bed that grabs my attention.

"What's that?" I ask.

Jigsaw glances at it and frowns. "Not sure. I didn't get a chance to look when I came up earlier."

I move closer to the nightstand. It's not actually a basket, more like a miniature steel tub. A sheet of white paper sticks up in the center. I pluck it out.

Welcome. I glance at Jigsaw. "I guess it's a gift basket?"

His eyes narrow with suspicion. "I'm afraid to ask what's in it."

I peer closer, picking up a hot-pink silicone bottle with a white cap. A plastic safety seal indicates it's new. *Gentle Warming Lubricant.*

Warmth spreads over my face. *Look at that—it's already doing its job!*

"Um, these are some interesting amenities." I run my fingers over the other items, heat building in my cheeks with each one I discover—buzzing cock ring, a package of condoms, an orange candle in a glass jar with a label that reads *Orgasmic Manifestation,* a twelve-sided die with a different sexual position engraved on each side.

"Uh, yup. Definitely new." Jigsaw steps up next to me and stares at the basket. "Or at least I've never had one of those left for me when I've stayed over before."

Chocolate hearts and a few more practical items like shampoo, soap, lotion, and lip balm round out the rest of the gifts. And finally, a small, white, rolled-up towel that was keeping everything tightly packed into the basket. I open it and blink at what's embroidered at the bottom in black.

Cum Rag.

"Well, that stole all the romance right out of this." I toss the cloth on the nightstand.

Jigsaw chuckles. "Now I feel like Stash helped put these together. I can't picture Trinity ordering these or handing them out." His lips quirk into a sexy smile. "Although, let's be honest, it might come in handy." He picks up the washcloth and drags it over my chest.

If I thought I was hot before, I'm on fire now.

I turn and crisscross my arms behind his neck, dragging him closer while standing on my tiptoes. He drops the cloth and wraps his arms around me.

"I warned you we could be crude at times," he says.

Before I can answer, he feathers a soft kiss against my lips.

I sigh and drag my fingers through his hair. He lets out a humming noise of approval. Our mouths meet again, soft and exploratory at first, as if he understands I'm still uncertain in this new environment. After a few gentle, reassuring brushes of his mouth against mine, our kisses intensify. He slides his hands to my behind, pressing me against him.

Breaking our kiss, he touches his forehead to mine.

"I'm happy you're here with me," he rasps.

"I'm happy too." Uncertainty still tugs at me. "I did okay at dinner, right? I wasn't too…much?"

He kisses my forehead and releases me. "You were perfect."

"Okay."

"I mean it."

Outside, people shout and whoop. Jigsaw moves toward the window and parts the curtains. "Looks like they have the fire going."

"Do you mind if I unpack my bag?" My hands nervously twist together. "I think I'll feel more…settled if I know where my stuff is." I wince at how weird that sounds. Easy breezy isn't my style.

"Yeah. Go ahead." He drops onto the edge of the bed and leans back on his hands, his gaze completely focused on me. "I'll enjoy the view."

"I know it's only a day and a half but…"

"Margot, it's fine. Do whatever makes you comfortable."

We've only ever spent time together in my space, where I know where everything is. He has no idea how particular I can be. But I guess if it's a deal-breaker for him, he should find out now.

I slide one closet door open, and stare at the few neatly hung flannel shirts. "You're sure this isn't someone's room?"

He crosses the room and peers over my shoulder. "I think Trinity just likes to make sure there are some extra clothes around in case anyone needs something." He quickly flips through the shirts, which range in sizes from XL to 3XLT.

"That's really thoughtful." I push the shirts aside and grab a hanger. I didn't bring much, so it doesn't take long to hang my jeans, tops, and the one dress I brought. I move to the dresser and open the first drawer—again finding a few items of clothing already stored inside. Unopened packages of plain, utilitarian cotton underwear for women and boxers for men, socks, and a few basic black T-shirts and tank tops.

"Shelby said if I needed clothes to attend yoga class with them tomorrow, they could probably find something for me. I guess she wasn't kidding." I close the top drawer and open the second. This one is empty. I drop my undergarments and socks inside.

"You should. The girls usually do yoga while we're in church."

"I might." I dig deep into my backpack again, my hand brushing against the velvet pouch, and finally find my pajamas. I fold them neatly and leave them on one of the pillows on the bed.

Jigsaw turns his head, watching me. His mouth curves in amusement. "I feel like a slob now. I was going to pull things out of my bag as needed."

I flinch and open my mouth to apologize but he tugs on my hand, pulling me closer. "I'm not criticizing. I think it's cute." He shakes his head. "I mean, I want you to be comfortable here. Do whatever will make you feel at home."

"Thanks. One last thing." I return to my bag and pull out a case with my toothbrush and other toiletries. "If I'd known there would be amenities, I wouldn't have bothered to pack this," I tease, holding up the case.

I cross the room, nudge the bathroom door open, and flip the light on. The white tile gleams. Clean towels are folded over a bar by the shower and a smaller holder by the sink. A skinny white cabinet with glass doors holds more towels and what looks like toiletries, tissues, toilet paper, and anything else a guest might need.

I set my case on the edge of the sink, turn off the light and return to Jigsaw. "It's well-stocked in there too."

"I feel like you're going to be *really* disappointed when we visit Downstate." He laughs and runs his fingers through his hair. "I keep the bare minimum of everything in my room."

"Well, if you're the only one using it, that makes sense." I shrug. "You already know what you need."

The pounding of boots over hardwood floors and voices from the hallway intrude into our room.

"It's not always quiet here." Jigsaw glances at the door.

As if to prove his words, someone bangs on our door. "Let's go, Jiggy!" someone shouts. "Fornicate later. Bonfire now!"

Laughing echoes in the hallway, then the sounds of footsteps running away.

Jigsaw rolls his eyes. "That had to be Stash. Surprised he even knows how to find his way upstairs."

"Why?"

"He usually lives in the basement." He holds up his hands. "Don't ask me why. He and Sparky have had their living quarters down there for as long as I've been in New York."

"Well, if he came all the way up here, then they must *really* want you at the bonfire." I return to the closet and drape my flannel over a hanger, my heart hammering a bit faster now that I know people are waiting for us outside. I know exactly what I want to wear. My hand brushes against my thick, black hooded sweatshirt and I tug it free. In the center, a cartoon of two burning matches lean into each other over a matchbox, with "we're a perfect match" scrawled in whimsical font above the image.

I smile at the cheesy, romantic pun, hoping Jigsaw won't find it too silly and slip it over my head.

I turn to face him, and his gaze immediately drops to my chest. A slow grin spreads over his face as he reads the front. He stands and closes the distance between us. "That is so fucking perfect. Did you plan that for tonight?"

I tug on the bottom of the shirt, pulling it away from my body to eye the image again. "Of course." My nose wrinkles as I lift my gaze to his face again. "Too cheesy to wear to a *bonfire*? Am I going to embarrass you?"

A flicker of something—disappointment, maybe—crosses his face. "No. Fuck no. It's adorable." He wraps me up in his arms and lifts me to kissing level. "It's perfect. You know how much I like your occasion-specific puns."

My lips wobble with the laughter I'm holding back. *Not all my puns.* He didn't enjoy my *fuckboi repellent* pin all that much.

He catches the look on my face and shakes with laughter. "Yes, even your little fuckboy pin was adorable. I didn't *love* that it was directed at me, but it still made me laugh."

I press my palms against his cheeks, holding him still so I can press my lips to his. "I love…I love that you get me."

His throat bobs with a hard swallow, and instead of answering, he sets me gently back on my feet.

That was close. All the feelings in my chest almost came shooting out of my mouth.

"We should get down there before all the s'mores are gone," he says, his voice rougher than before.

"I don't want to miss those," I agree.

He curls his hand around mine, and I follow him to the door. He opens it part way, then stops. The weight of his stare lands on me. Like maybe he knew exactly what I almost said, and he wasn't ready to hear it.

Or worse, it's not something he wants to say back.

CHAPTER SIXTEEN

Margot

The air outside is cooler now, carrying the scent of pine and burning wood. Light still lingers in the sky, but the parking lot is shadowed by the surrounding trees.

We pass several of Jigsaw's brothers. Men who hadn't been at the dinner but are just showing up now, backing their bikes into the long line of bikes against the fence. Many have women with them, dressed just a little differently than the ol' ladies who'd been at the dinner table earlier. It's not just the clothes—or lack of. It's their entire attitude. Touchy and clingy with the guys. Laughing too loud. Attention seeking.

Jigsaw glares at the scene, but I can't tell if it's any one person in particular he's annoyed about.

These must be the muffler bunnies he promised me wouldn't be here tonight.

He doesn't say anything, but his hand tightens around mine, his grip firm and reassuring. I squeeze back, silently letting him know I'm fine.

Ahead of us, a couple is about to dip into one of the forest paths.

"Grinder!" Jigsaw calls out.

The older gentleman's pushing a large, all-terrain-looking stroller and easily bring it to a stop before turning around. His hard expression softens when his gaze lands on Jigsaw. The younger blonde woman leans over the stroller to check on whoever's in it.

Jigsaw picks up the pace, pulling me along. "I want you to meet Serena," he says to me in a low voice.

"Hey, Jigsaw." Grinder gives him a quick hug and a fatherly pat on the back.

Jigsaw returns the hug, then steps back and nods at Serena. "How're you doing, sweetheart?"

She sighs but forces a smile. "Tired."

"You're not going to the bonfire?" Jigsaw asks.

"I don't think Lincoln's up for it," Serena says, reaching into the stroller to adjust the blanket covering her son. "We're staying at Z's place. We said we'd watch the twins so Teller and Charlotte could go to the bonfire for a while."

"*You* offered." Grinder smiles at her affectionately. "*I* didn't volunteer to watch two more babies."

She grins at him and nods toward Lincoln. "Well, it's good practice if you want more any time soon."

"Whoa." Jigsaw holds out his hands. "That's more information than I needed." He slides his arm around my shoulders. "I just wanted Margot to meet you. I thought we'd get to hang at the bonfire, but if you're not going…"

Serena smiles warmly and reaches to embrace me. "Shelby told me what a sweetheart you are," she says against my ear. "I'm sorry I didn't get to talk to you at dinner." She pulls back, still smiling, but there's a teasing lilt to her voice now. "I caught the tail end of your banter with Ravage, though, and thoroughly enjoyed you going toe to toe with him."

Grinder ducks his head and rumbles with laughter. "He keeps instigating these battles of wits when he's unarmed."

Serena shakes her head slightly. "It's his way of welcoming you, Margot."

Jigsaw snorts. "Welcome, or haze?"

"Well, both, probably."

Serena's so pretty it's hard not to stare at her as the three of them chat. Then recognition hits me. *This is* the *Serena.* The woman behind Tranquil Sparkle—my favorite YouTube channel. I open my mouth to tell her how much I love her content, then snap it shut. *Nope.* That would be too weird. Borderline stalkerish. Not the time or place.

"We're probably heading home early tomorrow," Grinder says. "But I hope you'll come to visit Downstate soon, Margot."

"I'd love that. Thank you."

We say goodnight to them, then continue to Jigsaw's vehicle.

"Are you sure I can't convince you to leave the cookies for me?" he asks, shooting me a hopeful look.

"I'm sure." I grab the container from the back seat, holding it close to my chest.

He heaves a dramatic sigh. "Okay."

Laughing, I tuck the container under one arm. "Do you need me to carry anything else?"

"No." He closes the back door and opens the tailgate. A few seconds later, he emerges with a thick blue blanket. "I didn't think about chairs, but I did bring a clean blanket. We can check the garage if you want a chair, though."

I step closer and slip my arm around his waist. "Cuddling on a blanket with you sounds perfect."

"Let's go cuddle, my little lady death." He captures my hand, intertwining our fingers as we make our way toward the path at the far end of the fence.

Small dots of light line the trail, flickering softly in the night. Even some of the trees are wrapped in dozens of tiny white lights, turning the wooded path into something almost ethereal.

"Oh, this is so pretty," I murmur, glancing up at the glowing canopy overhead. "Like a magical forest."

Jigsaw chuckles. "I think Murphy started this for Heidi and Alexa." He waves a hand toward the lights. "But everyone liked it, so they keep adding more."

"Pretty *and* useful."

The path forks with a narrower trail veering off to the left.

Colorful balls of light hang from the trees on the new path but the same lights on the bottom mark the trail. Faint voices and music drift toward us.

Jigsaw steers us onto the new path. "That way continues to Rock and Hope's house, and all the other guys' houses."

"They wanted to divert traffic away from their homes?"

He huffs a laugh. "Yeah, probably."

We push through a denser group of trees, and suddenly, the space brightens. The low hum of voices grows into lively chatter, laughter, and the occasional pop from the fire.

Clearing a small hill, the bonfire comes into view—tall orange flames licking toward the sky, encircled by a wide ring of cinderblocks. Shadows flicker over the faces of those gathered in a loose circle around the fire.

Couples are sprawled out on blankets spread over the ground. Others settle into camping chairs, coolers nearby. A few tents are nestled between the trees, one strung with glowing lights similar to the ones marking the path.

Jigsaw follows my line of sight.

"For the kiddos," he explains. "They usually conk out early."

"It's nice that they're included." Leaves rustle under our feet and we snap a few twigs as we approach the circle.

Rooster leans lazily against a tree, while Shelby sits cross-legged on a blanket next to a bag and a cooler. She turns at our approach and lifts her hand. "Over here!"

Jigsaw's steps quicken, and I match his pace.

Rooster pushes off the tree, motioning toward the open space beside them. "Saved you a tree."

"Thanks." Jigsaw claps Rooster on the shoulder before spreading out our blanket next to Shelby's.

Shelby's gaze drops to the container in my hands, her eyes lighting up with curiosity. "Whatcha got there, Margot?"

I grin. "Cookies."

She flips the lid of the cooler open. "We've got water, seltzer, beer, grapefruit juice, lime juice, and," she pulls out a large plastic jug,

"Emily and I made this." She holds the jug high in the air like a trophy.

"I'm afraid to ask," Jigsaw says.

"It's sweet tea and limoncello," Emily calls out from a few blankets over.

"Sure is." Shelby grins, shaking the jug enticingly. "You wanna try it?"

I don't usually drink, but we're staying here tonight. *One cup shouldn't be enough to pickle my liver, right?*

"Sure."

"Yay!" Shelby finesses a clear Solo cup from her bag, fills it halfway, and hands it to me.

"We've got ice over here, Margot!" Murphy calls out from across the fire.

I take a cautious sip. The sweetness hits first, then the tang of lemon, followed by a slow warmth sliding down my throat. "It's… um, good."

Jigsaw takes the cup from my hand. "I'll grab some ice for you."

"Thanks."

After we settle onto our blanket, I hand Jigsaw a handful of cookies, then I pass the container to Shelby and Rooster. Shelby stares at them like she's trying to decode their contents.

"They're chocolate with white chocolate chips," I explain. "No nuts. Butter, sugar, egg, vanilla, cocoa…" I try to list any ingredient that could be an allergen.

"They look *so* good." Shelby carefully selects one, then passes the container to Rooster.

"I begged her to leave them in the truck for me," Jigsaw teases. "But she *had* to share them."

As soon as he says it, a container of Rice Crispy treats gets handed to Jigsaw from someone behind him. He lifts it in the air between us. "See, I told you there'd be plenty of treats."

"These are so good, Margot," one of the guys who'd been at dinner shouts from across the fire. "Thank you for not listening to Jigsaw!"

Laughter ripples through the group, followed by a chorus of

similar thanks. It sounds more like they're messing with Jigsaw than actual gratitude, but I lean into his side anyway, grinning.

"See?" I murmur, voice teasing. "Isn't it nice to share?"

Jigsaw's arm tightens around me, his lips brushing my forehead. "No," he whispers, his tone all playful defiance.

I laugh softly, letting the warmth of the fire, the steady weight of Jigsaw beside me, and the easy camaraderie of the group sink into me, grounding me in the moment.

Trinity moves around the circle, handing out sticks and bags of marshmallows. Z's son follows close behind, his little hands gripping a stack of graham cracker sleeves like he's on an important mission. Right next to him, Heidi's older daughter clutches packages of chocolate bars with the same level of seriousness.

"Whatcha got for me, Chance?" Jigsaw asks when the little boy stops in front of us.

Chance holds up a sleeve of crackers. "Uncle Jiggy, you only get *one*," he insists, his little voice firm with authority.

Jigsaw raises an eyebrow. "One? But I'm a big boy."

"One." Chance nods, expression grave. "That's the rules."

Jigsaw exhales dramatically, like the restriction is just too much to bear. "Fine. But only because you said so, little man." He takes the crackers and tucks them into my lap. "Guard these with your life, little lady. Apparently, we only get one."

"We'll share," I promise Chance, earning a single approving nod before he marches on to Shelby and Rooster, his job far from done.

The little girl stops in front of us next, eying Jigsaw with suspicion. She glances over her shoulder, then back at Jigsaw. "I'll give you two chocolate bars, Uncle Jiggy. Don't tell, though," she whispers loud enough for everyone around us to hear.

Jigsaw's lips twitch, but he keeps a solemn face. "I won't say a word, Alexa." He holds up his hand. "Swear." He wiggles his fingers. "Now, gimmie."

She giggles and tosses two large Hershey bars at him, then hands me one too.

"Oh boy, we really lucked out," I whisper, setting the bar between us on the blanket.

"It pays to stay on the kids' good side. They always have excellent snacks."

Something warm squeezes around my heart. He might be joking about the snacks but it's the way he talks to the kids like they're people instead of annoyances that has me melting inside. They obviously like and trust him too.

Kids—like cats—in my opinion are good judges of character.

We all take turns approaching the fire with caution to roast our marshmallows. Rock carefully holds his daughter, allowing her to wave a long stick with several marshmallows at the end near the flames. But as soon as they droop and catch fire, Hope's right there to scoop the stick from her daughter's hand and rescue the gooey mess.

Laughter ripples through the group as the little girl smooshes sticky marshmallows into her mouth. As soon as everyone has at least one s'more assembled, someone tosses another log onto the fire, sending a fresh burst of golden sparks toward the sky.

The bonfire's roaring now, flames twisting and crackling as the logs collapse inward, embers glowing hot beneath them. A few guys shift closer to the fire, settling onto a large log that's been pulled up as a makeshift bench.

"All right!" The guy who'd quizzed me about Jigsaw's boyfriend qualities at dinner stands and claps his hands.

"Brace yourself," Jigsaw whispers in my ear. "Whatever Rav's about to say will be thoroughly obnoxious."

"Shelby tried to warn me when she called earlier." I tip my head and catch his lips for a quick kiss.

His eyes widen. "What's that for?"

"I'm having fun."

He curls his arm around my shoulders, drawing me closer.

A shrill whistle halts the remaining chatter.

"It's time for our favorite campfire game," Ravage announces.

A mixture of groans and chuckles ripple through our wide circle.

"It doesn't sound like it's everyone's favorite game," I whisper to Jigsaw.

He shakes his head. "That's because we don't *have* a favorite 'campfire game.'"

"Nope! No way, Rav," Shelby shouts. "If you're talkin' 'bout us all sharing 'first time' stories, I'm out. I already know way too much about y'alls sex lives as it is."

Laughter follows her declaration.

"He's just collecting material for his wank bank anyway," a big burly biker across the circle from us adds.

"Ewww," Shelby moans. She leans against me, her warm tea and liquor breath spilling over my cheek. "He's right, though," she whispers loudly in my ear. "Don't fall for it like I did. Keep it to yourself."

I snort with laughter. "It's not much of a story, anyway."

"Girrrl," she drawls. "Same." She collapses into a fit of giggles, falling against Rooster's chest.

Jigsaw turns, his body shifting slightly behind me. "I don't think I've ever seen you drunk, songbird."

"I'm celebrating," she says.

"Margot," Ravage calls out, pulling our attention toward the fire. I squint and blink through the smoke. "Since you're new to the circle, you *have* to go first."

"No, she doesn't," Jigsaw says in a low, warning growl.

"Didn't you harass Margot enough at dinner?" Rooster shouts.

"Come on," Ravage whines. "It's a rite of passage. Give us your best first-time sex story. We're all adults here."

"Um." Heidi raises her hand and waves it. "The kiddos are right over there." She points to a tent next to the blanket she's sharing with her husband.

"They're sleeping. Besides, that's *your* problem." Rav turns toward me again and flashes a mischievous grin. "Margot, you're up. First time..."

"That feels like fifth date conversation, at least," I answer. "Since this is my *first* date with the club, I'm going to pass."

A few chuckles go around the circle.

"Good call, Margot." Lilly nods and lifts the bottle in her hand.

Jigsaw hugs his arms tighter around me.

"Technically, it's your second," Sparky says. "Teller's wedding would've been your first."

Teller groans and rolls his eyes. "Don't bring my wedding into this degenerate wank bank collection festival."

"Doesn't count anyway," Stash argues. "We had other clubs and civilians there. She's right."

"Teller." Rav's dopey grin swivels toward his brother. "I don't think you've ever shared *your* story."

"And I'm not going to, either."

"Fine. I'll go," Ravage says.

Before he gets a word out, he's cut off by boos and heckles.

"No one wants to hear whatever vintage *Penthouse Forum* story you're going to regurgitate," Z says, waving a hand toward Ravage.

Ravage's eyes widen with innocence, and he cocks his head. "What's *Penthouse,* Grandpa?"

"Ask your mom," Hustler says, then snickers into his hands.

"Emily?" Rav draws out her name until it sounds like a dirty invitation. "You're newer to our circle as well. Time to give it up." He wiggles his fingers at her in a *hand it over* gesture.

"Um, pass." The woman with the shoulder-length red hair sits up. "Pass is an option, right?"

"Yes," Dex says. "Move on, Rav."

"All right, all right." Ravage rubs his hands together and focuses on me again. "We'll save first time stories for another bonfire. How about *scary* stories?"

"That sure beats *weirdest way you've ever injured your balls* stories," Dex groans.

Behind me, Jigsaw erupts in laughter, his body shaking against my back. "Those were classic. But let's not subject the ladies to it, please."

I turn my head and squint at him. "I'm scared to ask."

"Murphy has the best one." Jigsaw laughs even harder.

"Stories shared on the road," Murphy shouts from across the way, pointing a finger at us, "stay on the road. You know this, brother."

"I didn't *share* anything," Jigsaw protests between fits of laughter. "I'm just saying, yours is by far the best."

Wrath, the big biker who usually looks so intimidating every time I've met him, snorts and breaks into an almost child-like fit of laughter. "It really is."

"Fuck you." Murphy holds up his middle finger and wags it in Wrath's direction, then Jigsaw's. "And you too."

"I'm just saying." Jigsaw's slow tone fails at hitting the serious note I think he intended. "It's a miracle you were able to go on and father another kid after that. Respect, brother."

"That didn't sound very respectful." I turn and give him a scolding headshake. The corner of his mouth twitches into an irresistible grin and he leans in to press a quick kiss to my lips.

"Thank you, Margot!" Murphy yells from across the circle.

"Can we not rehash this tonight?" Rock's grave tone cuts through the laughter, carrying the weight to make it sound more like an order than a request. His irritated glance at Rav seals it.

"Fine." Ravage's lips scrunch into a pout that lasts all of two seconds. "Okay, okay. We'll stick with scary stories." He snaps his fingers. "Who has a *true* tale of personal terror?"

"You realize some of us have been stuffed into literal boxes by their stalker, right?" Shelby says.

Her calm delivery freezes the conversation. My throat tightens, choking off my gasp of surprise. Poor Shelby. She's been nothing but sweet and kind to me. I had no idea she'd endured something so horrific.

Everyone sits in sudden silence. Even Rav winces, his perpetual jovial smirk gone.

Jigsaw leans into me, pressing his lips to my ear and says, "That stalker is very, very *dead*."

A thrill of satisfaction shoots through me. "Good," I whisper back.

"Rav," Charlotte says, with an impressive amount of patience—

almost as if she's used to explaining things to him slowly, "can we *not* use our loved ones' trauma as entertainment, please?"

A couple of the other women murmur their agreement.

Next to us, Shelby rises, quickly slapping loose pine needles and a few dry leaves off her jeans. Rooster plants one hand on the ground, pushing himself to his feet at her side. He protectively curls his arm around her waist, leaving his hand resting on her hip.

Jigsaw leans back, his head tipping slightly as he reaches out, his knuckles grazing the leg of Shelby's jeans. "You all right?"

She nods and flashes a quick smile at him. "I just need to go for a walk."

Jigsaw frowns at Rooster who shakes his head and shoots a murderous glare at Ravage.

The three of them are awfully close.

It's nice the way Jigsaw cares about Shelby. A much friendlier brotherly relationship than he seems to have with his actual sister Jezzie. A nicer relationship than I've ever had with my own brothers.

Am I jealous?

No. That's not quite it. Wondering how I fit into their trio? If I'll fit in...permanently?

Maybe.

CHAPTER SEVENTEEN

Jigsaw

FUCKING RAVAGE. BROTHER HAS NO COMMON SENSE SOMETIMES. Knowing the horrors some of the ol' ladies have been through, it's insensitive as fuck for him to ask them to share personal scary stories. Never mind, I have my own. Part of me would like to give a detailed account of my time in Daddy's dungeon when I was a kid, bleeding out on the floor, not knowing if I'd live to see the next day. Maybe it would stop Rav's story time requests for good. But probably not.

I cast a quick glance around at my brothers and their ol' ladies. At least I have the comfort of knowing most of the people who've harmed anyone in this circle are six feet under—many of them at the club's hand.

I didn't hesitate to tell Margot that Shelby's stalker is dead. She should know if anyone ever fucks with her, I'm not the only one who will kill to protect her, the whole club will. The only guilt I have about that fucker's death is that I only cut off part of his pinky finger before Rooster had to turn the lowlife over to the FBI.

"Okay, maybe *true* horror stories was too much," Rav says. "How about scary campfire stories? Someone *must* have a good one." His sneaky gaze slides to Margot again.

Margot's lips twist into that slightly evil, borderline unhinged smile that's starting to turn me on more than it should. "Do you assume because I grew up in a funeral home, I must have lots of creepy dead body stories?" she asks sweetly.

"Well..." Guilt flashes over Rav's face, followed by interest. "Yes."

I will gut you, I mouth to Rav, making a point to pat my side where my hunting knife rests.

The fucker smirks and holds out his arms, practically daring me to make good on the threat.

"Let's see, I was slapped by a dead body once." Margot taps her finger against her chin like she's flipping through a long list of events. "Few things scare me anymore."

"What the fuck?" Z asks, half shocked, half laughing.

"It's just a muscle contraction," Margot explains in her usual kind but professional way. "It happens. My father's had bodies actually sit up while he was wheeling them around the prep room. That's always a wild sight."

Silence falls over the circle.

Margot focuses on Rav again. "But you asked for a scary campfire-type story, right?"

"Yup." He nods. "Ghosts haunting the hallways or zombies popping out of coffins? Give it to us."

"Okay. I have one." Her voice lowers, the words hanging in the smoky air. "A good one."

"Yes!" Rav claps his hands and briskly rubs his palms together.

Margot glances around the fire. Her eyes widen and cheeks flame when she realizes everyone's watching her. Then a slow, deliberate smile curves her lips. "It's really creepy though."

A hush falls over the group, broken by the occasional crackle and pop from the fire.

"We can handle creepy," Z says. "Give it to us."

She shifts forward.

"No, come on up here." Ravage slaps his hand against the thick log he's been using as a chair. "Come take the storytelling seat."

"You don't have to," I say against Margot's ear.

"No, it's fine. The smoke's starting to irritate my eyes." She flicks her hand in the air toward the smoke that's blowing directly at us.

"All right." I stand, hold out my hand, and pull her up off the blanket, then walk behind her until we reach Rav.

I casually thrust my palms against his shoulder, knocking him off the log. He lands in a clump of dry leaves with a satisfying thump.

"Dick." He sits up and sweeps his hands over his cut and jeans, knocking the crinkly leaf particles loose.

"Oopsie." I slap my hand over my mouth.

Margot bites her lip and shakes her head. I curl my hands around her waist and boost her up onto the log, then perch right next to her.

She squints into the fire, then glances out at everyone gathered in a circle. Rav climbs over the log and settles at the far end, facing us.

"So, this happened a few years ago, right after I graduated from mortuary school," she says, her steady voice carrying over the crackling fire.

I brace myself. She won't share the story of murdering that pedo, will she? No. There's no way Margot would talk about that, even as a joke.

"We had a woman come to us who needed to bury her mother," Margot says.

"This is already sad, not scary," Dex says.

Margot nods at him. "It *was* sad. Her mother wasn't that old. She got disoriented at night and apparently drowned in the lake near their house."

"This is gonna *get* scary, right?" Rav asks.

From the woods, someone snorts and I squint into the darkness, catching a glimpse of Rooster's light-blue T-shirt leaning up against a tree, Shelby at his side. I wave for them to join us, but he shakes his head.

"You asked, bro," I say to Ravage. "Shut up and let her tell the story."

Margot glances at me and raises an eyebrow, as if she's asking if she should continue. I'm too curious to see where the story goes to stop her, so I nod.

"Well, we took the mother into our care. I was the one who met with the daughter to go over her wishes for the funeral."

"What about the husband? He didn't help out his daughter?" Murphy asks.

"He wasn't in the picture as far as I knew. There was just the daughter, and she was an only child."

"That's so sad," Heidi says.

"You're bumming us out, Margot," Rav says.

"Shut up," Teller snaps. "You asked for a story and she's trying to tell it. Jesus."

"Well, Heidi's right," Margot says. "That's why my dad had me handle things. He thought she'd be more comfortable with someone her own age helping to make the arrangements. But since it was one of my firsts, he hired my friend April as a consultant."

"Is this April chick hot?" Rav leans forward, vibrating with degenerate anticipation. "Girls named after months are always smokin' hot."

"I can confirm." June lifts one hand and lets out a giggle. Her laughter and bright smile are nothing like the quiet, skittish girl she'd been when we rescued her from the South of Satan MC's campgrounds.

"Virtue names as well." Trinity raises her hand, then points to Hope, who lifts her hand in agreement.

"Amen!" Rav raises his hands toward the sky.

"Is there any category of woman you *don't* find hot?" Z asks Ravage.

"No." Rav points at me and my stomach twists, anticipating what he's about to say and not wanting Margot to hear it. "I'm with Jiggy on this one. I appreciate and enjoy women of all shapes, sizes—"

"We get it," Sparky shouts. "Can you *please* let Margot finish her story?"

I lift my chin at Sparky, and he nods.

Margot's watching my brothers' antics with a faint smile, like she finds all of this amusing instead of obnoxious. Or maybe she missed what Ravage said about me.

"To answer your question, yes, April's very pretty," Margot says.

"But is she single?" Birch shouts.

Margot ducks her head and laughs. "Yes, she is."

Time to get things back on track. "So, it was just a small, simple funeral?"

"Not exactly." The glow of the firelight dances over Margot's face, highlighting the seriousness of her eyes. "She was so nervous. Throughout the whole consultation, she kept wringing her hands. Like she was carrying something heavier than grief."

"She murdered her mother!" Hoot shouts.

Margot rolls her eyes. "No."

The fire crackles, emphasizing the silence. Is she waiting for more guesses or trying to come up with more pieces of the story? I haven't decided if she's telling a true story, something she made up, or a combination.

"April and I discovered that the woman had a number of what she told me were Slavic superstitions and rituals she wanted us to follow."

Lilly groans. "I can guess a few of them."

Margot nods. "This wasn't that unusual. We have a lot of different clients with various backgrounds. It's important to us that we respect people's traditions. But the fear the daughter had as she listed each ritual was...unnerving."

"What were they?" Hope asks.

"First, we had to cover all the mirrors in the funeral home with black cloth."

"To make sure the spirit doesn't get trapped between worlds?" Lilly asks with raised eyebrows.

Margot nods quickly. "That's what she said. We'd done that before, so it wasn't a big deal. I have black velvet cloths to fit each mirror in the house."

Lilly nods with approval. Z leans in and whispers something in her ear and Lilly shrugs.

"Then, she asked for a window to be left open during the service." Margot pauses, waiting to see if anyone will take a guess. When no one pipes up, she adds, "For her mother's soul to escape in case it was trapped. That one was odd but doable."

Rav rolls his eyes, and I shoot him a death glare. *If he interrupts Margot one more time...*

"Then she asked for a bell to be tied inside the casket," Margot says. "She told us it was a tradition."

"No," Z groans. "I sense where this is going."

"I wish," Margot mutters. "Then she asked for coins to be placed in her mother's hands."

"Not on her eyes?" Teller asks.

"No. Just her hands." Margot takes a breath. "There were other things, but these are the most relevant. She also stressed the body could *not* cross the threshold twice. This one was trickier but also not unusual. Fun fact—that's why the viewing room has two entrances."

I picture the layout of Margot's house. Except for the bathrooms, *every* room I've been in on the first floor has at least two entrances. The basement has three, if you count the rickety elevator as an exit.

"The final request was to bury her mother with a doll. At first I thought, aw, that's sweet, maybe it was something from her childhood that she treasured."

"Was it a Cabbage Patch kid?" Sparky asks.

"That would've been preferable." Margot shivers. "We bury people with jewelry, photos, love letters—someone even tried to bury her dad with his hunting rifle one time. And of course, children are usually buried with cherished toys." She stops and takes a breath.

I rub my hand between her shoulder blades.

Swan kneels up on her blanket and raises one hand. "Was it a Matryoshka doll?"

Lilly nods enthusiastically. "That's what I was thinking too."

"Kind of." Margot lifts her hands and shrugs. "A Russian nesting doll. That's what I thought at first. But it was bigger." She holds her hands vertically in the air, about twelve inches apart. "It was a dark wood color with intricate carvings. None of the colorful paint I'd seen on nesting dolls before. And, most importantly, it didn't open. It was very heavy, like it was solid, not hollow with other dolls inside."

"That's weird," Lilly murmurs.

"The weirdest part," Margot lowers her voice, "was that the mouth was carved wide open—"

Rav lifts his hand and a dirty smirk spreads over his face. "Like—"

"Don't," I warn.

"Like she was screaming," Margot finishes without acknowledging Rav's interruption. "And she had three small, rusty nails hammered into each eye, sticking straight out."

"Jesus Christ," someone mutters.

Margot touches her stomach. "And three nails sticking out of her belly button."

"Gross," Z groans. "And she wanted her mom buried with that thing?"

Lilly shakes her head vigorously. "Did she tell you it was a Kikimora doll?"

Margot's eyes widen and she sits back. "Yes," she breathes out.

"Bullshit!" Rav shouts. "I call bullshit." He points to Lilly, then Margot. "You two conspired ahead of time."

Lilly holds both hands in the air. "I swear we didn't."

"Watch where you're pointin' those fingers, brother," Z growls at Ravage.

"Jesus Christ," Birch moans and stares up at the sky. "Nothing scary has even happened yet in this story." He flashes a quick grin at Margot. "No offense." His gaze shifts to Rav. "What are you getting so worked up about?"

"Nothing." Rav crosses his arms over his chest.

"She said it was a good luck doll to help her mother find lost relatives in the afterlife," Margot continues.

Lilly and Swan both shake their heads vigorously.

"The daughter requested two viewings and a wake before the burial." Margot holds her hands up. "She was paying, so we did exactly as she requested. But because of the threshold rule, we had to leave the casket in the viewing room overnight."

"Here we go." Hoot rubs his hands together like he's excited we're closer to the scary part.

I'm less enthusiastic about where this story's heading.

"The doll was supposed to remain in this black velvet bag," Margot says. "I placed it in the casket with her mother myself. April took care of the coins. And I sewed the bell into the satin lining."

The bonfire pops and hisses, dragging out the tension. I squirm on the log, wishing Margot would finish the story.

Margot turns toward me. "I hadn't finished my apartment upstairs yet. So, I was sleeping in my old bedroom on the second floor. April had her own apartment in Empire and was commuting."

She turns toward the group again, the fire casting shadows over her face. "The only people in the house were my dad, my cousin, and me. Well, the only living people."

Someone groans.

"I woke up to the sound of running water." Margot shrugs. "It's an old house. I'm used to odd noises all hours of the night. But never anything like this."

I shift my gaze and catch Ravage hugging himself tighter.

"Scared something might be wrong—a busted pipe or a faucet someone left on, I got up to investigate." Margot takes a deep breath, then continues. "As soon as I opened my bedroom door, the air felt so heavy. Like the pressure you feel in the air before a storm. I searched the second floor—short of busting into my dad and cousin's rooms. Nothing. But the sound continued."

"Did you wake your dad up?" I ask.

"No, I really thought it was something simple." Margot tilts her head like she's trying to get each detail right. "I ran downstairs, checked the kitchen, the prep room, I even ran to the basement and checked all over. I checked every water source I could think of."

"Nothing?" Z asks.

"Nothing. But that heavy feeling in the air persisted." Margot pauses and her lips tilt slightly. "Then something banged on the first floor." She claps her hands, the sharp slap ringing through the air. "I nearly jumped out of my skin. I was terrified something happened to the box holding the casket up. I ran to the viewing room and turned on the lights."

"And?" someone shouts.

"The casket was as we'd left it, and I breathed the biggest sigh of relief." Margot presses her hand to her chest. "But the room reeked. Damp and earthy. Then I noticed a dark stain on the carpet and my heart jumped right back to terror. I was scared we botched the embalming or something. In school you're taught about all these nightmare scenarios, and I swear every one of them flipped through my brain."

"Was the woman *pissed* about her coffin?" Hustler slaps his hand over his mouth and giggles like he said something really clever.

"No. It was just water." She pauses, a sinister smile curving her lips. "And the doll was sitting in the middle of the puddle," she finishes in a low voice.

"Oh, hell no!" Ravage shouts. "Bullshit."

Margot holds one hand up toward the sky. "I swear." She nods at Hustler. "I almost peed *my* pants when I saw it."

"Nope. That's when I would've run screaming from the house," Heidi announces. "No way."

"I wanted to, believe me," Margot says. "But I was more worried about the water, that a pipe might have burst or something. I placed the doll back in the casket and woke my dad up to help me find the source of the leak."

Lilly's eyes widen to saucer size. "You *touched* the doll after that?"

Margot sighs. "I didn't want my dad to see it and think April and I screwed something up. So, I only told him about the puddle."

"What was it?" I ask. "A burst pipe?"

"No," Margot answers. "That spot on the carpet was the only place we found any water. The casket wasn't wet, the ceiling wasn't either. Nothing dripping anywhere. Just this puddle in front of the casket."

"It had to come from somewhere," Z says.

"We couldn't figure it out." Margot shrugs. "We cleaned it up and my father went to bed. I was on my way upstairs when I heard the tiny jingle of a bell."

"Oh, fuck no," I blurt out.

"Exactly." Margot takes a deep breath. "My heart was in my throat. But I tiptoed into the room, convinced the woman was going to be sitting up in her coffin…"

"And!?" Ravage shouts.

"The coffin was closed." Margo's gaze scans the crowd. "But the doll—"

"Noooo," Lilly moans. "Don't say it."

"Yup," Margot confirms. "This time she was sitting *on top* of the casket."

"Bitch really wanted some attention," Birch quips.

Nervous laughter rolls through the group.

"*Help meeee!*" A high-pitched voice echoes from the woods.

"Fuck!" Rav jumps off the log and comes closer to the fire. "What the fuck was that?"

Shelby's muffled giggles follow Rooster's fading cries for help.

"It's Rooster, dipshit." Rock laughs and jerks his thumb over his shoulder. "Story gettin' to you?"

"No." Rav runs his hands through his hair a few times, then glances around the circle.

Bonnie and Lala motion for Rav to join them on their blanket and he happily plants his ass between them.

"Aww, look at Rav gettin' protection from two sweet lil' bunnies," Birch heckles.

"Ignore them, Margot." Z waves his hand in the air, like a conductor instructing her to continue.

Margot flicks her gaze to the sky for a second. "So, now I'm looking at this doll and thoroughly spooked. Questioning my sanity."

"Did you tie the bag shut the first time?" Swan asks.

"The first time, no. I just placed her in the casket," Margot says. "But you bet your ass I tied it shut the second time."

Lilly winces.

"Was the first bang from the window closing?" Charlotte asks.

Margot points at Charlotte and nods. "Yup. I didn't realize that until the next morning, though."

"Had it rained that night?" Teller asks.

Margot claps her hands together. "Yes!"

Z slides his gaze to Teller. "Okay, that might explain the puddle, but not the doll."

"There's a logical explanation for that too," Teller says.

"The fuck there is!" Rav shouts. "That's creepy shit."

"After that, everything was calm for the rest of the night." Margot slides her hand through the air in front of her like she's smoothing out a bedsheet. "When I told April the next morning, she didn't believe me."

"I hope you made her stay over the next night," Wrath says.

"Oh, I didn't have to make her." Margot nods at Wrath, then Teller. "She wanted to stay to prove to me it was just something *logical* that happened."

Teller chuckles "And?"

"Same thing. Just as we were falling asleep—"

"Wait, were you sleeping together?" Ravage asks with hopefully raised eyebrows.

"Shut up." I reach down, wrap my fingers around a pinecone and fling it at Rav, hitting him squarely on the forehead.

"No," Margot says. "We weren't." She clears her throat. "I was falling asleep when I heard the loud bang again. April obviously heard it too, and we both met in the hallway."

"Wait, your dad and cousin never heard it?" Trinity asks.

"Nope." Margot shakes her head. "April thought I was messing with her, so she checked my room first."

Lilly huffs. "She didn't find anything, right?"

"Nope. This time, I didn't bother checking all over." Margot holds her hands up in the air. "We went straight to the viewing room."

"Do *not* say that creepy doll was out again." Ravage points a finger at Margot. "Don't."

Margot falls against me, laughing. "Unfortunately, yes."

A chorus of disbelief echoes around the fire.

"I'm serious." Margot presses her palms together like she's begging them to believe her. "She was sitting on top of the casket again. But this time with the two coins that April had put in the woman's hands."

"You've gotta be kidding," Z groans.

"Nope. April ran to get my dad—"

"Splitting up is a classic horror movie no-no," Emily tsks.

"I know!" Margot shouts. "But I knew my dad wouldn't believe us. He'd think we were playing a prank on him."

Everyone's silent and watching Margot now.

"I followed her up the stairs," Margot says. "And we heard another banging noise, so we both ran back to the viewing room." She waits, letting the silence further spook everyone. "The doll and the coins were gone."

"Oh, come on," Rav moans.

"No, seriously," Margot says. "We opened the casket and everything was back inside—well, the doll wasn't in her pouch, so I put her back in and tied it again."

"I'm starting to think she didn't like being in the bag," Z points out.

"I think you had a bad Kikimora," Lilly says. "She must have felt disrespected or insulted that she was taken out of the woman's house."

Z just stares at her.

I can't decide if my president's wife is trying to bolster Margot's story or if she believes in this stuff. But Rav's looking uneasier by the second, so it's a win either way.

"You might be right, Lilly." Margot closes her eyes briefly, as if it's hard to relay this part of the story. "The next day at the funeral, I took the daughter aside and asked if she was sure she wanted us to bury the doll. This terrified look came over her face and she asked if anything weird had happened."

"Uh, yeah!" Heidi says. "Did you tell her?"

"Well, I didn't want to seem unprofessional, but I did end up telling her about the water and the doll getting out." Margot glances up at the sky. "She was so upset and insisted we double-check that the doll was in the casket when we buried her mom. So, at the gravesite, we unfortunately had to do just that."

"What'd your dad think of that?" Teller asks.

"He's used to odd requests from family. We just had to make a few adjustments, so it was okay."

"The doll was in there?" Ravage asks.

"Yup." Margot nods. "And I stayed with the daughter while they buried the casket."

Rav stands and brushes off his jeans. "Well, that was definitely spooky. Thanks, Margot."

"Wait, I'm not done."

Rav freezes in place, staring at her. "What do you mean you're not done?"

"Oh my God," Z mutters.

"Imagine my surprise that night, when I'm getting ready for bed…" Margot stops and takes a dramatic breath. "And find the doll sitting on my nightstand."

Different people shout, "No!" or "No way!"

Margot holds up a hand like she's swearing an oath. "I swear to everything under the sun."

"There had to be more than one of these dolls." Wrath's smug face suggests he thinks he's unraveled the whole story. "Right? This lady was just fucking with you."

Margot tilts her head as if she'd once considered that idea, then discarded it. "I thought it might be a possibility."

"There's no way." Teller frowns. "That's fucked up."

Look at Mr. Logic getting all flustered.

"I thought so too." Margot's lips twist with amusement. "I tried calling the daughter to ask about the doll—if she wanted it back."

"And?" Hope prompts.

"Her number was disconnected."

"What a bitch," Trinity sputters. "She stuck you with her family's creepy, haunted doll?"

"Seemed that way," Margot agrees. "I'd had enough. I marched outside and threw her in the crematorium and cranked it high."

Rav stands again. "Great story. Thank you, Margot." He slow-claps.

Margot purses her lips, like she's trying not to laugh.

I have a feeling she's still not done.

"Don't say it," I mutter.

Margot turns her mischievous gaze on me, her lips curving into a faint, wicked smile. "Yup. It should've been burned to ash. But when I went back to my room, she was sitting right on my nightstand again."

CHAPTER EIGHTEEN

Margot

I HAVE TO STOP MYSELF FROM GIGGLING AT THE CHORUS OF "BULLSHIT!" the brothers yell at me.

"I'm serious," I insist. "The back of it was charred a little but otherwise it was perfectly fine."

Wrath stares at her. "What. The. Fuck?"

I turn my palms up and spread them wide.

"No fucking way!" Ravage explodes. "Of all the things that never happened, that never happened the most."

"No." Lilly sits up, tossing her long black hair over her shoulder. "Kikimoras aren't something you want to mess around with. If that's what it was, you're lucky she wasn't more destructive, Margot."

Lilly grins and winks at me, clearly enjoying the chance to give my story credibility.

"Maybe she was confused because she was in a home with a lot of spirits moving in and out?" Swan suggests.

Ravage stares at Lilly, then Swan, like they've lost their minds. Then he shakes his head. "All right, enough of that. Who else has a story?" He stands and glances around the circle.

"Wait." Rock holds up one hand. "*If* this is true. Where is the doll now?"

Jigsaw glances at me. "Please don't tell me it's in your house somewhere?"

I bite my lip to stop from laughing. "Well, I wasn't going to bother burning it again. Burying it seemed out of the question." I pause, wanting to make sure this next part sounds authentic. "So, I called someone I knew from school who collects haunted objects. He has stuff from all over the world that he tries to authenticate. I called him and he picked up the doll. She lives in a sealed glass box now. He keeps a wreath of dried flowers around her and *that* seems to have stopped the mischief."

"Road trip!" Sparky yells. "I want to go see this haunted objects museum."

"Not that I want to discourage you from taking a road trip." Dex stares at his friend like he's lost his mind. "But do you want to risk having that kind of negative energy attaching itself to you?"

"You might have a point, brother." Sparky thrusts his hands in front of his face, slowly turning them over to examine his fingers as if he's already forgotten about his road trip.

"No one's going to top that." Stash stands and claps his hands with more sincerity than Ravage. "Nice job, Margot."

"Thank you."

"I've got one." A tall, thickly built man steps forward, his features obscured by the flickering glow of the firelight. The flames cast fleeting highlights over his full head of wavy hair, the exact shade elusive in the shifting shadows. The cut of his square jawline and high cheekbones becomes clearer as he approaches us. Somehow, he's both handsome and rough at the same time.

"That's Birch," Jigsaw whispers to me. "He hasn't been a full-patch upstate for that long."

"Ah, okay." I work that out in my head. "So, the guys still probably rag on him extra hard?"

His lips quirk. "Something like that."

Birch ambles up to our log. Jigsaw slides off, then helps me off the log. He waves his hand toward the seat in an "all yours" gesture.

"I'm not sure I can top yours." Birch nods at me. "It's a little more light-hearted."

"Light is good," I assure him.

Jigsaw rests his hand on my lower back and guides me back to our blanket.

Rock, Hope, Z, and Lilly all either smile or nod at me as we pass them. Rooster and Shelby have returned to their blanket next to us. Shelby grins at me as I drop onto the soft flannel.

"That *was* a good one." She tilts her head. "Was it true?"

I press my hand to my chest and bat my lashes. "Of course it was."

She grins even wider.

"Let's go!" Rav claps his hands, drawing everyone's attention. He points to Birch. "This better be good, bro."

Birch shrugs. "Let's find out."

"No random creepy dolls either," Ravage warns.

"Are you going to heckle him or let him speak?" Rock asks.

Rav slaps his hand over his mouth and widens his eyes to a cartoonish size.

Chuckling, Birch shoves his hands in his pockets and leans against the log. "This happened my sophomore year of high school. I was fifteen or sixteen. The year we had that big blizzard up and down the East Coast."

"There's been more than one," a heavyset guy who'd been quiet most of the night says.

"That's our treasurer downstate—Hustler," Jigsaw whispers to me. "He's a stickler for details."

"Good quality for the treasurer." All of his reminders and prompts to help me keep track of everyone melt my heart. I tip my head and brush my forehead against his soft, cotton shirt. "Thanks."

Ignoring the interruption, Birch continues. "It was early morning. Before school. I put on my snow-shoveling pants." He bends and rubs his hands over his thighs, down to his knees. "They had this warm, fleece lining that made it almost tolerable to be out in the cold for so long."

"Nice. I love those," Teller says.

Birch ducks his head and lets out a huff of laughter. "Yeah, I did too. So, it was dark-ish when I started but as the sun started coming up, the neighborhood got busier. Lots of folks up early to make it to work on time. Driving slow through the barely plowed street. And I'm out there clearing the driveway for my mom." He touches his chest and curls his lips into a neighborly grin. "I know most of the neighbors and stop to wave as everyone passes by."

"You used to be *friendly*?" Sparky asks with exaggerated curiosity in his voice.

Birch playfully snarls at Sparky. "It's cold out, right? But like, I'm unnaturally cold…down south." He drops his hands in front of his body, framing his crotch. "But I've got a long sweatshirt on and my big puffy coat. I'm thinkin' I'm all covered, maybe it's just colder than I realized."

"Oh no," Rav moans. "I know what's coming."

"My next-door neighbor was a cutie," Birch continues. "She lived alone with her grandmother." He presses his fingertips to his chest. "I'm a nice guy. Thought I'd go over and score a few points with Grandma by shoveling their driveway when I was done with my own."

"Grandma got an eyeful, didn't she?" Charlotte asks.

He holds his hand out in a *slow down* gesture. "Easy, Sunshine. I'm getting there."

"Wait, this was in the middle of a snowstorm? How was your dick not shriveled up?" Stash asks.

"He's a shower, not a grower," a red-headed, freckled guy says with an approving nod.

"Thanks, Hoot. But actually, I'm both," Birch insists, a slow grin spreading across his face.

The girls across from us fall into a fit of giggles.

Jigsaw leans close to me. "I should've warned you—half the stories my brothers tell end up being sagas about their dick or balls."

"Men obsessed with their genitalia. You don't say," I tease.

His expression melts into something warmer and less tense. "Glad that's not a deal-breaker for you."

"I'm having fun," I assure him.

"As I'm walking over to the neighbor's," Birch is saying as I tune back into his story, "I waved at someone passing by. Instead of waving back, they shouted at me and drove off. And I'm like, whatever. I was kind of walking out in the road, so I thought they were just pissed I was in the way."

"Here we go," Shelby mutters.

Shaking with silent laughter, I duck my head.

"Like a gentleman, I clear a path to the front door." Birch's voice lowers so most of us have to strain to hear him over the crackling fire. "As I'm finishing..." He pauses for a few beats. "Grandma comes to the door and calls me over to thank me and pay me a few bucks—which I was going to turn down."

"Yeah, yeah, Saint Birch, we know," Z chuckles. "Come on."

"I'm gettin' there, Prez." Brich grins at him. "Okay, where was I?"

"Grandma saw your dick!" someone shouts from the other side of the fire.

Birch laughs, grinning so hard crinkles form at the corners of his eyes. "I'm cold by this point. I've been shoveling for like an hour. My legs are numb. I had gloves on, but they were wet and cold. Grandma calls my name. And like a dumbass, I stomp my way up to the porch, grinning like an idiot. Here I am, thinking I'm gonna get patted on the head and told I'm a good boy." He runs his hands over his face. "And as I approached, Grandma's sweet, angelic old lady face transformed into this look of horror and then anger."

A low murmur of laughter ripples around the fire.

Birch stops and squeezes his eyes shut as if he regrets bringing up these memories. "She starts yelling at me, 'Everest! Put your penis away, young man! What's wrong with you!?'" he finishes in a scratchy, high-pitched tone.

"I think my soul left my body." Birch wraps his arms around himself and shivers. "In slow motion, I glanced down." His head drops as if he needs to reenact each movement to tell the story right. "And there's my dick. Poking through my broken zipper, bobbing free in the ice-cold morning breeze."

Everyone who's been following the story explodes with laughter.

The ones who'd tuned out now turn toward Birch, checking to see what they've missed.

It's as if the laughter's infectious. Once I start, I can't stop. I pause for a breath, then Shelby's giggles set me off again. Behind me, Jigsaw rumbles with laughter. Rooster's deep bellows add to the merry soundtrack.

"My zipper broke. My damn sweatshirt wasn't long enough." Birch's outraged voice barely carries over all the noise.

Tears leak out of my eyes, and I can't catch my breath. The giggles just keep coming every time Birch says a word.

He knows it too and starts drawing out the story, adding more and more absurd details.

Shelby falls against me, shrieking with laughter.

"You weren't wearing underwear?" Sparky shouts.

"Nooo," Birch answers slowly. "I got dressed quickly that morning. Had my super-warm fleecy pants. Didn't think I'd need undies."

Undies. He didn't. This guy, who's as big as the tree he's named after, said the word *undies*. I can't. A few more snickers tumble past my lips.

Slowly, I catch my breath and sit up. Shelby's wiping beneath her eyes. Anyone not still caught in a fit of laughter has their attention focused on Birch.

"Wait," Lilly says. "Obviously it was an accident. That's not nice that she yelled at you."

"Awww!" Some of the guys heckle Lilly for being too soft.

"I mean, I *knew* I was cold—down *there*." Birch gestures to his crotch again. "I should've checked sooner."

"Probably the first cock granny had seen in years," Hustler says. "Shocked her."

"Probably the ugliest too." Stash grins. "Gave the poor old gal nightmares."

"So, after she yelled at you, what happened next?" Hope asks.

"Are you sure you don't miss being a lawyer?" Wrath lifts his chin at Hope.

"What?" She gestures with one hand toward Birch. "I need the mental image of him standing there in the freezing cold with his privates on display resolved in my head." She taps a finger against her temple.

"We all need it scrubbed from our brains," Rock says in a dry tone.

"This is *so* much worse than the time I went to Chemistry class with the back of my skirt tucked into my tights." Heidi huffs a laugh.

"Thank you for the acknowledgments of my suffering, ladies." Birch nods at Lilly, Hope, and Heidi. "Okay, so I'm standing there, staring at my poor chilly willy, a teeny, tiny icicle dangling from the head."

A few of the guys hiss in a pained breath or murmur "ouch" while the rest of us titter with laughter.

"I tried to turn and tuck myself away, but I slid…" Birch waves his arms in the air like he's teetering on a ledge, trying to catch his balance, "…and fell in the snow dick-first."

Another chorus of sputtering laughter pops off around us.

"I'm not ashamed to admit, I started crying at this point," Birch says in a *fuck it* tone. "My zipper was wide open, so not only was my dick cold but now all this snow and ice got pushed up against my balls." His body trembles with a violent shiver.

"It just keeps getting worse," I whisper to Jigsaw.

He hums a sound close to agreement. "I never knew Birch was this dramatic."

Birch grins wide as his brothers hurl jokes at him. "Yeah, yeah. I finally dug myself out, tucked my dick away, took off my sweatshirt, and tied it around my waist."

"Phew. That's what I needed to hear," Hope says. "Thank you!"

Birch glances at Lilly. "You're right. I think when Grandma realized I hadn't been doing the pervy swagger up the sidewalk on purpose, she took pity on me. Invited me in, gave me a pair of too-small sweatpants to wear, and fed me breakfast."

"Awww, see, that's what I was hoping happened," Lilly says.

Birch dips his chin. "She fixed the pants for me too."

"Bet the granddaughter told the whole school," Jigsaw shouts. "And never looked at you again."

Next to us, a short snort of laughter pops out of Rooster.

"Look at you so confidently *wrong*." Birch raises on his toes and points to Jigsaw. "I totally got with her in the spring." Birch winks. "I think her grandma told her I was well hung, and she should give me a test ride."

"Gross," Shelby moans.

"Bullshit!" Eazy shouts. "You went one too far."

"That's Eazy," Jigsaw whispers to me. "He's a member of my charter downstate."

I nod quickly. "I remember talking to him at Teller's wedding." My cheeks flame hot. "I wasn't *that* stoned."

Jigsaw shifts his body and clears his throat. "Yeah."

The air around us seems to change.

While the party carries on, I turn and roll until I'm kneeling between Jigsaw's outstretched legs. I rest one hand on his thigh. He drops his gaze to my thumb slowly stroking the rough denim of his jeans.

"What's wrong?" I ask.

"Nothing." He lifts his chin toward something behind me. "He thought you were cute."

Is he still talking about Eazy? "So?"

He swallows hard and stares into my eyes. "I never wanted to punch a brother so much in my life when I saw him talking to you."

"Yeah." I duck my head and laugh softly. "It was kind of obvious when you walked up and *kicked* him."

"Since I didn't give you an answer right away, I was worried you might ask him to…you know…" he lowers his voice and leans in closer, whispering against my ear, "tutor you."

His warm breath sends a shiver of pleasure down my spine. A second later the words that came out of his mouth penetrate my brain.

I sit back on my heels and scowl at him. "Why would you think that?"

Did he assume I was so desperate I'd ask any random biker to help me?

He frowns and shrugs.

No way. I don't want him to think anyone else would've made me happy. "I asked *you* because I liked *you*."

He stares at me for a few seconds, studying my face in a way that squeezes my chest. "Yeah, I know that now."

"Good." I poke a finger in his stomach, and he grinds his teeth like he's trying to hold in his laughter. "Are you *ticklish*?"

"What? No."

I tap my fingers along his side. "Are you sure?"

His lips tilt into a lopsided grin, then he grabs my hand, tugging me closer. "Tell me again."

I think I know what he wants to hear but teasing him is too irresistible. "That you're ticklish?"

He clamps his hands over my hips and pulls me into his lap. "No."

I cup his cheeks with my hands. "That I liked you?"

He nods slowly, his bristly cheeks rasping against my palms.

"I liked you then." I lean in and brush my lips against his. "And I like you a *whole* lot more now."

His lips quirk. "Good."

"Awww," Shelby sighs. "You two are the cutest."

We both glance over at her. Anywhere else, I'd probably be mortified at being caught in what I consider an intimate moment.

But it doesn't bother me here. This is what Jigsaw promised, a fun night with people who won't judge me. Where I can be myself without harsh criticism.

Would everyone be as accepting if they knew my favorite hobby? Something tells me the answer might be *yes.*

Jigsaw

After story time, the party takes a rowdy turn. Rock and Hope are the first ones to say goodnight, collecting their daughter from Heidi's tent with minimal fuss. Wrath and Trinity disappear into the woods with barely a wave goodbye. Z and Lilly check in on their son and talk to Heidi for a few minutes before following the same path Rock and Hope took.

Once the presidents and their ol' ladies have left, the few club girls who'd been invited start putting on a show. Rav cranks up the music, encouraging them. Swan, Bonnie, and June hold hands and start shaking their asses like they're expecting us to stuff dollar bills in their shorts.

Dex snorts with annoyance and helps Emily off her blanket. Keeping Emily tucked close to his side, Dex makes his way over to us.

"I get enough of this at work." Dex jerks his thumb over his shoulder toward the wanna-be strippers prancing around the bonfire. "We're heading to the clubhouse. You got a room for tonight, right?"

I lean all the way to my right and slap Rooster's outstretched leg. "Right next to my favorite mothercluсker."

Rooster chuckles.

"Good." Dex squeezes Emily to his side. "If you need something, let me know. We'll be up for a little while."

Emily's lips curve and she peers up at Dex.

I'm not all that fond of Emily, but Dex seems to think she's *the one* for him, and will probably patch her soon, so I make an effort to be nice. Well, nice for me.

"You having a good time, Red?" I ask her.

"I *was*." She flicks a glance toward the fire, but Dex is blocking her view. Swan had been a bit of an asshole to Emily when she realized Dex was planning to patch her. Guess that's still an issue. *Upstate's problem, not mine.*

Emily sighs. "I'm getting tired anyway." Her gaze shifts to Margot and she flashes a friendlier smile. "I loved your story." She wraps her arms around Dex's middle and hugs him. "We probably should've left after you were finished."

"Yeah, I could've lived happily without hearing Birch's dick in the snow drama," Dex says.

"I meant, Margot's story was a showstopper." Emily grins. "You need to write a book about that and have it made into a movie."

"I never thought about it." Margot presses her hand to her collarbones. "It was so freaky, no one ever believes me when I tell the story."

They chat for a few more minutes and by the time they're done, I dislike Emily a little bit less.

After they leave, I'm about to ask Margot if she wants to head back to the clubhouse.

Bonnie saunters over from Rav's blanket and drops to her knees in front of us. "Hey, Margot, right?"

Instantly wary of Bonnie's intentions, I wrap my arms around Margot. "What do you want?"

Margot cranes her neck to peer at me over her shoulder.

Bonnie shrugs. "I just wanted to say hi. We're all a lil' sad Jiggy found someone." She lifts her gaze and stares right at me. "But happy for him too." Her tone couldn't be farther away from *happy* if she tried.

Margot stiffens.

Well, at least I warned her.

"Nice to meet you," Margot says. "No reason for anyone to be sad." She clamps her hand over my thigh. "I keep him pretty happy."

Bonnie titters with laughter that borders on evil. "Sure you do, hon."

"Time for you to git," Shelby says, shooing Bonnie away like she's a stray cat.

Bonnie stands and saunters away. She doesn't return to Ravage's blanket though; she disappears somewhere behind the tree line.

"Who brought her up here?" I ask Rooster.

He shrugs. "How the fuck would I know? Probably that dipshit." He jerks his chin at Butcher. "He brought a couple different girls up after dinner. Was trying to talk Dex into letting Bonnie audition at Crystal Ball earlier."

I blow out an annoyed breath. "That's a hard no. She'll never show up on time."

Margot squirms and wriggles out of my hold.

Why am I still babbling about Bonnie? Margot's probably pissed.

Margot

That Bonnie girl thought she was clever, but I saw right through her not-so-subtle hints. If that's the worst I have to deal with tonight, I'll be fine.

"I don't suppose there are bathrooms around here?" I dart a nervous glance into the woods.

"We're surrounded by nature." Jigsaw sweeps his hands in front of him, then winces at the horrified expression on my face. "Most of us just grab a tree."

I wrinkle my nose and stare at the tree we're currently sitting under.

"Not here." He jerks his thumb over his shoulder. "Out there."

"Come on, Margot." Shelby grabs my shoulder and uses me for leverage to pull herself out of Rooster's lap. "I ain't copping a squat in the woods, either. I'll walk back to the clubhouse with ya."

Embarrassed she'd overheard us, I open my mouth and shake my head. "I'm okay."

"Wait a second," Rooster protests. "We'll go with you." He stretches out his leg and kicks his booted foot against Jigsaw's thigh.

"We'll be fine," Shelby insists, holding out her hand to me. "We can't get lost. Path's lit all the way to the parking lot."

I take her hand and stumble away from the blanket. "I think my butt fell asleep."

"See, it's time to stretch our legs," Shelby says.

We walk past different couples getting…carried away in the woods. I avert my gaze and follow Shelby's steps. At the clubhouse, a bunch of girls, including Bonnie, are sitting on the front steps vaping and laughing. The air around them reeks of sickly sweet apples.

"Hey, Lala," Shelby says, ignoring the other two girls.

Bonnie and the other one glare at me but I follow Shelby's lead and don't say anything.

Inside the house, Shelby marches straight to the bathroom, throwing a wave at a few brothers who say hi to her. "Lala's one of the girls who usually hangs out downstate," Shelby explains. "She's nice. The other two, meh." She shrugs and pushes her way inside the bathroom.

Now that we're here, I suddenly have to pee really bad. I all but knock Shelby down to get to one of the stalls.

The sound of the door opening and closing again reaches me. A gut feeling says it's one of those girls. I wait until I hear Shelby finish, then join her at the sinks.

I'm right. The girl pretending to fix her lipstick had been sitting next to Bonnie outside. She has short black, choppy, cropped hair that drags to her shoulders in sad little wisps, and freckles dotted along her nose. She'd be cute, except for the dumbest haircut I've ever seen on a woman. I wash my hands and don't bother saying anything.

As Shelby's finishing at the sink, the girl tries to step around her.

"Don't start trouble, Dee-Dee," Shelby warns.

I turn off the water and grab a paper towel, watching their interaction in the mirror.

"What?" The girl widens her eyes to a comically innocent degree. "I just wanted to say hi. I'm trying to be friendly. I haven't had a chance to talk to Margaret, yet."

The little smirk at the corner of her mouth suggests getting my name wrong was intentional, so I don't bother to correct her.

"You can sprinkle all the sugar you want on that bullshit, Dee-Dee," Shelby wiggles her fingers in the air like she's decorating a bunch of pastries, "but you ain't gonna convince me it's an apple turnover."

I burst into laughter, then clap my hand over my mouth.

Dee-Dee frowns in confusion. "What?"

"Don't mess with my friend," Shelby warns.

"It's just so *unusual* for Jigsaw to bring a lady friend to a clubhouse party." Her voice drips with syrupy sweetness. "He usually has more than he can handle." The veneer of politeness drops from Dee-Dee's face. "That man has a large and voracious appetite. And he likes it rough, something you don't look like you'd be good at."

Vomit crawls up the back of my throat and suddenly I wish I hadn't eaten so much chili at dinner.

If Jigsaw hadn't warned me and I hadn't already practiced my fuck-off face on Bonnie, I'd probably burst into tears.

Instead, I adopt Shelby's disinterested posture and turn back to the mirror, pretending to check the makeup I'm not even wearing.

"Jigsaw almost had you banned from Downstate for tryin' to fill my ears with tales about Rooster," Shelby warns. No wonder she doesn't like this woman. "Whaddya think he's gonna do when he hears you talking trash to *his* ol' lady?"

"Don't the guys have a saying, Shelby," Dee-Dee teases in a slow, cruel tone. "Snitches get stitches?"

"Yeah?" Shelby squares her shoulders. "Well, I got my own saying—*bitches get stitches too*."

Enough of this. I whip around and pull the pocketknife Jigsaw gave me earlier free. I hook my nail in the notch, trying to casually flick it open and failing miserably. It had been so easy in the truck when my hands weren't shaking.

Finally, I open the blade and wave it in front of me.

"It's okay, Shelby." I look Dee-Dee right in her heavily made-up eyes. "Did you have something else you wanted to say to me?"

Dee-Dee shifts her gaze from Shelby to me and her eyes widen. She stumbles back a step. "Are you threatening me with a *knife* just for telling you I sucked your man's dick?"

I gag but keep the knife in front of me. "You actually hadn't said *that* part out loud yet."

She lifts her chin in defiance. Her shiny red lips part.

"Girrrl, I'd quit while you're ahead," Shelby drawls. "Margot ain't playin'."

Dee-Dee snaps her mouth shut.

"My man warned me one of you…*bunnies* might give me a history lesson," I say, proud that my voice isn't shaking. "And then tonight, he gave me this pretty, shiny new knife as a present. I wonder if the two things are related?" I cock my head and stare at Shelby.

"I'm thinking, yeah. They sure are." Shelby crosses her arms over her chest and nods.

"You see," I lift my gaze, meeting Dee-Dee's shocked eyes and give her a slightly unhinged smile. "I handle dead bodies all the time. So Jigsaw knows nothing scares me."

Dee-Dee blinks rapidly, then turns and flees, sneakers slapping and sliding over the floor. "You're both crazy!" she screams as she hits the door so hard, she leaves it swinging violently in her wake.

Shelby hoots and slaps her hands against her thighs. "Dang, you're fearless."

With the confrontation over, all my bravery drops into my boots. I click the knife closed with trembling hands. "Maybe it was a bad idea to threaten her."

What if the guys get mad and ban me *for shoving a knife in someone's face?*

"Don't start none, won't be none." Shelby dips her chin dramatically. "You didn't start it, but you sure did finish it." She wraps her hand around my arm. "I *swear* that doesn't happen all the time around here. Most of the girls are nice."

"Jigsaw *did* warn me." I shrug. "I thought Bonnie would be it, though."

Shelby's gaze shifts sideways. "Well, I wasn't kidding. Girls get banned from coming to the clubhouse if they antagonize the ol' ladies."

"I don't want to be responsible for that."

"Like I said, if she didn't start trouble, she wouldn't be in it. That's on her." She frowns and stares at the door. "To be honest, I thought Dee-Dee *had* already been banned."

The door squeaks open. *What now?* Someone else stopping by to tell me they've slept with my boyfriend?

"Ladies, everything okay?" Rooster's rumbling voice asks.

"We're good. Be out in a sec," Shelby calls out. She turns and touches my arm. "You okay?" Her lips quirk with amusement. "You're a flock-star."

Her flamingo pun is a welcome bit of comedic relief. I let out a chuckle. "Guess I ruffled a few feathers tonight, huh?"

Shelby snorts, shaking her head. "Oh, big time." She grins, eyes shining with approval. "Proud of you, girl."

"I never really stuck up for myself when I got bullied in school." I shrug apologetically, feeling kind of silly sharing this with a woman I barely know. "I'll be dammed if I'm going to put up with it as an adult."

"I hear that."

My nose wrinkles. "Is what she said even true?"

Does Jigsaw really like bitchy women with bad haircuts?

Shelby takes a deep breath. "To be honest, I don't know. I try not to pay attention to who the guys hang out with, unless it looks like it's gonna be real, ya know?"

"I guess."

"I *can* tell you, I ain't seen Jiggy with anyone for quite a while." She waves her hand through the air. "Like, way before he even came clean with me and Rooster that he was seein' ya."

"Oh." My lips form a shaky smile. "That's good, I guess."

"And now that *we're* friends, I'll surely kick his behind if I ever catch him with anyone else."

She's so tiny, the mental image of her trying to kick Jigsaw's ass would almost be funny—if it didn't sting so much.

If I ever catch him with anyone else.

She said it so casually, like she expects it to happen eventually.

Like I should prepare myself for the inevitable.

CHAPTER NINETEEN

Jigsaw

"Let's just go in and get them." I grab Rooster's arm, pulling him toward the ladies' room.

He jerks out of my hold. "Fucking relax. Shelby said they're fine." He glances over his shoulder. "Dee-Dee's gone. Pretty sure she's not coming back." He laughs. "Ever."

"She shouldn't have been up here anyway," I growl.

His casual shrug pisses me off.

"She better not have tried to tell Margot the same lies about me that she told Shelby about *you,*" I grumble.

He scowls as that memory sinks in. "Who brought her up here again?"

"That's what I'm asking *you*, VP."

He shrugs like he's completely blameless in the situation. "Serena must've told Grinder she was cool."

"Don't blame Serena." Hell, why am I taking this out on Rooster? It's my own damn fault. I should've gotten off my ass and walked the girls to the clubhouse sooner.

He sighs in exasperation. "I'm not."

Finally, the door opens. Shelby steps out first. Her gaze lands on

Rooster and she beams. Margot peeks out and gives me a sheepish sort of smile.

All the tension that gathered in my chest releases. She's fine and she's not mad.

Shelby glances toward the clubhouse living room and giggles. "Dee-Dee better've run off to warn the other bunnies that Margot is *not* to be fucked with."

"How's that?" I ask.

"I don't know." Margot shrugs and stares up at me with innocent eyes. "All I did was show her the shiny end of the pretty knife you gave me."

Rooster chokes out a confused laugh.

I stare at her. Is she serious? Fucking with me?

More importantly—is there actually a heaven? Because Margot has to be sent from above.

Margot shrugs again. Tension drags the corners of her mouth down. Shit, she's trying to act cooler than she's feeling.

I curl my arm around her waist and drag her closer. "We're going to head upstairs. I'll talk to you guys tomorrow."

"Okay," Rooster says in a *whatever* tone. "Night."

"Night, Margot," Shelby calls out.

"Thank you, Shelby," Margot says over her shoulder.

The few bunnies we pass on our way to the stairs take one look at us and avert their eyes. Maybe word has spread—my woman is ferocious. Cross her at your own peril.

I'm grinning from ear to ear by the time we reach our room. Margot, not so much.

As soon as I close the door behind us, she turns and faces me. "I shouldn't have done that." Her bottom lip wobbles. "I'm sorry."

"Done what?"

She lifts her gaze, and I can't tell if that's genuine remorse or sinister satisfaction in her eyes. I'm kind of hoping for the second one. "Threatened dumb-haircut girl with my knife."

Laughter bursts out of me. "What?"

"I don't want your brothers to be mad that I threatened someone in their clubhouse."

Ah, that's what's bothering her. Not the confrontation with the girl.

She purses her lips into a remorseful pout. "It was a little extreme."

"Yeah, I don't care about that. And no one else will either. Did you actually stab her?"

"God, no."

"Then we're good. She shouldn't have cornered you." I hold out my arms. "Come here."

She's slow, tentative to embrace me. What the fuck did that girl say to her? "Tell me what happened."

She exhales a long, slow breath and slides her arms around me, cuddling up tight. *That's better.*

"Nothing. Just implied a bunch of gross stuff about you. I don't really want to dissect the conversation." She tips her head back. "Just promise me whatever you had with any of those girls is in the past."

"Uh, I told you. There hasn't been anyone *but* you since we got together. I wouldn't lie about that, Margot."

She nods slowly. "That's what Shelby said too."

Thank you, songbird.

Doesn't matter if she trusts Shelby's word more than mine. All that matters is that she believes it. That she believes in me. In *us.*

"She won't bother you again," I promise. "Neither of them will."

She snorts and pulls away. "Why? You'll have them banned? Shelby said crooked-hair girl shouldn't have been here at all."

"Yeah. That's exactly what I mean. I'll find out who brought her and make sure it doesn't happen again."

"I don't want to be responsible for that." The corners of her mouth curl up. "Let her stay. She can spread the word to the other bunnies—you're *mine.* Period."

Holy fuck.

A slow heat rolls through me, settling deep in my bones. I've had women fight over spending time with me, eager to please me, desperate to keep my attention. But this?

This is different.

Margot isn't trying to impress me to secure a place at the clubhouse. She isn't looking for bragging rights or validation. She doesn't want to use me, then hop into bed with one of my brothers. Hell, she's not even angling for a property patch. Nope. None of that. She sees me—all of me—and wants me to be hers.

And damn if that doesn't feel better than anything else ever has.

Who knew I'd ever like the sound of a woman claiming me this much?

"I'm yours," I promise her. "Every bit of me."

"Good." I still detect a hint of petulance in her tone. Those two girls did some damage tonight. Maybe staying here isn't the best idea. Everything always seems less complicated when we're at her place.

But it doesn't work that way. I love my club and they're my family. Besides, Margot fit in perfectly tonight. "Everyone loved your story," I say. "Well, everyone who matters."

In my arms her body shakes. Shit, did I make her cry?

But no, she pulls back and she's laughing. "When Shelby warned me that Ravage likes to tell stories around the bonfire, I just *knew* if I had a chance, I wanted to tell *that* one."

"Was it true?"

Her gaze slides to our bedroom door. Instead of answering my question, she asks, "Which one is Ravage's room?"

"Uh, why?"

"Can I show you something?"

A prickling of awareness travels over the back of my neck. It can't be.

"I'm afraid to ask."

She grins even wider and tiptoes to the corner where she left her backpack. She unzips one of the front pockets. After a second or two of rummaging through the dark depths, she pulls out a black velvet satchel with a triumphant smile.

My stomach clenches. *She's fucking kidding, right?* "That's not…"

She unties the bag and pulls out the freaky statue from her story.

Solid dark wood, a little charred on one side and a bunch of nails poking out of its eyes and belly button.

I stare at it, thoroughly creeped the fuck out. “That story was *true*?”

She shrugs. “A client gave it to me. It’s kinda spooky, though. Right?”

Hail Satan, could this woman be any more perfect for me?

Uncertainty dims the excitement in her eyes when I don’t answer right away. “You also warned me that the guys might mess with me. I figured if I had the chance to tell that story, I’d leave this as a gift for one of the guys to find…” She drops her gaze. “Sorry, that’s silly and childish, huh?”

“It’s fucking perfect, is what it is.” Pure glee bubbles through my blood. This will haunt Rav for at least a few hours. Serves him right for picking on my girl the first time she visits the clubhouse. “Where should we leave it?”

“Oh, I thought right in front of his door would be funny.”

“Nah, we can do better than that.” I pull out my phone and thumb through my texts until I find the group chat with Wrath, Trinity, Murphy, Heidi, and Dex.

Me: Anyone know code to Rav’s room?

A few seconds later, Wrath comes through for me. No questions asked.

“Put her back in the bag.” I nod to the statue in Margot’s hands. “We’re taking her on a lil’ trip.”

Murphy sends a follow-up.

He’s still at the bonfire.

Perfect.

Giddy with the thought of scaring the piss out of Ravage tonight, I lead Margot out of our room and across the hallway. He’s not an officer yet, so his room’s closer to the staircase. I hurry Margot to his door, punching in the code fast, hoping to avoid anyone seeing us and ruining the surprise.

Margot giggles as I shove the door open and usher her inside.

Her laughter cuts off as I close the door behind us and flip on the overhead light.

"Goodness, I thought I was nose blind from all the chemicals I use at work, but it reeks of…" Margot wrinkles her nose in the cutest way.

"Cum and disappointment?" I suggest.

"I was going to say bodily fluids and weed." She sniffs the air again. "But yours is probably more accurate."

My gaze ping-pongs around Rav's messy room—open closet door with clothes drooping from hangers, boxers and shirts dripping from dresser drawers. Nightstand drawer open with strips of condoms dangling from all directions. "All right, where are we leaving it?" I cast another look around. "Where he'll actually see it at some point this weekend?"

She purses her lips and studies the room. "Top of the nightstand? If he comes in late, he might not notice it until morning."

"Perfect." I hold my hand out, offering her first crack at prank placement.

She plucks at a box of tissues with her thumb and index fingers, gingerly shifting it aside, then plants the statue right in front of it.

"Nice." I let out a cackle. If Rav's as drunk or high as I think he'll be when he turns in tonight, he might not notice it until morning. From the angle it's sitting, it should be the first thing Rav sees when he opens his eyes.

And to be sure he doesn't see it until the sun's up, I walk over and unplug the lamp on the nightstand. "Give me that chair." I point toward the desk.

Margot hesitates, eyeing it for a second before shifting a pile of clothes onto the floor and dragging the chair over.

"Hit the light switch," I say, stepping onto the seat.

She flicks the switch off, plunging us into darkness. A second later, the glow of her phone's flashlight slices through the shadows.

"Thanks," I murmur, carefully unscrewing the overhead lightbulb. "There. That'll keep him from seeing it until morning."

A sharp gasp. Then Margot slaps a hand over her mouth, her shoulders shaking. "Oh my God. You're evil."

While Margot keeps the room illuminated with her phone, I hop off the chair, set the bulb on the dresser, and return the chair to the desk. She sweeps the light across the space again, pausing on the statue.

"You realize he might actually destroy it when he finds it, right?" I feel compelled to make sure she's thought this through in case the creepy statue actually has some sentimental value to her. "It's not like a priceless piece of art or family heirloom, is it?"

That wicked, scheming smile spreads across her face again, lighting something warm and dangerous inside me. "It'll be fine. Don't worry."

Her grin doesn't fade as we slip back to the room we're crashing in for the night. "You're sure this is okay?" she asks. "You're not going to get into trouble with your club because of me, right?"

I've never been so sure about anything in my life—Margot Cedarwood is exactly my kind of chaos.

CHAPTER TWENTY

Jigsaw

Hours later, I'm dangling in that hazy space between sleep and wakefulness.

Faint music and chatter drift upstairs from the hardcore partygoers. Lots of times that had been me, but I'm way too content holding Margot in my arms to worry about my brothers' antics or what I'm missing out there.

"Mmm." Margot sighs in her sleep and wiggles, settling herself into the pillows and pushing her ass against me.

I have everything I need right here.

My arm's carelessly slung over her, my hand resting on her stomach. Her movements pull me away from sleep. I slide my hand lower, dipping under the waistband of her shorts to stroke her skin. So soft all over.

The next time I hover close to awake, the barest hint of dusky sunlight's peeking around the curtains. Pain in my wrist draws my attention to my hand wedged between Margot's thighs. Even in sleep I can't get enough of her. Her wetness coats my fingers and I slide them up, slowly working them around her clit.

"Mmm." She sighs and her hips twitch.

Can I make her come in her sleep?

Intent on finding out, I rub harder.

She moans louder. Her eyelids flutter and her lips part but I'm pretty sure she's still asleep.

Bam!

"Ahhh! What the fuck!?" someone screams across the hallway. "Holy shit! Holy shit!"

More heavy thuds and banging.

More screaming. "Get it away! Get it away!"

Margot startles awake and lifts her head. "I guess he found it."

I bury my face in her hair and laugh. "You're brilliant." My lips find their way to her neck and suck. "Beautiful and diabolical. So fucking perfect," I whisper against her skin, inhaling the subtle peppermint scent from the soap we'd used in the shower before bed. My dick perks up.

"Mmm," she moans and turns toward me. "I was having the best dream. What were you doing?" She squeezes her legs together, trapping my hand between her thighs.

"Trying to make you come in your sleep." I scrape my teeth lightly against her neck. "Is that okay?"

"God, yes," she breathes. "I think I was close."

I pull my hand out of her pants and drag it up under her shirt to cup her breast. She arches her back, pushing her gorgeous full breast into my hand. I flick my thumb against her hard nipple, painfully aware of the fabric in my way.

"I need this off." I tug at the hem. She sits up and I help her strip off the shirt, then I yank her shorts down. "That's my girl. Nice and naked. No more clothes on your body when we're here."

She shivers and stretches against me. "Okay."

Fuck, I don't have enough hands or tongues to touch everywhere I want to touch.

I slide my hand over her hip and down her leg.

Her body shudders as if she's close to orgasm. "If I sleep naked, will you promise to wake me up in a special way?"

"How special?" I tease my tongue over her nipple, then suck it into my greedy mouth.

She hooks one of her legs over mine. "You were on the right track."

"You're the fucking best," I groan against her throat. "Yup, spread your thighs nice and wide for me." I take my hand away to lick my thumb, then bring it to her clit. "I'd happily sleep with my cock buried in you all night."

She gasps as I shove two fingers inside her.

"Oh my God, I think I'd like that. A lot."

Slowly, I pump in and out of her. "I'm so fucking horny for you, I woke up with my hand wedged between your sweet little thighs." I kiss her breast. "I think you liked it; my fingers were soaked."

"I do," she answers in a breathy little cry. "I really do."

"Show me, then." I push deeper, curling my fingers inside her, searching for that special spot. "Come on."

She squeezes her eyes shut and shamelessly grinds herself against my hand. "Good girl." I kiss her temple and work faster, so crazed to be inside her, I might end up coming on her leg before I get the chance. She rocks her hips in time with my thrusting fingers.

Her body tightens and quivers. She tips her head back, moaning toward the ceiling, louder than she's ever been before. "That's it," I encourage.

Shrill, unintelligible shouts, followed by laughter, flow from the hallway. I can't tell—and don't care—if the sounds are directed at us or something else, I just need Margot.

"Oh, oh, oh." She clamps her thighs tight, trapping my arm. A pleasurable shiver races down my spine as she moans through her orgasm.

When she's finished, I pull my hand free, and she whimpers.

"What do you want?" I whisper in her ear. "Tell me everything you want."

Her lashes flutter and she stares up at me with desperate eyes. "Fuck me." Her husky voice is somewhere between a plea and a command.

My star student has come a long way.

Margot

While still breathless and dizzy from being woken up in the best possible way, Jigsaw climbs over me, bracing himself on either side of my shoulders. His cheeks are flushed, pupils blown wide with desire. His cock grazes my leg, and I tilt my hips, desperate to get closer.

He groans and presses just the tip inside me. "Yes, yes, yes. More," I plead, then gasp as he pushes in deeper.

"Shhh, we both know you can take all of me." He hooks one arm under my thigh, spreading me wider. "Open for me. Let me all the way in your pretty pussy." He teases his thumb against my clit, while pushing deeper. "You're so fucking wet and hot for me, aren't you?"

"Yes." I reach down and cover his fingers, pressing them against me harder.

"That's it. Show me what you like."

"You," I pant, unsure how to put it into words with my mind spinning in a thousand directions. "God, you feel *so* good."

He growls as if he's lost his last thread of control and snaps his hips forward. He grabs my other leg, holding me the way he needs, setting a steady rhythm.

"Keep rubbing your clit for me. Don't stop."

I'm frantic now, overwhelmed with him. Desperate to come again. He drags himself against a spot that curls my toes with every thrust and finally, I bow off the bed, eyes closed, throat raw from screaming.

His movements falter. "Margot. Oh, fuck." The alarm in his voice snaps my eyes open. "I forgot…a condom." His face twists with agony as he drags himself free of me. A few seconds later wet heat explodes over my hip and stomach. He groans through his release while I try to absorb his words.

"I'm sorry, baby." He kisses my cheek and reaches for the nightstand, grabbing the cloth. "I guess this came in handy anyway." He carefully cleans me up, then tosses the cloth on the floor.

"Margot?" He brushes my hair out of my eyes. "I didn't mean…I think I was still half asleep." He drops more kisses on my cheeks and shoulder. "I've never gone without one before, I swear. And I get tested before I take a fight. I've always been negative. And…I haven't been with…Margot?"

I blink and slowly sit up. "Yeah, I get tested regularly too…because of work…bodily fluids and all. But, uh, I'm not on the pill or anything." We *really* probably should've had this conversation sooner.

"What?" His eyes widen and he pulls away. "Why not?"

My jaw drops. "Excuse me?"

"Well, condoms aren't a hundred percent. Don't you think…" He scrubs his hand over his face. "Fuck."

"I hadn't been with anyone in a while, so I didn't *want* to be on it," I say through clenched teeth. "Then we…I don't know. It didn't occur to me."

"Okay." He circles his arms around my waist and drags me against his body, burying his face against my neck. "I'm sorry." He kisses my shoulder and neck. "I'm sorry," he whispers again.

Tears prick my eyes. "For?"

"For being a dick. I shouldn't have assumed. I should've asked sooner…" His gaze strays to the nightstand. "For fuck's sake they were *right* there."

His obvious frustration with himself cracks the ice around me. "I thought something felt different."

He closes his eyes. "Yup. That's my excuse for why it didn't last long."

Laughing, I press my palm against his chest and push. "Long enough to make me come twice."

He rests his chin on my shoulder and stares at me. "Where are you…" He drops his hand to my stomach. "Do we need to worry?"

I arch a brow and turn my head. "Am I ovulating? Is that what you're asking?"

He blows out an annoyed breath. "Yes, I guess that's what I'm asking."

"I don't think so." Heat blasts my skin. We've been intimate for months. There isn't a part of my body he hasn't explored. Why is this so awkward? "I can grab the morning after pill on our way home tomorrow. But I just finished my period."

"Okay. Good." He sighs and runs his hand through his hair. "Will you…keep me updated?"

I slant a look at him. "What? You want me to send you an, 'I just got my period text' or something?"

He rolls his eyes. "Yes, actually. Is that so terrible?"

"No," I whisper.

"I told you I've never…but I assume that's what a good boyfriend does? Pay attention?" He looks so frustrated, or angry with himself, like he's afraid *he* messed up somehow.

That makes it easier to admit, "I wouldn't know. I've never had a good boyfriend."

If anything, Daniel acted like I had an infectious disease and should be quarantined if I was having any "female-related issue" as he called it. *Nope.* I'm having too good of a time this weekend to even think of that man.

"Hey." I rest my hand over his and shift my gaze to the floor. "While the cum rag did its job, I still feel a little sticky. Will you take another shower with me?"

He lets out a low chuckle. "Yeah, I can do that."

After a quick shower—and another orgasm Jigsaw insisted was necessary—we're both under the covers again. His hot, naked skin pressed up against mine. He strokes his fingers along my side, lulling me into a sleepy, contented state.

"We're going to be fine. No matter what." He brushes his lips over my shoulder.

I assume he's referring to the missing condom. I can't even let myself think about that right now.

"Thank you," I whisper.

"Can I ask you something?"

Still floaty from the shower orgasm and half asleep, I'd pretty much agree to anything Jigsaw asked of me.

My lips curve into a dopey smile. "Always."

"What did your ex say to you?"

Well, that's enough to wake me right up.

I flip over and stare at him. "What?"

"Why…or how did someone make you feel like you were 'broken in the s-e-x department?' That's what you said to me." A deep frown creases his brow as he studies my face. "When you asked me for lessons? Will you tell me now?"

With one question my lovely afterglow bursts into flames of mortification.

"Why?" I yank the sheet up over my body, tucking it around my breasts. "Everything has been so nice this weekend. Why would you bring up something bad?"

"I love having you up here with everyone." He lifts one shoulder. "I thought you trusted me enough by now."

"I *do* trust you. I've told you things *much* more important than *that.* So, why does it matter?" It's not the fear of him agreeing that I'm boring in bed holding me back anymore. I can't stand the thought of him knowing that someone *else* saw me that way. I don't want to remember anything about Daniel. Especially not *now.* "Are you afraid that we wouldn't be together if I hadn't asked for your…assistance?"

His frown deepens. "Not exactly."

I trace my finger over his cheek and along his jaw. "I liked you the first time I met you."

Which *was* right after I saw Daniel and he brought up all those awful feelings for me again.

It doesn't matter.

I still liked Jigsaw when I ran into him at the wedding. Trusted him enough to make my ridiculous request. Daniel has *nothing* to do with us.

And God help me, I think I'm *in love* with him now. Even if I am too chicken to admit it and terrified he doesn't feel the same way.

He captures my hand in his and brings it to his lips, dusting a light kiss against my inner wrist. "I liked you too." One corner of his mouth slides up. "Well, I *lusted* after you. Deeply."

Daniel always made me feel as sexy as a bag of frozen cauliflower. That Jigsaw found me instantly attractive melts some of my hesitation. "Even in all my protective gear?"

"Yeah," he answers in a solemn tone. "You were so careful and caring with the person you were working on, but then you got all cute and flustered when I tried talking to you."

"You didn't *try* anything. You invaded all my senses." My lips twitch. "In an electrifying way."

"Electrifying." He nods slowly. "That's how I felt. Your eyes. They're like staring into a storm—powerful, beautiful, and possibly dangerous."

"You made me feel seen for the first time in a very long time."

He dips down and presses his lips to mine. "I see nothing *but* you."

CHAPTER TWENTY-ONE

Margot

THE NEXT MORNING AFTER THE GUYS ATTEND CHURCH, WE ALL SETTLE in for breakfast in the dining room.

Thick slices of French toast and platters of eggs, sausage, and bacon are all spread out on the table. A whiff of maple syrup tickles my nose and my stomach growls.

"Hungry?" Jigsaw asks.

"Yes." I lean up and kiss his cheek. "Someone gave me an intense workout all night long. I'm starving."

His wide grin borders on smug. "We'll bring some snacks and drinks upstairs tonight. Need to keep you fed and hydrated."

"Agreed."

When the line moves, I pick up a plate.

"What do you want?" Jigsaw asks, grabbing a set of tongs.

"I can do it."

He squeezes the tongs open and closed. "Chop, chop. We're holding up the line."

Laughing, I point to a piece of French toast. "One of everything."

He drops *two* of everything on my plate along with a heaping pile of scrambled eggs. "I'll eat whatever you don't," he promises, leaning down to kiss my cheek.

One of the guys—Hustler, I think—walks up and slaps Jigsaw's back. "Bro, do you want to have some pie with your bowl of pussywhip instead of that French toast?"

Jigsaw bares his teeth in a maniacal grin. "Tastes fucking delicious. You should try it someday."

My skin warms with embarrassment. I don't want to be the reason Jigsaw's brothers tease him. Although, the more I'm around them, it seems like they'll take any opportunity to hassle each other.

"No offense, darlin'." He winks at me before strolling away.

"Lots taken," I mutter.

Jigsaw shakes his head. "It's a compliment as far as I'm concerned." He jerks his head to the side. "Let's grab a seat."

We find our way to the same chairs we'd sat in last night. Shelby beams as I sit next to her, then winces. "Those sweet teas snuck up on me." She pokes her fork into her eggs. "I'm only eating so I can down some Advil."

"Ugh. I'm sorry." Now I'm glad I switched to drinking water last night.

Rooster sets a cup of coffee in front of her and leans over to whisper something in her ear.

"Good morning." Ravage stops behind my chair and stretches over me, slamming my statue next to my water glass with a thud against the table loud enough to draw everyone's attention to us. "I think you left something in my room last night," he announces.

I mash my lips together to stop laughter from pouring out.

"No fucking way." Z stands at the end of the table and leans forward. "It's real?"

Sparky arranges his fingers into a cross and hisses at the statue.

Jigsaw's laughter rises from a deep rumble to a high belly laugh. He rocks sideways, clutching his stomach and almost falls out of his chair.

"I take it those were *your* manly screams we all heard echoing through the hallways early this morning, Ravage?" Dex asks.

Emily glances down at her plate and snort-laughs.

"I didn't *scream*," Ravage protests.

"Uh, yeah, you did," Birch says.

I tug the black velvet satchel out of my sweatshirt pocket. "Well, thank you for finding her, I was wondering where she wandered off to." I scoop the doll up and stuff her in the pouch, securing the ties at the top.

"It scared Bonnie half to death," Ravage says. "She left."

A sly smile curves my lips. "So, it served *two* purposes."

Rav rests his hand on the back of my chair and leans over, his morning coffee breath hot against my cheek. "I play pranks too, you know."

"No, you don't." Jigsaw shoves Rav sideways. "Not on my girl."

"Oh, so she can leave that freakish statue next to my bed and mess with my nocturnal activities?" Rav throws his arms wide, laughing as he backs up a few steps. "But I can't retaliate?"

"That's right," Jigsaw confirms without hesitation.

"Those are the rules," Wrath adds, his grin wide and unapologetic.

"Why do you assume she did it and not me?" Jigsaw challenges, arching an eyebrow.

Rav smirks. "Well, all the ladies want to get into my bed..." He drags out the words before flicking a slow, exaggerated wink—one of those smug, over-the-top gestures that probably works for him fifty percent of the time.

An embarrassingly loud snort-giggle bursts out of me.

Jigsaw's mouth twitches with amusement. "You're lucky she's laughing," he mutters, his face hardening and voice carrying an edge of menace. "Or I'd choke you for even suggesting my girl wants to get anywhere near your sad, cum-soaked bed."

Now that was a little too mean. I frown at Jigsaw and give Rav an apologetic smile. "Sorry, there's only one bed I want to be in." I reach over and squeeze Jigsaw's arm to make it clear in case Ravage is slow.

"Can we see the doll?" Lilly asks.

Trinity nods. "Do you mind passing it around?"

"Not all. Just be careful, the nails are sharp and rusty." I hand the bag to Shelby on my right. She passes it to Rooster without looking inside, like it's a prop for a horror movie she'd rather not star in.

"Did it really survive the crematorium?" Teller asks.

"Awww," I protest. "You're going to unravel my story piece by piece?"

Teller lifts his head and stares at me like he expects me to come clean. I sigh. "She came to me that way. But I was told she was tossed in an incinerator and that was all the damage she sustained."

When Lilly accepts the pouch, she pulls the doll completely out. She turns the doll over in her hands, studying the smooth wood, the intricate carvings, and each rusted nail with an almost reverent curiosity. "My grandmother had something similar," she muses. "It didn't have the freakish nails poking out of it, though. She told me her mother-in-law gave it to her as a wedding gift and if she kept a clean house, it would bring good luck. *But* if the house was messy, the husband was lazy, or the kids misbehaved…" She trails off, raising an eyebrow. "It would haunt her and cause problems."

I shiver. The way she says it doesn't make it seem like a quaint folktale. More like a warning.

"That covers an awful lot of issues," Z jokes, his voice an easy rumble that cuts through the moment.

Lilly's red lips twist with humor. "Be happy that thing got lost. She wanted to pass it on to *me* when I got married. I said no thank you."

"Sounds like it would've brought us good luck," Z says, the warmth in his tone unmistakable.

She gently grips his chin, tilting his face toward her, staring at him with so much affection, I feel like we're intruding on a private moment. "I was a little girl who had *no* intention of ever getting married. If I'd known *you* were in my future, I would've accepted it."

A few guys groan. Someone makes a whip-crack noise.

Another guy mutters, *get a room.* But no one really seems cruel about it. Z's a club president, and it's obvious the guys all have a lot of respect for him. It doesn't hurt that he's utterly unapologetic about his open affection for his wife.

I glance at Jigsaw, almost expecting him to be rolling his eyes at the display.

But he's not looking at them.

He's focused on me.

A quiet warmth spreads through my chest. I reach over, sliding my hand over his knee. "They're sweet."

"Sweet's not the word I'd usually use for Z, but with Lilly, yeah."

Before I have a chance to ask anything else, a woman on the other side of the table asks, "Where did your grandmother's end up?"

"No one knew." Lilly lifts her chin in my direction and passes the statue to Z. "Now I'm wondering if it was buried with her because no one else in the family wanted it either."

A few more people inspect the statue or ask me questions about it but most just take a quick look and pass it on. Jigsaw finally hands her back to me. I lean sideways, placing her under my chair.

"Does she really live in the house?" Jigsaw asks, his voice low and skeptical.

"Of course."

The guys pounce, teasing Jigsaw for sleeping near a "murder doll."

"She's never murdered anyone," I protest, barely holding back a smile. Then, for dramatic effect, I add, "That I *know* of."

Sparky's hand shoots in the air. "Wait, wait—does this mean there isn't a haunted objects museum?"

I laugh and shake my head. "No, there is one that exists. Someone I went to school with really does run it. He didn't like the mortuary business, so he did that instead."

Sparky sighs dramatically, slumping back in his chair. "Could you imagine tripping balls in a place like that?"

Stash stares at his friend like he's lost his mind. "No fucking thanks."

Jigsaw huffs a quiet laugh beside me, sliding his hand over my thigh and squeezing. "You're full of surprises."

I lean into him. "Well, you already knew that."

Jigsaw

Everything about Margot fascinates me. Even her creepy little statue-doll that apparently lives in her house somewhere. She could have a closet full of cursed objects and tokens from her kills and it wouldn't dull what I feel for her.

I'm stopped from asking a follow-up question by Hoot and Eazy running into the dining room and tipping a laundry basket full of underwear over Birch's head.

Z and Wrath stand up and fling packages of what looks like even more underwear at Birch, hitting him in the chest.

"Ow! What the fuck?" Birch shouts through his laughter, swatting the laundry basket and underwear away. "That better be clean laundry."

June's shaking with laughter. "It is. Promise."

Wrath remains standing. "We wanted to make sure you're always covered."

"Your chilly willy story gave us nightmares," Z adds.

Brothers laugh and hurl jokes at Birch. Hope, Trinity, and Lilly are howling with laughter. Rock's just shaking his head.

"You couldn't have done this at church?" Birch protests. "You gotta embarrass me in front of all the ladies?"

"Who do you think gave them the idea?" Trinity asks.

I reach behind Margot and Shelby to tap Rooster's arm. He turns and raises an eyebrow. "Why didn't we get in on this?"

Something hard hits my arm and lands on the table. *Fruit of the Loom Men's Micro Stretch Boxer Briefs.* I glance up at Wrath's serious face.

"We tried to tell you, but the noises at *your* end of the hallway indicated you were busy." He chucks a package at Rooster who catches it mid-air.

I pick up the package and wag it in front of me. "Joke's on you. These are my size *and* my favorite color scheme."

Margot's red-faced but laughing.

Behind us, Swan carries out a tray of cookies. Lala's carrying a basket of muffins. They set them near the coffee station.

"Coffee and cookies!" Swan announces.

"You stay and check out your new underwear," Margot teases. "I'll grab a cookie for you."

"More than one."

"You got it."

I should've just gone up with her since all I do is watch her move across the room.

Something hard smacks my arm. "Ow." I turn and glare at the offender—Rooster. "Why is everyone so *violent* this morning?"

"Are you going to be at Margot's this week?"

"Probably. Why?"

"Want to meet up at Zips one of the days?"

"Maybe. I'm supposed to ride out and visit Jezzie."

He raises his eyebrows. "Yeah? Everything okay with her?"

I shrug. "Just some brother-sister bonding."

Rooster stares at me for a few seconds. "That's good. That'll be good for both of you."

Uncomfortable talking about this here, I just nod.

Shelby and Margot return, putting an end to the discussion.

Margot rests her hand on my shoulder and leans so close her warmth washes over my cheek. Her lips brush my ear, sending a shiver of contentment over my skin.

"Here you go." She sets a small plate of chocolate chip cookies in front of me. The chocolate chips are still shiny and look warm and gooey.

I pull Margot into my lap, curling my arm around her waist. "Thank you."

The chatter around us cuts out. I pick up my head. Everyone's staring at us.

"What?" I snap.

"Bro, are you actually smiling?" Hustler asks like he's ready to call an ambulance and have me transported to the closest emergency room.

"Yeah…" Butcher elbows Hustler and frowns at me. "It's not that scary serial killer smile he usually wears," he murmurs just loud enough for everyone to hear.

"Oh my God, are you *happy*?" Hustler yells.

I level a bored, dead-eyed stare at Butcher, then Hustler. "You blow more hot air than two hamsters farting in a wool sock, you know that?"

The whole table erupts into laughter. Some of the guys return to poking fun at Birch for the willy story.

I still can't believe he willingly shared that with everyone. They'll never stop bringing it up. You couldn't have water-boarded that story out of me.

"How does it feel to be one of the *castrated brethren* now, brother?" Dex asks with a shit-eating smirk.

Fuuuck, I should've known Karma would come to collect for all the times I've thrown that joke around.

I lift my coffee mug and return the smug expression. "Warm and delicious, thanks."

Dex throws his head back, laughing like a big brother proud to witness his little bro choke down a big slice of humble pie. *Dickhead.*

Shaking her head, Margot slides out of my lap and into her chair.

"I'm going to refill my coffee." I pick up my cup, then hover my hand over hers. "You want?"

"Sure."

I stand, then lean over to whisper in her ear, "Don't eat my cookies while I'm gone."

"Or… you could bring more back with you." Staring at me with a dead-serious expression, she slowly reaches for the plate, grabs a cookie, and takes a big, obnoxiously sexy bite.

Fucking hell.

"I'm going to do very dirty things to you later," I promise.

She licks a crumb from her lip, as if daring me to make good on that threat.

My little lady death will be the death of me yet. "I have better uses for that tongue."

She licks her lips again. "Can't wait to hear them."

I shake my head and turn toward the coffee station, weaving between a few people on my way. The long folding table is stocked with white mugs, a few carafes, and cartons of creamer. I set my cup down and pick up a carafe.

Shelby slides in beside me, nudging me with her hip.

"I thought I'd never get ya alone," she teases.

I arch a brow, keeping one eye on the cup so I don't end up spilling coffee everywhere. "Oh yeah?"

She grabs a mug and a paper napkin. "I like Margot. A lot."

A warm grin spreads over my face. Not that I need Shelby's approval—but I still like hearing it. "Yeah?"

"Oh, yeah. And she sure seems sweet on you." She squeezes my arm.

"You think so?"

"I can tell." She rests her hand over her heart. "No tarot cards necessary." A devilish grin lights up her face. "And even if my intuition *was* on the fritz—that knife she pulled on Dee-Dee was a dead giveaway."

I can't hide my smirk. I'm not even one bit upset Margot did that. "Our energies match, right?"

"I'd say so." The smile melts off her face. "I like that for you, Jiggy. You *should* be with a woman who wants to fight for you. Who's proud to be with you and *only you*."

I can't tell if this is secret code for she's glad I'm no longer interested in her mom, or if she never approved of me hanging around with muffler bunnies. I like what she's saying too much to ask for clarification. "I really, *really* like her, Shelby."

"I can tell." She cocks her head, her serious eyes drilling into me. "I like her too, Jiggy." She steps closer and lowers her voice. "So, I wanna be straight with you, bestie."

"About what, songbird?" Amusement colors my voice. I love when Shelby's serious about something.

She flicks her gaze to the crowd around the coffee and clamps her hand over my arm, tugging me to a less busy corner of the room. "You know I love you, right?"

"You just dragged me away from my coffee, so I'm not sure."

"Jiggy, I'm serious!" She blows out a breath. "You're such a good friend to Logan." She touches her chest. "And to me. So please understand what I'm about to say comes from a place of love."

Feeling less amused now. "Go on."

"If I ever catch you with one of those bunnies…or anyone else… ever again, I will kick your ass to hell and back."

There's a cute image. "That right?"

"Yup." She nods once, one hundred percent not fucking around. "And I don't care what Rooster says or what club code is, I'll tell Margot. I ain't playin', Jiggy."

"There's something so heartwarmingly adorable about a tiny woman threatening me." I rub my hand over the top of her head and laugh when she swats me away.

"I'm *not* that tiny." She stomps her foot the way she does when she's really steamed. "And I'm not kiddin'."

"I know you're serious." I exhale a long breath. "I *could* be insulted you think so low of me."

Her jaw drops for a moment, then she shakes it off. "I think the best of you, and I *want* the best for you, but—"

"I've run my mouth a lot."

She rolls her eyes and adds a head roll for dramatic effect. "A lot."

I drop the joker act. "I like her, Shelby. More than any other woman I've ever known." I wave my hands in front of me, trying to force my brain to shove the right words into my mouth. "I can actually see a future with her. Like, I can't picture *not* having her in my life. Ever. That's never happened to me before."

"Awww." Her forehead wrinkles like she's about to burble baby talk to a fluffy puppy.

I lean down and keep my voice low. "I like her so much, I'm scared shitless she's going to wake up one morning and realize she can do better than me." I can't believe out of all the people I could've admitted that to, it's Shelby.

"Jiggy," she sighs and wraps her arms around my middle, giving me a quick hug. "That's not gonna happen. There's no one better."

"You just threatened to kick my ass," I remind her.

"Well." She pats my chest and tilts her chin up. "I apologize."

"Not a fan of whatever's going on here," Rooster's voice cuts in.

"Stop." Shelby releases me and steps back. "We were just having a chat."

I point at Shelby. "She threatened me with bodily harm."

"Tattletale." She smacks my side and gives me a playful scowl.

Rooster narrows his eyes at both of us, then shakes his head and focuses on Shelby. "Do I even want to know?"

Shelby grins, linking her arm through his. "You already know."

Rooster nods, like they'd been up all night plotting what she wanted to say to me.

"I don't like being the topic of your conversations," I say.

Rooster snorts. "You're really surprised? She's been buzzing about this since your tarot reading."

So glad I can provide entertainment for them. Shaking my head, I return to the bar, grabbing our coffees, a muffin, and a handful of cookies.

I *am* insulted Shelby thinks I might cheat on Margot. But I understand it.

If only she understood, infidelity isn't what scares me.

What if Margot wakes up one day and realizes she's made a mistake? That a man like me doesn't fit into her life.

I'd never cheat on her. I'm in control of my dick. I care about Margot too much to ever hurt her like that.

It's all the other darkness that lives inside me I'm worried about.

CHAPTER TWENTY-TWO

Margot

Sunday morning, the clubhouse is quieter. Jigsaw said most of the guys from downstate went home. Dex and Ravage went to work their shifts at Crystal Ball.

We say goodbye to Rooster and Shelby after breakfast. She hugs me extra tight, murmuring a promise to check in soon. I feel like I've actually made a friend this weekend and I'm sad to see her go.

In the living room, Teller, Charlotte, and their twins are sprawled on the sectional with Rock, Hope, and their daughter Grace.

Grace can't stop staring at the babies, her little face scrunched in determination as she repeatedly asks to hold one. Finally, she settles into Rock's lap, and he helps her cradle the girl twin.

"They're so cute," I whisper to Jigsaw.

He nods slowly. "We sure have had an explosion of babies in the club lately."

His tone isn't exactly full of joy for his brothers.

It's way too soon to ask him how he feels about having kids. And I think I already have my answer based on the way horror washed over his face when I said I wasn't on birth control.

"Hey, Margot." Hope waves at me. "Hey, Jiggy."

Rock glances up. "You two heading out?"

"In a little bit," Jigsaw answers.

I drift closer to Charlotte. "I haven't really had a chance to see the twins. Is it okay if I say hi?"

The words stumble out awkwardly. I'm not technically family. Is this weird to ask?

"Of course." She shifts closer to her husband, patting the empty space beside her. "Come sit."

"This is Ivan." Charlotte gently rocks her son in her arms. Up close, I notice his navy blue onesie is covered in tiny chickens. I flick my gaze to the other baby. She's wearing a teal onesie with pink flamingos.

"I feel like these outfits were gifts from Rooster and Shelby?"

Teller rumbles with laughter. "What gave it away?"

Instead of sitting next to me, Jigsaw's standing at the end of the couch. Watching from a distance.

He'd been so cute with the older kids the other night.

Do babies make him nervous? Or is it the unprotected sex making him uncomfortable?

Hope stands and moves closer to us. Teller leans in.

The way everyone's watching me so closely, maybe I should've waited until later to ask to hold the babies. Charlotte doesn't seem to mind. She's already focused on transferring baby Ivan into my arms.

A soft, warm weight settles against me, heavier than I expected.

"Aren't you a cutie," I coo, adjusting my grip. "A big boy, too."

Ivan blinks up at me, tiny feet kicking, happy little noises burbling from his lips.

"His sister's gaining on him," Teller says. "Right, Grace?"

Rock's daughter grins and bobs her head up and down.

After a few minutes, Grace peeks over at us, like she's suspicious that she's missing out on the more interesting twin. "Ivan." She points.

"You wanna trade?" Teller asks.

She nods quickly.

Teller gently shifts his daughter into his arms and gives me an apologetic smile. "Switch?"

"Sure."

He smoothly scoops Ivan from me, then carefully places Ivy in my arms.

Ivy's quieter, her body smaller but solid, her serious blue eyes studying me like she's trying to decide if I'm worthy.

"I'm not sure she likes me," I whisper.

"Nah, she's suspicious of everyone at first," Teller says. "Just like her mom."

"True," Charlotte laughs. "Do you want kids, Margot?"

I tear my gaze away from Ivy and search for Jigsaw.

Good Lord, we haven't been dating long enough to field that kind of question. I find him standing just outside the circle around me, his eyes round with…terror? Whatever it is, it doesn't look like the expression of a man eager to leave a genetic legacy behind.

Ivy sighs softly, her tiny body going limp against my chest. As if she's decided I'm a safe place to take a snooze. I graze my knuckle against her peachy-soft cheek.

"I haven't given it a lot of thought. Someday. Yes," I whisper. Heat burns my eyes, and I tilt my head, focusing on Ivy.

Do I want kids? Babies are cute, sure. But they only stay babies for a little while. Would I want to raise kids in the same house I grew up in? With all the weirdness and death surrounding them, the way it's surrounded me my whole life.

No.

The thought—the absolute conviction behind it—steals my breath.

No.

Even before I met Jigsaw, when I pictured a theoretical husband, our future children, I never once imagined us living in that house.

What would I do? Buy a house nearby? Commute to work?

I've never lived anywhere else.

Dad bought the property next door and moved himself out. But that was after I finished school, and he knew at least one Cedarwood would be in the home.

Would he be devastated if I left?

"See, she trusts you," Charlotte says gently.

"They're so adorable," I whisper. "How do you get anything done? I'd be busy staring at them all day."

"We don't," Teller says. "They never seem to want to sleep at the same time."

"Twins are a two-person job," Charlotte says. "I don't know how anyone handles triplets or more."

"Hush, woman," Teller scolds with a teasing lilt in his voice. "Don't jinx us."

Charlotte laughs. "I'm happy and blessed we have our two. I'm *not* ready for any more." She reaches up and squeezes Hope's hand. "You and Rock have been lifesavers, though. Everyone's been amazing but…"

Hope leans down and hugs Charlotte.

Ivy stirs, her delicate features tightening. She blinks, then her mouth works like she's preparing for a full-blown scream.

Charlotte immediately leans forward. "I can take her, Margot."

I carefully transfer Ivy back to her, and the baby instantly settles.

My lips form a weak smile. "Thanks."

"No, thank *you*." Charlotte rolls her shoulders back. "Feels like I've been holding a baby non-stop some days." She flicks an amused glance at Teller. "We trade off when we need to."

"You're doing all the hard stuff," he says in a low voice.

"I want to see." Grace places one hand on my leg and climbs onto the couch, wiggling herself into the space between Charlotte and me.

"Grace," Hope says. "Say *excuse me* to Margot."

"Or even a hello would be nice," Rock adds.

Grace turns, peering up at me with wide eyes and a sheepish smile. "Hi, Maw-go. Dis my cousin." She proudly points to Ivy.

"I bet you guys are going to have a lot of fun together when she's bigger."

She bobs her head up and down enthusiastically.

I lift my gaze, expecting to find Jigsaw.

But he's gone.

CHAPTER TWENTY-THREE

Jigsaw

Nope, nope, nope.

Why the fuck did Charlotte ask Margot about having kids now?

Seriously?

Fuck.

I stab my fingers through my hair as I walk down the hall into the dining room. Coffee. I'll say I just left to get some coffee.

Although, it would've been nice if I'd asked Margot if she wanted something before I ran away like a—

Like a coward.

Like a man who just got hit with a question he's got no fucking answer for.

I grab the coffeepot, pouring a cup I don't even really want, scowling into the dark liquid.

I didn't just run away from the conversation.

I ran away from her *answer*.

Wrath's at a table in the dining room by himself—for now. I take a quick look around. I won't get a better opportunity to talk to him than this.

Am I really going to Wrath for advice? Christ, I'll never live this down. I'd ask Rooster but he and Shelby seem to be in the "not right now" stage of the kids discussion. Wrath and Trinity seem to firmly be in the "no fucking thank you" stage.

"Hey, I thought you went to work today?" I ask as I approach. Casual. Just having a casual conversation with my brother. Not at all freaking out.

"I made Murphy go open for me." He grins and takes a sip of coffee. "Heading out in a bit."

"Can I talk to you for a second?"

He sets his coffee down and turns his cell phone over. "What's on your mind, brother?"

Christ, I must look really rattled.

Fuck it.

I pull out the chair next to him and sit down.

"You and Trin are pretty firm on the 'no kids' thing, right?" I ask, deciding to just go for it. Circling the question will just piss Wrath off.

"Yeah," he answers slowly, his sharp gaze searching mine.

"You both don't want them, right?"

Wrath's head tilts slightly. Only this big fucker can express sarcasm with a head tilt.

"What?" He lifts both blond eyebrows, his slow question edged with dry amusement. "Trinity's a woman, so she must want babies?"

I scrub my hand over my jaw. "That's not quite what I meant."

"Neither of us want them," he says. "We talked about it before we got married. I think we were both relieved." He lifts his massive shoulders. "Every now and then we check in with each other." His face breaks into a wide grin. "Or we see what the others are going through." He lifts his chin toward the living room. "And we look at each other and say, 'thank fuck we're not doing *that*.'"

I snort with laughter, thinking of the few times I've caught them exchanging that exact look.

"What's wrong?" He nods toward the living room again. "Did Margot stop to see the twins and it freaked you out?"

"Yeah, kinda," I admit. Why the fuck else would I be asking?

"Did you bother to talk to Margot about what *she* wants?"

"Didn't occur to me until, well, this weekend."

"You don't want *any*?"

I open my mouth, then stop. "I grew up in a really fucked-up household."

He hums with a sound of commiseration.

"My father was a religious nut," I continue, "and since I don't believe there's a magical sky daddy watching my every move, I'm not worried I'll whip them raw to save their souls or anything but…" I can't believe I put my feelings into such visceral words.

Wrath nods, like he understands exactly what I mean. "You don't want to risk taking out that anger on your kid?"

"Yeah."

He's shaking his head before I finish. "I've seen you in some stressful situations. Fucked-up shit that would test a lot of people. You're a sick, bloodthirsty fucker for sure, but only to people who deserve it. Otherwise, I suspect Ravage and Eazy would be missing a few fingers by now."

"Appreciate you acknowledging my bloodthirsty side."

"We all have one." He rolls his eyes. "Obviously. But some people can't turn that shit off at home. I think you're very aware of the difference." He cocks his head, studying me with the same kind of scrutiny as a researcher in a lab full of rats. "I've seen you on the road. On tour, the way you looked after Shelby. Hell, the way you're so protective of her here. And I've always watched you treat club girls with respect."

My lip curls. "I'm not getting the comparison."

He blows out an annoyed breath. "You're not a shitty human that takes advantage of people weaker than them. Hell, the fact that you haven't run Remy over yet tells me you have a metric fuck ton of patience."

I snort with laughter. "True."

Another question forms in my mind.

Fuck, he's really not going to like this one. "What if one of those times you check in with Trinity she changes her mind?"

But instead of angry, Wrath looks pained. He glances over his shoulder like he wants to be sure Trinity's nowhere in the vicinity. "I don't know. Before we got married…it would've been a deal-breaker for me. Now…I don't know. I think I'd do anything she asked of me."

We sit in silence for a few seconds, then his lips tilt into a half smile. "Nah, I don't have to worry about that. Before you guys got here the other night, Teller shared a charming tale of little Ivan pissing in his face during a diaper change. Trin gagged more than she laughed at that one."

Checkmark in the no-thank you column.

"I'm sure *you* laughed your ass off." I snort.

A wide grin stretches across his face. "With all the shit that's come out of Teller's mouth over the years, having his son pee in his face feels like Karmic justice or something."

Harsh laughter bursts out of me. "You're evil."

"Seriously, though," he says. "I get what you're saying about your family." He takes a deep breath, the lines on his forehead shifting down. "But for some people, having your *own* family, doing it right and with the right person…it can be healing in a way? Murphy and Heidi both had shit parents, and it's just made them determined to do everything right with their kids. Give them the childhood they never had, you know?" He waves a hand toward the door. "In fact, they're *all* doing that. Every one of us comes from one fucked-up situation or another."

"It seems wrong to use my kids as an experiment, though," I point out. "Like, spit some out and hope I don't fuck them up."

"Yeah, well, that's why if you're going to have kids, you need to have them with a good partner. Margot seems kind and she must have a deep well of patience to put up with *you*," he finishes with a smirk.

"Yeah," I scoff. "Thanks."

His lip curls. "Would she still want to live in the funeral home, though? If you two…" He waves his hand in front of him as if he's trying not to spook me by saying the words *married* or *kids.*

Would she?

"I don't know. Like I said, it's not something we've talked about, yet." I roll my shoulders back. "I didn't think…I never thought I'd—"

"I get it. For what's it's worth," he says, "Margot's special. Good ol' lady material."

I blink and sit back in my chair. I don't think Wrath's ever "pre-approved" an ol' lady before. "You think so?"

"Hell yeah. She handled herself well with the guys." His lips twist with amusement. "Heard she stood up for herself with your muffler bunny fan club too."

"Bro, I swear I didn't give her that knife thinking she'd have to use it here."

He slaps his hand on the table. "Seriously, if you really don't want kids, don't do it. There's enough unwanted, fucked-up people on this planet. Don't let anyone pressure you into it. But you should probably have that conversation sooner than later, yeah?"

My throat's too tight to answer, so I nod.

"It might not be easy but if you both want different things…"

We should go our separate ways.

Unthinkable.

"Thanks, brother." I hold out my hand and he takes it, pulling me in for a shoulder bump. "I know this was kinda weird. Didn't mean to get so personal. Appreciate you listening and your advice."

"Don't mention it." He scowls and tightens his grip, nailing me in place. "Seriously. *Don't* mention this conversation to anyone. I don't need all our brothers thinking Daddy Wrath is handing out life advice. The rest of 'em need to keep annoying Rock with their dilemmas."

Daddy Wrath. The joke's practically writing itself. But if I utter it, I risk him snapping my wrist like a chicken bone. "I'll keep your secret, Papa Wrath."

He snarls and releases me with a sharp shove.

Then, after a beat, he nods once. Like he has one more piece of wisdom to share. "You're not your father, Jigsaw. Ignore whatever fucked-up shit is still lingering in your head from your childhood and listen to what I'm telling you. You're not an abuser. You're a protector."

The words hit hard.

I respect Wrath's opinion. A lot.

But I wonder if he'd still feel that way if he knew how I abandoned my little sister and left her with my monster of a father.

CHAPTER TWENTY-FOUR

Margot

Later in the afternoon, we return to our room to pack up our stuff. I take a quick shower and wrap myself in a towel. As I step out of the bathroom with my toiletries in my hand, I find Jigsaw at the closet, flipping through the few items I'd hung up Friday night.

I stop and stare at him. "Why are you looking through my clothes?"

Jigsaw tugs a garment off one of the hangers, leaving it swinging on the bar, and turns to face me.

"I saw this." He holds up the one dress I brought in case Saturday dinner was a more formal affair. It's nothing fancy. Black flowy material with white roses dotted over it and a row of buttons down the front.

"I think it'll be a little small on you but give it a try." I giggle and drop my stuff on the end of the bed.

"Margot." He draws out my name in a seductive, teasing tone. "You have any idea how many times this weekend I've thought about getting you alone in the woods while you're wearing one of your sexy dresses?"

The simmering desire in his eyes and his low voice spikes my pulse. "Not as many times as I have."

He hums a low, delicious sound of disagreement and slowly shakes his head. "No. In my version, I'm chasing you, and when I catch you, I fuck you so hard you scream loud enough to chase the birds from the trees."

"Oh." I gasp. A vivid picture slides through my mind and my core throbs with approval. "I like your version."

"Great." He tosses the dress on the bed. "Put it on."

I reach for the dress, dragging it closer. "Now?"

"Look at me." His voice is low and commanding.

I shift my gaze from the dress to him.

"Right fucking now."

My fingers tighten around the fabric, anticipation coiling through me as all the different ways this will play out flicker through my mind.

"Uh, those are really sexy on you." I nod to his simple black sweatpants, hanging low on his hips and doing nothing to hide the sharp cut of his V-line. Bare-chested, every carved muscle and inch of inked skin stands out. The ridges of his abs, the flex of his shoulders. Standing so casually yet looking effortlessly lethal.

Who knew sweatpants could be such a turn-on?

He lowers the waistband and grips his hardening length, showing off. "Easier to free my cock." He snaps the waistband into place. "Now, hurry up." He reaches into the dresser drawer and tosses a bra and panty set to me.

Keeping my gaze fixed on him, I drop the towel.

His chest rises and falls faster.

I slowly slip on my bra and clasp it into place. My hands shake as I step into my panties and drag them up my legs.

"I usually wear something else under my dresses," I admit, embarrassment nudging my desire aside. "I'll feel a little naked in just this underneath."

"Like what?"

I point to the dresser. "Little shaper shorts." I rub my hand over my tummy and hips. "To smooth everything."

"Margot, it's just you and me. Going to play in the woods." He slides his hot gaze over my body. "And I love your *everything*."

I open my mouth to protest, but why? We're about to indulge in a mutual fantasy and I'm worried about my tummy bulge?

Without another word, I slip the dress over my head and carefully work each tiny button closed.

The scrape of a dresser drawer pulls my attention up. Jigsaw takes out a dark blue hooded sweatshirt. He slings it over his arm. "I'm bringing this just in case."

"Just in case what?"

"Your dress doesn't survive."

It takes a second for his meaning to sink in. "Oh." I stare down at the black floral pattern and shrug. It's for a good cause.

"One more thing." He picks up the little pink bottle of warming lube on the nightstand. The click of the cap seems louder than it should. "Lift your dress for me."

"What? Why?"

He tilts his head and stares at me until I comply.

I drag it up slowly, the soft fabric rustling against my legs.

"Higher."

I bunch it around my waist.

"Good." He steps closer and dribbles a few beads of the clear fluid on his fingers. "Let's spice things up a little."

"You're about to chase me through the woods and mount me like a wild animal. Already seems kind of spicy."

"Funny." He slips his hand into my panties. I inch my feet apart and tilt my hips without him even asking. He inhales a deep, shuddery breath. "Good girl. You're as eager to try this as I am."

I lick my lips, then gasp as he gently rolls his slippery fingers around my clit. I'm already so worked up, dizzy, and excited, it doesn't take long to bring me close to orgasm.

"Not yet." He withdraws his hand and kisses my cheek.

"That's mean." I rub my thighs together. "I don't feel anything...different."

He glances at the bottle. "I don't want to use too much the first time we try it. In case it's too intense for you."

"Intense?" I raise my eyebrows. Why hadn't I thought of that?

He turns the bottle toward me, so I can read the label. "It's supposed to be edible. If it starts to bother you," his voice lowers to a deep rasp, "I'll lick off every drop."

My knees buckle.

He grabs a strip of condoms from the nightstand and shoves them in his pocket. "Don't want to forget these."

I almost open my mouth to say, *since we already forgot them once this weekend, why ruin the fantasy*? But after the way he reacted to me holding the babies earlier, it doesn't seem like something to joke about.

Instead, I slip my sneakers on while he shrugs into a T-shirt.

"Let's go." He opens the door.

Downstairs, we run into Sparky and Stash, hanging out in the living room. I feel like I have a glowing sign above my head that announces *off to fornicate in the woods.*

But Jigsaw's smooth and calm. He gives them a casual greeting and keeps right on walking toward the front door.

As we step outside, warmth spreads from my center. More than what I already feel. "I think it's starting to do something."

Jigsaw stops at the bottom of the stairs. "Good something or bad something?"

My eyebrows draw together in concentration. "Good for now."

"Okay."

Jigsaw glances inside the big garage. None of the trucks or SUVs that had been in it Friday night are there now. He keeps moving toward the same path we took to the bonfire.

When we reach the cinder block circle and charred remains, he stops.

"You ready?" He cups my face and presses a gentle kiss to my lips, stealing my answer.

The warmth and tingling intensify. Is it the arousal gel, or just him?

Breathless, I pull away.

"Do we need some rules?" I ask, my voice quivering with excitement. "Are you going to count to ten? Your legs are a lot longer than mine. To make it fair, you should give me a good head start."

"Margot, it's just a game." He strokes his knuckles over my cheek. "It doesn't matter where you run or how fast. We both know when I catch you, I'm going to fuck you," he says in the most maddeningly seductive tone possible. "That's the only rule."

Need throbs between my legs. If he keeps talking to me like that, I won't be able *to* run. This clearing actually looks like a perfectly good spot. He could sit with his back to that tree while I pull my dress up, straddle his lap and…

He sets his hands on my shoulders and turns me around. "If you go up this hill and to the right, you'll eventually come to a clearing where there's a semi-circle of tiered stone benches and a big slab of stone."

I peer at him over my shoulder. "Sounds very Roman Empire."

His lips tilt. "*If* you make it that far. Don't keep going. The path will narrow again and hook up with the trail that leads right to the parking lot."

"Wait, what if someone sees us?"

He tilts his head toward the path. "Garage was empty. They brought the kids down to Teller's earlier. Wrath went to work." He shrugs. "I don't think anyone goes out there unless there's a formal event or something."

Wow, he gave this a lot of thought. My desire ratchets up about a thousand degrees. "But you don't know for sure…"

"That'll be part of the fun."

I frown, hating that I'm asking this. "You've never done this before, right?"

"No." He shakes his head. "You're the only woman I've ever wanted to chase." He presses his lips to my ear. "To hunt down. Fuck like a savage. Only you."

I'm breathing hard but my nose tingles, like I'm on the verge of crying for some reason. How can something so crude also be so sweet?

He squeezes my hips, then releases me, almost like a wild animal he's setting free.

That's exactly how I feel as my feet start moving. *Wild.* Absolutely nuts. A little silly. And frantically praying he catches me soon.

My sneakers crash and pound over the mossy earth. My pulse is so loud in my ears, it feels like I'm covering more ground than I actually am. I'm tingling all over. Desperate for him to catch me but also afraid of our game ending. My heart's on fire.

How long will he wait before coming after me?

The crunch of a stick echoing behind me propels my feet faster.

Don't look back.

Another snap of a branch.

I squeal and dodge around trees, leap over branches, and skitter over pine needles.

But I keep going.

More crashing through the woods. Leaves crunching. Twigs cracking.

Heavy footsteps accelerating.

My heart pounds.

My clit throbs.

The clearing Jigsaw mentioned must be ahead. Tall, gray stones and overgrown grass are just barely visible through the trees.

Will I make it?

My body trembles with the thrill of being captured. Can't wait to feel his arms around me. But I still keep running.

He's close.

So close, his heavy breathing is a growl in my ear.

He's right behind me!

He slams into my back, the force knocking the breath from my lungs. His arms wrap tight around my waist, stopping me from falling forward. A squeak of surprise bursts past my lips. He's a solid wall of muscle against my back. Strong enough to lift me off the ground, while my legs flail in the air.

"Gotcha," he says against my ear. He noses my hair out of his way and licks the sensitive spot between my neck and shoulder, then grazes his teeth against my skin. "You gave a good chase."

What a liar, he's barely out of breath and I can't catch mine.

He carries me easily to a small rectangle of blue stone at the base of a tree—only large enough to be a bench for woodland fairies or a resting spot for a bunny.

"Put your feet down." He lowers me until my toes touch the rock. It's just big enough for my sneakers, leaving my heels hanging off the edge a bit. "There you go. Good girl." He pats my behind.

He gently presses his hand between my shoulder blades. "Brace yourself."

I grasp the trunk, my nails scratching against rough bark.

He kneels behind me and slowly lifts my dress, trailing kisses behind my knees and higher. I shift my feet, embarrassed my thighs are so slick. I moan and shiver with excitement when he hooks his fingers in my underwear and drags them down to my knees.

He brushes his lips against the backs of my legs, then slides his hand between my thighs.

"Fuuuck," he breathes out. He teases his finger along my slit. "You're so wet. You liked being chased?"

"Only by you." I sag against the tree, hugging it more than bracing myself against it. "I want you so much." I don't even care how desperate I sound.

"That's good." There's a crinkling and rustling of fabric. "Because I'm so fucking hard for you." He taps my hip. "Stick your ass out for me a little more."

He nudges my entrance with his cock and I gasp, lifting on my toes.

"Easy," he warns, sliding in slow. Taking his sweet time. He groans and curses. Rough fingers dig into my hips.

With the first hard push, my cheek scrapes bark, and I wince. "Ow."

"Aw, shit." He pulls out. "Come here." He captures me around the waist again, bunching my dress up against my stomach while he carries me away from the tree.

I kick my legs, my underwear falling to my ankles. Keeping me tight to his body with one arm, he slips one hand between my legs.

"Look at you showing off your pretty pussy to the entire forest," he teases as he strokes two fingers over my clit.

A mixture of laughter and moaning bubbles out of me.

The man must have abs, glutes, and quads of steel. He lowers us to the ground where I end up on top of him, then quickly rolls us. Keeping one arm under my head, protecting me from the ground, he hooks his other one behind my knee, spreading me wide. He settles between my thighs and thrusts in all the way.

"Oh!" I yelp.

"Take it." He covers my mouth with his, kissing me deep.

I wrap my arms around his neck and my other leg around his waist. He hums encouraging noises into my mouth, his tongue licking and stroking mine. He breaks away panting, staring down at me with an absolutely feral gleam in his eyes.

"Tell me you like this." He pumps in and out of me at a frantic pace. "You like your man hunting you down." His thrusting slows but he stops to grind himself into me. "Fucking you out in the open."

"Yes, yes, yes." My hands fall to his shoulders.

He growls and slides his hand out from under my head. I fall back on soft earth and stare up at him as he gathers my wrists in one hand and pins them above me.

"Yes." His eyes widen with satisfaction. "That's nice." He releases my leg.

"Please," I whisper. "I want to come."

He kisses my forehead. "Come, baby." He squeezes my thigh. "Lock your legs around me."

I lift my hips and cross my ankles, finding a new delicious angle. With my arms still pinned, I use my legs for leverage, working myself against him.

"That's it," he encourages. His fingers play with the buttons of my dress. They're too tiny to undo one-handed. He dips down and bites at the fabric, tearing at it with teeth and fingers until buttons go flying. He scrabbles with the cup of my bra, tugging it down until he frees one breast.

His desperation to see my body outside in broad daylight triggers something deep inside me. My thighs tremble.

"Fuck yes," he growls as he sucks my nipple between his lips and flicks his tongue against the tip. The zip of electricity from the wet suction of his mouth travels straight to my core. Brutal pleasure throbs from my clit, spreading down my legs and through my body. I spasm around him so hard, he groans.

The sensations intensify. I grunt and scream with the overwhelming, painful pleasure.

"That's it," he groans. "Come for me. Be as loud as you want. I got you."

The pressure builds and builds, another scream ripping from my throat. A sound unholy in its intensity. Terrifying. I've never been comfortable being loud or demanding in any way. But I can't stop.

The contraction doesn't end—it subsides, then intensifies. It goes on and on, leaving me shaking and tears spilling from the corners of my eyes.

I'm gasping for breath when Jigsaw releases my wrists and rolls us until I'm on top of him.

"Fuck yeah," he groans and yanks my dress open wider, frees my other breast from my bra. "Don't stop moving." He squeezes my thighs. "Ride me like a good girl."

"I…I…I…am." I gasp and shudder, pressing my palms flat against his abdomen and working my hips like a maniac. "Oh!" My body stretches tight and slows. Bone-melting bliss soars through me.

Jigsaw groans and clamps his hands over my hips, rocking me up and down. His body shakes and jerks under me as his release hits him.

I grin like an idiot when his eyes finally drift open. I've never been so thoroughly pleased with myself. This strong man who effortlessly chased me through the woods and manhandled my body is now spent and shaking beneath me.

He cups my cheeks. "Dream come true."

Me, or what we just did? "That was…I don't know. You fucked the words out of me." Giggling, I fall against his chest. He wraps his arms around me and kisses the top of my head.

"I don't know if I can move," he mumbles after a few heartbeats of silence.

"I didn't hurt you, did I?" The angle his body's sprawled on the ground at doesn't seem comfortable or supportive.

"No." He grabs my elbow, lifting my arm and inspecting my skin. "Did I hurt *you*?"

I roll my wrists a few times. "No." I stretch my neck and kiss along his jaw. My body's buzzing and languid at the same time.

I sit up and carefully disentangle myself from him, kneeling awkwardly on the ground by his side.

"Sorry about your dress." He grips the edges and tries to close it but without the buttons it hangs loose. The satisfied grin on his face sort of negates the apology.

Laughing, I tuck my breasts back into my bra. "You *did* warn me." One bra strap loosens and swings free. "Oh no." I gasp and giggle at the same time.

"And your bra." He reaches for my hair, plucking leaves, twigs, and pine needles from it.

He sits up and carefully tugs off the condom and rolls his pants up in a move that shouldn't be as sexy as it is. Everything this man does makes me want to jump on him.

"Give me a second." Twigs snap and leaves crinkle as he walks into a grove of trees.

"You don't happen to see my panties anywhere, do you?" I call out.

His warm, rumbling laughter floats back to me.

The sweatshirt he brought is mashed flat against the ground. At least his back had some protection while I rode him like a crazed cowgirl. I stand on wobbly legs and shake them out.

"Found 'em." Jigsaw dangles my underwear over my shoulder. Leaves and dirt cling to the plain white satin. "Not sure you want to put them back on, though."

"Give me those." I grab them and ball them up in my fist.

"Stand still." Soft, gentle tugs on my hair keep me straight as an arrow as he pulls more debris from each strand. "Maybe try flipping your hair and shaking it out."

"How bad is it?" I bend at the waist and sweep my hair forward, wiggling my fingers through it. Dirt and pine needles flutter to the ground.

I flip it back and try to tame the wild waves with my fingers. "Better?"

He presses his lips together, like he's trying not to deliver bad news. "Less leaves. But you still look like you copulated with a wild animal."

I poke my finger in his side. "I did." I snort-laugh and raise my eyebrows. "Copulate, huh?"

"I loved the dictionary when I was a kid." He grins and tugs the zipper on my sweatshirt up over my open dress. "I was keen to know each and every synonym for sex."

"As are most kids."

"Come on." He holds out his hand. "Let's go clean up. I want to get you home before it gets late."

I try not to pout that our weekend's over. As we walk back to the clubhouse, I'm not self-conscious or worried about running into anyone while looking so rumpled and messy.

It feels like I left that piece of myself behind—shed the shy, nervous part of me and left her with the leaves and moss.

And what's left of me feels free, wild, and untamed.

CHAPTER TWENTY-FIVE

Jigsaw

I'm really not ready to say goodbye to Margot when I pull into the parking lot behind the funeral home.

A car I don't recognize is parked in a space at the edge of the lot. 'Think your dad has a consultation?"

She frowns. "No, that's Henry's car. I wonder if he's out at a pickup with Paul."

My hands tighten on the steering wheel, barely holding back a shudder. Pickup means they're coming back with a body.

Shit, I still don't want to leave Margot.

"Where should I park, so I'm not in the way?"

She blinks a few times. "You're staying?"

"Well, I want to at least walk you upstairs."

"I thought maybe, you know, after spending the whole weekend together, you'd..."

"What? Be tired of you? Not a chance." I reach over and rest my hand on her leg. "We've spent longer stretches together here."

"That's true."

"Do you want me to go?"

She stares at me with the most serious, almost sad eyes. "I really don't. I hope that doesn't seem too..."

"It's perfect." I lift my chin. "Where should I park? I don't want to be in the way when the hearse gets here."

"Silly, we don't use the hearse for pickups. We use a minivan." She points to the car. "Park next to Henry."

We get out and Margot walks around to my side.

She holds out her hand for my bag. "I can take that." Her lips tilt with amusement. "My murder doll is in there, after all."

"I'm not scared of that thing." I grab my bag and lift her backpack onto my shoulder. "Let's go."

Margot's father greets us inside the door. His gaze shifts from Margot's backpack slung over my shoulder to the duffle bag in my hand.

Christ, it probably looks like I'm moving in. Not that he doesn't already know I spend a lot of time here.

"Hi, Margot," he greets her. "Did you have a good weekend?"

"I did. The property up there is really pretty."

I bite the inside of my cheek.

"Good." His gaze shifts to me. "Jensen…well, I'm glad you're both back."

You might feel differently if it turns out I knocked up your daughter.

Why can't I stop thinking about that? Between the condom fuckup and our time in the woods, I'm thinking about fucking Margot one hundred percent of the time, instead of my usual ninety-nine percent.

I clear my throat. "Just wanted to help Margot in with her bag." I pull my shoulder with her backpack on it forward.

He nods once, then returns his attention to Margot. "Unfortunately, we got a call—"

"I figured, since I saw Henry's car out back," she says.

"Her name's Mrs. Penny." He waits as if Margot should recognize the name. When she doesn't say anything, he continues. "She lived in the same community as Daniel's grandmother. I think he made the referral."

Margot's entire body goes rigid.

Who the fuck is Daniel?

"What do you need from me?" she asks, her tone and posture stiff as a board.

If her father notices the shift in her demeanor, he doesn't mention it. "Her granddaughter will be here in the morning. Would you take the consult?"

She blows out a breath, her entire body relaxing. "Sure. Of course."

"Thank you. The information's on my desk."

"I'll come back down and go through the file tonight."

I trail up the stairs after her, trying to come up with a way to ask her who the fuck Daniel is that won't sound unhinged and territorial.

CHAPTER TWENTY-SIX

Jigsaw

THE PERFECT DAY FOR A LONG RIDE.

The kind where I let the machine take over and the roar of the engine drowns out every nagging question swirling in my head.

Like why the fuck Margot went stiff at the mention of *Daniel.*

Or that I suspect Daniel's her shitty ex-boyfriend.

Or why, after a weekend that was near perfect—explosive sex, Margot getting to know the club, my brothers accepting her as my ol' lady—I'm still turning over certain things in my mind.

Like the forgotten condom.

Like the way she looks so natural holding a baby in her arms.

Like the way I need to buy a house with a lot of acreage so I can hunt her down and fuck her outside every day for the rest of our lives.

Ow. I better save that last thought for later.

I stand on the pegs, lifting and repositioning myself, then sit farther back in my seat.

This isn't an aimless joyride.

Today, I know exactly where I'm headed.

To find clarity with the only blood relative I give a shit about?

Maybe.

Although my relationship with my sister is hardly smooth and uncomplicated.

Jezzie said she was free this afternoon. I'm hoping we can actually enjoy some time together instead of squaring off like opponents in a cage match.

I back my bike into a spot near her apartment and kill the engine. The courtyard outside her building is full of college-age kids sprawled across the grass, soaking up the sun like reptiles while staring at their phones. A few glance my way, widen their eyes, then quickly return to their incessant doom-scrolling.

I yank out my own phone.

Me: Here.

I hit the button for her apartment once and she buzzes me in right away. At least the building's safe.

I jog up the stairs, yanking off my riding gloves, and wrinkle my nose at the thick, skunky scent of weed clinging to the hallway. My clubhouse usually reeks about the same, but we're not spending thousands on tuition while we're getting baked.

Her apartment door swings open as I approach and an excited smile spreads over Jezzie's face.

"Jensen!" she squeals and rushes into the hallway. I barely have time to brace myself before she's throwing her arms around my neck and squeezing tight.

Hey, look at that. She's happy to see me.

"Hey, kiddo." I return the hug. Coconut and pineapple shampoo or perfume clings to her hair, fresh and sweet—at least it's not weed. "How've you been?"

"Good." She releases me, bouncing on her toes a few times, then backs up into the apartment. "Come in. Come in. How was the ride?"

"Not too bad."

She eyes my black leather cut. "You wore your colors?"

"I rode here. Why? Worried I'll embarrass you in front of your college friends?"

Her smile falters. "No. I worry about *you* since you're riding alone."

"I told you this is a…gray area between us and another club. We're friends with them. It's fine."

She nods quickly but her forehead remains wrinkled. Is she really worried about my safety, or is she worried her fancy college friends will find out she has a dirty biker brother? The one who funds her lifestyle, but whatever.

"You want something to drink?" she asks, already moving toward the small kitchen. "It was a long trip."

"Sure." I walk up to the counter dividing the living room from the kitchen.

"Is iced tea okay?" she asks.

"That's fine."

She pulls a glass pitcher out of the fridge and two glasses from a cabinet and stands facing me on the other side of the counter. She pours and slides a glass my way.

I take a quick sip, wincing at the bitterness. "Thanks."

"So, Margot didn't come with you?" she asks, bringing her glass to her lips but keeping her eyes on me.

"Nah, she's working."

"I like her." Jezzie sets her glass on the counter with a soft thud and pins me with a pointed look. "She's really sweet."

"She is," I agree.

"She seems very…sensitive. Thoughtful." She tilts her head, her face screwing into a frown. "You're not going to break her heart, are you?"

"I hope not." I lift an eyebrow. "You done with the interrogation?"

"Not even close." She snorts with laughter. "You've never had a *real* girlfriend that I know of."

How awful that my little sister knows me that well. "No one worth introducing to you." No need to explain my former love 'em and leave 'em approach to women with my little sister, for fuck's sake. "Enough about me. What's going on with you?"

"Wellllll." She draws out the word to a playful degree. "I found a job."

My shoulders stiffen with annoyance. How many times are we going to have this argument? "You're supposed to be focusing on school. I thought you were taking classes over the summer?"

"I *am*. But only two. It's not a lot of hours." Her forehead scrunches as she casts a guilty glance around the apartment. "Not enough to cover my rent, but I'll pay for my utilities or something."

"Jezzie," I sigh, pressing the heel of my hand against my chest. "Just put it in a savings account…so you'll have a deposit for an apartment or whatever after graduation when you're on your own." *As if I won't still help her out.*

Her eyes widen and she claps her hands together. "So you'll let me take the job?" she asks.

"Let you? How am I supposed to *stop* you when I'm like two hours away?" I let out a frustrated snort. "Wait, tell me what the job is, first."

"Oh, it's waitressing in this tiny pizza place nearby. My friend Erin works there. Her uncle owns it. They need someone to help out part-time. It's close enough to walk there."

"Yeah, how late you going to be walking home?"

"Erin will give me a ride."

"All right." I pick up my glass and drain the rest of the iced tea. "Let's go."

Her gaze narrows as she eyes me with suspicion. "Go *where*?"

"See the place." I pat my stomach. "I could eat a slice or two. I'm starving."

"Jensen, no! You're not going to terrorize my friend's uncle."

"I'll be nice." I push away from the counter and walk toward the door. "Since you told me about it, you obviously want my opinion. Let's go."

"Ugh. Let me grab a sweatshirt."

It could be another ten minutes of her searching through her closet and the walls of the apartment are already closing in on me. "I'll meet you outside."

Her grumbling answer gets muffled as I close the door and jog down the stairs.

Outside, I slip on my sunglasses and take a slow glance around the area. Well-kept buildings, small, niche shops. A mix of college kids and locals.

"Hey, do you need directions?" a soft voice purrs.

I glance down and find a girl wearing what looks like a fuzzy, sleeveless, peach-colored onesie, flip-flops, and way too much self-tanner, twirling a piece of crunchy-looking blonde hair around one finger.

"I'm Mila." She thrusts a hand tipped with shimmery peach three-inch claws at me.

Not interested in getting stabbed by her knife-shaped talons, I jam my hands in my pockets. "I'm fine. Waiting for my sister."

Her gaze flicks over me like she's assessing whether I'm a bad decision she wants to make this afternoon. "Who's your sister?"

Aren't you a nosy little tramp?

I'm about to tell her to fuck off when Jezzie crashes through the door, bumping into me.

"All right, let's go." She stops cold, eyes narrowing. "Hey, Mila," she says, her voice dripping with irritation.

Mila flashes a half smile, half sneer at my sister.

I don't have time for this shit.

"Later." I nod to the girl and rest my hand on Jezzie's back, steering her around the girl and onto the sidewalk. "Which way?"

She casts a glare over her shoulder. "Why were you talking to her?" Jezzie whispers.

"Uh, she started talking to *me*. What'd you want me to do, backhand her?"

"Yeah, kinda." Jezzie giggles, then threads her arm through mine, leading me to the left. "It's this way." She glances over her shoulder again. "I can't believe you have a sweet, decent woman like Margot at home and I caught you talking to that deep-fried witch."

I stop walking, jerking her to a stop.

She turns to face me. "What?"

"You need to chill the fuck out. I wasn't trying to pick her up. Christ, Jezzie. You got that low an opinion of me?"

Her tough-girl expression wobbles. "Well, I told you, I like Margot."

"Yeah," I answer slowly. "So do I." I wave one hand in the air. "I still have to, you know, *talk* to other human beings sometimes. Doesn't mean I want to fuck 'em."

"Well, *she* probably wanted to fuck *you*. She has a boyfriend back home but brings a different guy to her apartment every weekend." She squeezes her eyes shut and gags. "Her bedroom's right above mine."

Shaking my head, I squeeze my eyes shut and count back from five. "I'm sorry to hear that," I say, using the most patient tone I've got. "You want to look for a different place?"

"What? No. I just don't want—"

I hold up a hand to stop her. "Even if I wasn't with Margot, I'm not interested in banging girls my sister's age. Thanks. I'm good. Can we go now?"

She glances at my road captain patch. "She's probably going to pester me for an invite to your clubhouse now. She'd fit in well with all the—"

"All right. Enough." I skewer her with my big brother glare. "I came to spend time with you, not argue about stupid shit."

She lifts her shoulders and drops her gaze to the sidewalk. "Sorry."

"What?" I cup one hand over my ear.

"Shut up." She smacks my arm. "You heard me."

"No, I didn't. It sounded like—"

"I'm *sorry*!" she shouts.

I blink up at the sky. "Am I dead? Hallucinating?"

"Oh…my…God," she spits out between giggles. "You're ridiculous."

"You're ridiculous," I mimic, walking ahead of her. "Let's go. I told you I'm hungry."

She hurries to catch up with me, looping her arm through mine again. We cross a small, one-way street and continue along the sidewalk until she stops at a narrow storefront with a red awning hanging over a few sets of tables and chairs set up on the uneven sidewalk in front of a tall, plateglass window.

"This is it." She grins at me as if we're about to step into a fine dining establishment.

I glance up at the red, white, and black sign announcing *Luigi's Slice* in red script. "Luigi's slice of what?" I ask.

"Stop it," she scolds. "Be nice."

I grab the door and hold it open for her. A wave of oregano-scented heat rolls over me. "You're going to sweat to death working here in the summer," I warn her.

"They have A/C."

Sure they do.

"J-bird." A girl who looks like she spent her high school years perched on top of the cheer pyramid calls out to Jezzie from behind the counter. She hurries over, her long, light-brown ponytail swishing down her back, and locks her arms around my sister in that bouncy, overexcited way that screams *cheerleader energy.*

J-bird?

Jezzie's not quite as enthusiastic but she accepts the hug. Laughing, she pulls back and grabs my hand. "I brought my brother. He wants to check out the place."

I scowl at her. How am I supposed to *check it out* if she announces that's why I'm here?

"Jensen, this is my *friend,* Erin." She stresses *friend* like she wants to make sure I remember my manners. "Erin, this is my big brother."

"Goodness." Erin's gaze travels up to my face. "You *are* tall." She flashes a blindingly white smile. "I'm so happy to finally meet you. J-bird talks about you all the time."

"Does she now?" I side-eye my sister again.

"All good stuff." Erin touches my arm. "Promise."

"Don't tell him that," Jezzie warns. "It'll go to his head."

More like stop my heart from the sheer fucking shock.

Jezzie approaches the counter with Erin, but I hang back and take in the place. Small, but clean. Narrow. Simple. Two red vinyl booths by the window, each big enough to hold about four people. Two smaller tables against the wall to my right and a counter with four barstools on the left. Assuming the counter is for people picking up their own slices, at most Jezzie'll be waiting on four tables? Six if she's supposed to cover the two outside.

Erin and Jezzie have moved to the far end of the counter, excitedly gabbing.

Beyond the counter, huge steel ovens and a long, shiny silver prep station take up most of the space. A big, broad-shouldered man slides a pie from a large wooden pizza paddle into the oven. The oven door clangs shut, and he makes his way to the register. A worn black T-shirt with *Luigi's Slice* scrawled across the front stretches over his large frame.

"How can I help you, sir?" he asks with a tired but polite expression fixed firmly on his face.

"Uncle Luigi." Erin hurries to his side. "This is J-bird's brother."

A more genuine smile lifts his cheeks. He holds out his hand. "Nice to meet you."

I shake his hand—firm but polite grip. Doesn't try to impress me with how strong he is. "You too." I shift my gaze to my sister. "Jezzie says you offered her a job?"

"Sure did." He tilts his head toward his niece. "She's here with Erin all the time, anyway. Might as well earn a few bucks, right?" he laughs. "Seriously, though. My last part-timer got married and left. So it's just Erin and me, and another guy who works the mornings. We get busy in the afternoons and weekends. Mostly a carry-out joint." He nods to the tables. "But we get a few dine-ins."

"So, she won't be making deliveries or anything?" I ask.

"Nope. Don't deliver. Most of our customers are from the college. They can walk their lazy asses down here. It'll do 'em good to get some fresh air."

"Can't argue with that." I like him already. Seems straightforward, no bullshit.

He eyes me up and down, his gaze lingering on the patches on the front of my cut. "You ride?"

"Hell yeah. You?"

"Used to. I got an old '95 Dyna Wide Glide that's been sittin' in my garage for years. Haven't had the time to fix it up. Can't seem to part with it, though."

"Don't. That's a great cruising bike. Reliable engine. Easy to modify."

"It's no fire-breathing powerhouse but it always got my big ass around. Never let me down or saw a trailer when I was running it."

"Sounds like you miss it. Gotta make some time to ride the wind."

"Yeah, I definitely wanna get back to it." He waves his hand over the glass display case covering the middle of the counter. "Whatta you having?"

I eye the pans of various pizzas. "Two pepperoni slices." I nudge Jezzie. "What do you want?"

"Cheese."

Luigi grabs our slices and tosses them in the oven, then nods at Jezzie and points to the cooler in the corner. "Grab whatever sodas you want."

I slide down to the register, but Luigi shakes his head. "Family doesn't pay."

He's not going to keep Jezzie employed for long with that policy. "Thanks." I drop the twenty in my hand into the tip jar and wait for Luigi to return with the warmed pizza.

Jezzie chooses the booth in the corner and starts tearing the crust off of her pizza as soon as we sit down.

"What do you think?" she asks as she stuffs small bits of golden-brown dough in her mouth.

"I haven't tried it yet." I pick up my slice, holding it in the air.

She rolls her eyes. "You know what I mean," she says in a hushed voice, her gaze darting to the kitchen and back to me.

"Nice place. Small. You sure he's got enough business to keep you employed?"

"I told you it's not a lot of hours." She glances around. "And yeah, believe it or not between five and seven this place is jam-packed."

"All right." I take a bite, savoring the hefty amount of gooey cheese, spicy pepperoni, thin layer of sauce, and extra-crispy crust. "It's good," I mumble. "Can see why they're busy."

We eat in silence. The occasional clatter from the kitchen or Luigi and Erin's conversation filling the space. Every now and then, I flick my gaze toward the door.

A group of four college-age guys shuffles in, their loud voices competing with each other as they argue about something.

"Settle down." Luigi's voice rumbles from behind the counter, silencing the kids. Not a request. A warning.

They immediately dial it back, bantering with him for a few minutes before finally placing their orders.

Jezzie cranes her neck to peek at them, then quickly drops her head and focuses on her plate.

I frown. "You know those guys?"

She nods, eyes still locked on her food. "I have a class with one of them."

The tallest one leans sideways, angling himself to get a better look at Jezzie. His gaze flicks to me and he freezes in midair—like he's Bambi staring into a semi's headlights on a midnight highway.

Then, like someone hit his *unpause* button, he swaggers toward us, hands stuffed into the pockets of his sagging, oversized jeans. The whole outfit looks like it was stolen from the skater kids I went to high school with. "Jay, that you?"

Jay?

Red spreads over her cheeks as she quickly grabs a napkin and swipes it over her mouth. "Oh, hi, Colt," she says in a forced, breezy tone.

She throws a please-don't-embarrass-me glare at me.

I shrug. *I'll do my best but can't make any promises.*

Colt stops at the edge of our table and nervously glances between Jezzie and me, then runs his hand over his light-brown buzz cut.

"How are ya?" he finally says to her.

"Good." She lifts her chin. "My brother's visiting, so I'm showing him all the best spots."

Colt's shoulders ease down, and his mouth curves up—like he's relieved to find out I'm her brother and not a boyfriend. If my little sister wasn't involved, I'd find this whole situation funny as fuck. Their interaction is so…innocently awkward.

Now I feel like a dick for the way I overreacted to her talking to Remy at the track. Maybe she hadn't been as into him as I'd feared. And, on second thought, maybe she'd be better off *with* Remy, so I could terrorize him on a regular basis.

Colt clears his throat. "Hi, I'm Colt." He waves his hand in the air like a Muppet getting his strings pulled.

"Jensen." I nod and resist my natural inclination to poke fun at him.

"I, uh…" He jerks his thumb over his shoulder. "Well, I saw you and wanted to say hi."

"Yeah." Jezzie stares up at him with a goofy, wide-eyed expression.

I bite the inside of my cheeks. *Must not laugh.*

"Nice to meet you." Colt does the awkward Muppet wave again, then shuffles back to his friends, the bottoms of his ridiculous pants dragging along the floor.

"Don't," Jezzie growls under her breath.

"What?" I widen my eyes. "I didn't say a word."

She mashes her lips into a flat line. "Yeah, I guess you were pretty decent."

"Later, Jay!" Colt calls out as he and his friends swagger out the door.

She whips around. "Bye!"

As soon as the door swings shut behind him, I squeeze my eyes shut and snicker in short bursts.

"Shut up!" Jezzie slaps my hand.

"What's with the Jay and J-bird?" I ask, still grinning.

She lifts one shoulder, twisting a piece of pizza crust between her fingers. "I dunno. I kinda hate my name. It's always embarrassing when people ask me what 'Jezzie' is short for. Who the fuck names their kid Jezebel?" She lets out a short, dry, humorless laugh. "She was supposed to be a whore."

The bluntness of that knocks the smirk right off my face.

I exhale and lean back. "Nah, I always thought she was kind of a badass who stayed true to herself. Whoever wrote about her in the Bible was kinda biased."

She frowns. "Yeah?"

Tugging on ideas and half-buried memories I haven't thought about in over a decade, I add, "Sure. The people writing about her were all men in power. She pissed them off. So they turned her into the villain."

A pained smile stretches across her face. "You remember Dad lecturing us about how Jezebel was the epitome of a *bad woman*. That used to make me feel like pig shit. Then he'd harp on modesty and obedience, controlling everything we wore, ate, learned…" She stares out the window.

I remember all too well. "Meanwhile, Ahab was out there being a weak-ass king and worshipping idols, but somehow, *she* was the problem. They couldn't see the double standard."

I reach over and touch her hand, drawing her attention away from the window. "She was a queen who was smart and strategic. Ruthless when she needed to be. But they reduced her to a harlot and used her name as an insult."

She pierces me with soulful eyes. "And I get to carry that insult around for life."

"They were all just stories he twisted and weaponized to keep us in line. But yeah, I know it was worse for you."

She picks at the cheese on her pizza. "You're lucky you got named before our parents went full-tilt Christo-crazy."

Relieved we're moving away from the Bible talk, I snort. "Jensen? You're kidding, right? You know how many kids picked on me in school? I got called Jenny, Jennifer, you name it."

A sly smile spreads over her lips. "Yeah, but if you ran into those bullies today, you'd make them piss their pants."

I snort with laughter. "I guess."

"Wow, I was *not* expecting this kind of Biblical feminist analysis with my biker brother today."

Coldness settles in my chest, our shared past pressing against my ribs like a slab of concrete. "None of those stories ever sat right with me. Not Cain's punishment, Eve's supposed inferiority, or Jezebel's vilification."

Jezzie exhales sharply. Her fingers tighten around her bottle of soda, the plastic crinkling under her touch. "Yeah," she murmurs. "Me neither."

My fingers curl into a fist against the table. "Our father tried to beat all those doubts and questions out of me, but the more he tried to whip the devil from my soul, the more I was convinced I was on to something."

Jezzie's throat bobs as she swallows. "I'm sorry, Jensen." She glances down at her plate. "He only got worse after you left," she whispers, so low I almost miss the words. They still strike like a hammer.

Guilt crumbles over me. I couldn't save everyone. "Have you ever heard from Ruth?"

She shakes her head. Hesitates. "No. I know she and—"

I hold up my hand, not wanting to hear the kid's name. Jezzie was my only responsibility.

"They relocated somewhere on the West Coast, last I knew," she finishes.

A chill creeps down my spine. The past has a nasty habit of digging itself up when you least expect it.

I never anticipated this deep a conversation with my usually prickly sister over pizza today. And I don't enjoy the demons of my past returning to take a bite out of me.

I exhale sharply, shoving those old feelings deep, deep down. "It's okay. *We're* okay. You're brave and smart and know not to fall for any of that bullshit now."

She nods slowly, then rolls her shoulders back like she's also shaking off bad memories. "I get the creeps anytime someone talks about going to church or religion of any kind."

"Can't blame you." I reach over and rest my hand over hers. "Why didn't you say something about your name? When I introduced you to Margot and my brothers...I would've used whatever name you wanted."

"I...I thought you'd think it's dumb." She tugs at the hem of her sleeve, her knuckles brushing against my thumb. "Or you'd make fun of me. I don't know."

Fuck, that stings—because she's right, I probably would have teased her. What kind of shitty brother am I that I had no idea her own name bothered her so much?

"Since I was starting over here, I wanted to test out something different." She wrinkles her nose. "I'm not sure I care for *Jay* either, it kinda sounds like a dude's name." The corners of her mouth turn up. "Erin came up with J-bird on her own."

I squeeze her hand once, then let go. "Well, when you decide on a name that fits, just tell me." I narrow my eyes and fake snarl. "I'll punch anyone who gives you a hard time about it."

A genuine trickle of laughter eases out of her. "Deal."

"You ever talk to Aunt Angela about this?" I ask, curious how she would've advised my sister.

Her jaw tightens. "Once."

"And?"

"She said my name was my connection to my family's history or some crap. Like, yeah. That's kinda why I hate it." She meets my eyes again. "Honestly, I think it was more about the difficulty in getting your name legally changed," she adds quickly, as if eager to defend our aunt from any criticism I might raise.

"Yeah, but better to do it when you're young, before you get established in a career or something," I point out.

She nods slowly. "That's true."

"You talk to her recently?" I ask, shifting from the topic of names. "She doing all right?"

She sets her slice down on the paper plate. "She won't text, so we talk every couple of days. I think she's good. She's got a nice group of women her age she's been hanging out with—they do a lot of volunteering and now they're planning some month-long cruise to Alaska this summer."

"No shit. Good for her." I shiver at the thought of being trapped on a boat for that long.

"Don't be mad. But she asks about you all the time. If you're doing okay. I told her you're seeing a really nice woman."

I roll my eyes and finish chewing. "I'm not mad. What'd she say?"

Jezzie glances away. "Just wanted to know if you're nice to her."

Motherfucker. The words and their implication slam into me harder than expected.

I lean in close, lowering my voice. "Why? She think I'm a monster like our father?"

She meets my stare head-on. "Yeah, probably." She holds up her hands in surrender. "*I* know you're not. I've told her that dozens of times."

Gee, I'm almost convinced.

Wait, dozens of times? So Angela harps on this a lot?

Fucking great.

My stomach's turned sour. *Damn.* We were having such a good conversation and actually bonding like adults instead of snipping at each other like teenagers.

I don't even know why I'm so annoyed.

I've spent my whole life making sure I don't become anything like my father.

And sometimes I think I'm even worse.

CHAPTER TWENTY-SEVEN

Jigsaw

I RIDE STRAIGHT TO MARGOT'S PLACE AFTER MY AFTERNOON WITH MY sister.

She meets me in the parking lot, looking adorable in a long sweater she has wrapped around her like a bathrobe.

"So, how'd it go?" she asks as soon as I get off my bike.

I set my helmet on the seat and run through a couple different answers, then go with the worst one.

"Well, I guess my aunt, and probably my sister, are worried I'll turn into a violent monster like my father, so that was a nice kick in the balls."

The words taste bitter on my tongue. I can't believe the first thing I'm doing is whining to Margot about my wittle hurt *feeeelings*.

But it gnawed at me the whole ride here.

"What?" Her eyes widen. "Why?"

"I don't know. Runs in the family?"

I move closer, reaching for her, needing to feel her warmth against me.

But she stops me with a hand against my chest.

My heart stutters. But as I stare into her determined eyes, I don't see rejection.

"Jensen, I realize I never met your father but from what you've told me and everything I know about you, you're the opposite of him in every way that matters." She cups my cheeks with her soft warm hands and leans up, brushing a kiss against my lips.

Such a sweet, simple gesture but it eases all the rage and shame that simmered inside me the whole way here.

"Thanks." I hug her close. "Jezzie claims *she* doesn't think that, and she told my aunt that's not true, but it still burned my ass..."

"I don't blame you." She purses her lips together, as if she's deep in thought.

"Come on." I tug on her hand. "I don't want to talk about this out here."

She nods and leads me inside, up the stairs, and into her apartment in silence.

"How was your day?" I ask as I'm taking off my boots.

"Long." She frowns and slips off her sweater, draping it over the chair in the corner. "You know, whatever your aunt's said probably feels especially offensive since it sounds like, from what you've told me, you've never spent a lot of time around her as an adult. So, she has no idea who you are as a person. I'd be annoyed too."

God damn. That's *exactly* it. Margot understanding what I'm feeling and confirming that I'm not being a sulky prick about it soothes the chaotic fire swirling in my chest.

"I missed you today. Wish I had you with me. Even Jezzie seemed disappointed you didn't come."

Margot's brows lift. "Really?"

"Yeah, she likes you a lot."

Margot bites her lip, then nods. "I liked her too. I'll go visit with you next time. But I think it's good you two had some alone time together."

I shrug. "Yeah. It was." All the bad feelings that got raised about my father almost blotted out the hilarity of running into Jezzie's crush. "You'll be proud of me. We ran into a guy she clearly has a crush on, and I didn't try to scare him or embarrass her."

"Awww, it's nice to be a grown-up sometimes, huh?" she teases.

“Heh.” The corners of my mouth turn up. “We covered lots of grown-up topics. It was kind of surreal.”

She doesn’t laugh or prod me for details. “I’m really happy for you guys.”

I wrap my arms around her, pulling her in tight, breathing her in. “Thank you for pushing me to go.”

She melts into me, arms sliding around my waist.

“Anytime,” she whispers.

I press a kiss against her temple, letting my lips linger.

I love this woman.

Every part of her.

I should tell her.

The words sit heavy in my chest, right there, waiting to be said.

CHAPTER TWENTY-EIGHT

Margot

"Margot," Jigsaw whispers, urgency in his voice.

I blink. My room's still dark. Only the suggestion of pale gray light glows around the edges of my curtains.

Jigsaw's bigger body's wrapped around me. Protective and possessive even though it's just the two of us in my bed.

My body shifts, stretches, my butt grazing him. Heat sweeps over my skin. He's hard. I roll my hips again. Between my legs I'm already aching for him.

A deep groan rumbles through his chest, and he presses himself tighter against my back. "Don't distract me," he rasps in his sleep-rough voice. "I need to tell you something."

Now alarmed, I roll over. He props himself up on one elbow, eyebrows drawn down. His serious expression pulls me fully awake. He's not waking me up for sex. "What? What's wrong?"

His frown deepens. "Nothing's wrong." Then he reaches for me, cupping the side of my face. "I just…I can't…"

I draw back, dislodging the covers as I go. Did he wake me up to… break up with me?

No. My gaze drops to his tight black boxer briefs. He wouldn't wake up hard and insistent with someone he wanted to break up with, would he?

His jaw's clenched tight and he's studying me with that burning intensity that leaves me breathless and excited.

Not a breakup. Then what?

"Talk to me." I reach for him, tracing my fingers over his shoulder and down his arm.

"Come back here." He coils his arm around my waist and drags me closer this time. So tight to his front that I drape my leg over his hip.

He groans and grinds his hard length against my center. "Fuuuck." He squeezes his eyes shut. "Don't distract me."

"How am I distracting you?" I ask with an innocent lilt. "You woke *me* up, remember? If it's not to give me this," I push my hips forward, gasping when his hardness nudges my clit, "then what?"

He breathes harder, like he's running a marathon in his mind. "I love you, Margot."

The heat simmering inside me explodes. "What?" I whisper.

"I think, no, I know, I've felt this for a while. But I've never… been *in* love." His frown deepens. "I love my club, my brothers, my sister…so I know what it is, I think. But this is…so different than anything else. I love you." He shakes his head. "I don't want to fuck this up."

His gaze studies my face. Questioning. Waiting.

He might be braver than I am, but he needs to hear this as much as I did. "I love you too, Jensen."

"You don't have to do that," he says. "You won't hurt my feelings if—"

"I love you," I repeat.

He slides his erection against me and takes a shuddering breath. "I'm already fucking this up. I didn't want to say it when we're naked."

"We're not naked."

"I very much *want* you naked."

I run my fingers through his hair and cup his cheek. "I love you."

He stares at me as if he can't decide if I'm telling the truth. As if he wants to believe but can't.

"I *love* you," I say, with more force behind it. "I've wanted to tell you that…I've almost said it…but I was scared."

"Of what?"

"Losing you. Scaring you away. Being too much."

He drops his forehead to mine and breathes a deep sigh of relief. "Too much? I love everything about you. You could never scare me away. I'm afraid I'll scare *you* away. I'm way too fucking needy when it comes to you." A sharp scowl crosses his handsome face. "And I hate that I just said that out loud. But I trust you."

"You're not needy." Or if he is, then so am I. I slide my body against his. His skin's so warm, searing through my thin camisole. "You can say anything to me." I press my lips to his. "Tell me anything. Everything."

He rains kisses over my forehead, my cheeks, my lips, and down to my neck. "I love you." He drags the straps of my top down my arms and kisses his way to the tops of my breasts. "I want to *make love* to you."

"You already are." In every touch of his lips against my skin. In every word he whispers, I feel it.

I don't ask what this means about our future. Of where we go from here. I'm too happy to ask any question that might ruin the moment.

Jigsaw

Why'd I wait so long to tell her I love her? Because now that I've said it, I can't stop saying it.

And by the fourth time she says it back, I actually believe her. But when she admits she held back because she was scared of losing me, that's when the sappy shit really starts pouring out of my mouth.

"You could never scare me away," I reassure her. "I'm afraid I'll scare *you* away. I'm way too fucking needy when it comes to you." *Fuck, I can't believe I just fucking admitted that.* "And I hate that I just said that out loud. But I trust you."

"You're not needy," she whispers, rubbing herself against my already painfully hard cock.

How wrong you are.

I think she misunderstood my level of neediness.

"You can say anything to me." She brushes her lips against mine. "Tell me anything. Everything."

Nope. Already came too close to admitting I want to be with her every second of the day. That even when we're in the same bed, I dream about her. How I never have a single fucking nightmare when she's sleeping next to me.

After visiting my sister and picking through all the garbage of our past, I thought for sure the nightmares would return with a swift vengeance. I should've been trapped in an endless loop of clawing at the locked door in my father's basement, his voice in my ear, commanding me to repent. Or the other one, where I find Jezzie broken and bloodied, unable to answer me when I scream her name.

But the nightmares didn't come.

It's because of Margot. Having her curled up against me, breathing slow and steady, grounded me with every inhale.

So I finally said it.

And then I said too much.

I keep my mouth occupied kissing every inch of her, but she still has clothes in my way. "I love you." I tug the straps of her top down and her breasts pop free. "I want to make love to you."

"You already are," she whispers in a breathless rush.

She pulls her arms free of the straps and I tug the material down, kissing each bit of skin I expose. I dip my tongue in her navel and her stomach quivers with laughter.

"Let's take these off." I twist her shorts down her legs, and she lifts her feet for me to take them all the way off. I sit back and admire her. All bare except for the little scrap of satin twisted around her waist. Heels on the mattress. Ready for me. "Fuck, you're pretty."

She shyly drops her knees together.

"No." I run my hands over her calves. "Open for me."

She spreads her knees wider.

"Good. Stay like that."

I slide off the bed and shove my boxer briefs off, then stop at the nightstand for a condom and toss it on the bed.

She rolls her head to the side, eyes on me the whole time.

I dive back on the bed, right between her thighs. My face inches from her pussy, her heat washing over me. I kiss her inner thigh and her breath stutters, body shaking.

I hook my arms under her legs, yanking her closer, and use my fingers to spread her open, exposing her glistening skin.

"I…I want…" She reaches down, resting her hand over mine.

I drag my tongue through her slit several times. Her body jerks and wiggles. Finally, I tease my tongue around her clit.

"Yes, yes, yes. Please," she begs.

The evil part of me wants to tease her but I want her too much. I suck at her clit, tracing the tip of my tongue against her until she's in a frenzy.

Her body tightens. Her hands claw at the sheets. She tries to clamp her legs around my head, but I press my hands against her thighs, keeping her spread open.

Harsh gasps and moans tear from her throat. "Right there. Don't stop. Please."

I groan against her wet skin, my promise not to stop.

She spears her fingers through my hair, pulling me closer.

Slowly, the tension drains out of her body. I suck and lick with less pressure until she lets out a contented sigh.

Desire wraps around my chest, pulling tight. I grab the condom, smooth it on and hook my arms under her knees again before she realizes what's happening.

"Jensen?"

I slowly ease inside her.

"Oh God." She lifts her head, watching with wide eyes while I sink all the way in. Her breaths turn short and choppy.

"Good?" I ask, shifting my gaze between where we're joined and her face.

"Yes," she moans, and drops her head back on her pillow.

Fire licks down my spine. Too soon.

Another tortured moan passes her lips. "Oh my God."

"Come here." I need her pressed up against me more than I need to breathe. I slip my arms under her and lift her into my lap, sitting back on my heels. Her tits squeeze against my chest, and she drapes her arms over my shoulders. "That's better."

She fuses her mouth to mine and starts rocking her hips.

I let out a sharp groan of surprise. The new angle and friction feel so fucking good. She breaks the kiss, panting and staring into my eyes.

"Don't stop," I warn her. "Don't you dare."

"No."

"Lean back. I got you."

She grabs my shoulders and arches her back, grinding herself into me.

White spots burst behind my eyes.

"I," she gasps. "I'm so close." She screams the last word.

Pleasure swells as she tightens around me. I groan and shudder, releasing her so she falls back on the bed. I fall over her, pounding into her so hard, the bed rattles. Groaning loud as I finally come.

I collapse over her, our sweaty bodies sticking together. She wraps her arms around me tight, kissing my cheeks, dragging her fingers through my hair. "I love you," she murmurs over and over.

"Thank you." I drop a kiss on her forehead and roll to the side before I crush her. "Give me a sec."

I sit up, head spinning, and drop the condom in the small trash can near the nightstand.

She's on her side, up on one elbow, beautifully naked when I turn around. I slide under the sheet and urge her closer. She eagerly settles against my side, running her hand all over my chest and abs.

"I love the way you touch me."

She slows her soft strokes and slides her fingers down my arm. "Just checking to make sure you're real."

CHAPTER TWENTY-NINE

Margot

We must drift back to sleep after that. Sometime later, my alarm rudely pulls us from sleep.

"I have to get ready," I whisper, lifting the sheet to take another peek at his magnificent body. "You can stay here if you want to."

"Can't." He reaches for his phone on the nightstand without opening his eyes. "Church."

How I wish I could go with him. I'd hang out with the women while the guys have their meeting. Maybe this time I'd ask Trinity if I could help her in the kitchen. I'd laugh while the guys teased each other at breakfast and…

"What's wrong?" Jigsaw frowns and sits up.

"Nothing." I shake off the longing. I have a job to do. "I was just…nothing."

"I wish you could come with me. But I know you have to work." He glances at his phone. "I have time. Let me help you before I go."

"You don't have to."

"I want to. Don't argue with me." He lifts his chin toward my closet. "Get dressed. I'll make you something to eat."

I try to give him a stink-eye for the bossy tone, but the twitch of my lips negates it.

Less than an hour later, I'm ready to head downstairs.

"You look really pretty." Jigsaw traces his finger over the lacy ruffle of my dark blue silk blouse.

Warmth glides over my skin. "You say that every morning."

"It's true every morning."

As if he's my bodyguard clearing a path, he heads down the stairs first.

Paul's already downstairs. He slides a knowing smile our way.

Jigsaw doesn't bother trying to hide that he spent the night. "Where do you need an extra set of hands?"

Paul raises his eyebrows at me, then answers. "Down here. Follow me."

"I'll be in the kitchen." I hurry in there, my heels clicking over the tile. After preheating the oven, I pull out several cookie trays and boxes of store-bought dough.

Wearing gloves, I drop dollops of dough on the trays and slide the trays in the oven. I snap the gloves off and set the timer on my watch, then hurry to the prep room to speak to my father.

Jigsaw catches me in the hallway on my way back to the kitchen.

"All done." His gaze shifts to the door, then the kitchen.

The buzzer on my watch vibrates against my wrist. "Let me grab the cookies out of the oven and I'll walk you outside."

"Cookies?" He wiggles his eyebrows and sweeps his hand in front of him. "After you."

Laughing, I return to the kitchen and grab a pair of oven mitts. I bend over and open the oven door. Heat blasts my eyes, steaming up my glasses for a second. Carefully, I slide the trays out and set them on top of the oven.

Jigsaw steps behind me, resting his hands on my hip, his warmth hotter than the heat from the oven against my skin. "There is nothing hotter than you bending over in this skirt to take cookies out of the oven." He slides one hand over my butt, patting me lightly.

I step back. "This skirt?" I gesture to the below-knee-length black pencil skirt that always makes me feel about as sexy as a nun balancing the church's checkbook.

"Yup."

"For that, I'll give you a few cookies to go." I lean up and kiss his cheek. "I even saved back extra dough to make some for you later."

He slips both hands around my waist, pulling me against him. "You're spoiling me."

"Happy to." I reach for a roll of paper towels and tear off a sheet. He releases me and I grab a thin spatula, peeling two still-warm, wobbly cookies from the tray. "They're not cooled enough."

"They're not going to last long." He takes the paper towel, carefully folding it around the cookies.

We step onto the back porch, holding hands. I still have a few minutes before visitors start arriving. My gaze scans the parking lot. Several attendants are parked in the back. The garage door is open. Paul will pull the hearse out soon.

"Paul said you're expecting a lot of people?" Jigsaw asks.

"Yes. Her death was kind of sudden. I mean, she was elderly but in good health. She was active in her church and did a lot of volunteer work."

His expression hardens at the word church. Briefly, but I catch it. Understandable.

Still holding hands, I walk him to his bike, reluctant to let him go. As if admitting I love him means I can't bear to see him leave. Or I'm afraid he won't come back.

He sets the cookies on the seat of his bike and pulls me into his arms again. "You know I don't want to leave, right?"

It's like he knows exactly what I needed to hear.

"I don't want you to go." I squeeze him tighter. "But I don't want you in trouble with your club, either." More seriously, I add, "Will you tell everyone I said hello? Will Shelby be there?"

"Uh, I think she's down in Tennessee recording." He scrunches up his face. "Rooster was pretty grouchy last time I touched base."

"Awww. They're so sweet."

He flicks his gaze to something behind me. "I hope you'll be able to come up again. Soon."

"Me too."

He steps closer, cupping the back of my neck, careful not to mess up my hair, neatly captured with a silver barrette. His thumb presses firmly under my chin, tilting my head as he lowers his face to mine. I curl my arm around his neck as his lips ghost over mine. His minty breath washes over me and he sweeps his tongue between my lips, sliding it against mine. I let out a startled moan. He sweeps his hands down my back, clutching my hips like he can't get enough of me and needs a reminder of how I feel under his fingers.

Somewhere behind us, I'm aware of a car pulling into the lot. We're right at the corner of the house where anyone could see us as they pass by.

Jigsaw kisses the corner of my mouth, then along my jaw to the sensitive spot on my neck. He sharply pulls back as if yanked by a leash of restraint. "If I don't stop now, I'm going to take you back upstairs…" he whispers, letting me fill in the blanks.

"I think I'd let you."

He captures my hand, lifting it to his lips. Dusting a kiss against my knuckles while holding my gaze, silently communicating all the other places on my body he wants to kiss.

"I better go before Dad comes looking for me." I squeeze my eyes shut. "Damn, I need to run upstairs and grab my planner."

His lips curve. "Go ahead. Let me watch you go inside."

So protective, even though it's broad daylight and we're about to have a hundred people in and out of this house.

I nod to his bike. "Be safe."

"Always."

Flushed and flustered from our searing kiss I turn and head toward the back porch. Time to put on my professional mask. I can't properly greet mourners with the lovesick grin of a giddy teenager plastered on my face.

"Margot?"

My entire body somehow freezes and recoils at the same time. A feeling I've only ever experienced with one man.

Daniel.

You have got to be shitting me.

His shoes scrape against the asphalt as he hurries to catch up to me. I force my face into something somber and professional. No matter how much I hate Daniel, I'm at work. He's just another member of the public I have to interact with.

He stops in front of me and smiles like he has every right to my time and attention. Then his gaze travels over me from head to toe.

"You look…different." His voice drips with the cold condescension I used to mistake for sophistication.

Different doesn't sound like a compliment or even a normal thing to say to someone. *Wait.*

Did he see Jigsaw and me kissing? Is that why he's making a face like a skunk pooped in his Cheerios?

I hold my breath—acutely aware of the stillness around us. The quiet of the neighborhood.

The absence of a certain Harley engine.

Behind me the air shifts. I don't have to turn around to know it's Jigsaw's aura of protection at my back. He rests his hand right above my butt and stands so close, we're touching from shoulder to thigh, making it obvious he's not some rando hanging out in the parking lot who just walked up and joined our conversation.

"What are you doing here?" I ask Daniel, although his perfectly tailored black suit should make the answer obvious—he's attending the service.

When my father said Mrs. Penny lived in the same area as Daniel's grandmother, I'd wondered if they'd been friends. I never expected *Daniel* to show up today, though.

His curious gaze flicks between Jigsaw and me.

My palms sweat. Should I introduce them? Jigsaw clearly isn't going to introduce himself.

"I, uh…" Daniel swipes his hand through his hair. What's wrong with him? I've never seen him…nervous? Is that what's making him sweat? Jigsaw must be giving him a lethal dose of his death stare.

Good.

I swallow a giggle. Jigsaw could crack Daniel like a saltine if he wanted to and Daniel seems to know it.

"Mrs. Penny was a good friend of my grandmother's," Daniel finally explains. "I left a voicemail to let you know I'd see you…" He frowns at Jigsaw again.

"She's been busy." Jigsaw's grave tone vibrates with the restraint of someone who wants to knock the man in front of him into next week.

My father must have gotten the message and not bothered to tell me. A warning would've been nice.

I don't care about Daniel anymore, so why am I slightly stunned and paralyzed standing here talking to him?

Honestly, I'm grateful our relationship ended. Everything in my life right now is good and some of it wouldn't have been possible if Daniel and I were still together. Like the man standing next to me.

The deadly expression on Jigsaw's face is so intense as he stares Daniel down, I'm almost scared someone else has taken over his body. Is this the same man who so sweetly cuddled under the sheets, told me he loved me, and made me come so hard I heard angels sing this morning?

Is that low, vibrating sound an actual…*growl* coming from him?

CHAPTER THIRTY

Jigsaw

The way I'm holding myself back from punching this motherfucker into next week can't be healthy.

Margot's pretty face is salt-pale and clenched with anxiety. This isn't a random guy here for the funeral. He has to be one of the exes who treated her shitty. There's no other reason for her rigid posture. I've seen her interact with quite a few clients now. She's always warm and friendly. So natural and effortless at putting people at ease. Now, she looks like she wants to melt into the pavement or punch him in the nuts.

His jaw flexes as he fixes me with an imperious glare. "I'm sorry, who are you?"

Your worst nightmare.

My hand strays to the hunting knife at my side.

"Oh." A short, choking sound stumbles out of Margot's mouth, as if she had to cut off an automatic apology.

Good girl. Don't you dare apologize to this fucker for a damn thing.

She tips her head back and smiles up at me. "This is my boyfriend Jensen. Jensen, this is Daniel." She waves her hand at him as if he's an insect she's trying to shoo.

So this is the guy who made her react so strangely the other day when her father mentioned him.

Definitely an ex.

Dan's mouth mashes into a thin line, his gaze darting between Margot and me. "You're…I see…"

One biker plus one mortician doesn't seem to compute in Dan's uptight brain.

Ignoring him for the moment, I curl my arm around Margot's waist, turning her toward me. "You need me to stay, babe?" I ask her in a low voice, not caring if Daniel overhears, but wanting to exclude him.

I've got maybe an hour and a half if I want to get to church on time. This douche canoe can't possibly stay at the service that long, can he?

She opens her mouth and hesitates, clearly wanting to say yes. "I know you have to meet up with—"

"I always have time for you. Let me grab that stuff you wanted from upstairs."

"Thanks." She blows out a relieved breath. "That'd be great."

"You got it."

"How did you two even meet?" Daniel blurts, barely keeping his tone on the polite side of snide.

"Jensen's a business associate of Dad's." Margot shrugs. "We ran into each other at a mutual friend's wedding and things sort of…"

"Yes, they did," I confirm with a low growl, pulling her closer and pressing another kiss to her cheek.

Margot laughs softly but doesn't pull away. I slide my arm around her waist and turn her toward the porch steps.

"Uh, is it possible to go in early?" Daniel asks, hurrying to catch up.

"Sure," Margot says over her shoulder.

Inside the back hallway, we run smack into Mr. Cedarwood. He actually smiles when he sees us, even though I'm basically mauling his daughter. The dude sure has accepted me dating Margot better than I thought he ever would.

"Jensen." He beams. "Good morning."

"He's helping with a few things," Margot explains, pulling slightly away from me. As if her dad can't look outside and realize my bike's been parked in the same spot for days. As if her cousin won't mention I came downstairs with Margot this morning.

"Good. Good. Thank you." His forehead creases into a scowl as his gaze lands on something behind us. Daniel, no doubt. The flicker of annoyance disappears as her father's face smooths into a professional mask of a welcoming smile. "Daniel, what are you doing here?"

Is that a hopeful note in his voice? Would he rather see Margot with that uptight prick? If he had the same suspicions that I do about the way Daniel treated his daughter, would he slam the door in the guy's face like I'm dying to do?

Nope. Within seconds, the two of them get cozy catching up and talking about Mrs. Penny. Cedarwood leads Daniel down the hall with a hand on his shoulder.

Who gives a fuck? Margot's too smart to be fooled by that guy. And she's not a pushover who bends to her father's will either. Gretel alone is a bundle of black, furry proof that Margot does what she wants.

"Who is he?" I ask.

Margot's gaze shifts away. "I really don't want to talk about him now."

"I assume he's an ex of some sort?"

The anxiety creasing her forehead confirms it even though she doesn't say a word.

She squeezes my hand. "Thanks for sticking around," she whispers.

"Not a problem." I bend down and kiss her cheek. "Where will I find your planner? And what does it look like?"

"Um, it's blue with a clasp. Next to my lounge chair in the living room. You're sure you don't mind?"

"Not at all." I flick my gaze toward Daniel and her father. "You want me to wait a minute?"

"No." She tilts her head toward the hallway. "I'll be in the service room. I need to check on the flower arrangements."

"Okay. I'll be right back." Without another glance at her dad or her ex, I jog up the stairs like I know my way around the funeral home and I'm perfectly at ease here.

CHAPTER THIRTY-ONE

Jigsaw

LEAVING MARGOT WHEN I KNOW HER SLIMY EX IS SLITHERING AROUND the house sends my heart into freefall—like it's trying to exit my body and get back to Margot.

That dread follows me to the upstate clubhouse.

She'll be fine. People will be in and out of the house all day for the service. Her dad's there. Her cousin. Other people who work for Cedarwood.

Except, no one else knows how shitty he treated her. Hell, I don't even *know*. I'm only guessing based on stuff Margot said. Based on the ways she reacted when we first started our "lessons."

She won't be alone with him.

No matter what excuse my brain throws at me, my heart smacks it away.

I should be with her. Protecting her.

As I back my bike into a spot along the fence, Z and Rock step out from the path leading into the woods. Z lifts a hand in greeting and both of them stop a few feet away from me.

Great, just what I need, both presidents in my face. Where the fuck is Rooster when I need him?

I take my sweet-ass time, shutting off the bike, taking off my helmet, placing it just so on my seat, adjusting my cut—anything I can think of to stall. But they stay where they are.

"Prez." I greet Z first, then force a smirk onto my face. "Prez." I nod at Rock.

Z narrows his eyes and stares at me. Rock tilts his head ever so slightly.

"Everything okay?" Rock asks.

"Yeah, why?" I frown and jam my hands in my pockets.

"You look all pinched and squinty," Z says, still staring at me like a target at the end of a rifle scope. "And not in your normal, healthy serial killer way."

"I don't even know what to say to that, Prez."

The buzz of an ATV interrupts our bizarre conversation. Has to be Teller arriving. He's the only one who uses an ATV to ride through the woods connecting his property to the club's. I inch toward the front door of the clubhouse, but Rock's hand shoots out to stop me.

"Stay put," Z orders.

What'd I do now?

Teller parks next to my bike and joins us. "We meetin' outside now?"

"No, knucklehead," Rock grumbles.

Teller punches my shoulder lightly. "What's up, brother?"

"Nothing." I lift my chin toward Z. "Prez says I'm not looking serial killer enough today."

Teller snorts and shakes his head, shooting Z a *what the fuck* face.

"How's Margot?" Teller asks.

Fucking hell. He's going to forever think his business deal with Margot's dad means he gets to stick his nose in my relationship.

I jam my hands farther in my pockets and glare at Teller. "We're fine."

"She working today?" Z asks.

"Yeah."

"That's too bad," Teller says. "I was hoping she'd come up again soon."

"Why?"

He frowns and shrugs at me. "Because she's your girlfriend," he answers slowly, like he's speaking to someone a few fries short of a Happy Meal. "She's funny. Everyone liked having her here."

I blow out a breath and relax. "She wanted to come today, but they have a service going on."

Rock's still staring at me with that intense expression that makes me feel like he can unscrew the top of my head and see the thoughts bouncing around inside my skull. "You sure everything's all right?"

"Don't you have enough kids to papa-bear?" I elbow Teller's side while meeting Rock's less than amused stare. "I'm fine."

Brothers do not let ol' ladies interfere with club business. I can't tell either president I want to skip church because I have a bad *feeling* that some guy might be mean to my girlfriend. They'd probably strip my patch.

Rock finally nods and starts toward the clubhouse.

Z moves closer to me. "You sure you're good?"

When I don't answer right away, Teller smacks my shoulder and walks around behind me to catch up with Rock.

From the corner of my eye, I note they're still standing outside.

Fuck it. I blow out a breath and answer Z's question. "I'm fine." I keep my voice low. "It's just…Margot's ex showed up for the funeral today and I didn't like leaving her with him around."

Instead of cracking a joke about my caveman need to mark my territory, Z scowls. "He hurt her or something?"

I take a long, slow breath, considering my answer. Unfortunately, Rock and Teller take the pause as an opportunity to walk the few feet and rejoin our conversation. "Not physically, no. At least, I don't think so. But I think he was emotionally or mentally abusive based on shit she's said and some of the ways she reacts to stuff." I shrug. "I didn't care for the way he spoke to her when I was standing right there with one hand on my hunting knife."

"So, he's a dumb motherfucker too," Z says.

I expel a huff of agreement.

"Her dad there today?" Teller asks with a note of concern.

"Yeah. And her cousin. It'll be a full house for the funeral. That's the only reason I was able to leave her," I admit.

Z glances at the clubhouse, then Teller, and finally Rock. "Church will be quick," Z says. "Winter's coming. We're not going on any major runs right now."

"Keeping things copacetic at Cedarwood's is kinda club business." Teller shrugs.

I open my mouth to protest that my relationship is absolutely the fuck *not* club business.

Teller's trying to help me out here.

I snap my mouth shut.

Z opens his mouth, but he's drowned out by the rumble of Rooster's bike rounding the corner of the clubhouse. He nods at the four of us and slowly backs his bike into a space a few feet away from mine.

"Nice of you to join us, motherclucker," Z calls out.

"Go easy on him. He's lost without his little songbird," I joke.

Z snorts. "So are we. Chance keeps asking when Aunty Shelby's gettin' back from Tennessee." He glances at Rooster, then me. "Gettin' real worried you're both gonna jump charters and take over Deadbranch eventually."

The thought *has* occurred to me more than once. Shelby spends so much time there, it'd make sense. And I always thought I'd go where Rooster goes. But Margot's family business is *here*. I doubt she'll want to move to Bumbfuck, Tennessee just because Rooster wants to stay attached to his girlfriend as much as possible.

Wife. Shelby's going to be his wife.

"Yeah, over Squiggy's dead body," I quip. "I don't think he'd be eager to have Steer's downstate brothers invade his little Deadbranch kingdom. He'd feel outnumbered."

"Don't be so sure," Z mutters. "It might not be up to him anyway."

Well, fuck. For whatever reasons, Rock and Z command a lot of our national president's respect and unfortunately, his attention. Of course, Z would know how pleased—or pissed—Priest is with Squiggy as the new president of the Deadbranch charter. Fuck, for all

I know, our last SAA Steer—Deadbranch's new SAA—is feeding information back to Z on the regular.

"You talkin' shit about me?" Rooster's boots scrape over the blacktop as he approaches us.

Z runs his hand over his chin, attempting to seem serious. Too bad his grin and accompanying dimples kind of undercut the stern president thing he's going for. "Now, why would you assume that?"

Rooster hooks his arm around my neck and yanks me to him, dropping a loud, sloppy kiss on my cheek. "Miss you, fucker. Had no one barging into my kitchen draining my coffeepot all week."

Laughing, I shove him away. "You wouldn't even notice my absence if Shelby were home."

"Not true. She'd be asking why there was so much leftover coffee."

Z's mouth pushes into a sad puppy pout. "Bro, if you're lonely, you can stay at our place." He pats Rooster's cheek a few times. "We could use a manny."

I snort, then cough-laugh into my fist. "How is our little songbird, anyway?"

"Good." Rooster rubs his hands together fast enough to light a fire. "Picking her up tomorrow."

I could crack a joke about all the noise they'll be making tomorrow night, but I'm not in a joking mood.

Z glances at me, frowns, then steps forward and taps Rooster's chest. "Church is going to be short. I want you to ride out to Cedarwood's with Jigsaw."

"Prez, he doesn't have to," I say, annoyed he's asking Rooster to do something I'd ask him to do myself, if I thought it was necessary.

The humor washes off of Rooster's face. "What's wrong? Is Margot okay?"

"She's fine." I aim a scowl at Z.

"Fill Rooster in later." Z slaps my shoulder, then Rooster's. "Let's sit down at the table."

CHAPTER THIRTY-TWO

Margot

THE SERVICE IS EVEN BUSIER THAN WE ANTICIPATED. I HAVEN'T HAD much time to worry about Daniel's whereabouts since he disappeared to chat with my father earlier.

Jigsaw helped Paul and me finish the last bit of prep work before guests started arriving. I hated saying goodbye with Daniel lurking about. But I couldn't ask Jigsaw to stay just because I didn't want to be near my ex.

I'm leaving the viewing room to check on guests in the parlor when footsteps snap against the floor behind me.

A strong hand wraps around my elbow and tugs. "Can we talk?" Daniel asks.

Why didn't I ask the priest for a vial of holy water before he left? Would Daniel sizzle if I sprinkled him with it?

I shake myself loose and glare at him. For his grandmother's funeral, I had to be polite and professional.

Now, I'm done pretending. "About what?"

"I need to speak to you."

I glance into the viewing room. The guests have dwindled down to a handful of folks. I catch Paul's eye and through a series of hand signals let him know I'll be in the kitchen.

Jerking my head to the side, I indicate Daniel can follow me.

A teenager dressed in black jeans and a black sweater is bent over staring into the refrigerator. "Can I help you?" My tone's sharp. No one's supposed to be in here.

"You got any snacks?" she asks.

Working with the public sure is a pain in the rump sometimes. I guide her into the parlor and point her in the direction of the table with cookies and a few other items.

Once we're alone, I turn and face Daniel.

And suddenly wish I hadn't chased the teenager away.

"What's on your mind?" I walk over to the refrigerator and pull out a cool bottle of water, stopping to roll it over my forehead for a second before uncapping it.

Daniel stares at me with his mouth agape, as if I'd rubbed the bottle through my cleavage.

"Your father told me to talk to you."

"About what?" I take a quick sip of water.

He steps forward and tugs the water bottle out of my hands, setting it on the counter.

What the hell?

"I miss you." He holds out his arms as if he expects me to leap into his embrace.

He wasn't that touchy-feely when we were an actual couple.

My glare remains in place until he slowly returns his arms to his sides.

I arch an eyebrow. "What about Danielle?" Last I knew he had a girlfriend. Not that I care one way or another. The question is my weak attempt to shame Daniel for telling me he misses me when he's with someone else.

"We broke up."

"Why? You seemed perfect for each other." *Oof,* that came out a few shades snottier than I intended.

He frowns, then shakes his head. "No. *You* were perfect for me. And I threw that away."

Bile burns the back of my throat. A year or two ago I would've relished this apology. I still wouldn't have wanted to get back together with him, but it would've felt vindicating.

Now, I just feel sick.

And angry.

"We make sense, Margot." He aims his scowling face in the direction of the back parking lot. "You can't be serious about dating some lowlife biker."

One thing I've learned in this business—guilty people are mean people. Relatives who are drowning in guilt because they didn't spend enough time with their loved ones are always awful. So are ex-boyfriends who suddenly feel bad about the way they treated you, now that you're with someone else.

When I don't react or comment on Daniel's insult he frowns and shoves his hands in his pockets. He'd wanted to bait me, and I won't give him the satisfaction. Instead, I keep my face blank. Emotionless. Letting him know he's not worth the effort.

The longer we go without speaking, the more Daniel fidgets.

"Your father said I should talk to you." He crosses his arms over his chest, then drops them to his sides.

"So you said."

"I want to get back together." He lets out a snotty chuckle. "He can't want *that* guy for a son-in-law." Daniel holds out his hands. "How could having a grungy-looking gangster hanging around here be good for the family business?"

Ignoring the insult, I keep my face smooth and calm. "Is that what you said to my father? *You'd* be good for our family business?"

"No. Not exactly. I just asked him why he was letting you run around with that guy—"

"You *what?*"

"He said he makes you happy." Daniel pulls an annoyed face, like the concept of happiness is too trivial to ponder. "Come on, Margot, I can make you happier."

Dad actually said that?

Finding out my father feels that way is more important to me than anything else I've learned in this conversation.

Time to wrap up our chat with a hard dose of the truth. "You made me miserable every second we were together, *Dan*." I shorten his name just to piss him off, then speak slowly, so he understands how serious I am about this next part. "I'd rather die alone and be eaten by mice than waste another second of my life with you."

His eyes widen, as if he's stunned I don't have fond memories of our time together. "Be serious, Margot."

"I'm deadly serious." I cross my arms over my chest. "Do you remember what you said about me?"

Red crawls up his neck and over his cheeks. He averts his eyes, maybe remembering the long, long list of shitty things he said to me during our time together. "We were engaged. We said lots of things to each other."

I step closer and lower my voice. "You compared me to a *corpse*. Which, in hindsight, is hilarious since *you* were the one who was so awful in bed," I finish in a harsh whisper.

"Wh…what?" he sputters. "What did you want me to do?"

"Gee, I don't know. Maybe give me an orgasm, just once."

He wrinkles his nose like a child who still thinks girls have cooties. "Don't be crass."

A wild thought pops into my brain and out of my mouth before I think it through. "Daniel, are you sure you actually *like* women?"

His face turns redder than a beet.

"It's okay if you don't," I say as gently as possible.

"Of course I like women," he says through clenched teeth. "Why would you even ask that?"

"Because everything about me seemed to annoy or disgust you." I swallow hard, debating my words. "You put me down every chance you got. For the strangest things. You were quite hateful."

He lifts his chin. "I don't sugarcoat the truth." He sweeps his gaze over me and his lip curls in disgust. "You're not a ten, Margot. You're adequate. You come from a good, traditional family. You'll make a good wife. And I've reached a stage in my life where that's more important. Getting married." He drops his gaze and sort of sneers at my body. Not the look of a man attracted to me—or any other woman. "Especially since you seem to have lost a few pounds." He raises a hand and slowly swirls his finger in the air around my midsection.

Ice crackles in my chest. Tears sting my eyes.

I don't care what Daniel thinks of me. I don't. But damn, who wants to be reminded someone finds you unattractive?

And why the fuck should I care that he's at a "stage in his life" where he wants to get married?

I swallow hard and gather all my courage. I have years' worth of things to say, and I won't allow him to rob me of this opportunity.

"Have you ever had a moment of self-reflection, Daniel?"

He frowns. "About what?"

"*You* have the personality of a baked potato." I gesture wildly to his perfectly styled—to cover his receding hairline—dirty-blond hair. "And your hairline looks like it's trying to run away from your face, yet you have the audacity to stand there and insult *me*?"

Instant heat sears my cheeks as my cruel words hang in the air. I shouldn't have stooped to his level of petty insults.

"I…I…" He runs his hands over his hair several times, as if checking that it's still there.

Instead of making me feel better, knowing that I rattled him makes me feel worse. The awful comments he always made about my breasts or hips or thighs stuck with me for way too long. I wouldn't wish that kind of self-doubt on anyone…well, except maybe Daniel.

His jaw works overtime to form words that won't come. For once, I've managed to leave him speechless, and the irony of it is quite tasty. This man, who always had something cruel to say, who never hesitated to pick me apart like a grapefruit, finally has no retort.

Good.

I take a deep breath, trying to steady myself, but the rage burning in my chest doesn't recede.

It's not about him anymore. It's about me and the years I wasted doubting myself because of him. Fury bubbles over. He *really* thought I'd give him another chance to tear me down again.

"You know what? I feel sorry for you, Daniel."

An angry scowl slashes his expression. "Excuse me?"

"It must be exhausting to be so hateful. Shredding everyone around you just to make yourself feel better."

Telling Daniel off should be more satisfying but this whole conversation is leaving a sour taste in my mouth.

"Are you insane?" He raises his eyebrows and steps toward me. "I make four times the amount of money that you could ever hope to earn." He waves a hand toward the parlor. "I'm not stuck in a backward little town playing with dead people all day."

I steel myself from flinching. What I do *helps* people. It's nothing to be ashamed of. He used to tell me it was a "respectable" career. How we could make so much more money if we didn't "get sucked in by charity cases all the time," as he put it.

"Money isn't everything," I say. "And if your life is so wonderful and I'm so pathetic, why are you trying to get back together?"

Who cares about his reasons? I'd rather gargle with formaldehyde than spend another minute in his company. I turn away, crossing my arms over my chest, as if the physical barrier can protect me from this conversation.

"Obviously, I've made a mistake. You used to be a nice woman—"

I turn and glare at him. "No, I used to be a doormat."

He's blocking my way to both doors. The closest leads into the parlor but I'll have to skirt right by him to reach it.

He frowns and runs his hand over his hair again. "I never thought you were a doormat."

A burst of outraged laughter explodes out of me. "Of course you didn't." *Why would he when he was busy wiping his feet all over me?*

The back door creaks open and bangs shut. I hope it's not people leaving for the church already. The last thing I want to do is be alone in the house with Daniel.

"No matter what you seem to think, I really did miss you and want to see you. After things ended with Danielle, I realized what I'd lost in you." His tone seems gentler, more reasonable, but alarm clangs in my chest.

Sounds like Danielle didn't want to put up with his crap either so he thought poor, pathetic Margot would be desperate enough to take him back.

Unhinged laughter bursts out of me. "You've got to be kidding."

"I'm very serious." He takes a step closer, holding out his hand like he's trying to trap a mouse. "I thought now that some time has passed and we both have clearer heads, we could reconcile. I still have your ring in—"

"She's spoken for." Jigsaw's low, deadly voice hits the walls of the kitchen like the racking of a shotgun.

His presence shocks me even harder than Daniel's desire for a second chance.

Jigsaw steps inside the kitchen, his heavy boots thudding against the tile. Then another set of footsteps thunders into the room. Rooster. Today, his usually jovial expression is ferocious and aimed at Daniel.

Joy leaps into my chest. Jigsaw not only came back, he brought Rooster with him. No doubt to scare the piss out of Daniel. I force myself not to cackle with glee and clap my hands together.

"Hi, Jensen." My face bursts into the most relieved smile.

"Hey, baby." Jigsaw pushes by Daniel, easily bumping him out of his way, and clamps his hand over my hip, claiming me in the best way possible. He drags me close, pressing a long, lingering kiss against my lips. The electric sparks shooting through me from his touch almost obliterate Daniel's presence.

"Hey." My breathless voice fills the space between us. "I didn't expect you to be back so soon."

"Can't stay away from you." He gives my hip another affectionate squeeze.

Daniel clears his throat.

We ignore him.

"I, uh..." Daniel mumbles.

I tilt sideways to see past Jigsaw's body. Rooster's leaning against the doorframe, taking up the entire space. With his arms crossed casually over his chest, the sharp angles of his face covered by his beard, and the black leather vest announcing his status as VP of a motorcycle club, he radiates menace.

Daniel's gaze flits to the door leading into the parlor. His body sways with indecision. As if he doesn't want to admit the two bikers intimidate him.

Jigsaw and Rooster's gazes meet. Rooster lifts a questioning eyebrow. The corner of Jigsaw's mouth quirks.

I'm enthralled by their unspoken conversation.

"You need to get by, bud?" Rooster asks in the most condescending tone possible.

I barely stifle a snicker as Daniel squirms. The red in his cheeks deepens to a shade of purple. He lifts his chin. "No, I need to finish my conversation with Margot." He swallows hard. "In private."

Rooster sneers.

"That's not going to happen." Jigsaw steps behind Daniel, crowding him forward.

Rooster eases away from the door, his boots echoing against the tile floor. "Looks like your conversation is finished. Say a *polite* goodbye to Margot."

Daniel's gaze darts between the two men, his expression flickering between indignation and fear. He's not used to situations he can't control. Too bad for Daniel, these men don't give a fig about his family connections or his bank balance.

"We were having a conversation. I'm not doing anything wrong," Daniel protests.

"You're breathing. But we can always change that." Jigsaw's warning seems calm but carries an edge. "Margot's done talking to you. And you're done wasting her time." He lifts his chin toward the hallway. "Go out there and pay your respects or whatever you came to do and then *leave*."

Daniel glances at me as if I'm going to offer him a reprieve. I meet his gaze with the coldest glare I can muster. Jigsaw's right. I've wasted enough time tolerating Daniel, letting him walk all over me. No more.

"We're done here." My voice stays steady, even as my stomach's in freefall.

Daniel's jaw tightens. "Well, then. Good luck, Margot." He rolls his shoulders and runs his hands through his hair, like he's trying smooth his dignity into place. "I'll, uh, have a word with your father on my way out."

"You do that," Jigsaw laughs.

Daniel's eyes narrow but his sense of self-preservation kicks in and he wisely keeps any smart-ass retorts to himself. He's used to lording his power over men who flinch at his family's name and influence.

Now, he's out of his depth—facing men who live by their own code.

Rooster remains in Daniel's way, forcing Daniel to squeeze by, rumpling his suit jacket in the process.

When he's finally out of sight, I blow out a relieved breath and brace my hand on the counter.

Jigsaw turns to me, his harsh expression softening as soon as our eyes meet. "You all right?"

I nod, my hands trembling. "I am now."

"Come here." He scoops me into his arms. I press my face against his chest, savoring his warmth, strength, and crisp outdoor scent.

I let out another shaky breath. "Thank you," I murmur against his shirt. I can't believe I said those things to Daniel. I didn't get out *all* the cutting remarks I'd rehearsed in my head over the years, but I hit the highlights.

I pull back and stare up at Jigsaw. "I think some of your brashness has worn off on me. I told him exactly what I thought of him."

His lips curve with pride and affection. "Good. Your calmness must've worn off on me too, because I didn't say half of what I wanted to say. Or punch him even once."

"Oh, stop."

"Nah, he's right," Rooster says, stepping forward and slapping Jigsaw's shoulder. "My brother showed a lot of restraint. Something about that dude—he's got a very punchable face."

I clap my hand over my mouth and let out a giggle that feels sublime after all the tension. "He does, doesn't he?"

My laughter fades as a sobering thought creeps in, erasing the smile from my face.

"You must think poorly of me for dating someone like that." My voice wavers, and I glance nervously at Rooster. What if he thinks I'm not good enough for his best friend?

If only they knew Daniel and I did more than date. I said I would marry him.

"Don't sweat it." Jigsaw snorts, then clutches his stomach like he's about to double over. "My bushy-bearded brother has you beat in the awful-ex Olympics, trust me."

"Shut up," Rooster growls, shooting Jigsaw a glare. Clearly, he's not finding this as humorous.

"Well, whatever happened, it brought you to Shelby and you two are clearly meant to be together," I say to Rooster.

That replaces the scowl on his ruggedly handsome face with a fond smile. "Yes, we are."

Jigsaw stops his silly antics, but a shadow crosses his expression. Briefly, but I saw it.

"I better get back to work," I announce to smooth over the awkwardness. "Daniel cornered me, and Lord only knows what's been going on out there."

How could I forget all my responsibilities?

"We'll let you get back to it." Jigsaw gently rests his hand on my arm, stopping me. "We're going to stick around, though. Just in case."

I smile up at him. "I'd really like that."

CHAPTER THIRTY-THREE

Margot

Rooster and Jigsaw remain in the background until the guests are gone. As soon as the last person leaves, I slip off my heels, allowing my throbbing toes to sink into the carpet in the parlor.

Jigsaw unfolds his big frame from the antique sofa. Restless energy seems to course through him as he shakes his arms at his sides and rolls his head from side to side. "What can we do to help you finish up here?"

He already rescued me from Daniel's annoying presence. I can't ask him to do more. And I really can't ask Rooster to pitch in. "It's okay. I can handle it."

"We're not *asking*." Rooster stands and claps his hands together in a loud *pop*. "Come on, point us in the direction of the heavy lifting." He lifts his arms in the air like he's eager to bench-press something substantial.

"The heaviest item has already been carried out." I walk my fingers through the air toward the back door.

Rooster winces as he seems to realize I mean *the casket*.

I sigh from exhaustion and the nagging voice that says I'm taking advantage of them.

"We're not going anywhere." Jigsaw leans in and whispers against my ear, "And the sooner you finish, the sooner I get you all to myself tonight."

I flick my gaze toward Rooster, then back to Jigsaw. "You can at least let me make you guys dinner before you send Rooster packing."

"I think you've done enough work today," Jigsaw says. "We can go out, or I'll order something."

"Okay." My gaze bounces around the parlor. "I usually clean up in here last. Follow me." I turn and cross the hallway into the viewing room and point to the dais. "The flowers need to be moved into the kitchen. We'll store them in the cooler in case the family wants to take them home tomorrow."

"On it," Rooster says.

I step toward the stand holding the guest book. "I need to put this in the office." I gesture toward the small, narrow door in the back corner of the viewing room. "There are cleaning supplies in there." I give him a list of things to wipe down while I run down to my father's office and take care of some paperwork.

A few minutes later, Jigsaw taps on the open door. "What's next?"

"We can leave the chairs for now." I close my eyes briefly, running over the list my father left me. "I think that's it. I just need to lock the doors."

Jigsaw leans into the hallway and gestures wildly toward the doors. "Lock those!"

"Got it!" Rooster shouts.

I shut the computer down and stand, stretching my arms over my head and yawning.

"Long day?"

"It was…a lot." I don't want to bring Daniel up again, but I think Jigsaw understands.

He holds out his hand. "Come on. Let's get dinner."

"Ugh." I glance down at my stodgy outfit. "I need to change."

Rooster's waiting outside the office with Jigsaw. "You guys can come upstairs." I glance up at Jigsaw. "Maybe Gretel would like to meet Rooster."

Jigsaw chuckles. "Okay."

Rooster frowns in confusion.

"Oh, you didn't tell Rooster you hijacked my cat?" I tease as I head for the stairs.

"I didn't *hijack* her." Jigsaw laughs. "She just has good taste in humans."

Jigsaw

Rooster follows slowly behind me.

I turn and stare at him a few steps below. "I'm not gonna ask you to join us for a three-way, bro."

He snaps his head up and frowns at me. "Maybe I don't want her dad pissed if he finds us *both* up here."

"Dad really doesn't venture up here that often," Margot calls down. "As for any other concerns, Jigsaw's already more than I can handle. Besides, I like Shelby way too much to invite you into my bedroom."

Rooster's eyebrows shoot up and he lets out a deep rumble of laughter. "Christ, you two are perfect for each other," he mutters.

I hurry up the last few stairs and wrap my arms around Margot's waist as she punches in the code to her apartment. "Am I too much for you?" I ask against her ear.

"I love every..." She lowers her gaze and her lips curve into a playful smile. "Second."

We push into the apartment, and Rooster follows us inside.

"I made more cookies after you left." Margot points to the kitchen. "And brought a plate up just for you. They're in the fridge."

In between tending to a busy service and dealing with her ex, she somehow found time to set aside cookies for me? "Thank you."

"I'm going to change." She squeezes my hand. "Help yourself to anything you want. There's coffee in the cabinet above the coffee maker."

"I got it." I glance at Rooster and nod to one of the stools at the counter.

Margot hurries into her bedroom and I head into the kitchen in search of the cookies.

In the fridge, there's a small black-and-white plate stacked with chocolate chip cookies and covered with plastic wrap.

"Get in my belly," I sing to the cookies as I flip the cover back and grab one off the plate, stuffing it in my mouth.

"They're so good," I mumble, spraying crumbs everywhere.

I plop the plate on the counter in front of Rooster. He lifts an eyebrow.

"What? You like cookies."

"Yeah," he answers slowly, reaching for one. "I don't sing to them, though."

He takes a bite and nods approvingly. "So, are we going to talk about that guy?" He keeps his voice low. "What's the deal?"

Cookie chunks lodge in my throat. I cough and take a sip of water. "I don't know."

"Better find out. He seems like a real asshole."

I don't want to share my suspicions when Margot's only a few rooms away. "No shit."

Gretel scurries into the kitchen and lets out a loud, "Mwraar" as she twines herself around my legs.

"Hey, girl." I bend down to pick her up and she purrs so hard, her sleek, fuzzy little body vibrates against my hands.

Rooster stares at me like I've grown an extra head.

"What?" I turn the cat toward him. "Gretel, don't be scared. He's all doodle-do and very little cock-a."

Gretel head-butts me and rubs her head against my chin as if she agrees whole-heartedly with my nonsense joke.

Rooster reaches out a hand, letting it hover in the air. "Can I pet her, or will she attack me?"

"I don't know." I walk around to the other side of the counter. "Let's find out."

"She hasn't attacked anyone, yet!" Margot calls out from somewhere down the hallway.

"That's reassuring," Rooster mutters, eyeing Gretel with suspicion. He hesitates, then slowly extends his hand. The cat gives it a cautious sniff before rubbing her head against his fingers, purring louder.

"Gretel approves," I announce loud enough for Margot to hear.

He pets her for a few seconds, and then she returns to rubbing her head on my chin.

He huffs. "Do you sneak her extra treats or something?"

"Don't be jealous." I shrug and set Gretel down. "I've always told you females of all species find me charming."

Rooster rolls his eyes. "Margot's such a saint."

Yes, but I've taught her how to be a good little sinner.

He glances around the apartment, his gaze skipping over the long bookcase taking up an entire wall. "This is nice up here."

"Were you worried I was spending all my time in the cold room downstairs?" I glance over my shoulder and lower my voice. "With the bodies?"

He pauses for a few too many beats. "No."

Somewhere in the back of the apartment water rushes from the shower into the tub. I force myself not to salivate and hunt Margot down in the shower. Instead, I grab another cookie off the plate and set it on a napkin, then break off a piece. "Where do you want to grab dinner?" I pop the piece of cookie in my mouth, savoring the sweet, chocolaty chewiness.

"I don't have to tag along to dinner with you two," he protests.

"Bro, I've literally third-wheeled it with you and Shelby multiple times. Across the country." I spin my finger in the air like a bus wheel. "Shared tight quarters in the RV."

"Don't remind me."

"You can at least have dinner with us." I pull my sad puppy face and lower my voice again. "Then I'll ride home with you."

"Why?" He frowns. "I figured you'd be staying here."

"Don't want you riding home alone."

He stares at me, a completely puzzled expression twisting his big, bearded mug. "You know I'm a grown-ass man who rides by myself all the time, right?"

"Yeah, but it's late. You're not used to these roads the way I am."

"You mean the giant *highway* that runs from here right through Empire and downstate? What are you worried about? This is all our territory now. There's no issue flying colors here at night or any other time." He grabs a cookie and chomps it in half.

Crumbs fly off his fingers as he munches on the cookie. I pick up a napkin and hand it to him.

"You seem awfully cozy here," Rooster says in a low voice, making it hard to figure out if he's pleased or concerned by his observation.

Gretel leaps onto the end of Margot's chaise lounge and meows loudly.

"Sorry, are we ignoring you, girl?" I walk over and rub my knuckles over the top of her head. She purrs louder and leans into the petting.

"Ahh, is this where you snapped the picture of Wrath's book?" Rooster asks, moving closer to Margot's bookshelf.

"It's not *Wrath's* book." I scoff. "It's a book his chin to navel happens to be on the cover of."

"Whatever." His lips quirk. "Did you tell Margot?"

"No, I'm waiting to see if she puts it together."

"Puts what together?" Margot reappears, wearing purple jeans and a bright black, purple, and pink sweater that hangs off one shoulder. Her long hair now flows loose and freely over her shoulders.

"I was saying, you have a really nice place here." Rooster quickly changes the subject.

"You didn't think I lived downstairs with our clients, did you?" Margot teases.

Rooster's lips twitch into a guilty smile. "Not exactly. As we were coming up all those steps, it brought Cinderella in the attic to mind."

I chuckle because I'd had a similar thought once upon a time.

Thankfully, Margot isn't insulted. She beams at Rooster.

Gretel chirps with impatience and thumps her front paws against Rooster's leg. He jerks back, then smiles down at her and gently scratches behind her ears.

"Gosh, I had no idea she was such a little hussy," Margot laughs, wrapping her arms around me. "She's hidden from every other person who's been in my apartment besides Jigsaw."

Gretel hops off the chair and rubs herself against Margot's leg, then throws herself on the floor and rolls onto her back, showing off her tummy. Margot squats down to pet Gretel for a few seconds. Then Gretel springs up and hurries into the kitchen, stopping to turn her head as if she's checking to see if Margot's picking up the hint or not.

"Oh, someone's hungry. Give me a minute." Margot returns to the hallway and Gretel races after her.

"She has like a theater room and kitty city down there." I point in the direction where Margot just disappeared.

He nods once. "You want to go to Remy's place for dinner? Kill two birds and all that?"

"Yeah, that's fine."

"I'll head home from there." His lips curl into a smirk. "Then you don't have to worry about me riding so far alone, *Dad*," he finishes with a sarcastic head bob.

CHAPTER THIRTY-FOUR

Margot

The morning after dinner out with Jigsaw and Rooster, I'm barely awake when I sense someone staring at me. By the feel of his body and the sound of his breathing, I know it's Jigsaw.

"What's wrong?" I whisper.

"Nothing." The weight in his voice strips away the last bit of sleep clinging to me. I roll to my side to face him.

His gaze is heavy, his features carved from stone—no teasing smirk, no playful glint in his eyes. Just quiet intensity that tightens the space between us.

"Why aren't you sleeping?" I ask.

He reaches over and brushes hair off my forehead. "You're my very own Sleeping Beauty."

"So, why didn't you kiss me awake?"

"You seemed peaceful."

I shift closer to him, my leg brushing against his. "That's because you're here. Why can't you sleep?"

A flash of pain creases his forehead but he doesn't answer. Just keeps his steady gaze on me.

I brush my fingers over the sheet draped over his hip. "Is there something *I* can do to help you sleep?"

Instead of answering, he captures my hand and presses it to his chest, halting my exploration.

Okay, so he's not up for early morning sex. What has him so tense?

"What is it?"

"Can I ask you something?"

His tone instantly sets me on edge. It's too calm. Too curious.

I push back, creating a little distance between us. "Not when you say it like that."

"Is Dan the Douchewaffle—"

I let out a giggle, even though Jigsaw mentioning my ex is already tensing my body with anxiety.

Jigsaw remains stone-cold serious. "Is he the one who—" He frowns and swallows hard, as if he can't put his thoughts into the right combination of words. "Is he the one who made you think you needed sex lessons." The corner of his mouth turns up in a weak attempt to add a little light teasing to the heavy question.

"I told you, none of my previous experiences were *good*," I hedge, sensing he won't stop this time. Not until he has answers, and I want to delay as long as possible.

"Yeah, I could tell."

My heart thuds. Is that his way of saying I *was* terrible when we first started? "You could tell?"

"Just…from some of the questions you asked." He frowns. "We've talked about this—you thought you couldn't come, didn't want me to go down on you, expected sex to hurt…"

Shame heats my skin as he lists all the little signs he picked up on that loudly announced how awful my prior experiences had been.

"Hey." He slides his arms under my body, pulling me closer. "Stop. None of that made me think badly of *you*."

"Just sorry for me?"

"No. Your…inexperience is one thing, but you were convinced you were broken. And then yesterday, I overheard how that guy spoke to you. Is he the one who made you feel that way?"

"Yes." I squeeze my eyes shut, scared that once I open the door to my past, I won't be able to close it.

"How? What'd he say?"

Why does he want to know so badly?

Will he use the information to judge how much abuse I'm willing to tolerate and change the way Daniel did?

"Just mean stuff."

"Like what? That you were broken because *he* couldn't figure out how your body works?"

"Pretty much." *Please, please stop asking.*

Maybe it would be a relief to finally purge it all to someone.

And Jigsaw's the safest person I know.

He's staring at me intently, waiting for more details.

"You promise you won't tell anyone?" I ask, hating the pitiful pleading in my tone. "Not even Rooster? I know he's your best friend and as much as I like him, I—"

"Promise." He presses his hand over his heart. "Not even Rooster."

Shame I shouldn't even feel wraps around my throat. I didn't do anything wrong. I'm *not* broken.

Why is it still hard to share something so embarrassing even though I trust him?

"It's okay." He lets out a long sigh. "You don't have to if you don't want to."

He doesn't try to guilt me into spilling my pain, just keeps his arms around me. The solid protection of his body surrounding me finally loosens the knot of embarrassment tangling my tongue.

"Daniel and I started out…nice. He seemed perfect at first."

"How'd you meet?"

"Through my dad's bank." I roll my eyes. It sounds so absurd. "He works in finance."

Jigsaw snorts. "Go on."

"He'd take me out to dinner. Invited me to meet his friends. Seemed very interested in getting to know my father." I pause, searching for details I've buried. "One time when we were at an event, one of his college buddies made fun of my job in front of everyone."

I scowl, the details of that awful night returning with painful clarity. "It embarrassed me terribly, but I laughed it off because I'm used to people saying stupid things about what I do." I stop and close my eyes briefly. "But Daniel seemed *really* bothered by it. Slowly, we stopped socializing with his circle. He started criticizing me a lot more. I wasn't smart enough. Or pretty enough. I dressed too weird. Wore too much makeup. Not enough makeup. Nothing I did seemed to make him happy."

"Jesus, Margot. All of that is bullshit. You know that now, right?"

I half-heartedly lift one shoulder and nod. "Even though he seemed to hate everything about me, he still asked me to marry him. Gave me a beautiful ring." I glance down at my bare fingers. "I had this uneasy feeling in my stomach. But like an idiot, I still said yes."

"You said yes to this guy?" he asks in a pained voice.

I shift my gaze to his, but there's no judgment in his eyes, only curiosity.

"I did. On paper, he seemed like a good fit for me. I'd never come close to feeling anything like I thought people in love were supposed to feel." I press my hand over my heart. "I kept telling myself that's because this is real life, not a movie or a book. I'm an adult, not a teenager. I didn't need to be romanced and smothered with affection all the time. He paid for our dates. Introduced me to his family…"

"Margot, that's the bare minimum."

"I know."

"Adult or not, you deserve to be cherished." He entwines his fingers with mine and pure affection flows through the simple gesture. I can't bring myself to agree with his statement, though.

"Once we were engaged, he ramped up the complaints. Suddenly, I needed to lose weight, my breasts were too squishy and big, my thighs too jiggly." Humiliation rains down over me as I list each small insult that, over time, added up to a mountain of pain.

He squeezes my hand. "None of those things are true. You're perfect the way you are."

I duck my head, allowing my hair to cover my face. "I mean, I know I'm not tiny. I'm not blind. But I started to feel really awful." I peek up at him through my hair. "I think you already know the sex was bad."

"Yeah," he says quietly.

"It had *never* been great for me." I scoff. "Another thing I thought was just reality versus fiction." Heat blooms over my face but I've told him this much, I might as well give him the whole story. "I bought some books. Did some reading about how to…I thought maybe it was his lack of experience too. So one time I asked if we could explore doing something to make it last…*longer*. So maybe I could, you know, *enjoy* it too."

I risk a glance at Jigsaw, expecting to find him laughing or smug. But his face is stone-cold serious. "Go on."

"He was…angry. *Really* angry." I press my hands to my face. "His cheeks got so red, I thought he might explode. He said it was *my* fault that our sex life was so bad."

He snorts a humorless laugh. "How so?"

Just say it. Get the words out. "He said I was as exciting in bed as a *corpse*. How working around dead people must've rubbed off on me because I was cold and boring…There was more, but I stopped listening. It wasn't just *what* he said. It was *how* he said it. So hateful and vicious when he supposedly loved me."

Tears of anger and humiliation burn my eyelids, but I blink them away. How did I allow someone like that into my life for so long?

"I will kill that piece of shit if I ever see him again," Jigsaw swears. He squeezes my hands again. "None of that is true. *None*."

He's the reason I know that now, but that sounds really pathetic and I'm already feeling low enough. "Since my prior experiences hadn't been stellar, I felt like the common denominator had to be *me*. And maybe he was the only one with the spine to say it."

"Bullshit. There are just a lot of shitty guys out there who don't know—or care to learn—how to please a woman," he protests. "That's not *your* fault."

I study his face, feeling all the shame and doubt bubble up again, waiting for a hint of doubt in his expression.

Nothing. He's serious and waiting for me to continue.

"The corpse comment hurt," I admit. "I'd told him how kids made fun of me for growing up in the funeral home. So, he kind of knew that was a sore point and used it against me." I let out a deep sigh. "That was it for me. I tugged the ring off my finger, left it on his kitchen counter, picked up my purse, and left."

He blows out a relieved breath. "Good."

"And I was afraid to get involved with anyone again until I 'fixed' myself."

"There is nothing about you that needs *fixing*," he says with venom in his tone. "I want to strangle this fucker for hurting you that way."

Jigsaw

Strangle is the polite way to put what I want to do to her ex. *Mutilate. Dismember. Butcher.* Those are all better words to describe what I want to do to him.

At the very least, cut out his tongue. A poetic punishment for his crime of using it to destroy Margot's confidence. And it would have the added bonus of stopping him from hurting anyone else in the future. A gift to the world. One less asshole offering his worthless opinions to a woman he claims to care about.

"Jensen." Margot's low, scolding tone halts the violent storm brewing in my chest. "You're looking murdery. Whatever you're thinking—stop. He's not worth it."

"You're worth *everything*."

She tilts her head. "If I wanted him dead, I could've done it myself."

Now why'd she immediately assume I jumped straight to murder? "I'm not plotting to kill him."

She studies me for a few more seconds, but I keep my face blank and un-murdery. Or at least I try to.

"Words aren't enough to take someone's life." She squints at me. "*Or* permanently disfigure them."

She knows me so well.

"Disagree. You spent, what? Three years doubting yourself because of this asshole? He deserves at least a few punches to the face, don't you think?" I fucking hate that he ever had any piece of Margot's heart

—he's not worthy to breathe her air, let alone touch her or hear her voice.

I take a breath and push back my need for vengeance. "Does your father know what a piece of shit Daniel is? They seemed kinda cozy earlier."

She stares at me like I've lost my mind. "No, Jensen. I didn't tell my dad I broke up with Daniel because we had a terrible sex life and he called me a corpse." She delivers each word with deadly precision. "We don't have that kind of father-daughter relationship."

"He should know the guy's a piece of shit."

"Daniel was always on his best behavior around my father—mostly because I think he wanted to manage my family business's finances."

I bet he did.

"Don't you dare tell my father what I told you."

"I'd never do that. I promised I wouldn't tell anyone. And I keep my word."

"Then promise me you won't seek Daniel out and try to murder him."

"Ahhh, no. I won't promise you that."

"I'm serious."

"So am I." I hold up one hand, pretending to be a man of reason. "Okay, I promise not to seek him out."

She stares at me as if she's planning to bargain for how much violence I can visit upon her ex. But it's not really up for debate. The need to put my blade to his throat rages inside me.

"I *mean* it, Jensen." *Satan save me, she's so damn cute when she's trying to be stern.* "It's in the past. There's no reason your paths should ever cross. So if something happens to him, I'll know you went against my wishes, and I'll be upset."

"Soooo." I tap my chin, pretending to work this all out in my head. "Does that mean if I run into him by chance, the universe is giving me the green light to fuck him up?"

"No." She laughs and presses her hands against my chest, attempting to shove me. "Now that we've had this conversation, and you know everything, I want to forget I ever knew him at all."

"As you should."

"Well, if you kill him, then it will be all over the news and it will bring all those awful feelings back up. You wouldn't do that to me, would you?"

God damn, if that isn't the best argument she could've made. No, I don't ever want to cause her any pain.

How much news coverage would a guy like that get if he just vanished off the face of the planet?

"Besides." She reaches up and runs her fingers through my hair, pulling me out of my plotting. Her touch is gentle but deliberate, like she's trying to soothe all my evil thoughts away. "If the universe is trying to tell us anything, it's that I'm right where I'm supposed to be."

She means with *me*.

The weight of all the cosmic events that had to take place to bring us together wallops me in the chest. Not that I'm sentimental, but I grew up on the other side of the country. A mortician and a biker? Our worlds shouldn't have collided. Shit like that doesn't happen unless the universe is trying to screw with someone. Maybe it's me.

The only reason we're even together is because she thought she needed someone to fix her. All I had to offer her was physical. She deserves so much more. And I want to be the one to give it to her.

Is it insane to think we can turn this into forever?

I'm so slow to respond, she snatches her hand away. "Well, you know what I mean."

My mind's spinning through all the reasons I'm selfish as fuck. Being with me will eventually drag her down. I stare at her and try not to let the thoughts spill out. That I want to be enough for her. That the world isn't big enough to hold the things I feel for her.

"The universe is smarter than I give it credit for," I finally say.

She laughs again; this time it's lighter. I want to keep that sound.

But the dark part of me—the part that knows what I am, what I've done, what I *want* to do—starts pulling me under. I'm *not* right for her. Not long-term. Not even close. Her moral compass might skew in a different direction than the rest of society, but it's for the right reasons. Mine was shattered years ago. I'd kill for her. I'd maim. I'd destroy the world if it meant keeping her safe.

Her hands twist together in her lap. "You okay?"

I swallow hard and force myself to meet her concerned gaze. "More than okay. As long as I'm with you."

If only she understood how *not* okay I am.

I'd kill a man just because he hurt her feelings.

Is that love or madness?

CHAPTER THIRTY-FIVE

Jigsaw

Margot: Got my period.

HAL-LE-FUCKING-LU-JAH

Me: Need anything?

Margot: Advil and Sleep. I'm exhausted.

Is she telling me not to come over?

I stare at my phone, waiting for, what? An invitation?

Fuck it, I'm halfway to her house anyway.

We haven't spoken about her ex again—except that I made her promise to tell me if he ever shows up at her house. I don't want him alone with her for any reason.

"You seem moodier than usual," Remy says, swiping a rag over the bar top way too close to my hands.

I swat his dishtowel away and glance around the bar. The place is quiet. No handsy assholes bothering Remy's little sister that I need to threaten with my hunting knife tonight. Just two old guys who look like they're capping off a day of fishing with a beer. Nothing that needs my attention. "You mind if I head out?"

He stops and stares at me. "You're asking my permission?"

This kid. Sometimes, I respect him almost as much as I want to punch him. "Well, I was supposed to be here helping you out."

He checks out the nearly empty dining area. "Yeah, I don't think we're going to get much more traffic tonight. Why, got a hot date?" His lips twitch like he thinks he's clever, then his eyes widen. "Are you still seeing Margot?"

Not as much as I'd like. Hell, I'd hover over her like the ghost of needy boyfriends present, all day, every day, if I didn't think it would drive her nuts. "Yes," I growl. "Why?"

He holds up his hands and backs up a step. "Just making conversation. She's a nice woman."

She's the *perfect* woman. Kind, sexy, smart, and deadly. My favorite blend.

Ignoring his comment about my woman, I ask, "You have cookies or anything chocolate back there?" I nod toward the kitchen.

"Uh, these gooey chocolate brownie things Molly insisted we add to the menu. You microwave them. And, if you want to go into diabetic shock, top it off with ice cream." He shrugs. "They're good but no one really orders them here."

"That sounds good. Can I get two of them to go?"

"Yeah, sure." He taps the bar top and swaggers down the hallway to the kitchen. "Hold tight."

I pull out my phone again, re-reading Margot's message. Advil and Sleep. I'd skipped over that first part.

Me: You need me to pick that up for you on my way over?

Look how easy that was to invite myself to spend the night.

Margot: No, it's okay.

Is that a "no don't come over?" Or "no, I have enough Advil?"

Fuck it. Unless she outright says *don't come over,* I'm going.

Me: I pass right by a drugstore.

Well, I will if Remy hurries the fuck up so I can catch a store before it closes. I check my maps app to see where the closest pharmacy is and how late they're open.

There's actually a small, hometown pharmacy not far from Margot's house. Perfect. Anything to avoid one of the big box stores. Hopefully the hours on their site are up-to-date.

"Here you go." Remy sets a small brown paper bag with handles in front of me. "I threw in some chocolate chip cookies Lynette made earlier too."

"Perfect. Thank you." I pull out my wallet. "How much?"

"Seriously? You've been coming by for weeks to play bouncer for free, at least let me give you food."

I realize Remy has his pride but I'm not really into accepting free stuff from people when I know they're struggling. "Fair enough."

I pull out a twenty and drop it in the empty tip jar on my way out.

Behind me Remy sighs. "Thanks, Jiggy."

"Night!" I call over my shoulder.

Outside, I hurry to my truck and set the bag on the passenger side.

After a quick stop at Clover Hometown Pharmacy, I have two different kinds of Advil, the brownies, and what I hope Margot will think is a cute surprise.

I jog up the stairs of the back porch. I open the screen door, then stop. *Shit.* She didn't hear my bike coming.

Me: on back porch.

A few seconds later something buzzes and there's a click. I twist the knob and push my way inside.

I'm already passing the second floor when her door at the top of the stairs opens.

Behind her, the apartment's mostly dark. But there's enough light to make out her halo of blonde hair, mussed after a long day, and the loose blue sweatpants and long, baggy T-shirt she's wearing.

As I reach the last step, her lips curve in a tired smile.

Dark circles ring her eyes, making her look paler than usual.

"How's my favorite girl?" I slide my arms around her, inhaling the familiar scent of vanilla and sandalwood in her hair. "Missed you."

"Missed you too." She backs up into the apartment, closing the door behind us.

"Brought you some things." I hand the bags to her and stop to take off my boots.

"For me?" A hint of her usual sparkle returns to her eyes.

"Well, I don't think Gretel's going to be into any of it," I tease.

She carries the bags to the counter and pulls the lava brownies out first. "Oh, these look so good. Are they from Remy's place?"

"Yup. I guess we have to nuke them, and they get all gooey."

"Yum." She pulls the cookies out next and sets them next to the brownies.

"Those were for me." I stuff my hands in my pockets and swagger over to her. "But I'll share because you're so cute."

She laughs softly. "I don't feel so cute today."

I move closer and push the pharmacy bag toward her. "Open this one."

The bottles of pills rattle as she pulls them out. "Two kinds of Advil?" She lifts an eyebrow in confusion.

"I wasn't sure if liquid gels or regular ones work best in this situation." I circle my hand in front of her stomach. "So I got both."

She studies the blue box of liquid capsules. "I've never tried these. Thank you."

She peers in the bag again and pulls out the flat, wide white box inside. "What's this? *Cuddly Plush Heating Pad*? Why is there a cartoon cat on the box?" She pries the flap of the box open.

"It's a Gretel-shaped heating pad," I explain. "You wrap her in damp paper towels and pop it in the microwave."

"Oh my gosh!" She laughs and pulls out the soft, flat, plushy black cat filled with some kind of seeds that warm when nuked and give it weight. "This is the cutest thing I've ever seen. How did I not know this existed sooner?"

I'm way too pleased with myself over a simple gift and try to wipe the grin off my face. "I thought it was cute and once I read that it was for cramps and you said…well, I thought it might help."

"Aw." She lunges forward, hugging me so fast, the heating pad whacks my cheek. "Oh! Sorry!"

"Heavy little thing." I rub my cheek. "Soft though."

"She really is." Margot rubs her cheek against the flat cat's belly. "I really love this. Thank you." She sets flat cat on the counter and loops her arms around my neck.

"You're welcome." I brush my lips against hers. "You want me to heat it up for you? It's supposed to stay warm for half an hour."

"Actually, yes." Her expression twists with pain and she reaches for the box of pain meds. "I'm going to take these and lie down if you don't mind."

"No." I take the box from her hand and tear it open, then break the safety seal. "Did you eat something?"

She nods quickly. "I had some yogurt and granola right before you got here."

"Okay." I twist the cap off and hand her the bottle.

While she gets ready for bed, I wrap the heating pad and nuke it, praying it actually does what the box promises.

Margot

The band of pain around my forehead tightens, while the heavy ball of misery in my lower abdomen refuses to go away. I'm not sure how I feel about Jigsaw seeing me like this but I'm too tired to ask him to leave.

And for once, it's kind of nice not being alone when I feel so awful. Instead of acting confused or telling me "it's just nature, get over it" or something equally infuriating, he brought what I needed and more.

Exhausted, I pull the covers back and climb into bed. *Oh, sweet comfy mattress and pillow.* I curl up on my side, willing the Advil to hurry up and do its job.

Behind me, there's a swishing of feet over floor.

"Flat cat is warm and ready," Jigsaw says in a low voice.

I groan and hold my hand out.

"I got it. Roll over on your back for a second."

I open my eyes and stare up at him. This tall, brutally beautiful man looming over me, concern etched into his expression, and what's basically a stuffed animal in his hands. "Thank you," I whisper, unable to come up with anything better.

I ease onto my back. He holds out the heating pad. "Is that too hot for you?"

I reach up and place the inside of my wrist on the warm, velvety material briefly. "No, it's fine."

He lifts my shirt and tugs my sweatpants down a few inches, then carefully spreads the heating pad against my lower abdomen. "Here?" he asks.

Mildly embarrassed, I reach for it. "A little to the right."

Once it's where I want it, he rolls my pants into place and lowers my shirt, then covers me with the blanket. The warmth slowly seeps into my body and a fraction of the achiness recedes. "That actually does feel a little better."

"Good." He stares down at me for a moment. "Do you want me to lie next to you for a while?"

Emotion wraps around my throat, holding my words hostage for a few beats. "I'd like that. A lot."

"You got it." He walks around to the other side of the bed. There's a rustle of fabric, the ticking of his zipper, and the whomp of heavy denim landing on the floor. The covers lift and the mattress dips. "Not trying to be frisky," he says as he eases closer and slides one arm underneath me. "Just don't want to get my dirty clothes all over your sheets."

A smile curves my lips. "You're so perfect," I murmur.

"What?"

"Nothing." I settle against his body. Cocooned by his warmth, I let out a contented sigh.

He drapes his free arm over me and rubs slow circles over the heating pad and up to my stomach.

"Mmm."

"Is that good or am I annoying you?" he asks.

"Good."

"Okay." He buries his face against my neck and inhales. "Get some sleep."

"I'm sorry."

"Why?"

"Well, it's early for bed and you came all this way…"

"Stop. I'm happy right here with you." He kisses my neck. "You're even being a good girl and letting me take care of you."

I shake with quiet laughter. "It's nice to be taken care of. You're good at it."

"Only for you," he whispers against my ear, his hand still rubbing a soothing pattern. "If I can't sleep, I brought my laptop. I'll go out in the living room and do some work. If you need anything, just yell."

"The Wi-Fi password is on a pink sticky note by my chair."

"I'll figure it out. You rest."

"Okay."

He's quiet after that. His hand keeps moving in slow, rhythmic strokes over my stomach. Each pass seems to drag the tension from my body, leaving a weightless calm. His steady breathing grounds me.

Sometime later, he slips his arm out from under me, and I settle into my pillow with a sigh. The bed dips. He presses his palm over the heating pad and tucks the blankets around me.

Eyelids too heavy to open, I mumble my thanks.

My thoughts drift, untethered, slowly pulling me into sleep.

Jigsaw

Satisfied Margot's asleep, I slide out of bed and out of her room, leaving the door ajar so I can hear her if she needs me. I pad to the laundry room, grabbing the sweats Margot seems to like me in and a T-shirt I left here last time. No need to risk Mr. Cedarwood catching me running downstairs to my truck in just my boxer briefs.

Once I have my bag, I'm back inside in less than a minute. No sudden appearances from her dad. No awkward small talk with her cousin.

Gretel yowls at me the second I step inside.

"Shhh." I press a finger to my lips as if she understands what that means.

I set my laptop on the counter and grab a bottle of sparkling water from the fridge before settling onto a barstool. The laptop screen glows as I open my email.

Gretel leaps onto the stool next to me, tail twitching, bright eyes focused on me, wide and unblinking.

"What?" I whisper.

More freaky staring.

This cat.

I swivel my stool sideways, and she places one paw on my leg.

"You want to sit in my lap?"

Another paw. Then her little nails claw through my pants as she scrambles into my lap.

"Ow, you little demon." I curl my arm around her and swivel back to the counter. She sits up, balanced on my leg and stares at the laptop as if she's about to start typing.

"I don't remember hiring you to be my assistant," I mutter, curving my arm around her to tap on the keyboard.

Gretel purrs and rubs her head against my wrist as I check my email.

The first one, sent about an hour ago, grabs my attention.

I'm torn between irritation and confusion.

Stella@StellaStarr.com

Request for funding.

The fuck is she sending this to me for?

Since Z got married, he hasn't had much contact with the MC's superstar porn girl. Rooster maintains her website—organizing her content, uploading new videos, keeping things running smoothly. Since Rooster never dipped his dick in Stella—the way Z and our old president, Sway, did—their relationship is strictly business. Although Shelby's not a fan of Stella's.

All I do is help Rooster with the messy parts of the website—fixing broken links, making sure the videos work, and sometimes troubleshooting login issues for her subscribers—although apparently, I'm not very "professional" in my responses. *Whatever.*

But the money side? Not my fucking domain.

Sway set up funding for Stella's projects and was never transparent with the club about the financials. Now that Z's president, every major expense goes to a vote. If Stella needs cash, she should be going through our treasurer—or Z.

I click the email open. *Big mistake.*

I almost gag. Both at the amount she's requesting and what it's for.

The MC's porn princess has been pitching wilder and wilder content ideas for her site lately. No doubt in a sad attempt to capture Z's attention again. Am I going to raise my hand at church and float that theory to my prez? *Hell fucking no.*

Not my business.

My phone buzzes against the counter.

I scoop it up and laugh when it's Rooster.

"Hey, motherclucker," I answer, keeping my voice low.

"You see this email from Stella?" he asks.

"I'm looking at it right now."

Gretel lets out a loud, "Meeow" and bumps her head against my elbow, purring like a race car.

Rooster snorts on the other end. "I take it you're at Margot's?"

"Where else?"

"Well, I just got off the phone with Z."

I flick my gaze to the clock on the kitchen wall. "Bet he *loved* you calling in the middle of the night about Stella."

"Oh, yeah. He was *ecstatic*," Rooster says, dragging out the words. "Pretty sure he's baking me a fucking cake as we speak."

I chuckle at the thought of Z doing anything in the kitchen.

"But he never let me give him the details," Rooster says. "We need you down here tomorrow afternoon for church."

"I figured."

"We need to discuss at the table, and we don't need to involve Upstate," he says. "Rock's pretty sick of Stella."

"It's not their action, either."

"Exactly." He sighs. "Sorry, I know it's a longer ride for you."

"It's not a problem, brother. I'll probably stop by the house first to grab some clothes and my bike."

"All right. Good." He hesitates. "She didn't call you, did she?"

"Who? Stella? I don't think so." I pull my phone away from my ear and scroll through my calls. "No."

"Good." He growls into the phone. "I spent thirty fucking minutes on the phone with her, listening to her lecture me about the 'merits of her proposal,'" he finishes in a pretty decent imitation of Stella's snotty voice.

"Z should bake you a cake for listening to that."

"Heh. Yeah."

We plan a time to meet at the house, then end the call.

I check the rest of my messages, take care of a few issues, then close my laptop. "Tomorrow's problem."

"Murrrp." Gretel rubs her head against my chest.

I set her on the floor and head into the bedroom. Margot's still sleeping on her side, her breath steady and even. I strip down to my shorts again and slide into bed, careful not to disturb her.

Margot

"You feel better this morning?" Jigsaw asks as soon as I walk out of the bedroom the next morning.

"I do. Thank you." I hold the kitty heating pad up. "I think she stayed warm for longer than thirty minutes."

"Good." He closes his laptop and shifts off the stool.

My mouth goes dry as he prowls closer in those low-slung black sweatpants and no shirt. I force my gaze up to his face.

A half smirk tilts his lips as if he caught me admiring him.

"Uh, did you sleep?" Was he afraid to sleep in bed with me because I have my period? *No.* He'd been so kind and gentle last night, not disgusted.

"I did. Guess that means I didn't wake you."

"No." I yawn and stretch.

"Good. I was on the phone with Rooster late. I tried to be quiet." He shrugs.

"Is he okay?"

"He's fine. Just some club stuff." He gestures toward his laptop. "Which is why I was up early and not in bed with *you*."

He pulls me closer, tucking me against his solid body, his palm warm against my lower back. "I need to get on the road early."

"Oh." I slide my arms around him to hide my disappointment. Resting my cheek against his chest, feeling the steady drum of his heartbeat.

From my bedroom, my alarm dings. I sigh and pull away. "I have an early consult this morning."

"Pre-planning or…" He pulls a face.

I let out a dark chuckle. "I *wish* more people pre-planned. It'd be so much easier on their families. But no, this is an elderly woman. Her niece was her only family, and she said it shouldn't be too much."

"That's good, I guess." He reaches for his T-shirt draped over the barstool and slips it over his head. "I'm stopping at my place to meet with Rooster and get my bike."

I glance down at my sloppy sleep clothes. "You want me to walk you out?"

"No. Get ready for your appointment." He leans down and kisses my cheek, then catches my lips.

I curl my fingers in his T-shirt and hold him. His kiss is slow and deliberate. "You know I hate leaving you, right?" he says against my lips.

I nod quickly.

He lingers for a moment, like he has more to say, then gathers his things and presses one last kiss to my temple.

CHAPTER THIRTY-SIX

Jigsaw

"All right. Settle the fuck down," Z rumbles, running his hands over the polished wood of the table. He pulls his coffee cup closer and takes a slow sip, like he's mentally preparing himself for the bullshit about to go down. "Been a while since we sat down at our own table."

"You gotta admit, Upstate's clubhouse is much classier," Hustler snort-chuckles. "No wonder we don't wanna meet here."

Z shakes with silent laughter and inclines his head in agreement. Prez is walking a fine line not to outright insult our clubhouse since he hasn't been our president for that long.

Hustler has a point, though. When Z took over our charter, he kicked our asses into gear. We upgraded large portions of our compound. Still—it's nothing like Upstate's property.

Since most of the time my brothers treat our clubhouse like it's an amateur porn studio, all the upgrades in the world can't hide its seedy, cum-dumpster-esque charm.

Z doesn't take the bait, just moves on. "First things first. Grip, Brew—welcome back to the table."

Grip grins. "Good to be home, Prez!" He slaps his palms against the table like an overexcited toddler. Brew follows, drumming his hands on the edge.

Z barely gives them a glance. "Try to keep the excitement to a minimum."

Grinder snorts. "That's a big ask."

Z covers club business: the laundromat break-in, our dirty cop's latest updates, the usual. Then he finally circles to the porn empire.

And Stella.

He sweeps a hand toward Rooster, who's sitting next to him, looking like he'd rather be anywhere else.

"Rooster, why don't you share with the club what had you squawking in my ear late last night?"

I bite my lip and tuck my chin to my chest to hide my laughter. Rooster's glare snaps to Z, but Prez is completely unbothered.

Rooster elbows me as he sits forward, a printout of Stella's email clenched in his fist, and sweeps his gaze up and down our long table. "Stella has a request for money." He throws a cranky look Z's way. "I know how much you're going to love this, Prez."

"Stop fucking around," Z grumbles, already exasperated. "Share her brilliant deviance so we can get it over with, please."

"She wants to..." Rooster closes his eyes and silently retches.

"Now, now. Don't be so judgmental," Butcher scolds, wagging his finger between Z and Rooster. "Aren't you two always saying she's the club's most profitable asset?"

"No. She's our biggest *pain* in the *asset*," Hustler corrects. He lifts his chin at Rooster. "Why'd she email *you*, anyway? I'm the money guy."

"That's what I said," I mutter.

Rooster shrugs. "Probably because I handle all her website stuff. I'll be more than happy to send her your way for this fuckery next time." He throws a stink-eye at Z. "She assumes *I'm* her club point-of-contact now that you're wifed up and won't take her calls."

Z's dimpled grin holds zero apologies. "Sorry about that, brother."

"No you're not." Rooster laughs.

"Uh, she looped me in as well." I raise my hand. "And I would like to officially unsubscribe, please."

"Aw." Butcher makes a kissy face at me from across the table.

"What's wrong, your pretty little girlfriend get mad that a hot porn star emails you in the middle of the night?"

"Shut the fuck up about my ol' lady." I lean forward. "She doesn't know, and I'd like to keep it that way."

Rooster snorts. "Amen. The fewer people who know, the better."

Loud banging vibrates against the table. I turn toward the far end where Grip and Brew are drumming their palms against the edge, drowning out any conversation.

"What's the porn proposal?" Grip shouts like an impatient three-year-old. "We wanna hear it noooow!"

"Settle the fuck down," Grinder snaps.

"You two need a snack and a nap or somethin'?" Eazy asks.

"Come on. It sounds like it's gonna be good," Brew says. "We wanna hear it."

Rooster shakes his head. "I assure you, it's not good." He focuses his stare on our two rowdy brothers until they're quiet, then stands.

"Christ, you need to stand for this?" Z mutters.

Rooster spreads his hands wide. "Give me a break, Prez." He glances at the pages spread out on the table. The last one's covered with his blocky handwriting. "She wants to 'expand' on her current genre of meeting up with one or two randos in a hotel to film them fucking."

Z sits forward, eyes narrowed. "Expand, meaning *what*?"

"Well, Prez." Rooster throws him a disgusted scowl. "Meaning *expand*. She wants to…" He scrubs a hand over his face like he needs to physically cleanse himself before saying it.

"We're not gettin' any younger, Rooster, spit it out," Grinder says.

"Some of us more than others," I mutter loud enough for Grinder to hear.

"Keep it up, you ain't gonna get *any* older."

I grin at him. Grinder's so fun to provoke sometimes.

Rooster stares at the paper like he's contemplating setting it on fire with the power of his eyeballs. "She wants to put out an open casting call—for one hundred guys." He glances down at the papers again. "No, I'm sorry. One hundred and *one*."

Silence.

Hustler blinks. "To do what?"

"To fuck her. On camera." Rooster slides his hands through the air in a conveyor belt gesture. "All in one day."

Grip and Brew explode into cheers, banging on the table again like drunk frat bros.

"Settle the fuck down!" Grinder snaps.

"Wait." Hustler waves his hand at Rooster. "Is that even possible? Time-wise?"

I stare at him. "Aren't you our numbers guy?"

"Gives every guy about fourteen minutes with her if she takes the full twenty-four hours and about seven if she wants to do it in twelve," Eazy announces.

"Seven minutes in heaven." Grip holds his hands up toward the ceiling.

Suds side-eyes Eazy. "You couldn't break a ten at the laundromat the other day, but sex math you can do?"

"Everyone has their talents." Eazy flashes a middle finger at Suds.

"Can I please share the whole proposal before we start discussing this?" Rooster asks with a heavy dose of sarcasm. "Or whatever's going on down there."

Grinder stares at him in horror. "There's *more*?"

Z still hasn't said a word but he's leaning sideways in his chair, rubbing his temple, like he'd rather go down a bottle of Advil than listen to another word. "Continue, VP," he says, absolute exhaustion weighing down his voice.

"She proposed posting an open casting call on all of her social medias, 'seeking male talent, eighteen and up only, current STI results, location to be determined.'" Rooster rattles off the list of requirements in an irritated tone. Stella's email had a precise list of demands.

A strangled noise of exasperation escapes Z. "Who's supposed to sort through the applications?"

Rooster glares at him. "Me." He jerks his thumb in my direction. "Jiggy."

"I beg your finest of pardons, motherclucker." My tone better be crystal clear that I'm not sorting through a bunch of gang bang applications. "No, the fuck I won't."

Chuckles from further down the table swiftly get covered with a loud fake cough.

"Can't forget my favorite part." Rooster taps one of the pages. "The applicants need to send in a headshot—because, and I quote—'she doesn't want any ugly guys.'"

"Yeeeah," I say, stretching out the word to draw attention to the obvious. "We all know that pile will be full of dick pics."

Butcher bursts out laughing. "The only guys signing up for that are gonna be ones who can't get laid otherwise." He points at Suds and Hustler. "Guess you two are off the gang bang list, you ugly fuckers."

"Pfft." Suds lets out a fuck-you snort. "Fine by me."

"Where is she planning to film this fuckfest?" Grinder asks. "From what Z's described, the kind of hotels she likes to film in are gonna notice a parade of peckerwoods rotating through their lobby, dicks in hand."

Rooster's lips stretch into a thin line. He's really dreading this reveal. "She wants to film it *here*."

"Absolutely the fuck not," Grinder practically shouts. "Is this broad insane? We're not taking the security risk of having a hundred civilians traipsing through our clubhouse."

Rooster raises one finger. "A hundred and *one*."

Grinder shakes his head and rolls his eyes. "Whatever."

"Grandpa has a good point," Hustler says. "I don't want a hundred perverts in and out of our clubhouse."

"You mean a hundred and one, *in addition* to the ones that already live here?" I say, circling my finger around the table.

A slow smirk spreads over Hustler's face. "Don't act like you're so innocent now that you've got a pretty young thing who lets you stick it in her on the regular."

Grinder smacks the back of Hustler's head. "Watch your fuckin' mouth when you talk about his ol' lady."

Hustler throws out a hand in my direction. "He started it, callin' us all perverts."

"You *are* a pervert," Z says. "Ol' ladies are off-limits." His gaze swings to me. "Sit the fuck down, Jiggy."

Hadn't even realized I'd gotten up and was leaning halfway over the table about to wrap my hands around Hustler's neck. *Ooopsie.* Still glaring at him, I drop back into my chair.

He finally holds up his hands. "Sorry, you know I'm just fuckin' with you, brother."

I nod to accept the apology.

Rooster glances down at me, his eyes squinty with annoyance. "Can I continue?"

I hold out my hands. "No one's stoppin' you, brother."

He blows out a breath. "I warned her filming it here wouldn't be an option. The alternative she suggested is renting a house through Vay-Kay.com"

"She's gonna need a *big* place for that," Hustler says.

Z holds up his hands. "Wait a second. We're not bankrolling this 'project' of hers. It's disgusting."

This must be the answer Rooster expected or was hoping for. He bobs his head up and down. "It doesn't fit her 'brand' of female-gaze, artsy porn, either. I feel pretty confident very few women want to watch this."

"Wait." Suds snaps his fingers. "Her films are supposed to be for *women?*" His face wrinkles with confusion. "Is that why they're all shot in that weird hazy sunlight and there's always so much pussy-licking in them?"

"Tell us you've never satisfied a woman without telling us," I sing.

Laughter ripples around the room.

"Wait, why are we being so judgmental, Prez?" Eazy grins like an idiot. "Clubs run trains all the time. Not much different than that."

"*This* club doesn't have a hundred strangers line up to drill anyone," Z says through clenched teeth. "The porn business is sleazy enough. Let's not make it worse."

That wipes the smirk off Eazy's face. "I'm just sayin'," he mutters, sliding down in his seat.

"What's wrong, bro? You want to sign up to be sloppy seventy-fifths?" I taunt.

"Only if you're number seventy-four." Eazy blows me a kiss.

"Fucker." I laugh and sit back.

"The amount she's requesting is in the mid six-figures." Rooster passes a piece of paper to Z.

"Hah." Z barks out an incredulous laugh. "In her fucking dreams."

"Uh." Grinder lifts one hand in the air. "I realize I'm old and maybe not 'with it' but should we be concerned?"

Z slides a cautious gaze toward our SAA. "About?"

"Seems to me like a sick cry for help, no?" Grinder turns, looking for one of us to agree.

Fuck it, I'm with Grinder on this one.

"Yeah," I agree. "All jokes aside, can we all admit, this ain't normal?" I hold my hands in the air. "Not trying to yuck anyone's yum but come the fuck on."

"Kinda feels like we'd be feeding a bulimic a sixteen-course meal," Hustler says.

"Hundred-and-one course," Grinder corrects.

No one laughs.

Butcher sits forward and clears his throat, all serious now. "Prez, you sure she isn't doing this as a way to get your attention?"

The icy-cold blast of Z's glare prickles against my skin as it travels down the table, landing on Butcher. "I don't give a fuck one way or another."

"She's a club asset," Hustler mutters.

Z slices a glance at Hustler. "By all means, feel free to give her a referral to a therapist if you're concerned."

Rooster jumps in before Hustler responds. "I think some of it is that she feels like she's getting older, so she has to do more extreme content to keep her audience."

Hustler flips through some papers in front of him. "Her site still brings in way more than any of the other girls'."

Rooster taps his fingers against the table. "I set her up with someone Teller recommended to talk to about her finances. Someone *outside* the organization."

"I thought she wanted to play director with the new talent she's bringing in?" Z asks.

"She does." Rooster turns and glances down the table at Butcher, then back to Z. "Don't get bent, Prez. But it *did* feel like she was hoping this idea would get your attention. In the thirty minutes I talked to her, she brought your name up a *lot*."

"Let's take a vote," Z says without acknowledging Rooster's theory. "I don't want anyone complaining we robbed the club of an opportunity."

We all seem to be on the same page, so taking individual votes feels like overkill. Z's been by-the-book since he took over.

"Yay or Nay, we fund Stella's 'hundred-and-one man' project?" Z rolls his eyes, then shifts his gaze to Rooster to cast the first vote.

"Nay," Rooster says without any additional commentary.

"Nay," I add.

Every brother at the table adds their no vote, finally ending at Z.

"Nay." He slaps his gavel against the block, signaling the Stella portion of club business is finished.

"I'll let her know if you want, Rooster," Hustler offers.

Z side-eyes our treasurer.

"We have a chain of command she should follow. She should be aware of that," Hustler explains.

"I'd appreciate it." Rooster glances at Z. "I'd rather keep my involvement focused on the IT stuff for her site. Not her funding…or anything else."

"Tell her she can do whatever she wants," Z says to Hustler. "We're just not paying for it *or* getting involved in any other way." He sends a look around the table. "That clear with everyone?"

Meaning, no one at this table better jump in that hundred-man line.

We run through a few other minor matters, then Z sets us free. Rooster's slow to leave the table, so I stick around too.

"You thinkin' of pulling us out of Stella's business, Prez?" Rooster asks once it's just the three of us.

Z frowns. "No, why? You heard Hustler. She still brings in a lot of money."

"No reason." Rooster slaps his palm on the table and stands. "Just want to make sure we're all on the same page."

I'm not *quite* ready to leave yet.

"With Sway fucking off in Florida, it sounds like maybe Stella's a bit…adrift, maybe?" I scrunch my face into one of thoughtful confusion. "They were a thing for a while, right? Maybe she's missing that older man mentoring Sway was so good at." It's a struggle to keep my face stuck in serious mode.

Z groans at the reminder that he dipped his quill in the same ink as our old prez.

My work here is done.

I follow Rooster into the main part of the clubhouse. The room's crowded, full of rowdy voices discussing the dirtier details of one hundred guys and one girl and the clink of glasses or popping of cans at the bar.

"You couldn't miss that opportunity, could you?" Rooster slaps my back a few times and laughs as we settle onto two barstools in the corner away from everyone else.

I widen my eyes to a shocked and offended size. "At least I didn't explicitly say he's basically crossed swords with Sway." I make an X with my index fingers to demonstrate.

"Nah, you were subtle as a brick." He squeezes his eyes shut. "Jesus Christ. Z might've shot you on the spot if you actually said that."

Lala stops by and Rooster asks her for two cups of coffee.

Once she's gone, I lean in toward Rooster. "If *he* wants to pretend he doesn't have history with Stella, that's fine and dandy, but he shouldn't expect the rest of us to forget."

He sighs. "Go easy on him. I think distancing himself has more to do with not wanting to rub Lilly's face in his past."

I open my mouth to spit out something quippy, then stop. Isn't that the same thing I was worried about with bringing Margot around the club? *Fuck.* A random bunny or two is a lot different than having a well-known porn star as your ex. "Lilly's made of strong stuff. She doesn't give a fuck about Stella."

"Yeah, I know but," he pulls a disgusted face, "if we start letting her reach out to him instead of running interference, that's a shitty thing to do to Lilly." He takes a sip of coffee. "Not that Shelby *loves* when Stella calls me." He shrugs. "But I don't have history with her."

"Hot or not, I straight up just don't like Stella. Shelby's right, she's condescending as fuck."

"You don't *have* to like her," he says, using his patient tone. "Just help me deal with the web stuff."

I'm not done listing my complaints. "Every time she asks me to 'star' in her 'biker series,'" I cover my crotch with both hands, "my dick wants to crawl up inside my body and hide."

"Same, brother." He rolls his lip in disgust and sets his cup down. "Jesus Christ, could you imagine if we allowed Stella to film a fucking gang bang here…or had a wrap party for it at the clubhouse. How fucking awkward would that be?" He turns on his stool slightly, surveying the room. "She'd try to fuck everyone here just to make sure Z got an eyeful."

"Probably." I glance over my shoulder at Grip and Brew over by the pool table, actually using it for its intended purpose for once. "A good portion of our brothers would do it in a heartbeat too."

Rooster stops and glances over his shoulder, then turns back to me. "Maybe it's for the wrong reasons, but I'm glad Z backed me on this. If she wants to film her little fuckfest safely, she needs to vet all of those applications thoroughly, find a suitable location—where she won't risk getting arrested—set up insurance, staff enough professional bodyguards…"

"Fuck, yeah. Otherwise she'll end up with bouncers who are trying to take a turn instead of controlling the crowd." I take that one further. "Or they won't be paying attention to make sure no one hurts her or does more than they agreed to."

"Right. How many times have we seen guys at Crystal Ball think a lap dance means the girls are down to fuck outside the club? Jesus

Christ, she needs security guys when she's doing one or two guys now."

I snort-laugh into my coffee. "And who the fuck's she going to hire to entertain all these guys while they're waiting in line?"

"Exactly. All those logistical details will cost a fortune."

I slap his chest with the back of my hand. "Look at you all lawyerly and shit."

"It's not lawyerly. It's common sense." He sighs. "I think it would alienate her current subscribers too."

"Or she might get a lot of free advertising for her site if that story went viral."

He shrugs. "She'd get an uptick in looky-loos checking it out for the shock value, but they won't stick around. It would damage her brand more than help it." He gestures toward the chapel and then to the rest of the clubhouse. "We're a bunch of dirty bikers who've hosted some questionable parties, and even *we* thought it was disgusting."

"Shit." I shake my head. "Priest already hates our porn business. Could you imagine how hard National would come down on us if that made it into the news and Lost Kings were attached?"

"Right, because if she does it the *wrong way*—doesn't vet all the guys thoroughly, or films it in the wrong place, it could be a *huge* liability. At best it ends up being an STI super-spreader event, at worst, multiple lawsuits and bad publicity for the entire organization."

"Uh, *worst* case would be she adds a random serial killer to the guest list and get murdered," I point out.

"Jesus Christ," He groans. "You're right. Out of a hundred people who sign up for something like that, odds are high one or more of them are psychos."

"Well, it's done now."

"Exactly. We voted it down. Hustler's going to give her the news." He rubs his hands together briskly like he washing off the entire filthy discussion. "Done. I just hope the other girls don't start coming up with ideas like this next."

A hand clamps down on my shoulder and yanks me sideways. I

glance behind me and find Z. He grabs Rooster and *yoinks* him closer too. "Are you *still* talking about this?" he asks.

I jerk my shoulder loose from his grip and spin my bar stool around to face him. "Just discussing all the many reasons it's a good thing we voted it down, Prez."

He glances at Rooster, then me, his jaw tightening while he drags his hand through his already messy black hair. "I'm sorry you have to deal with her. I thought you'd only be working on her website. Maybe connect with her when she sends you content to upload. Not get into stuff like this."

Rooster leans his elbows back on the bar. "I don't mind, Prez," he says, his tone easy, but his pinched expression suggests something more. "Well, unless she asks me questions about *you*." He holds up his hands, palms up like he's preparing to ward off Z's wrath. "I tell her I'm not gonna discuss your personal business with her but she always tries."

Z's face darkens, his eyes narrowing. "What the fuck for?" he snaps, his voice rising enough to draw the attention of a few brothers. "Once she found out I had a kid, she was thrilled I dumped her." Z squeezes his eyes shut, pinching the bridge of his nose like he's trying to push a bad memory away. "She jumped back on Sway's dick so fast, I thought she was over it."

Rooster shrugs. "I'm just letting you know."

Z's eyes narrow. "She talk shit about Lilly?"

"Never," Rooster says. "Kinda acts like she doesn't exist, honestly."

"For fuck's sake. I don't need this."

"Sorry, Prez." Rooster pats his shoulder. "Hustler and I will handle it."

"Anyone hear from Sway recently?" I ask. "Maybe he can talk to her?"

Z scowls at me. "He's the one who got us into this mess in the first place."

"Yeah, I know," I answer slowly. "Maybe that's why *he* should deal with this." I tap the patch on my chest. "He 'retired.' He didn't get excommunicated."

"If I talk to him, I'll mention it," Z says. "You sticking around?"

I really should put in some facetime with my club. I've either been at Margot's or at Upstate's clubhouse lately. "Yeah, for a little while."

"Good." Z slaps my back. "I miss your witty commentary."

"Don't encourage him, Prez," Rooster groans.

"It's good to have you home," Z says before taking off.

Too bad it doesn't feel like home anymore.

CHAPTER THIRTY-SEVEN

Margot

My consultation earlier in the week went well and I've been nonstop working on the arrangements, fighting with suppliers to get the right casket here, drafting the obituary, and preparing the legal paperwork. There are so many pieces involved in putting a funeral together, and I enjoy working my way through the chaos so the family doesn't have to.

But by midweek, I hit a snag.

I can't finalize any of the arrangements.

As much as I hate having to ask my father for assistance, I'm stumped.

I stop in his doorway. "Dad?"

He glances at me and sets his pen down. "What is it, Margot?"

"I still haven't received a signed death certificate from the medical examiner's office for Mrs. Baker."

"Did you call them?"

I grit my teeth. *Why does he always assume I messed up?* "Yes, but they won't give me a straight answer and can't tell me when they'll release the body. Has that happened to you before?"

His eyebrows draw down, deep furrows lining his forehead. "Only in unusual circumstances. Let me call and check."

It'll burn my ass if the cranky old medical examiner gives my father answers he wouldn't give me. But we need that certificate. No certificate means no burial.

He picks up the phone on his desk and dials the number from memory. I drop into the chair in front of Dad's desk and slide my hands over the wrinkles in my dress pants.

My phone buzzes in my pocket and I discreetly pull it out.

Jigsaw: Missing you.

How can two simple words instantly quell my anxiety.

Me: Miss you too. Weird day here. In a meeting with Dad.

Jigsaw: Call me later.

I wish I could call him now. His voice, his presence, have a way of grounding me.

"Yes, Ed." Dad's sharp tone pulls my attention away from Jigsaw's text. "We've already spoken with the family. We're in a holding pattern, waiting for that certificate, though."

I slip my phone back into my pocket and lean forward.

His eyes widen and he rubs a spot in the middle of his forehead—a sure sign that whatever the examiner's explanation is, it's giving him a headache.

"You're kidding? I thought she was…" He exhales sharply. "No, I understand. Please keep Margot updated. Thanks, Ed."

He rests the phone in its cradle, his fingers still lingering on the receiver as he stares at me. "They're not releasing her because they found something suspicious."

"Suspicious?" I blink. "What? Her niece didn't mention any concerns."

Dad stares at the phone. "Apparently her doctor raised some questions. She had a large estate, and he said she'd just had a physical and was in excellent health."

"Dad," I say with tired patience. "How many times do we hear that? We both know after eighty, it's a gamble whether you wake up every day or not."

His lips purse in disapproval. "You're awfully cynical."

I reach for the file on his desk and flip through the documentation, studying the death report. In the corner of the folder a scribbled note in my father's handwriting reads—*D, ref.*

"She didn't have a lot of family. Her niece says most of the estate is going to charity. Is this doctor upset he's not in the will or something?"

"Don't be ridiculous."

Well, this doctor just made my week a whole lot more difficult.

"I'll call Colleen and let her know we may need to pick a different date."

"Just say there's a backlog at the medical examiner's office. Don't mention anything about the doctor raising suspicions."

"Of course." *I'm not stupid, Dad.*

I glance at the address in the file one more time. The street name sounds familiar. But I can't place it.

"All right," I murmur, pushing my annoyance at the delay aside. "While I'm waiting, I'll help Paul with the Allen case."

"That would be good." He flips open the planner on his desk. "I have a consultation at nine tomorrow I'd like you to sit in on."

I hesitate. "Okay. Any particular reason?"

He closes his calendar with a decisive thud. "No, you'll understand once you meet them."

Jigsaw

The problem with our upstate and downstate charters being so intertwined these days? Being called for church twice in one week. Not that it didn't happen before, but it seems to be the norm instead of the exception lately.

Rooster and I ride up together. I've missed this. We've ridden together for so long that we automatically move in sync. Weaving through traffic, a slight dip of his shoulder and I know to anticipate a lane change. We learned how to ride together. Friends of his uncle taught us, then brought us into the club out in Washington. Years of club runs, high-speed chases, back roads cruising, highway miles—we've done it all.

We arrive at Upstate early and back our bikes in close to the clubhouse.

"Surprised we're not meeting at the new clubhouse in Empire," I say to Rooster. "It would cut, what—thirty minutes off for the guys coming from Union."

"I'll let you suggest that to Rock." He sets his helmet on the seat, then tips his head back, staring at the cold, gray sky. "I'd rather be here, honestly. It's crowded and noisy down there." He side-eyes me. "What's wrong, you longing to hit up Crystal Ball after church?"

"Fuck no. I helped Dex out the other night and remembered all the reasons I'm not interested anymore."

He rumbles with laughter, shaking his head as he circles around the bikes to meet me.

The skitter of a stone over pavement is the only warning I get before a thick, inked arm snakes around my throat and yanks me back into a viselike grip.

"What the—ack! Fuck," I choke out.

Rooster—asshole that he is—busts up laughing.

"Look who it is bright and early, my two favorite fucknuggets," Wrath says against my ear.

"Not…feeling…the…love, brother," I gasp.

"You should be able to get out of this move easily," he taunts. "I thought you were a master cage fighter?"

"He meant masturbator," Rooster adds, grinning like a dick.

I roll my eyes, or at least I try to, seeing as Wrath's forearm is steadily cutting off my oxygen.

"I don't want to hurt you, bro," I manage.

Wrath shakes with laughter, his chest rumbling against my back, his hold shifting just enough to cut my air further.

He asked for it.

I plant my feet and immediately go for his wrist, gripping it hard. Instead of fighting against his strength, I drop my weight while twisting my torso sideways, pulling his arm forward as I duck under it.

It's not the cleanest or the prettiest escape, but I break free, gasping for air as I put some distance between us.

"Not bad." Wrath shakes out his wrist, rolling his shoulders like he's evaluating my technique. "Figured you'd go for the knee sweep."

That *would* have been better. *Damn, I'm getting rusty*. "Told you I didn't want to hurt you, *old man*."

He wags a finger in my face. "*Old man* who just almost put you to sleep in the driveway."

Rooster snorts. "This how you're planning to greet us for church now?"

"Just trying to teach you situational awareness." He reaches out and slaps Rooster's cheek a few times. "Always be prepared."

I pat the hunting knife strapped to my belt. "Bro, you came at me on the street like that, I'm not using an evasive maneuver, I'm straight-up stabbing you."

Wrath's eyes glint with amusement. "Duly noted."

Great, he took that as a challenge.

A rustling in the trees grabs our attention, and Z, Rock, and Murphy emerge from the woods, making their way toward us.

"Aw, what's wrong, big boy?" I ask Wrath in a high-pitched baby voice. "You weren't invited to the presidential summit?"

"No, he heard you two coming and ran through the woods like Tarzan to ambush you," Z explains, lazily circling his arm in the air.

Wrath crosses his arms over his chest and nods.

"You need to get out more," I suggest, shaking my head. "Socialize with people. Go on some playdates or something."

He screws his face into a mask of pure disgust. "I see enough people at work."

Rock, Murphy, and Z step into our circle, exchanging looks.

"A heads-up woulda been nice, Prez," I say, slapping Z's shoulder, "that fuckin' Tarzan was coming to get me."

Z smirks wide enough to show off dimples. "I wasn't sure which one of you he was gonna target."

"Thanks, Prez," Rooster says.

I lace my hands behind my back and rock onto my heels—the picture of innocence. "So, did Z fill you in on Stella's *hundred-and-one men in one day* film proposal?"

Murphy turns to the side and gags. "What the fuck?"

Z shoots me a glare.

Rock arches an eyebrow, then shrugs. "You know what? I don't wanna know." He holds up a hand, already done with the conversation. "I'm not volunteering as security for that gig."

"We voted it *down*," Z says, his glare still locked on me.

"Why…How…What?" Murphy sputters.

"It's as disgusting as you think," Rooster says.

A thunderous chorus of bikes echoes up the driveway. "Guess that's the rest of Downstate," I shout to Rooster.

It's not just Downstate, though. Dex is at the front of the pack.

He parks in the garage and jogs over to us. "I was worried I was going to be late. Had the inspector down at Crystal Ball."

"What inspector?" Z asks.

"Fucking fire marshal," Dex mutters, scrubbing a hand over his jaw. "It was just a routine check."

"Was it Keegan?" Wrath asks.

"No." Dex shrugs. "Wouldn't have mattered. That guy's un-bribable." He grins. "And it didn't matter. There weren't any issues for him to ding us on. He wanted to give me a hard time about the back door since we prop it open a lot, but it's clearly marked. And obviously if we're propping it open, people can get out if they need to." He lifts his chin and taps his fist on my arm. "Thanks for helping me get ready for the inspection."

"Any time, brother."

A few of the other guys walk over to us and Rock lifts his arm, waving everyone toward the clubhouse. "Let's go inside."

We file straight into the war room.

I take a seat on the far side of the middle of the table, between where Rock's guys usually sit and where our downstate brothers sit. Seems like an appropriate spot given how I've been splitting up my time lately.

I reach across the table and slap Eazy's hand, then Butcher's as they take their seats.

Sparky shuffles in and lifts his chin at me before sprawling on the couch tucked into a corner at the end of the table.

"All right." Rock stands at the head of the table. "Settle down."

The door pushes open and Grinder hurries inside, walking straight to the empty chair on Z's right-hand side.

"Where you been, G?" I tease as he squeezes behind my chair.

He flicks the back of my head in response and keeps moving.

"Welcome to our downstate brothers," Rock starts off the meeting. "I'm going to run through a few of our matters, then turn things over to Z."

Z's eyebrows shoot up in a *what now* expression.

"Dex—fire marshal visit to Crystal Ball?" Rock asks. Even though we already discussed it outside not everyone was there.

"It was good. No issues. I think the guy was disappointed." He glances down to the end of the table. "All the recent upgrades met with his approval."

"Good." Z nods.

"And," Dex adds. "I want to say thanks for letting me borrow Jiggy. He was a big help in getting stuff moved and out of the way."

I curl my arm and slap my bicep. "You know it."

Rock goes over a few more things that only concern his guys. Finally, he glances up. "I've got a meeting with Loco. He's specifically asked for Z, Grinder, and Rooster to join me."

"Aww, he doesn't want to see my pretty face?" Teller jokes.

"I told him you're busy," Rock says, still looking down the table at Z.

"Yeah, all right. When?" Z asks.

"Sometime this week. I'll let you know when I've got a date."

Z's silent for a few seconds. "I'll probably just stay up here at the cabin, then." He points at Dex. "Promised Dex I'd watch CB for him while he and Emily are away."

"Thank you, brother," Dex says. "Girls will be very excited to see your pretty face."

"The ones who even remember him," Ravage adds. "We've had a lot of turnover since he was there."

Z grinds his teeth. "Can't wait," he says in the least excited tone possible.

"Uh, Lilly all right with you working at Crystal Ball?" Hustler asks. "I mean, I can do it if…"

"Worry about your own wife, bro," Z snaps. "Oh, wait, you don't have one."

"Ouch." Hustler claps his hands to his cheeks. "That stung."

We run through a list of other items, then Rock excuses everyone except the officers.

I'm already halfway to standing. "RC's too?" As I'm asking the question, I note Dex's ass still firmly planted in his seat.

Fuck.

Rock points to my cut. "That road captain patch just for decoration?"

"No, sir."

"Good." He nods to the vacant chair next to Murphy. "Come sit your ass down."

"Clown," Rooster mutters against my ear.

"Dickface."

Once we're all rearranged, Rock nods to Wrath.

Elbows on the table and hands clasped together, he leans on the table like we're about to discuss a bank heist.

This should be good.

"I have a source who says when Griff's done with that shitshow reality nonsense he's going to be offered a pro fight in Vegas."

"No shit." Murphy whistles and sits back, crossing his arms over his chest.

"You think this is an investment opportunity?" Teller asks.

Boy, he sure got there fast. Always looking for ways to make bank.

"I do."

"Wait," I cut in, frowning. "I've been helping out at Remy's place, and he hasn't mentioned it."

"He doesn't know yet. It's not final. That's why I didn't want to discuss it in front of everyone yet," Wrath explains. "Griff still has to agree to do it."

"Not a chance he's saying no to that," Murphy says, shaking his head.

"Did you *watch* the show?" Dex leans forward, expression twisted with disgust. "From the bits I saw, it's fucking awful. Doesn't have much to do with fighting. I tried to warn him…"

Wrath shakes his head as if that part's unimportant. "The fights they *did* show? He's by far the best fighter in the whole house." He points at Murphy, a smirk tugging at his mouth. "Reminds me of you when you were younger. If you'd been more disciplined."

Murphy bristles. "Well, I didn't have the luxury of being *disciplined* when I was younger."

"Easy, Jolly Green. It wasn't an insult."

I jerk my thumb at Murphy. "Is that new? Are we calling him Jolly Green now, because I can get on board with that."

Wrath's deep laugh shakes the table.

"Is there a point to all of this?" Z asks.

"Yes, there's a point." Wrath nods to Teller. "Bishop Babymaker was right."

Teller groans.

I grin. *Glad that stuck.*

"It's an investment opportunity," Wrath says slowly, like he's trying to dazzle us. "Griff will be the underdog. The odds will be against him."

"Because he's unproven," Grinder points out.

Wrath's already shaking his head. "Yeah, in a *professional* cage, sure. But he's been fighting for years. Fought for his life at The Castle."

Teller's jaw tightens. "They should've burned that place to the ground."

"*Now* he's been professionally trained, and he'll have to train nonstop for that fight," Wrath continues. "Plus, he still needs money. Once the government takes its bite of whatever shitty prize money he wins, he won't have the nest egg he wants."

"What does any of this have to do with us?" Rock asks in his usual *move it along* tone.

"I think we should nurture this opportunity," Wrath says. If he were a cartoon character, there'd be dollar bill signs in his eyes. "Offer our support. Offer our protection at the fight."

"You want the whole club to swarm into Vegas?" Z asks, raising an eyebrow. "The *club we don't name* still runs that territory. We show up in force there, law enforcement will be all over both clubs."

"No, not the whole club," Wrath says. "I'm sure Remy and Eraser will be there. We only need a couple more guys who Griff can trust to have his back."

"Dawson's really into MMA," Rooster chimes in. "*Watching* the fights," he clarifies with an eye roll. "Betting."

"Does that guy have his own personality?" Hustler asks.

"Yes," I answer in a dry tone. "Being so stupid-rich that he picks up hobbies like babies pick up seashells."

Rooster rolls his head to the side and gives me the questioning eyebrow/eye roll combo.

"What?" I shrug. "It's true."

"Weird comparison, but okay," Z says.

"He goes to Vegas all the time," Rooster says. "I'll ask him what the security situation is at those events."

"I *know* what it's like." Wrath circles a finger in the air. "Those fights are on pay-per-view, you know."

"Yeah, that's not the same," Murphy says. "Some of those so-called pro fighters are gutter rats. Griff might not get a warm welcome as an outsider. They don't air all the squabbles that go on backstage between the fighters and their entourages."

I pull back and stare at Murphy. "Look at Jolly Green with the big words today."

"Fuck off." Murphy laughs and punches my shoulder.

"Exactly." Wrath nods like he's happy someone's finally getting his point. "We should be there to make sure no one fucks with him."

"The odds will be so against him, the payoff could be huge. If he pulls it off," Teller says, practically salivating at the thought of a major influx of cash. He turns to Rock. "We could take a portion of club funds."

"You want to bet club funds on a *fight*?" Rock asks with a raised eyebrow, clearly not sold on the idea.

Teller dials back his enthusiasm. "Let's see what Wrath finds out. Obviously, I'd ask for a vote. I wouldn't touch club funds for something like that without approval. And I wouldn't risk more than we can afford to lose."

Rock scowls at him. "I know that."

"I'm in." I raise my hand like someone's taking attendance. Margot said she wanted to travel. Maybe our first trip together will be Vegas.

"Let's get a date and more information first," Rooster says. "But I'll probably go too."

"If Remy's going, I assume he'll need someone to watch the bar," Dex says. "I'll do that for him."

"I wouldn't mind seeing Vegas," Grinder says with a casual shrug. "And I'd like to support the kid after everything he's done for me."

"Good." Wrath slaps the table. "That's all I wanted. See if there's interest and if Teller thinks it's worth an investment."

"Wait a minute." I hold up my finger. "Is this why you greeted me with a choke hold?" I swivel my head between Rock and Z. "Is attacking us his new way of saying hello from now until Vegas?"

"I told you." Wrath grins, pure evil. "Situational awareness."

"Oh, it's *on* motherfucker," I promise.

"All right." Rock slaps the table, signaling the conversation's over. "This could be interesting." He nods toward Wrath. "Thanks for bringing it to the table."

But Wrath's distracted with his phone lighting up. He scowls at the screen. "Let me take this," he mutters, already pushing away from the table.

Rock stands and dismisses everyone.

Rooster and I stop in the living room.

"Vegas, huh. It's been a while." Rooster slaps my chest. "You remember our first long ride? Boone and his buddies taking us through Nevada? Supposed to be this epic scenic three-day ride—"

"And my balls went numb on day one?"

Rooster barks out a laugh. "Well, yeah. Same. But when we reached that town with—"

"The biblical plague of crickets everywhere!" I shudder with disgust. "I can still hear the crunchy noise they made when we ran over them. Felt like driving on gravel."

"There had to be millions of them on the road." Rooster shakes his head. "Remember the woman at the gas station telling us they used snowplows to get them off the road."

"No, I remember her warning us that bikers wipe out every year because the road gets slick from all the cricket goo."

"And the guys thought she was full of shit, and we kept going."

"Jesus, it was like rolling through a massacre."

Rooster closes his eyes and runs his hand over his face. "Oh, the smell."

"Rotting fish and zombie brains." That's the only way I've ever been able to describe it. "That shit stuck to my tires forever. Fucking disgusting."

Rooster shakes his head. "I know he was a good friend to Boone, but Monkeybutt was the *worst* road captain. That's not the only time he made a bad call."

My mouth turns down at the memory. "Yeah, he fucked around one too many times and found out the hard way."

After a moment of silence, I ask Rooster, "We're not riding out if we go out for the fight, right? Wrath can't take that kind of time from Furious." And *I* can't get Margot on the back of my bike for a ride down the block. She's definitely not riding cross-country with me.

"Doubt it." He raises his eyebrows. "Maybe we can borrow Dawson's private jet."

"In your dreams," I scoff.

Behind us, the war room door opens.

"Jiggy, fuck I'm glad you're still here," Wrath says, his scowl deeper than usual.

I turn toward him. "What's wrong?"

"I need you to head out to Margot's. Now."

CHAPTER THIRTY-EIGHT

Margot

Well, now I understand why my father wanted me to sit in on this consultation.

The woman here to bury her father is about my age but that's where our similarities stop.

"For fuck's sake. Can we please bury my dad without all your biker bullshit?" Abby explodes, pounding her palms against the arms of the chair in front of my dad's desk. "Why are you even here?" she screeches at the burly man in denim and black leather.

"'Cause the club's paying for the funeral, darlin'," the man who's only ever been introduced to me as *Ulfric* answers smoothly, ignoring her outburst. "Whisper was clear, he wanted to be buried here."

"Whisper! Jesus Christ, enough already. Can we please use his real name now?"

Ulfric casts a sideways look at her. The first sign his patience with her outbursts has a limit. "No one will know who we're talking about, then, Abigail."

Ouch. Full-naming her. That's harsh.

"We can, of course, craft his obituary to include any other names Mr. Hall was known by," I say. "We do it all the time."

"See? This is why your father wanted Mr. Cedarwood to handle the arrangements." He nods to my dad.

Pretty sure any funeral home would do the same.

Wait. Is that his subtle hint he'd like me to get lost?

"Well, I hope you're prepared for a parking lot full of Harleys, loud men, and a shoot-out or two," Abby says, her gaze shifting between Dad and me.

"There ain't gonna be no shoot-out, Abigail," Ulfric sighs. "Stop trying to scare the Cedarwoods. But there will be a lot of bikers in attendance. Some from different clubs."

I shoot a glance at my dad, and he lifts one eyebrow. Does he think dating Jigsaw means I'm the outlaw biker whisperer or something?

"We can certainly handle any…delicate relationships," I assure Ulfric without revealing my personal involvement with the local motorcycle club. "It shouldn't be a problem. But if you prefer, we can add security—"

"Nah, we got a good relationship with the dominant club in the area. Their enforcer was Whisper's business partner for years."

Huh. How about that.

"Dominant club," Abby mimics with a nasty sneer stretched across her burgundy-painted lips. "Jesus Christ, you're all still so ridiculous. No *one* owns upstate New York. I don't need permission from a bunch of boys in leather to bury my father."

Ulfric takes in a long slow breath. A prickling sensation travels down my neck. Like if my dad and I weren't here to witness it, Ulfric's friendly Grandpa veneer might melt, and he'd smack the attitude right out of Abby. "It'll be handled. You focus on your family, Abigail."

"I plan to." She rips her purse open and yanks a long cream-colored envelope out. "Dad had a list of demands…*requests* that he wanted for his funeral." Abby's gaze skips between my father and me.

"We're more than happy to handle any special requests Mr. Hall might have had." I sit forward and hold out my hand. She flicks a glance at my father in a *going once, twice* sort of way, then hands it to me.

"We already had a plan worked out with your father." Dad taps the glossy white folder in front of him. "Is that list dated?"

I pull out a thick sheet of cream paper and unfold it, reading the date to my dad.

He nods once. "I'll have you compare the list to what's in here and we'll adjust as necessary." Dad tilts his head toward Ulfric. "Mr. Hall already pre-paid a portion of our fee."

"Of course he did," Abby grumbles.

She should be thankful her father thought ahead. I bite my tongue from lecturing her about how many families we see who have no arrangements, slim finances, and leave the burden of sorting it out to their loved ones.

I run my gaze over the list from Mr. Hall.

Music: Led Zepplin

Coffin: shiny, black with black leather accents and silver hardware. Wolf Knights MC engraving.

Flowers: black and silver arrangements.

Transportation: Harley Davidson Hearse Funeral Chopper.

Traditional biker funeral.

My questioning gaze lifts, catching my father's attention. "I'm not sure if we'll be able to accommodate *all* of these requests, but we'll do our best."

"The Harley coffin trailer?" Abby snorts. "Fuck it. Do whatever's safest, even if it's not on his list. I don't want his coffin hitting the pavement and his body rolling out before we get him in the ground."

Horror shivers over my chest. A catastrophe of that nature would ruin our reputation if not bankrupt us. Great. New nightmare unlocked. *Thanks, Abby.*

"Whisper could be dramatic when he wanted to be," Ulfric says with a sad but fond smile. "Keep safety in mind. But money isn't a concern."

Sure, people say that all the time. Right up until we present them with the bill. "The funeral chopper will be our biggest logistical challenge. I'll research our options and consult with you." I glance at

Ulfric, then Abby. Although, if Ulfric's paying, he's the one my dad will go to for approval on any expenses.

With the number of specific requests Mr. Hall has it's going to take more time than usual to plan the funeral. I try to say that as gently as possible without sounding like I'm being critical.

"The custom casket with the engraving may take one to two weeks," I say. "I'll reach out to our supplier immediately."

"We have something here I can show you," my father says to Ulfric. "It may be close to what you want and then we can have an engraved piece added."

"That sounds good."

Flowers might take longer if the florist needs to order special dye but not as long as the custom casket. Damn, I bet that funeral chopper will require an extra permit. If I can even get my hands on one.

"As I said, there will be a lot of bikers in attendance." Ulfric shifts his big body and rests his ankle on the opposite knee. "We like to escort our brother in our traditional biker procession."

More special permits and probably an escorted road closure or two.

"And at the cemetery, we'll want to send him off with a final rev," he finishes.

We'll all be deaf by the time the funeral's finished.

"I think we can accommodate all of those things. It will take longer than usual, though," my father says.

"That's fine." Abby opens her purse and sticks her hand in, digging around and finally pulling out a small brush and quickly flicking it through her long brown hair. "I need to deal with Dad's house. I'm hoping the tenants will want to buy it. I don't want to manage it from California."

"If you need a referral to an attorney, we can help with that," my father offers.

"No, Dad had someone."

My father takes them into the show room, while I follow, pen and notepad in hand, jotting notes as we go.

When we're finished, I walk them outside, the same comforting platitudes and reassurances I give all our clients rolling off my tongue with practiced ease.

At the bottom of the porch steps, Abby hesitates.

Then, she turns and throws her arms around me, dragging me into a crushing embrace. The force of it knocks me off balance and squeezes the air from my lungs, but I return the hug.

"Thank you, Ms. Cedarwood," she murmurs against my hair. "I'm sorry. I'm not angry with you. You've been very kind, and I appreciate it."

A sharp sting prickles behind my eyes.

"It's okay to feel everything you're feeling." I ease away, enough to meet her tearful eyes. "You can't fast-forward your way through grief. There is no way to skip the messy parts—no way around the anger, sorrow, and frustration of all you've lost."

Her breath hitches.

I gently squeeze her hands. "Every tear you shed, every painful memory you share are all steps toward healing. Allow yourself to feel it all and I promise you, eventually peace will settle in."

She nods so fast I'm not sure my words sank in, but that's okay.

Her fingers tighten around mine. "My dad and I had a complicated relationship. I don't mean to take it out on you." Her voice wobbles and she pulls a tissue from her pocket, dabbing it under her eyes.

I swallow over the lump in my throat. "I understand completely. I promise we'll take good care of your father and help you honor his memory."

Her gaze slides toward Ulfric, and she lets out a sharp, angry breath.

"That's the problem, all those things he wants, they're a reminder of how he abandoned my mom and brother and me, in favor of *'the club.'*" Her lips twist into something bitter, a half smile that doesn't reach her eyes. "But I still want to honor his wishes."

I hang onto my professionalism with both hands. Clients unload years of family trauma on me all the time. I listen, I absorb, and I offer them comfort where I can. But this? This one hits differently.

"I understand." I pause, choosing my words carefully. "Relationships with our parents can be… complicated."

She inhales sharply and glances at the funeral home then back to me.

"You have my number," I remind her. "Reach out if you need anything at all or shoot me an email. Even if you think it's something trivial."

"Thank you, Ms. Cedarwood." She wipes under her eyes and sniffles.

"You can call me Margot." My lips curve into a warm smile.

"Margot," she repeats, then smiles. "That's pretty."

"Thanks."

Ulfric pulls her into a hug next. She stiffens at first, arms locked at her sides. But after a few seconds, her posture softens, just barely, before she steps back.

"Thank you for everything you're doing, Ulfric." Her voice is raw, thick with unshed emotion. She sniffs and presses the tissue against her nose, gathering herself. "Dad could be stubborn." A weak smile flickers across her lips. "I know you two had your disagreements. The… club stuff."

She swallows hard. Given how she seems to feel about the club, the words must be like splinters stuck in her throat. But she gets them out. "But he loved you like a brother. Respected you." Her voice wavers, but she pushes through. "And Dad… he didn't respect many people."

Ulfric's warm rumbling laughter feels like a truce between them. "That describes him well, sweetheart."

They share a few more words and then Abby hurries to her car, sliding behind the wheel and slamming the door. She doesn't look back as she pulls away.

Ulfric sighs and jams his hands in his pockets, watching her car turn left, then disappear. "Some men are better at *talking* about being family men, than they are at *being* family men."

I'm not sure what to say to that. I clasp my hands in front of me, tilt my head up, and study him. Waiting to see if he has more to say.

"Thank you for being so understanding, Margot." He lifts his chin in the direction Abby just drove off. "What you said to her was really nice."

Gee, it's almost like I do this for a living or something.

"I meant it." I gesture toward the house. "Obviously, I see people moving through grief all the time. It's complicated. Especially if they had unresolved issues—which many parents and children do."

"Yeah, he tried healing those wounds a little too late. Moved across the country to be near her but I'm not sure that went so well." He lets out another heavy sigh. "He was a good brother. Loyal as they come. To the club, anyway. I want to give him the best send-off possible."

"Absolutely." I rest my hand on his forearm. "Relationships are complicated." I nod toward the house. "We've seen it all. We don't judge. Bringing Mr. Hall's loved ones peace and comfort during this difficult time is our only concern."

"Thank you, darlin'." He lifts his chin toward the house. "Your dad's handled funerals for us before. I trust you."

"Well, we appreciate that."

"What she said about a shoot-out ain't gonna happen." He lifts his chin toward the road. "I just want to put your mind at ease."

"I wasn't worried." That seems like the safest thing to say.

"Lost Kings MC is the other club around here," he says. "We won't have a problem with them, though. I've already spoken to their enforcer." He grinds his teeth as if he's debating whether to speak his next words. "But Whisper had some other…business associates who might attend. I'll make sure there're no issues. Wrath already said he'd assist."

Guilt prickles over my skin.

I'm not *obligated* to disclose my relationship with Jigsaw's club, am I? Is it dishonest to stand here and act like I don't know who he's talking about? This feels like a hypothetical that would've been on one of the exams in my *Funeral Service Ethics* class.

Why is he even sharing all of this with me now? Is he worried my father would tell him to take his business elsewhere? If only Ulfric knew. We've had family showdowns that make a biker brawl look quaint.

"We can coordinate with whomever you'd like." There. *That's a perfectly neutral answer.*

The deep rumble of an engine rolls through the streets of the usually quiet neighborhood. I cock my head. Is that Jigsaw's bike?

A faint smile lifts the corners of Ulfric's mouth, as if the throaty engine is music to his ears.

The sound grows louder, until the sidewalk under my feet trembles.

Jigsaw lifts his chin as he approaches the house. Instead of riding around back to park in the lot, he pulls up right at the curb.

"Speak of the devil," Ulfric murmurs, his gaze locked on Jigsaw as he swings his leg over his bike. "A Lost King right here in Pine Hollow."

His tone holds curiosity, not hostility, but guilt still ties my stomach in knots. I should've told him sooner.

"Yes, uh…" All my professionalism seems to be leaking out through my shoes.

Jigsaw strides over the sidewalk, his gaze locked on my face, although I don't doubt he took a good look at who's standing next to me.

Without hesitation, he slips an arm around my waist and leans in, pressing a warm, deliberate kiss against my cheek. "Hey, sweetheart."

No need to disclose anything to Ulfric, now.

I flash a brittle smile. "Hi."

Jigsaw turns to Ulfric and extends his hand.

"Ulfric," he greets smoothly, his grip firm. The kind of handshake that carries the weight of respect. "Long time."

Ulfric studies him for a second before clasping his hand. "Jigsaw, right?" His gaze flicks to me.

Is that disappointment on his face?

Annoyance?

My entire body clenches with anxious embarrassment.

"Well, no offense to Ms. Cedarwood," Ulfric says, his voice rough as weathered stone. "But visiting a funeral home isn't usually under good circumstances."

"Sorry to hear about Whisper, brother." Jigsaw's smooth tone carries the weight of understanding and respect. "Everyone I know always had a lot of regard for him."

Ulfric's shoulders and posture relax a fraction. "Thank you. The Cedarwoods have all the details. I hope you'll be at the service."

That sounds more like a command than an invitation.

"You know it," Jigsaw says. "Wrath wanted me to tell you not to hesitate to reach out if you need anything. We built a new clubhouse down in Empire. Next to Crystal Ball. If you've got brothers coming in from out of state who need a place. We have some extra rooms there."

Ulfric stares at him for a few seconds, then nods. "That's generous. Appreciate the offer. I'll keep it in mind."

I can already picture it. A gathering of bikers drinking whiskey and telling stories about Whisper in the middle of a strip club, half-naked dancers weaving between them while they mourn.

Barely containing my eye roll, I fold my arms over my chest as Ulfric swings a leg over his bike and starts the engine.

As soon as he's out of sight, I step back, slipping free of Jigsaw's hold.

"Do you remember when I told you the funeral business was kind of conservative?"

A furrow forms between Jigsaw's brows. "Yeah."

My voice sharpens with frosty precision. "Please don't walk up and stake your claim on me in front of a client like that again."

He clenches his jaw and stares at me as if he's debating my seriousness. Annoyed—at him *and* myself—I turn and head up the sidewalk. I hate conflict. I see enough of it at work.

"Hey." Jigsaw's hand closes around my shoulder, halting my escape. Before I can shake him off, he moves in front of me, cutting off my path.

I glare at the hand still resting on my shoulder and he backs up a step, lifting both in the air. "If I hadn't known who he was, I wouldn't have done that. I would've assumed it was a client and waited until you were finished."

A bit of my fighting flame dims, and I relax my shoulders.

One corner of his mouth turns up, but I don't think he's amused. More like he's trying to mask his own annoyance. "You also need to understand, in *my* world a biker standing that close to someone's ol' lady is asking for trouble."

My temper shoots from mild annoyance to outrage. "Well we're in *my* world and he's a client of my family's business."

He sweeps one hand through the air between us as if he's the oh-so-reasonable one here. "Did you see me punch his teeth down his throat?"

"Oh, be serious! He's old enough to be my grandfather."

"I'm dead serious." He slides his gaze over me. "You're a beautiful young woman."

Ignoring that I press my hands to my hips and glare at him. "I've stood closer to some of your brothers, and you didn't punch any of them."

He taps the shoulder of his black leather vest. "Key words: *my brothers.* We share a patch."

I'm still waiting for his playful grin to break loose, signaling that he's joking. "Are you an actual caveman?"

The corners of his mouth twitch. "Descended from cavemen."

Do not laugh. Don't encourage him. I huff and push past his tall, hulking frame, hurrying to the porch steps.

"Get back here."

"No," I toss over my shoulder.

As my foot hits the second step, two strong arms wrap around my waist and yank me backward.

"Put me down!" I shriek.

"Not a chance, lady death," he breathes against my ear as he turns us in a circle. "You know how much I love chasing you."

Liquid heat shoots through my body.

"My father's right inside," I hiss.

"Good." He lowers me until my feet land on the sidewalk and turns me to face him. "He should know how crazy I am about his daughter."

A charming, lopsided grin sneaks over his face.

It's impossible to be annoyed but I can't give in this easily. "Crazy being the operative word."

He shrugs. "I'll own it." He leans down. "Don't forget, I know where Ulfric's club has dropped a few bodies. I'm just worried about you," he says against my ear.

I slide my gaze to his and find all humor gone. He's dead serious. I guess I shouldn't be shocked. Maybe the two motorcycle clubs used to go on murder sprees together instead of cruising New York's finest scenic highways.

"Fine." I curl my finger, inviting him to lean down again so I can whisper against his ear. "But don't forget, I know how to drop bodies too."

CHAPTER THIRTY-NINE

Jigsaw

My feisty lady death.

Fuck, I love her.

She has no idea how much I wanted to punch Ulfric the second I saw him standing too close.

Not based on anything logical.

He wasn't leering at her. Wasn't crowding her space in a way that set off alarms.

Didn't matter.

Something primal and stupid in me still wanted to knock him back a step. Thankfully, I didn't since that would've been the exact opposite of what Wrath asked me to come out here and do. Offer support. And try to find out exactly how many Wolf Knights will be coming into town.

Ulfric was too smart to fall for that when I offered the clubhouse for his guests. At least I tried.

"Why are you really mad?" I ask Margot. It can't just be because I walked up and kissed her cheek.

"I'm not mad." She huffs and brushes a stray curl out of her eyes. "I just…he mentioned your club and I felt awkward not saying that I… that we…I don't know. It felt like a weird conflict of interest."

"You embarrassed to be with me?"

"No!" she shouts, then sends a sneaky glance around as if someone might be watching. "Whisper's daughter has…strong opinions about her father's club. Ulfric was just trying to reassure me there wouldn't be any issues. I felt weird not saying, 'yeah, I know, my boyfriend is a member.' That's all."

I've never had a "professional" job like hers, but I think I understand what she's saying. "You realize it was going to come up eventually, though, right? Better now than at the service."

She glares at me.

I give her a smug smile in return. "It's okay. You don't have to agree with me. We both know I'm right."

"Ugh." She clenches her fists like she's physically restraining herself from smacking me, then stomps up the front stairs.

Laughing, I follow behind her. My smugness dies a quick death when we cross the threshold and run into Mr. Cedarwood.

Margot stops, absolutely rigid. I just avoid slamming into her back.

"Jensen." His usually somber face actually flexes into a smile. "I was hoping that was your bike I heard."

You were?

I straighten my shoulders. "It was me," I answer like a doofus.

Mr. Cedarwood nods, his assessing gaze lingering on me for a beat too long, like he's working something out in his head. "Did you run into Ulfric outside?"

"Our clubs are friendly. Have been for years." I pause, then choose my next words carefully. "Wrath asked me to check in, see if he needs anything."

His gaze stays fixed on me. "Well, Mr. Hall had a long list of items. It's going to keep Margot busy for several days."

Margot's placid expression shifts to outrage.

Wait, is this his polite way of telling me to get lost?

His gaze flickers to Margot then back to me. "One request was a bit unusual. I was hoping you could assist Margot with it? We have another case that's…stalled and—"

"Yeah, of course," I answer, relieved there's something I can do to help Margot.

"Wonderful." His gaze shifts to Margot. "I'm sure you know which item I'm talking about."

"Well, I assume it's not the floral arrangements."

What am I getting myself into? Did Whisper request a gaggle of strippers to gyrate over his grave or something?

"You can use my office. I need to run out for a bit," Cedarwood says. He reaches out and pats my shoulder. "Thank you, Jensen."

"No problem, sir."

Margot sighs as she watches her dad stride down the hall to the back door. "Come on."

Once the door closes behind Mr. Cedarwood, I slide my arm around Margot's waist and let my hand stray to her ass, giving it a gentle squeeze. "Tell me what you need."

She slants an exasperated but affectionate look my way. "Have you ever seen a Harley Funeral Chopper?"

"Now we're talking." I clap my hands and rub them together. "I'll make some calls."

Margot

I settle into my father's chair behind his desk and go through my list of vendors.

Jigsaw's on the couch, legs stretched out, crossed at the ankles, phone pressed to his ear.

The contrast between his rough-cut biker energy and my father's neat, methodical workspace shouldn't work. But he somehow fits right in. I thought he'd be annoyed at my father imposing on him. Instead, he's eager to get started.

"What's up, Steer?" he speaks into his phone. "Yeah, of course we miss you." He flicks his gaze to the ceiling.

I open my laptop and log into one of our vendor accounts. I might as well start with the smaller items that aren't as time sensitive until we figure out the vehicle situation.

I glance over at him as he laughs into the phone, the deep, warm sound curling through the room.

"No, brother, I don't need it for myself," he says, amusement lacing his voice. "You've seen them before, though, right?"

I bite back a smile.

His hand lazily drags over his jaw as he listens, his gaze landing on me every so often. He raises an eyebrow or smiles at me every time our eyes meet.

It's distracting. But I like it.

He ends the call and scratches out some notes on a pad of paper.

"Find anything?" I ask.

"Sort of. Our charter in Tennessee can get one easily but that's going to be a pain in the ass and probably really expensive to ship here. But one of the guys down there knows of a place in Vermont, so I'm going to try them next."

"Great. Vermont will be a lot easier." I stand and walk around to his side. "Thank you. This is a big help."

"You got it." He curls one arm around my legs and drags me closer, until I topple into his lap. "Only payment I need is a kiss from you."

I press my lips against his bristly cheek. "I'll give a lot more than that later," I whisper in his ear.

"I'll happily accept." He turns, catching my lips.

The chime of the front doorbell echoes through the house.

Frowning, I slide out of his lap. "You think Ulfric came back?" I ask.

He shrugs. "Got me. You don't have any other appointments today?"

I check the small black-and-white video monitor with a wide view of the front porch. Two men in suits peer up at the camera, then glance at the door.

It's not the same men who questioned me about Laurel. But they definitely look like cops.

My stomach plummets to the floor.

"Margot, what's wrong?" Jigsaw's concerned voice pulls me away from the screen.

"I don't know," I whisper. "They look like cops."

He leans down, staring at the screen. "Fuck."

In a matter of seconds, his entire demeanor shifts. My relaxed, cocky biker trying to cop a feel—gone. Replaced by this protective, watchful, *dangerous* man.

He rests his hands on my upper arms. "All right. Relax. You're fine." He glances at the screen again. "Are those the same cops from last time?"

"No." I shake my head.

"Good. Do you want me to answer the door?"

"I don't think that's a good idea." I shake my head. "Do you?"

He runs his hand through his hair, clearly torn between wanting to protect me and wanting to keep our relationship away from the police.

"I'll be right in here. Bring them into the parlor so I can overhear the conversation." He pauses. "This time if they ask if anyone's here, just say yes, your boyfriend. My bike's right out front. They're going to figure it out eventually."

"Okay." I nod quickly.

The doorbell chimes again.

"Go," he urges.

I hurry to the front door and slowly open it a fraction. Two men in dark blazers stand on the porch. "Hello? Can I help you?"

"Are you Margot Cedarwood?"

My stomach tightens.

"Yes. How can I help you?" I stare at the two men. One older with cartoonishly bushy eyebrows, making him look like a runaway from the Muppets. The other one's younger and more polished—his eyebrows impeccably waxed and shaped. What an interesting duo.

The younger one—smooth brows—flashes a badge at me. "Investigator Thomas with the Empire Police Department."

I unclench about fifty percent. The other officers were from Slater County. I haven't killed anyone in Empire, have I?

"...My partner," Mr. Thomas finishes. I missed the name of his partner. Damn.

"How can I help you?" I ask, opening the door wider.

"Do you know a Daniel Muldoon?" the smooth-browed detective asks.

Annoyance immediately twists in my chest. "Unfortunately."

Shoot, why'd I have to say it like that? What if Daniel's dead or something? I'll be their number one suspect.

Creaking over the floorboards behind me draws my attention. I glance over my shoulder.

Did Jigsaw kill Daniel after I *explicitly asked him not to*?

The older cop raises his bushy eyebrows. "You were romantically involved?"

"Yes," I answer more respectfully this time. "Engaged, actually."

"Who ended it?" Thomas asks.

"I did." I frown. "Why are you asking me about Daniel?"

The younger cop tilts his head, peering past me into the foyer. "Can we come in?"

Refusing will make me look suspicious.

"I suppose." I open the door wider and step back. "Let's talk in here."

I lead them into the parlor. They settle onto the couch, while I perch on the edge of a chair, my posture deliberate—poised, alert, in control. Like I might have to jump up and attend to business any moment now.

The smooth-browed detective leans back, crossing one ankle over his knee. "Can you tell us more about your relationship with Mr. Muldoon?"

"I already told you. We were engaged. I broke it off. There is no *current* relationship."

The older detective nods, tapping a thick finger against his knee. "But you arranged his grandmother's funeral here, correct?"

"Yes." My voice tightens. "Well, he called my father to arrange it, but I ended up handling most of the preparations for Mrs. O'Leary."

"How would you describe their relationship?"

A chill slides over my skin, sweeping away my annoyance. I sit up straighter and clasp my hands in my lap. "From what I remember, it was...cordial. Mrs. O'Leary was a very nice woman. Daniel was...respectful..."

"Respectful?" Thomas asks. "Not affectionate?"

I snort and look away. "Daniel's not an affectionate person."

"Is that why you broke up?" the older detective presses.

I stare him dead in the eyes. "Has something happened to Daniel?"

The older man's eyes widen. "No. No. He's fine."

I blow out a breath. I may hate Daniel, but I don't wish death on him, and I certainly don't want the cops thinking I murdered him. "So, what is this about?"

"Why did you break up?" he asks again.

I smooth my hands over the arms of the chair, the soft, worn velvet grounding me. "We weren't compatible. He was very... critical of me. And I grew tired of it."

"Was he abusive?" Muppet-Brows asks.

I hesitate, choosing my words carefully. "Not physically, no. But he could be vicious with his words. I didn't want to stick around and find out if the behavior would escalate to physical violence one day."

Thomas studies me, his expression carefully blank.

Muppet-Brows nods approvingly. "Smart woman."

I dip my chin in response.

"How about a Mrs. Penny? Do you know her?"

I stiffen, my pulse stuttering. "We recently handled her funeral. Why?"

The older detective nods. "Daniel attended the service, correct?"

Unfortunately.

My mouth moves before my brain catches up. "Yes."

The older cop leans in, crowding his partner. "Did you speak to him?"

"Yes."

"About what?"

I grit my teeth, remembering the awful conversation. Then bite my cheek to stop from grinning when I remember Jigsaw and Rooster scaring the crap out of Daniel. "Normal catching up stuff at first. But then he wanted to talk about getting back together."

"But you said he was critical of you."

"Yes. And I reminded him of that fact when I told him absolutely not."

Muppet Cop grins so wide, I feel bad for referring to him as *Muppet Cop* in my head.

"Did he say he'd changed?" younger cop asks.

I snort a laugh. "No. He didn't understand what my problem was." I rub the arms of the chair again. "But I finally got a few things off of my chest. Overall, it was an unpleasant conversation. My boyfriend walked in on the tail end of it and told him to leave."

"So, you're seeing someone?"

"Yes."

Investigator Thomas opens a small notepad and clicks a ballpoint pen. "And his name?"

"I don't see any reason to bring him into this."

The cop's pen hits his notepad with a soft clunk. His jaw works but he doesn't seem to be able to come up with a good enough reason I should give him a name.

"Did Daniel react violently to being told to leave?" he asks.

I snort even harder. "No, he reacted like all bullies act when faced with someone bigger than they are. He scurried out like a roach who'd had the overhead lights turned on."

The older cop nods again, a small smile tugging at the corners of his mouth. I seem to be confirming a lot of opinions he's made about Daniel.

The younger cop doesn't seem to find me as entertaining. I wipe the smirk off my face and pretend their questions aren't a waste of my time.

"Do you know a Mrs. Ellen Baker?" the younger cop asks.

Surprise drops my jaw for a moment.

"I do," I answer slowly. "We were contacted by her family to take her into our care and have a service for her. I had the consultation with her niece earlier this week. But we've run into a snag at the M.E.'s office."

"Are you aware Daniel is the one who recommended your funeral home to the Bakers?" Investigator Thomas asks.

My heart stops.

What?

I blink and sit back. "No, I wasn't. My father did the intake for that case. He didn't mention Daniel had anything to do with it. The niece didn't mention him when we spoke."

That's the third client Daniel's sent our way this year.

And the police are here to ask me about it.

Holy shit!

The older detective exhales slowly, watching me carefully. "That's the third client in the past year that Daniel has directed to your funeral home," he says, echoing my thoughts.

My heart pounds.

"How much do you know about Daniel's job?" the older cop asks.

"Uh, not much, honestly. He manages money for people. Retirement accounts, I think? He was always after my father to invest with him."

"Did he?"

"Not to my knowledge." My father may have been okay with Daniel as a son-in-law, but he didn't trust him with his money. "Daniel wanted to manage money for me, as well. Kept trying to tell me how much I could earn if I started young. It all seemed too complicated, though."

"Is that all?"

I purse my lips, thinking over my answer and the gut instinct I always had when Daniel harped on me about investing with his firm —*No*. "I might not have seen his behavior as abusive right away, but I guess I subconsciously knew he wasn't right for me. I didn't trust him to invest my money."

"Did that make him angry?"

"Yes," I answer, a surprising flood of memories washing over me. "If he wasn't criticizing my appearance, he criticized my intellect."

"You seem like a very bright young woman to me," older cop says.

"Thank you."

"Is it possible he referred these last two clients to your funeral home as a way to get back into your good graces?" younger cop asks.

I blow out a long, thoughtful breath. "I doubt it. I mean… referring someone to us makes sense. His grandmother's funeral was here. If someone needed a recommendation, we'd be the first name he thought of. We appreciate the business, of course. But I really can't say *why* he'd recommend us."

"Maybe to convince your father to talk you into getting back together with him?" the cop suggests.

"That seems a bit far-fetched." I hesitate. Daniel *did* say he spoke to my father about us getting back together.

Investigator Thomas uncrosses his legs and sits forward. "What's wrong, Ms. Cedarwood?"

"Uh, yes. Actually, Daniel said he spoke to my father and my father told him to speak to me." I shrug. "My father knows I'm seeing someone else."

The night my father handed Jigsaw the keys to his Cadillac springs to mind, along with a few other interactions they've had but I don't want to share any of that with the police. "He wouldn't try to interfere in my love life. Daniel should've known that."

The older one stares at me, then casually slides his gaze to his partner. "And were you aware that both Mrs. Penny and Mrs. Baker had sizable estate funds managed by Mr. Muldoon's firm? Not to mention his grandmother's estate."

My blood runs cold.

I barely stop myself from gasping. My fingers dig into the velvet arms of my chair.

"No," I force out.

Muppet-Brows gives me a measured look. "That doesn't strike you as… unusual?"

My pulse roars in my ears.

"I…I don't know. They were both elderly…" My gaze strays to the other side of the parlor. "Unfortunately, I see so much death. I'm not a good judge of what might be considered *unusual*."

The older cop nods slowly. "I can understand that, Ms. Cedarwood."

The younger cop scribbles something in his notebook. Then, without looking up, he says, "Do you think Mr. Muldoon is capable of harming someone for financial gain?"

The question punches the air from my lungs.

They suspect Daniel murdered these women.

"I—" My gut is screaming *yes.* His lack of empathy and compassion. The way he could tear me apart with so many cruel words. The way he talked about money like it was the only thing that mattered.

"I don't know if I'm the best person to ask. I told you we didn't have a good relationship."

The older cop's eyes narrow. "That wasn't your first answer, was it? What's your gut reaction."

"Daniel's a jerk," I whisper. "I…I want to say no he wouldn't harm anyone, but…I really don't know."

The older detective nods slowly. Like he expected that answer.

"Thank you for your time, Ms. Cedarwood," he says, standing.

I barely register them moving toward the door.

Is Daniel capable of murder?

Not just murder, but preying on three innocent, elderly women for something as banal as money? When he already comes from a wealthy family?

Yes, I think he is.

CHAPTER FORTY

Margot

"I GOT THE GIST OF YOUR CONVERSATION," JIGSAW SAYS ONCE WE'RE SAFE inside my apartment.

"Oh?" I kick off my shoes and head straight for the bedroom, my mind spinning.

Daniel might have killed his grandmother?

Mrs. O'Leary was so nice. She didn't deserve whatever happened to her. Did she see Daniel coming? How did he do it? I never saw any signs of foul play on her body.

This is why the Baker autopsy is being held up.

Does my father know? Does he suspect Daniel?

I stop and turn.

Jigsaw didn't follow me into the bedroom.

I find him in my kitchen. He holds out a bottle of water to me, his expression serious. Protective. "Drink this. You look like you're about to faint."

"I'm not sure what I am." I uncap the bottle and take a long swallow, the cool water soothing my dry throat. "Tell me what you heard?"

"They asked you about your ex. Douchwaffle Dan."

I snort, but the humor dies quickly.

"I can't believe it. But also, I can." I stare at Jigsaw, feeling sick. "I can't believe I ever… oh my God."

"I couldn't get every bit of the conversation. My takeaway is they think he's knocking off little old ladies for profit?" Jigsaw says with a questioning lilt.

I scowl. "*Little old ladies* seems disrespectful given the circumstances. They were women who lived full lives, who had families, who…"

"Okay." He curls his hand around my upper arm and steers me into my theater room. "He may have killed *three elderly women* who couldn't easily fight back, in order to steal their money."

I sink onto the couch, my stomach twisting. "It seems that way."

His jaw tightens. "They must have a solid case. They shared an awful lot with you."

My pulse spikes. I press my fingers to my temples. "Oh my God, what if they think my dad was involved? Or me? And that's why they told me so much, to see if I alert Daniel?"

"Margot. Stop." He clamps his hand over my thigh, his firm grip grounding me. "I think the younger cop might have been a little suspicious. But the older one definitely wasn't."

"What if they were lying to me? Cops love to play games with suspects."

"True," he agrees. "But I really don't think that's the case. You were honest and helped give them some context for the kind of person he is."

"But who even told them we dated?"

"You said you met his friends and family. I'm sure one of them remembered you." He sweeps his gaze over me, slow and deliberate. "I'm guessing there aren't a lot of beautiful, blonde, female morticians under thirty who work for family funeral homes in the area. Even if his friends didn't remember your name, they'd remember those details. Put it together with where the grandmother's funeral was held, and they probably just went from there."

I blink. *Oh.* "That makes sense."

How can he be so calm and reasonable?

He nudges my knee with his. "We have contacts in Empire. I can try to find out who they're investigating."

I shake my head. "No, that seems like a bad idea."

Jigsaw watches me, eyes sharp and assessing. "What are you thinking? Talk to me."

I let out a short, humorless laugh. "I'm thinking about how I ever let that man touch me."

Jigsaw tilts his head, considering. "I mean… yeah. Can't blame you there."

I swat his arm. "Not the time."

The amusement slides from his expression, leaving something darker.

"How awful." I swallow hard. "I thought he just had a vicious mouth. But…to kill your own grandmother?" I tip my head up and stare into Jigsaw's eyes. "She was a nice woman. I only met her a few times, but she was very kind to me. How could anyone…how could he hurt her?"

Jigsaw stares at the ceiling. "Uh, because he's a greedy fuck? Money makes some people do evil things."

"I know. Believe me." I wave my hand in the air. "I've seen enough fights break out over money or family heirlooms. But this? And then two more women? Friends of his grandmother, I suppose."

Jigsaw presses his palms together like he's praying to the Lord above. "Can I kill him now? Please?"

He's so utterly sincere, I can't help laughing. "No! You still want to do it for the wrong reasons."

"Nope." He leans forward, all serious expression and convincing eyes. "That's an added bonus. Killing defenseless old ladies is fucking *low*. It's not like they were suffering and he was trying to help ease their misery. He wanted to hurry them off the planet to steal their money. That's absolutely death-worthy."

He's not wrong.

I sigh, rubbing my forehead. "Honestly, I'd rather see him arrested and disgraced first."

"First?"

"Before he dies. Remember, *my* criteria includes a failure of the justice system as well."

He growls, low and frustrated. "All right. But if he gets acquitted or too light a sentence, it's game fucking on for that motherfucker."

I don't argue, but the dark satisfaction that flickers in my chest is enough to tell me I won't try to stop him.

I might even join him.

Jigsaw

The bombshell about Margot's ex lingers like a bad snowstorm. I definitely thought he was an asshole. But a killer—no. A piece of shit who murders old women deserves to die. Never mind that I already hated the guy. I'd feel the same way even if he hadn't been so cruel to my woman.

Margot still seems so rattled.

"Come on. You need to eat something," I pat her knee and stand, holding my hand out to her.

"I need to change." She stares down at her all-black outfit. "I feel gross."

"Go ahead. I'm going to order a pizza."

"Ohhh," she moans and closes her eyes. "That sounds perfect right now."

"Good. Meet you in the kitchen."

"Deal." She leans up and kisses my cheek. "Thank you."

I pull out my phone and place the same order I did last time. Then we'll have leftovers for tomorrow.

Gretel scurries into the living room and hops up on Margot's lounge chair. *"Mroar."*

"You gonna eat some pizza with us, G-kitty?"

She plops her paws on my leg and stretches.

"Come here." I pick her up and she rubs her head against my chest.

Margot finally wanders out in red plaid flannel pants and an oversized red sweatshirt with a black cat face on the front. It kind of reminds me of one of the patches our Virginia charter hands out. I open my mouth to say that, then stop. The pussy patch has a bit of an unsavory backstory. Although now that I'm with Margot, I kinda want to call Ice and see if his club's doing the pussy patch challenge again.

"You look good in that." I pull her into my arms, and she rests her check against my chest.

"You say that with everything I wear."

I shrug. "Then it must be true."

She laughs softly.

My phone vibrates and I pull it out. "Food's here."

"That was fast tonight."

"I'll be right back."

After we eat, Margot leans back and stretches her arms overhead, letting out a contented sigh. The weight of the afternoon still seems to cling to her but at least she has more color in her cheeks.

I reach over and settle my hand on her thigh. "Feel better?"

"Much."

"Should we—"

"I don't want to talk about it anymore tonight. Tomorrow morning, I'll need to tell my dad. And I still have so much work to do for Whisper's funeral." She slides off her stool and moves closer, pressing her body against my side. "I'd like to do something else tonight," she finishes in a low rasp.

Her voice. Her eyes that lower as she sweeps her gaze over me.

Whatever she has in mind, I'm in.

I finish my seltzer in one swallow and set the glass on the bar. "What'd you have in mind?"

"Well." She curls her hand around mine and tugs. "Remember the first time you came over?"

She pulls me toward her lounge chair, a playful smile dancing over her lips. "For my first lesson."

"Fuck yes. How could I forget?"

"Well, I think about it a lot." She stops at the foot of the chair.

"As do I." I curl my arm around her waist and yank her against me. "Loved every second with you. Already knew a few lessons weren't going to be enough."

"Really?" She pushes against my chest.

She'll have to push a lot harder to move me. "What do you want?" I ask. "You want me in the chair? You want a repeat?"

"Sort of."

I strip off my T-shirt and settle all the way into the chair. "Come show me."

She pulls a condom out of her pocket and slaps it on the side table.

"Ooo, look at you all prepared," I tease.

She presses one knee into the chair and slowly lowers herself until she's straddling my thighs.

"Come closer." I cup her butt and slide her right up against me.

"Oh," she gasps and rolls her hips. "You're already…you're so…"

"Hard for you," I supply the words. "Yes. Yes, I am."

She laughs, then gasps again.

"You like that?" I whisper, holding her gaze.

"I do."

"Keep going. See if you can make yourself come grinding in my lap." I sneak my hands under her sweatshirt and tug it up. "First, while this is cute, it needs to go."

"Okay." She keeps rolling her hips while I struggle with the sweatshirt.

"Ah, fuck. This is sexy." I slide my finger under one strap of her sheer black bra.

"Jigsaw, I'm…" A little V forms between her eyebrows, and she lets out a frustrated grunt.

"Give it a minute, woman. I know my cock is magic but still."

She laughs, rocking herself against me a little *too* hard.

I hiss in a pained breath. "Not enough room in my pants for what you're doing to me."

"I'm sorry!" she yelps and slides back a few inches.

"It's fine." I dig my feet into the cushions and lift my hips. "Undo my jeans and take me out of my denim prison, please."

"Those sexy black track pants should be mandatory when you're with me," she grumbles, attacking the button but carefully lowering the zipper. "Much easier access."

My phone—firmly lodged somewhere inside my pocket—starts vibrating against my leg.

Who's bothering me now? "Fuuuck," I groan.

I have to slide down more and wedge my hand inside until my fingers finally find the edge of my phone, then drag it out.

The buzzing stops.

Missed call: Zero

I stare at the screen. Call my president back or give my girl her orgasms first? Maybe sneak one in for myself.

I set the phone on the side table. "Where were we?"

"Who was it?"

"Z."

She raises her eyebrows. "Shouldn't you call your president back?"

"You want your orgasm or not?"

Instead of answering with words, she reaches into my briefs and brushes her thumb against the head of my cock.

"Fuuuck, yes," I groan. "He'll call back or text if he needs me that bad."

"*I* need you bad," she says, curling her fingers around me.

"Yes, you do."

My phone rattles against the table.

"Godfuckingdammit." I pick it up.

Z: call me now.

"Why is he being such a cockblocker?" I whine.

Margot giggles.

"You think that's funny, huh?" I shove my hand down her pants and encounter nothing but skin. "No underwear, dirty girl?"

She lets out a sharp breath of surprise as I drag my fingers through her wetness.

"Not laughing now, are you?" I stop and roll one finger around her clit.

"No," she gasps and rocks her hips against my hand.

"Good girl. Keep doing that while I call him back."

"What? No. I can't do that." Her mouth protests but her body keeps moving.

"Yes, you can." One-handed, I hit Z's number.

"Jigsaw," Z answers in a tight voice.

Maybe it's because all the blood from my brain has relocated to my cock, but I steamroll over the warning in his tone. "This isn't the best time. What'd you need?"

"Where you at?"

This time, his tone penetrates through my lustful fog.

"Margot's. Why?" Shit, is the clubhouse getting raided by the cops again? I slip my hand out of Margot's pants and motion for her to hang on.

Pressing her hands on the arms of the chair, she carefully extracts herself from my lap.

"I need you to come down to Crystal Ball," Z says.

There is *no way* I'm leaving my girlfriend unsatisfied so I can go babysit a bunch of strippers tonight. Absolutely the fuck not. "Crystal Ball? Why?"

Z hesitates. Just for a second. But it's enough.

Something is seriously fucked.

"Because I've got a kid here who came in asking for you."

Kid? Lead settles in my gut. *Don't like the sound of that.* As a late bloomer with the ladies, I haven't been fucking long enough to have a son old enough to walk into Crystal Ball without a fake id. "What kid? Who?"

Z's exhale is heavy, like he's bracing for my reaction. "Says his name is Cain Killgore. And he's your brother."

Margot and Jigsaw's story concludes in
Scatter the Bones (Lost Kings MC #26)

THE LOST KINGS MC® WORLD

by *USA Today* bestselling author
Autumn Jones Lake
This is my suggested
suggested chronological reading order
For all of the books in the Lost Kings MC World

1.Kickstart My Heart (Hollywood Demons #1)
2.Blow My Fuse (Hollywood Demons #2)
3.Wheels of Fire (Hollywood Demons #3)
4.Renegade Path (A Lost Kings MC World Novel)
5.Slow Burn (Lost Kings MC #1)
6.Corrupting Cinderella (Lost Kings MC #2)
7.Three Kings, One Night (Lost Kings MC #2.5)
8.Strength From Loyalty (Lost Kings MC #3)
9.Tattered on My Sleeve (Lost Kings MC #4)
10.White Heat (Lost Kings MC #5)
11.Between Embers (Lost Kings MC #5.5)
12.Bullets & Bonfires (A Lost Kings MC World Novel)
13.More Than Miles (Lost Kings MC #6)
14.Warnings & Wildfires (A Lost Kings MC World Novel)
15.White Knuckles (Lost Kings MC #7)
16.Beyond Reckless (Lost Kings MC #8)
17.Beyond Reason (Lost Kings MC #9)
18.One Empire Night (Lost Kings MC #9.5)
19.After Burn (Lost Kings MC #10)
20.After Glow (Lost Kings MC #11)
21.Zero Hour (Lost Kings MC #11.5)
22.Zero Tolerance (Lost Kings MC #12)
23.Zero Regret (Lost Kings MC #13)
24.Zero Apologies (Lost Kings MC #14)

25.Swagger and Sass (Lost Kings MC #14.5)
26.White Lies (Lost Kings MC #15)
27.Rhythm of the Road (Lost Kings MC #16)
28.Lyrics on the Wind (Lost Kings MC #17)
29.Diamond in the Dust (Lost Kings MC #18)
30.Crown of Ghosts (Lost Kings MC #19)
31. Throne of Scars (Lost Kings MC #20)
32. Reckless Truths (Lost Kings MC #21)
33. Deeper You Dig (Lost Kings MC #21.5)
34. Rust or Ride (Lost Kings MC #22)
35. Agony to Ashes (Lost Kings MC #23)
36. Fighting the Forbidden (Ruthless & Royal #1)
37. Repairing the Wreckage (Ruthless & Royal #2)
38. Twist the Knife (Lost Kings MC #24)
39. Collect the Pieces (Lost Kings MC #25)
40. Scatter the Bones (Lost Kings MC #26)

...and many more to come!

ABOUT THE AUTHOR

Autumn Jones Lake is the *USA Today* and *Wall Street Journal* bestselling author of over twenty novels, including the popular Lost Kings MC series. She believes true love stories never end.

Her past lives include baking cookies, bagging groceries, selling cheap shoes, and practicing law. Playing with her imaginary friends all day is by far her favorite job yet!

Autumn lives in upstate New York with her own alpha hero.

www.autumnjoneslake.com

facebook.com/autumnjoneslake
goodreads.com/autumnjoneslake
pinterest.com/autumnjoneslake
instagram.com/autumnjlake
bookbub.com/authors/autumn-jones-lake

www.ingramcontent.com/pod-product-compliance
Lightning Source LLC
Chambersburg PA
CBHW050916030726
47503CB00007BB/2313

* 9 7 8 1 9 6 1 8 4 8 1 7 7 *